I0762855

Praise for *Aubrey Wants to Die*

'Aubrey is the ultimate hot mess vampire, and I inhaled her story in a night. Sexy and laugh-out-loud funny, full of delicious drama and surprisingly moving—Aubrey's chaotic undead rollercoaster of a journey had me cackling, yearning and questioning my entire existence.' **Anna Downes, author of *Red River Road***

'There's nothing quite so charming as a vampire having an existential crisis. *Aubrey Wants to Die* is full of dark romance, quirky neuroticism and ancient lore. Knight has created a fresh and feisty take on an old genre. I loved Aubrey, who feels both mysterious and known—your bestie and your worst nightmare all wrapped up in one. This character-driven story has lashings of existential angst, black humour and a romantic heart. It's cool, hypnotic and addictive. I loved it.' **Vanessa McCausland, author of *The Last Illusion of Paige White***

'I was absolutely hooked on this smart, sexy thriller, devouring it in a day. Aubrey is in constant danger as she chases her happy-ever-after and tries to find the meaning of life, alongside us mere mortals. You can sink your teeth into this delicious vampire thriller!' **Petronella McGovern, author of *The Last Trace***

PIP KNIGHT

Aubrey wants to Die

HANOVER
SQUARE
PRESS

Recycling programs for this product may not exist in your area.

Trigger warning: This book contains some sensitive material, including suicidal themes and sexual assault, which may be triggering for some readers. If you or someone you love is experiencing hardship, contact the Suicide Crisis Helpline (9-8-8).

ISBN-13: 978-1-335-00143-6

Aubrey Wants to Die

Hanover Square Press
22 Adelaide St. West, 41st Floor
Toronto, Ontario M5H 4E3, Canada
HanoverSqPress.com

HarperCollins Publishers
Macken House, 39/40 Mayor Street Upper,
Dublin 1, D01 C9W8, Ireland
www.HarperCollins.com

Printed in U.S.A.

For Mickey—
Who, when I said, 'Am I crazy to want to write a vampire book?' replied, 'So be crazy.'
Without you, this book might not exist.

And for the Aubreys. Every single one.
For you, this book does exist.

It is as if I had a string somewhere under my left ribs, tightly and inextricably knotted to a similar string situated in the corresponding quarter of your little frame …

Charlotte Brontë, *Jane Eyre*

Aubrey wants to Die

1

Every once in a while, there's a winter fog so thick you can barely see in front of you. It rolls in with the mulled wine and the fake Santas and the Christmas lights on Oxford Street, around the time everyone starts mumbling about seasonal affective disorder like it'll kill you. It rolls in with no warning and casts an intoxicating magic, the kind that belongs in story books. The kind that makes you want to stand still forever, lose yourself and just breathe it in.

He was like that fog.

He stopped me in my tracks and reminded me of what it was to have a heartbeat. So that's how I ended up here, at Archway tube station, wearing huge sunglasses at 9.07 pm in case I cry.

I look up at the board: *three minutes*. The next train is due in three minutes.

I just need to hold it together for three more minutes. Then I'll be on my way home. *I can do this.*

The platform reeks of urine, and I can hear rats scuttling in the distance. A woman arrives, earbuds in, scrolling through her phone. A roll of silver wrapping paper pokes out the top of her bag, which makes sense. It's five days before Christmas and she, unlike me, probably has people to see. Presents to wrap. Tinsel and little blinking lights to twist around branches, and little rocking horse ornaments to hang. I bite down on my lower lip, staring at an advertisement on the wall opposite me. It's for a telephone company—a couple talking to each other on FaceTime. I think it's meant to be long distance. I can see the love in their eyes.

And me? I'm going to be alone forever.

Don't cry Aubrey, don't you dare cry.

I look up to the board again: *one minute.*

Flashes from tonight flicker through my mind. Jonathan, looking at me as he said, 'Aubrey, you texted me one hundred and four times this week … It's not your fault, it's a beautiful thing that you're so loving. And we were both swept up by it, like we'd lost our minds, but it's all too much now …' His voice cracked. 'I think we need a break … before it gets toxic.'

As I looked into his eyes, all I wanted was to tell him *everything*, to make him understand … but I couldn't.

So instead, I said, 'A break? For how long?'

He sighed. 'I don't know, but … a while.'

I knew what that meant: we were breaking up. How could this be happening? But shit, now my lip was quivering—I was going to cry. And if I did that, he'd *definitely* think I was toxic.

I needed to get out of there.

So I just said, 'I … think I should go.'

Then he walked me out of the kitchen, through the living room, past the red and brown floor rug, the rug we'd slow-danced on, and across to the front door. All while his roommate-slash-business partner, Baxter, watched on silently from the sofa.

He opened the door, looked at me one last time and something tugged at my ribs as he said, 'bye', and I said, 'bye' and then he closed the door. I just stood there for a moment, staring at the heritage-green paint, and then I heard him say to Baxter, 'Fuck, I really thought she was the one.'

And that was it. The moment my heart broke. Because, for a brief moment, I had been in the warmth, basking in the light. Now I was back out in the cold night air, where I have always been.

Where I always will be. Where I belong.

Because I'm broken and I can't be fixed.

A rumble sounds in the distance. Lights flicker in the tunnel. I take a deep breath and step forward to the edge of the platform.

There's a rush of dusty air. I close my eyes.

And then …

I jump.

There is this elastic moment that stretches and bends and all I can feel is … lightness. Hope. Redemption.

But then: the high-pitched screech of brakes.

A big bang.

The world goes dark.

Pitch black.

And I am dead.

Okay, I don't jump, but I want to. I want to do things like that a lot, to be honest. Anything to escape this world. But I already know how that would play out.

I'd feel the heat of the train above me. The darkness around me. Voices would be yelling from the platform, calling for help, security people would arrive. And me? I'd be lying on the tracks with not a scratch on me. Or if I *did* have a scratch, it would heal within moments. There would be no broken bones. No blood. The CCTV hanging from the ceiling would have captured it all. As I crawled off the tracks, I'd have to explain how I survived completely unscathed. If I couldn't do that to their satisfaction, if they ever figured out what I was, I'd end up in a scientific testing facility, with tubes up my nose and wires stuck to my skull for all of eternity. Which, frankly, sounds like a fate *worse* than death.

It's not worth the risk.

I know all this because I've tried it before.

And … I can't die.

I can't die because I am already dead.

I'm a vampire. And you'd think, after more than a century, I'd have life all figured out.

2

I woke up 150 years ago in a low-lit room, a gasolier hanging from the ceiling above me, my pale blue dress wet with blood. As my eyes flicked open, I knew nothing, but I could sense *everything*. A conversation taking place through the walls somewhere, the buzzing of a fly before it landed. And if I stared at it, zoomed in, I could see the veins on its wings, the green metallic sheen of its body.

Where am I?

I scanned the room. I was on a bed. There was a dark wood armoire, a free-standing wash basin, a dressing table with a brass vase and an oval mirror, and I was … hungry. Ravenous.

My jaw ached. My mouth watered.

I stumbled out into the hallway, my head throbbing, that hunger inside me growing. 'Hello?' I called, even though I didn't know who I was calling to. All that came back was silence.

Holding onto the banister tightly, I made my way downstairs to the living room. There was a newspaper on the oblong coffee table: *The London Evening Standard. May 5th, 1876.*

As I stared at it, I tried to make sense of everything. I knew what a newspaper was. I knew the months of the year and the days of the week. I knew the fundamental working parts of the world. I just had no recollection of my place in it. I—the version I had been before—had been erased.

Who the hell am I?

'Hello?' I called out again as I surveyed the furniture in the room, searching for some memory of it.

It's just me here. A twinge of fear rippled through me, but that hunger was getting stronger and stronger.

My nostrils flared as I picked up an intoxicating scent: rust and lust mingled together. *Blood.* An electric jolt rolled up my spine and I rushed towards the smell, into a kitchen, and scanned the shelves.

An icebox. In the corner.

I ran towards it, and wrenched open the door.

Now the scent was so strong I could almost taste the iron. I felt my upper jaw tingle, a strange sensation on my gums … *What is that feeling?*

But then I didn't care what the feeling was, because: meat. Raw meat. The hunger took over. I held it in both hands and sucked on it, but it was almost dry and made me gag.

I looked around wildly, searching for more. But there were just jars of grain and beans and bowls of fruit, and my head was throbbing now. I needed *blood* … *blood* … *blood* …

It rolled round my head like a mantra.

I ran to the front door and as I pulled it open, I was hit by the stench of horse dung, the sound of hoofs. A carriage was passing, and there were people walking up and down the darkened street. I wasn't in a city, I was in a village. The people I could see were well dressed and none of them were covered in blood like me. Panic gripped me.

I'm different from these nice, normal people. And not in a good way. I can't let anyone find out.

The panic grew stronger, and I shut the door.

I ran back up the stairs, searching for a clue, something

that would help me make sense of this, tell me what to do, and then there, in the mirror at the dressing table, I saw myself for the first time. My golden hair was pinned up, but pieces had come loose, were red with blood and hanging in my face. And my dress … I'd known I was covered in blood, but I hadn't realised how *much* blood until I saw myself. It was everywhere. Was I injured? I checked my body, but nothing hurt. I leaned in to inspect my face, searching it for memories. *What the hell happened to me?* There were golden rings around my irises that seemed to glow, and my skin was pale and translucent … But as I leaned in closer, my eyes caught on my mouth, on my teeth. I flinched.

Do I have … fangs?

A flicker of memory; that feeling in my gums when I saw the meat, smelt the blood, fed. Horror rolled through me as I traced the sharp tips with my finger. What was going on? I knew what a vampire was: a monster from books, from folklore. Not real.

Oh god.

I pressed against my fangs, trying to push them back into my gums, but they wouldn't budge.

Frantically, my hands moved to my chest. *Where the hell is my heartbeat?* I raised my fingers to my neck to feel my pulse, my actions instinctive. But thank the lord, it was still there. Just very, very weak and slow.

How did this happen? Did someone do this to me? Where are they?

But the only thing I knew for certain was that whatever had happened, I needed to hide it.

I stripped off my clothes, found a sponge and cleaned the blood off myself as best I could. And when I reached for a towel to dry myself afterwards, there, embroidered onto it was the name *Aubrey*.

Is that my name? Or my family name?

It had a familiar ring to it. Either way, it was the only name I had, so I took it.

I went over to the armoire and pulled it open. It was full of shoe boxes, petticoats and dresses—bodices, skirts—some plain and made of cotton, others ornate and silk, decorated with embroidery and beads. *Where did I wear these?* I had no idea.

But there was a plain navy dress, so I put it on quickly, then some simple boots, and a bonnet to cover my hair, still damp from trying to get the blood out. I packed some underclothes into a small suitcase along with a second dress and my silver hairbrush from the dressing table.

I carried the case downstairs and stepped calmly outside—*Keep your mouth closed, no smiling*—then walked down the cobbled street and crept into a garden. I huddled on a bench out of sight, trying to figure out what the hell to do next. I was helpless. Alone. A tear rolled down my cheek. I wiped it away, then glanced at my finger and it was … blood. I was crying blood.

Honestly, could anything else go wrong?

And I was still hungry, so, so ravenously hungry. I licked the tear from my finger but it did nothing for me. What was I going to do? How would I survive? I knew I needed blood but what kind of blood? And how would I get it? It felt like I didn't have a chance in hell.

Then a man appeared and sat down beside me.

I quickly wiped my face. My shoulders tightened as I took him in. *Would he be able to tell? Should I run?*

He was almost entirely bald with a dark beard, wearing a well-cut grey suit. His eyes were brown … as I studied him, my breath caught. There were golden rings around his irises, just like mine. And then he smiled, revealing pointy canines.

'I'm Hans,' he said. And I didn't trust him, not at all, but in this world that made no sense, he was the only one holding out an olive branch. What else was I to do but take it?

I replied with the only name I had: 'I'm Aubrey.'

We travelled to London that same night without so much as a backward glance.

The nights that followed were a smudge of waking up as grey dusk fell, catching glimpses of flower sellers with baskets and men in top hats driving carriages and buskers playing harpsichords in the street outside the window. Then the inky night would descend and we would make our way out into the dimly lit street, full of soot and smoke—a perfect setting for vampires like us.

Hans was kind—it seemed he was as relieved as I was to find another vampire. He helped me with the basics and answered my immediate questions.

Was he my sire? 'No, but it was probably a man,' he'd guessed. 'A woman wouldn't have abandoned you. Whoever he is, he must have been far older and more powerful than me to turn you.'

Why couldn't I remember anything of my human-self? 'That happens to all of us when we're turned. It makes the transition easier.'

Soon, he'd given me my first fake birth certificate, and opened a bank account for me with a bank manager on Lombard Street. It was something I would have struggled to do without a man by my side. He'd also made my first sizeable deposit and then got me a job in a dressmaker's shop. Luckily, it turned out I could sew.

And, of course, he'd taught me to feed.

Our first victims were all middle-aged men, for no reason other than there were a lot of them out alone at night. Drinking blood was addictive, it felt like glitter in my veins, like I was plugged into a wall and lit up from within. Colours were brighter, sounds were musical, and I felt almost weightless. Pure, undiluted euphoria.

Life was nothing but sparkle and bliss, until our fifth night together.

In the hour before dawn, we walked through a small street, Hans trying each door, gently rattling the handles. And then—*click*. One opened.

We crept inside. It felt fun, naughty, like we owned the night. Upstairs, we found a man in the master bedroom, sleeping alone. Hans leapt forward and attacked him in the darkness. As soon as I smelt the blood, I felt my gums tingle and my fangs emerge. I joined Hans, feeding eagerly.

With the taste of salt and rust came the electric lightness that I had come to crave. My senses sharpened, and I could hear everything, feel everything. Bliss pulsed through me … I never wanted it to stop.

I think I heard the footsteps a moment before Hans did, but I was too busy gorging myself to look.

Then came the sharp inhale of breath, a small whimper. I swivelled towards the door.

Watching us was a small boy of maybe nine years old. He was clutching a stuffed bear, its legs dangling. And the look in his eyes was of absolute terror.

Hans let go of the man and grinned, blood dripping from his chin as he threw himself at the boy. I heard teeth puncture skin.

A harrowing yelp pierced the air.

It hit me in the chest like an arrow. And the moment it did, something hot burst inside me. I could almost hear it. My vision blanched for a moment—like I was staring at a bright white screen—my ears rang and a heat, a white-hot fury I'd never felt before, rushed through me. It was dizzying.

I had to save the child. It was an urge stronger than hunger or self-preservation. It was like a wildfire burning through my veins.

I lunged at Hans.

But he swatted me off—he was older and stronger and faster than me. I tried again, but he just held me back as I flailed against his grip. I clawed at his face.

'Do NOT!' he boomed.

He grabbed me by the shoulders and threw me across the room. I hit the wall and crumpled to the ground. He stood over me, the little boy laying in a pool of blood behind him. And all I could do was glare up at him.

'How dare you,' he growled, his eyes flaming. 'You're on your own.' With that, he turned and stormed out.

I rushed to the boy and cradled him in my arms. As I carried him to the bed, I caught sight of my reflection in the window. My hair was a mess and I was covered in blood, so much blood. My eyes were wild, the rings around my own irises glowing like fire.

It was the first time I saw myself with total clarity.

I was a monster.

When I looked back down at the boy, he was dead, all the light gone from his eyes.

The hunger that had consumed me just minutes before was nothing but an echo now, the spell broken. And in its place lay a deep sense of shame and self-loathing. And, for the first time, my conscience ignited.

As the nights passed, I couldn't shake that image of myself, standing holding that child, stained black-red with blood. I was terrified. Terrified of my hunger, of becoming like Hans. Terrified of the searing rage that had come out of nowhere, that I didn't understand, that I had no control over. Because when would it come out again? And what would I do? What if I lost control and attacked a child myself next time?

How bad would I become?

And also, I was all alone again. Hans had left me after just five nights, my sire had left me instantly. Everyone would leave me if they ever saw my rotten core. I was barely a vampire, no longer a human. And I could see exactly what kind of life I would have: always hiding, always running from my darkness, a monster that nobody could ever love.

That was the first time I tried to die.

I stood on Waterloo Bridge, staring down at the black water. I could smell wrought iron as tears gathered in my eyes and whatever was left of my threadbare soul realised this was it. The end. Soon I would be gone. As I peeled my fingers away from the railing one by one, my insides twisted and my head got light. I clenched my eyes shut as tears rolled down my cheeks. And then I … let go.

Icy air hit my face. My eyes flicked open—a blur of lights in the distance—and then *crash*.

The arctic water sucked me in and down, swirling me as though in a drain. I waited for the water to fill my lungs, for oblivion to find me … But oblivion did not come. Instead, I bobbed to the surface.

As I swam towards the shore, I thought: *I must have done it wrong.*

And then: *Maybe it wasn't high enough?*

But I tried again and again and again—altering my methods each time—and still, it didn't work. It dawned on me that there must be something I didn't know.

There must be a *specific* way I needed to die, a vampire way, I thought. Without Hans around to ask, I turned to books. But, if there *is* a way for me to die, I've yet to find it. Which is why, after 150 years, I'm still here.

3

I stumble home from the Tube, across the Thames and London Bridge, my sunglasses on the whole way in case I cry. Now I'm on my street, not far from Borough Market and the flat where Bridget Jones lived in that movie. I can see my building just up ahead. It's brown brick with black awnings and old Dickens-style lights on the walls, and right next door to a pub called Bunch of Grapes. Usually there are flowers hanging in baskets outside that pub—a burst of pink, orange, yellow and red. But right now, those flowers are covered in snow, the pavement outside, iced over.

I pass the pub and the bins, pull open the flimsy black wrought iron gate, and rush down the stairs to the front door of my basement apartment.

The neighbour's cat is waiting on the mat by my door—a little ball of white fluff. Animals like me, and I feel like that's a good sign—surely that means I'm not a bad person, no matter what the books and TV shows say about me.

'Hey, Cat,' I say, my voice cracking as I fumble the key into the lock then push the door open. She meows and runs in after me, purring and rubbing against my shins as I close the door, take off my coat and sunglasses, and drop my bag on the beige leather sofa.

I move through the darkened living room, past my bookshelves, full of my favourite dog-eared novels (*Hunger, Bonjour Tristesse, Frankenstein*), a bunch of beloved romances, a few self-help books (that clearly didn't work) and my first edition copy of *The Vampire in Europe*, which I bought the day it was published in 1929 and which has taken an active role in the destruction of my mental health ever since.

In the kitchen, I pull open the fridge. Light spills out, cool air hits my cheeks and I look inside: a mini carton of lactose-free milk, a small bag of artisan cat treats, a few bottles of nail polish (there was a trend a while back to keep it in the fridge and I have to use the storage space for something), and a turquoise Fortnum & Mason biscuit tin.

Just for the record, it turns out I *can* eat human food. I can also drink alcohol, smoke cigarettes and the like, but the only thing I *need* to sustain me is human blood.

And I still hate that about myself. I'd still give *anything* not to be a vampire. To be human-me again. It's not like I'm suddenly okay with being the blood-sucking villain of my own story.

But how can I be human-me again when I still don't know who I was?

I reach for the biscuit tin and lift off the lid. It's one of those musical tins that you twist and then it plays an eerie tune. But I don't use it for biscuits.

I pull out the almost empty bag of blood, pour what's left into a mug and put it in the microwave. As it spins round and round in its lit-up cage, I grab a nappy out of the middle drawer, wrap it around the empty blood bag and drop it into the rubbish bin. Nobody opens a dirty nappy.

This is my life: a carefully constructed set of rules and rituals to keep me safe. Hidden. A functional part of society.

I get my bagged blood, I go to work, I go for long nighttime walks and then I sit at home with Cat, watching the world through my phone, my laptop, through the bars on my windows. Pushing down my darkness. Hiding my bags of blood like an alcoholic hiding vodka bottles. There's not a lot of meaning or hope in it—or at least, there wasn't until I met my boyfriend, Jonathan. Sorry, *ex*-boyfriend. Fresh tears well in the corners of my eyes.

Cat meows a little louder, pushing against my legs as I grab the bag of cat treats and put some into a saucer, then add a little milk. It's lactose-free, so according to the internet it shouldn't harm her, but apparently it's not great for her either. Problem is, she loves the stuff. She begs for it. She always wants more. Even Cat has a self-destructive vice, it seems.

I put the saucer on the ground and she purrs and eats as I open the freezer and reach into a spinach box for another bag of blood to defrost for tomorrow. But all I can feel is cold cardboard. *It's empty*.

Great.

Just what London needs over Christmas: a heartbroken vampire who's run out of blood.

But then: *Beeeeeeep*.

My dinner is ready.

I pull out the warm mug and take a sip. A calm moves through me, the fatigue lifts. As I take a second sip, I feel a little less dead inside. It's not the same as drinking from the vein, not even close, but it does the job, and this way no one gets hurt. Because, after 150 years of trying to be good and sometimes slipping, here is what I know for certain: when I drink from the vein people *always* get hurt, and once I start I can't stop. Which is why I can't have even a single taste. I *never* want to go back to that. Thankfully, it's been so long now, that I'm no longer tempted—I'm happy with my bagged blood, and I have my darkness totally under control.

Well, unless I get really, really angry. Then my darkness controls me.

I carry my mug to the sofa by the misted-up window. Cat jumps up and settles down on my lap and starts licking my hand with her rough little tongue, looking up at me now and then, like she can tell something is wrong. I stroke her and look out the window.

This is my favourite spot in the flat, especially at night. If I look up, I can see the street through the bars, see couples falling in love, see the leaves on the trees turning rust-red and amber, illuminated by streetlights—but nobody sees me. Nobody knows I'm down here. Right now, a couple is standing at the top of my stairs, leaning against the railing, kissing. His hands are in her hair.

And that was us.

Until just a couple of hours ago.

I look around my little flat now: my windowless bedroom, the TV, the low ceilings, the chipped beige tiles in the bathroom, the front door with the rickety lock, the toaster and kettle that came with the flat but I've never used yet keep on display for the same reason I keep tampons in my handbag: optics' sake. I mean, I have a rental inspection every six months and I'll be damned if after all these years of hiding, I'm outed by the absence of domestic appliances. I've lived here for the last four years and never had a problem with it—living humbly helps me fly under the radar, blend in—but now I'm thinking, *Is this really all there is for me?* Because, for a moment there, I'd imagined a life. A real life. With complications and make-up sex and throw pillows and dinner parties and shared memories in photo albums and *him* …

And how can it just be over?

I pull my phone from my bag and stare at the screen, willing it to light up with his name. For this to all be a big mistake. But nothing comes. And now all I can think about is the afternoon we met. And how is it, that someone can come into your life, with no warning at all—one person out of hundreds of thousands, one moment in 150 years—and then *boom*, nothing is ever the same again?

4

I first met Jonathan on a Sunday afternoon in late autumn, five weeks ago.

Yes, I know that five weeks doesn't sound like a long time, but Jonathan isn't just some guy. He's my soulmate. And I don't mean that the way people usually say it, I *mean* it. I have proof. Our souls are genuinely linked.

Usually, I'd have still been sleeping. I go to bed just before dawn and, if left to my own natural circadian rhythms, I sleep until dusk. But there are two churches near me, and maybe it's true, maybe the church bells really do drive away demons, because even with earplugs they *always* wake me on Sundays just before eleven, and I can never get back to sleep. So I was wide awake when Daphne's text came in: *At Borough Market. Need drink and chat. Emergency. Where are you now?*

I work with Daphne at Selfridges and she's one of my three friends. She's mildly alcoholic, always dishing out dating advice to anyone who'll listen, and sidelines as a part-time model and a 'sugar baby'. How else is she meant to get into the property market in this economy? While nobody knows where I live—so she couldn't just turn up on my doorstep—

she'd said it was an emergency. And I might not be perfect, but I *am* a good friend.

So, through blurry eyes, I replied: *Bunch of Grapes on Thomas Street?*

I sent her a link to the pub next door, got dressed, threw on my coat, my big sunglasses and a pair of gold birdcage earrings, which have since become my lucky earrings, then rushed out the door and up the stairs to the pub.

It was crowded, the lights all decorated with plastic autumn leaves twisted around them, and the bottles behind the bar flashed amber and blue and brown.

Daphne wasn't there yet, so I headed straight over to the one free table in the darkest corner. I sat down, pulled out my phone so nobody would come and talk to me, then messaged with Sally while I waited. We're members of the same … umm … online community.

Over the next fifteen minutes, Sally sent a few furious texts wishing her husband, Frank, 'dead' because he'd asked her in-laws over for Christmas and she was a vegetarian so why the hell should she have to cook a turkey? Then it was my turn. I didn't want her to feel guilty about what she'd said about Frank, so I wished my lecherous boss, Kenny, 'dead', then complained about the upcoming Christmas rush at Selfridges, and the fact that I couldn't get up to order anything without losing my seat, all while I anxiously scanned the door for my friend.

Then, finally, Daphne arrived and got us drinks. Over an acidic glass of malbec, I learnt that Daphne's 'emergency' was that she was bored and thirsty and had a blister. Soon our glasses were empty and it was my shout, so I left her there, eating crisps and frowning down at her phone screen as I headed to the bar.

I was three people from the front of the line when I heard: 'Can I get you a drink?'

I turned to look.

Beside me stood a man in a black T-shirt with John Lennon glasses on his head. He smelt of pepperoni, the kind of deodorant that has a metallic panther on the label and A-negative blood. And all I could think as I took him in was: *Ah, shit.*

Men really, *really* like me—and it's not just because I have golden blonde hair to my shoulders, amber eyes, skin so pale and unblemished it looks like it belongs to a statue and a face that remains eternally twenty-two.

It seems natural selection has equipped me with some sort of scent that would make it easy as all hell to feed off the guys who hit on me—if I wasn't entirely non-violent. I could lure them to their fate like a beautiful, poisonous flower. But I *am* non-violent. Since I never date, never even hook up anymore—I can't risk letting anyone get close in case they learn my secret—the attention is nothing more than inconvenient.

Still, I've had this problem for a very long time, so I *have* developed ways of dealing with it: don't be rude, don't engage, and leave as soon as possible. And … if that doesn't work, talk about Jesus. Which was exactly what I planned on doing with Pepperoni Guy.

'I'm okay, thanks,' I replied, keeping my eyes on the bar.

'You have a boyfriend?' he asked.

I smiled sweetly, still not looking at him. 'Yes.'

'Where is he then?'

'He's almost here,' I lied. *Eyes forward, eyes forward.*

'Nah, you don't, love. I can tell. I think you're going to have a drink with me.' Like if another man didn't own me, I was up for grabs.

And then he did just that: he grabbed me tight around the waist, hard enough for it to hurt.

That dangerous heat—a darkness, a fury—swirled in the space beneath my ribs, and I imagined myself baring my fangs. Just to scare him off. Make him leave me alone.

Don't, Aubrey.

I pushed it down, like I always do, and tried to pull away again. But, unlike the vampires in pop culture, I'm not particularly strong at the best of times and I'm downright weak while the sun is still high.

I looked behind me for Daphne, trying to catch her eye to silently beg for help, but she was smiling down at her phone. And then I saw a man, a beautiful man, in a mustard jumper, coming back from the bar, and he was looking right at us. He was tall with good shoulders and thick, dark blond hair, and the bluest eyes I'd ever seen. Two lines deepened between his eyebrows as he frowned.

I swallowed hard as his eyes moved from me to Pepperoni Guy, then to the hand grabbing my waist. The beautiful man mouthed: 'Are you okay?'

One hundred and fifty years of hiding has taught me to never rock the boat, never cause a scene, so I nodded—I'd deal with it myself. But then Pepperoni Guy grabbed me even tighter and I squirmed instinctively. That was that. The beautiful man strode towards us.

'Hey,' he said gently, as his gaze held mine. 'I was looking for you.'

It was the first time I'd ever heard his voice, but it sounded almost familiar in a way I didn't yet understand. He had a slight Northern accent and it gave him a certain charm, like an uncut diamond.

'Who's this?' Jonathan asked, looking straight at Pepperoni Guy, who let go of me immediately—*oh sorry, your property, my bad*—and wandered away.

I looked up at Jonathan and whispered, 'Thank you.'

He gave me a small, mischievous smile, and then whispered back, 'My pleasure, that was fun. I felt like a right hero.'

He started to laugh and I laughed too because he was right, it was just like how Edward had saved Bella from that oncoming car in *Twilight*, or how Sookie had saved Bill from the addicts in *True Blood*—but I didn't say that. I wasn't sure he'd appreciate the references.

'Are you here with anyone?' he asked.

I nodded back at Daphne who was now watching from our table and gave us a little wave. 'Just my friend.'

'Well, do you both want to come and have a drink with me and my friend, Baxter?' he asked. His face changed suddenly, like he'd just realised maybe I'd think he was as bad as Pepperoni Guy. 'No pressure though, only if you'd like to,' he added.

I could have so easily turned him down. While I considered myself a 'theoretical' romantic (I believed in true love and soulmates for humans and fully endorsed it), I was also a realist: I knew that wasn't an option for me. Because love—real love—is when someone sees your darkness and loves you anyway. Despite it. Because of it. Whatever. And my darkness, has always been just a little too … much. The only place someone like me finds a love like that, is between the pages of novels or on TV.

But as I looked into his eyes something tugged in my chest and told me he was *different*. It felt like there was an invisible cord that had always been linking us, rib to rib, but now that he was close, I could feel it tugging harder. Needing me to follow, logic be damned.

I'd never experienced anything like it, and it was impossible to turn away from. So, when I opened my mouth to reply, I said: 'Sure.' As I followed him over to his table and Daphne quickly joined us, I thought, *It's just a drink, no big deal, one little drink.*

One little drink turned into a mind-blowing afternoon. Three days later, after following each other on Instagram and sending a few flirty texts, I sat across from Jonathan in a little Italian place in Shoreditch for our second date, listening to his heart beat—a melody I would soon come to recognise anywhere. Jonathan wore a jumper the exact same shade as his eyes, and I was wearing a thin white lace top that Daphne had helped me pick out.

When we were halfway through our meal, the waiter reached for the breadbasket and knocked my glass of wine, spilling it all over the table and splashing up onto my torso.

'I'm so sorry,' the waiter said, his face going puce.

'It's okay, don't worry about it,' I replied in the most soothing voice I could, moving aside and helping him mop up the mess with some napkins.

When the waiter left, I looked back over at Jonathan, who was watching me with a soft expression in his eyes. 'You're really kind, you know,' he said.

I smiled—it was nice to have a compliment that wasn't about my body or my face.

He really looked at me then, thoughts moving behind his eyes, thoughts I wanted to know.

'What?' I asked.

Then he narrowed his eyes a little. 'Aubrey, what do you want from this?' he asked gently, his voice a little shaky. 'I mean, you're so young,' he said, never guessing the age difference was not quite as he thought. 'Are you looking for fun or …'

'I …' I didn't know what to say. Because I knew the answer, I *knew* it. I'd known it since the first afternoon we'd met. But dare I say it? Wasn't it insane?

'It's okay,' he said. 'Whatever it is. I'm a big boy.' His eyes searched mine, and it felt as though they were staring straight into the centre of my soul. I could tell from the timbre of his voice that he was asking a question he wanted an honest answer to.

So, I did the bravest thing I'd ever done. I looked him square in the eye and said, 'I'm looking for … well … true fucking love, of course.'

I held my breath and watched for his reaction. That moment between saying it and him replying seemed to stretch a decade.

I was just about to laugh it off and say I was joking, but then his cheeks flushed, and he smiled and reached for my hand. Our eyes met. I could hear his heart beating a little faster. And then, in a slightly husky voice, he said, 'It's so refreshing to have someone just tell the truth.' He paused for a moment. 'Me too, for the record—not that I'd ever usually admit it. God, it really feels like I've known you a lot longer than I have.'

As he said it, the wariness that had been tightly coiled inside me for as long as I could remember, began to unwind.

Then we changed the subject. But something had shifted between us in that moment. Something that never shifted back. I knew it at the time, but even I could never have predicted how close we'd get, or how quickly.

I went home with him that night and we made love for the first time, his hands on my hips as I moved on top of him. His eyes on mine.

Afterwards, as I lay in his arms, wearing his The Doors T-shirt—I would come to claim it as my own every time I slept over—and pretending to sleep while his breath grew heavy behind me, it felt as though the entire universe was expanding. Everything I'd come to believe impossible for me—true love, soulmates, all of it—was within reach. Turns out, there was nothing 'theoretical' about my romanticism in the end, I'd just been too scared to hope.

For the first time ever, I didn't want to die at all. I felt safe. Because if anyone could tether me to my humanity, save me from the darkness inside me, it would be Jonathan.

And now he's gone.

While I'm here in my flat, just me and Cat and my mug of blood. And there on the coffee table is the unfinished blanket I'd just started knitting when I first met him. Big wooden knitting needles. Mauve wool. The most recent in a long line of hobbies I've taken up to distract me from my existential angst. Knowing that's what I'm going back to, that I found my soulmate and lost my soulmate and now it's back to knitting …

It makes me want to die even more than before we met. Like, double as much.

5

I know I'm not supposed to admit any of this. That being single is a perfectly fine lifestyle choice, and that the general consensus is that if a guy breaks up with you, you should get over it and move on. But it's just … I've been alone for such a long time. Also, is it even possible to just 'get over' your soulmate? I don't know. All I *do* know is that I can't text him for the 105th time this week.

Instead, I check my phone is connected—the 5G reception in my flat is patchy and only works half the time, the other half it connects to the wi-fi from the pub next door automatically—and then tap through to Jonathan's Instagram profile. Maybe seeing his face might make it hurt a little less? I chew gently on my cheek, waiting for it to load.

Then there he is, smiling back at me: Jonathan Sanderson. In the first picture, which he posted last Wednesday, he's shiny with sweat and wearing workout clothes, clinging to a fake rock face in a rock-climbing gym with Baxter.

I glance to the right, to a picture of us together from just two weeks ago. We're sitting on the stones of Brighton Beach, the tangerine of the setting sun giving us a warm glow. I'm wearing huge sunglasses, and his cheeks are pink from the cold air and he's holding onto me so tight—our first night away. We stayed up until three am, just talking about everything and making love.

Then right beside that is another picture, from just three weeks ago: we're in the dark of an arthouse movie theatre, and the photo is blurred, his eyes bright and my hair falling over my face as we laugh. We'd gone to see a screening of *Dirty Dancing*, and as he went to take the photo, Jonathan had whispered, 'Nobody puts Baby in a corner.' Someone had hissed, 'Shut up,' and we couldn't stop laughing.

But I was wrong, looking at his profile isn't helping at all.

And look, I know it wasn't all perfect. Jonathan works too much and was always saying things like *smoking will kill you* every time I lit a cigarette, so I gave them up just for him, but being with him was the first time I believed I might not always be alone.

Because sure, I have friends, but they'd all run screaming if they ever found out the truth about me. But Jonathan would have stayed if I'd given him a chance, if I'd just trusted him enough to tell him the whole truth. But I was too scared. It felt too soon. So instead, I sent him 104 texts and now he thinks I'm unhinged, and he's gone, and I can smell rust and my lower lip is quivering …

My breath gets quicker and quicker and finally, those fat tears I've been holding back roll down my cheeks. I wipe them away; now there are blood tears on my hands. It's disgusting—*I'm* disgusting.

My phone pings with a message from my hand and I almost drop it.

Hope floods my veins—*what if it's him?*

But it's not him.

Daphne: *How did the date go? X*

I sniff back tears and stare at her message. Daphne told me not to double-text, triple-text Jonathan, she told me we were going too fast and to play it cool or something like this would happen. But I didn't listen, I was following my fucking heart.

I swallow hard, take a deep breath and type back: *He said he thought we should have a break … am so sad.*

Typing bubbles flare … They stop, then start again.

As I watch them, I need Daphne to write back with *Oh that's not so bad* or *give him a week, he'll be back.*

Beep.

Daphne: *Argh. Are you okay? You can do better anyway! Xxx*

And I know she's trying to make me feel better, but the problem is, I *can't* do better.

It's Jonathan or nobody.

So, as the boiler bubbles and hisses from the kitchen and Cat purrs, I quickly reply to Daphne: *Can you help me get him back?*

Typing bubbles flare again …

I bite down on my lower lip as I watch them flare, then: *Beep.*

I squint down at her reply, almost scared to read it.

Daphne: *Maybe. Let's talk tomorrow. But Aubs stay chill ffs. DO NOT TEXT. DO NOT CALL. I MEAN IT!!!*

And thus, sitting in my darkened living room, staring down at the blue-white light of my phone screen, I think: *Okay.* Because she's right. I tried listening to my heart, and look where it got me. From now on, I will listen to my head. Or, at the very least, I will listen to Daphne.

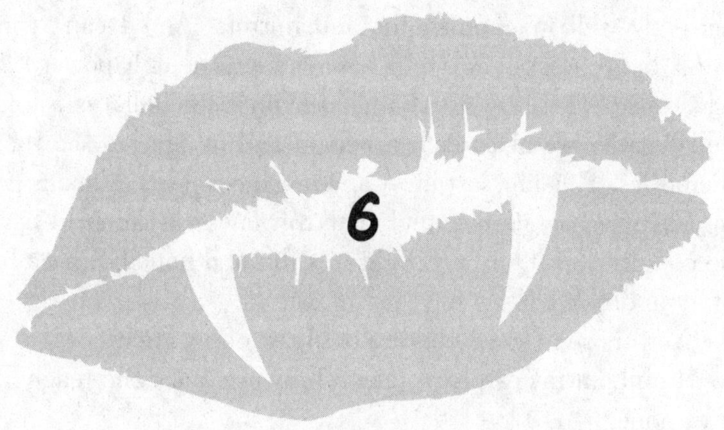

6

When I wake to the sound of my alarm the next afternoon, I'm spread-eagle in the middle of my queen-sized bed, the fitted sheet coming off the mattress and a random striped sock on the floor in front of me. Just like anyone else. Because, disappointingly, I don't sleep in a pretty satin-lined coffin, despite what books and movies might say.

In fact, I should point out right now, that pop culture vampire lore gets as much wrong as it gets right.

I mean, yes, obviously I cry blood and drink blood. I don't age and sometimes my little fangs emerge. Yes, I can hypnotise people (though it's a bit hit or miss, so I'm pretty sure I'm doing it wrong). Yes, my senses are more finely tuned than most—I can smell a person's blood type, hear their heartbeat, see in the dark, and zoom in on details—but mainly it's nothing sunglasses, deep breaths and a good pair of noise-cancelling headphones can't fix. Yes, my circadian rhythms are totally messed up, and yes, fine, I'm a teensy bit obsessive …

But that's about it.

I run cool, not icy cold. I can't fly. I'm not that quick, nor strong—I'm downright clumsy at times. I don't need an invitation to go inside. I can bleed. I feel pain. I show up perfectly well in photographs and mirrors. And I can't turn into a bat or mist or anything else. In fact, the only power I *do* have (aside from my questionable hypnotism skills) is a total dud—sometimes I'll touch a person and be able to see their memories. This life, last life—anything goes. (Yes, humans get multiple lives while I'm stuck with this one—so unfair.) I have no control over it, no idea what it is for, and honestly, it's a bit of a mindfuck.

Yet, those inaccuracies are the least of my grievances.

I pull out my earplugs, take off my eye mask and reach for my phone.

No new messages.

But the little white digits on my phone say it's 3.30 pm. I do some quick maths. That makes it eighteen and a half hours since we last spoke; and my hair still smells like the cedarwood and musk of his cologne. Everything aches.

I swallow hard as I look through my bedroom doorway towards the living room window. A thin band of late afternoon light creeps in around the edges of the heavy-duty blinds. And as I look at it, I think: *Here we go again, for the 55,016th time*. Another dusk, another moon, another night just like every other night that's gone before and every night that will come after, forever, and ever, and ever and ever …

Lucky me.

Because I have what everyone thinks they want, eternal life, and all I want, even after all these years, is to die.

Which brings me to my *major* bugbear with vampire stories.

If this were a book or a TV show, I could just wander out into daylight right now and explode or burst into flames or something. Sunlight is supposed to kill me.

But nothing in real life is ever that simple.

Turns out, I *can't* die. Ever. Not even in the ways vampires routinely die in literature. None of it works. Not a stake through the heart, not beheading, not crucifix nor holy water, not garlic, not silver, not starvation, not fire and certainly not sunshine. All sunlight does is make me tired, foggy and even more irritable. It's like putting my head underwater—everything, every sense, is muffled and I can't think straight.

And yes, I'm *sure*. Following my foray into the river and subsequent attempts after Hans left, I made it my mission to figure out how vampires die. *How hard could it be*? I thought. But I've tried almost everything now; every method more than once. I am quite literally stuck here on this earth. Just me and AI and Tinder and every other money-making advance that masquerades as 'progress' until it screws up the world even more than it already was. Stuck here, watching the oceans fill with plastic and waiting for the apocalypse to finally come.

But as I lie in bed, staring at the strip of sunlight that won't kill me, I think, *Okay, so it is what it is. Let's assess the damage.*

One: Jonathan is my soulmate; the only person who could ever love me despite what I am. Two: I went a little hard and fast and scared him off. Three: I have to get him back. Four: I can with Daphne's help.

Because Jonathan didn't plan on breaking up with me last night. He was getting a bottle of wine for us to drink when I pushed him to it. I think back on the scene, assessing it for signs of hope.

I was following him into the kitchen, looking at him, wondering why he'd been so quiet all week. Telling myself it was just because of work—he and Baxter had been developing a property app and were in the thick of getting funding—while also telling myself it was important to share my feelings, tell him when I was hurt.

Then … I tripped.

The contents of my bag scattered all over the kitchen tiles and Jonathan crouched down to help me gather everything up.

'Are you okay?' he asked, gently touching my arm, like I was a delicate flower, not dead inside with bones that never break and flesh that heals in moments.

I nodded, and I should have just left it there. But instead, as he handed me my lipstick, a rogue business card and two loose tampons, I said, 'It really hurt my feelings that you didn't reply to my texts this week. It's not hard to text back, Jonathan.'

And there was an edge to my voice as I said his name, an edge I'm not proud of.

An edge that wouldn't have been there if I were well adjusted and didn't have abandonment issues of epic proportions. But the thing is, I *do* have abandonment issues of epic proportions. Hans left me the moment I stepped out of line. Freddie (my only other relationship before Jonathan—more on that later) left me.

And, worst of all, my sire left me. Because he never did come back. So yes, I have issues.

When Jonathan wasn't replying to me last week, I assumed it meant he was going to leave me too.

Not great. Not healthy. But I can't change any of that.

I can only do better. Which means letting Daphne help me.

But right now, I need to get ready for work.

I trudge to the kitchen to get some breakfast. But as I get to the fridge, my gaze catches on the bin. Poking out the top is the nappy from last night, the one with the empty blood bag inside it. I really don't want to go and get blood right now, I'm seriously not in the mood, but it's already 21 December. And Es—my blood connection and friend—is finishing up work today and won't return until the 27th. I'll have to go get some before work. I really can't afford to be hungry over the holidays, especially not when I'm feeling like *this*.

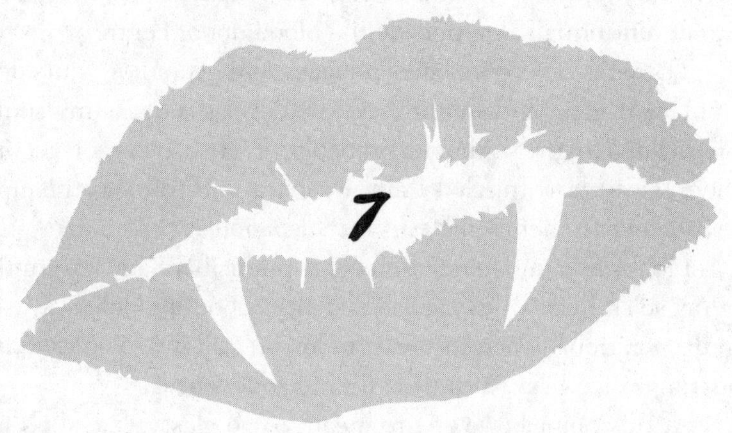

7

Winter is my favourite time of year—the days are short, the nights are long, and everyone else is pale and has the morbs too. But the second half of December, when the Christmas rush hits … not so much.

As I emerge from Bond Street tube station into a thick holiday crowd, I clench my jaw, turn away from Selfridges and rush towards Oxford Circus instead. The sky glows indigo, and all around me shop windows are lit up with Christmas displays, spilling green and red light out onto the pavement. It would almost be scenic—tourists in winter coats and woollen hats and gloves tottering along slowly, exhaling clouds of fog and staring into shop windows—if I wasn't already running late for work.

Stay calm. All you have to do is get some blood then go to work and Daphne will help you fix this, I think as I rush towards the blood bank where Es works. Luckily, it's not far away. Though, to be candid, that's less by luck and more by design.

Four years ago, when I got my job at Selfridges, I cased the place out and managed to befriend Es at a local cafe. But what started as necessity is now a real friendship—insofar as I can have a real friendship.

I turn left up Regent Street, then right down Margaret Street, until finally I'm outside the blood donor centre.

There's a goth-looking teenage girl standing outside, smoking a vape and wearing eye shadow as dark as my soul. *She'll do*. I figure I should probably practise before I get in there, given how frazzled I am. I can't afford to mess this up. I stride over to her as she eyes me suspiciously.

I look deep into her eyes, feel my pupils flare and a warmth in my solar plexus. I can sense that she's about to look away, so in desperation I reach for her arm, muster all my focus, and in a strong voice I say, 'You will give me your vape.'

At this point her eyes are meant to go glassy, like she's in some kind of trance. And then I'm supposed to be able to tell her what to do. But that's not what happens. No, instead, my other dud-power fires up because … this is my life. My stomach clenches. I brace myself. And in come a stream of images.

It's like watching a silent black and white movie, that's slightly sped up: *wooden pails of soapy water … laundry hanging up … clothes I recognise from the 1880s …*

Ahh, a memory from her last life, I think.

Thankfully, she pulls her arm away and the images cut to black. Her nose crinkles. Then her forehead. 'Fuck off,' she says.

As I watch her strut away, I know what she's thinking: I'm some weird young woman who tried to steal her vape. Not a vampire trying desperately to get bagged blood because she's committed to being a good person. And *this* is why I feel so misunderstood.

Still, at least now I know my hit-or-miss hypnotism powers are a total 'miss' today. Which may make what I'm about to do a little more challenging, but it's better to know up front.

I pull open the door, move inside, take a deep breath of what smells like antiseptic, and walk through the reception area. I smile at the receptionist—she knows me now, I'm not sure if that's a good or a bad thing—and head down the hall to where Es will be.

Even when I'm not frazzled and heartbroken, this next bit is a bit tricky. Let's just say getting blood from a blood bank is a lot more complicated than they make it look in vampire movies. To start with, I need whole blood, and donated blood doesn't stay whole for very long. Soon, it's separated into red cells, platelets and plasma, so I need to get to it before any of that happens. And you can't just walk up to a quarantine fridge and help yourself to a nice bag of AB negative. There are swipe cards and CCTV. Honestly, you'd think they knew vampires existed, the way they've got it locked down. Each year, with the advancement of tech, it just gets more and more complicated. And I have to be careful not to implicate Es.

My mission, therefore, is to get to the blood between when it is drawn and when it is put in the fridge. Not an easy feat.

I get to the room where they take blood and peer through the window. I can see Es, she's standing by one of the reclined donation beds, smiling and chatting to someone she's just hooked up to a needle and bag. Her light brown hair shines under the overhead strip lighting and a silver cross hangs around her neck, reminding me a little of Buffy. That, coupled with her true-crime fascination, her biological knowledge and her disturbing ability to join dots, means if anyone actually *believed* in vampires, being friends with her would be very risky.

Luckily, Es is entirely scientifically minded and evidence based.

My gums tingle as I look at the bags of blood currently being filled; they almost glow neon red, while everything around them dulls to greyscale. I swallow hard, then reach for my phone and text her: *Here xxxx*

I watch her glance at her phone, then up at me. She grins and I smile back, then my gaze shifts to the cooler box beside her, the words *Blood Products* written on the side.

Reach for the handle, please reach for the handle …

She's talking now, and I strain to hear her voice through the door. I can just make out her thick Liverpool accent saying, 'I'm just going to go to the fridge.'

Yes.

The other technician nods and then, seemingly in slow motion, Es reaches for the blood cooler and starts to wheel it my way.

Yes, yes, YES.

Step one accomplished.

As she comes out the door, she grins at me again and looks around—it's just us. We head quickly down another hallway, towards the room the big fridges are kept in, then slip into a storage room and shut the door. *Click.*

I know this room well; we do this handover a lot.

Now comes step number two.

'Do you have them?' she asks, her deep blue eyes wide and sparkly. She's twenty-eight and has the beginnings of the fine lines I'll never have. Oh, how I want life to leave its traces on my face, for people to look at me and know I've *lived*. Instead, they look at me and assume I know nothing.

From my pocket, I pull a small bag of five weed gummies. The ones I buy from Brendon, who tends the bar at Bunch of Grapes. Paying Brendon for them and then giving them to Es for free makes me feel marginally better about using her for blood. It's a finely tuned moral ecosystem I have going on. Now comes the pièce de résistance, step number three …

As I go to hand them to her, I stumble a little, then lean against the cool plaster wall. 'Oh wow,' I say. 'I'm so dizzy.'

She frowns. 'Are you okay?'

Most of the time I'd hypnotise her now, or at least give it a shot. Make an excuse if it failed ('Just joking!'). But given how badly it went with Goth Girl, and given how close I am to tears, this seems like a safer bet.

'I haven't eaten today,' I say. 'I think it's low blood sugar.'

'Aubs, eating is important,' Es says. 'Wait here, I'll get you some biscuits.'

I nod.

As soon as the door clicks shut behind her, I pull open the cooler. There are six blood bags inside. As cool air rises, I rifle through them, ignoring the first bag, which is labelled O negative. I never take that—it's the universal blood donor type, the type that saves lives. But the second and third are B negative and A positive … I grab them, shove them into my bag, then quickly close the cooler again. I've barely zipped my bag shut when I hear Es coming back, her footsteps quick on the linoleum.

'Here,' she says, handing me the biscuits and shutting the door behind her. I make a big show of unwrapping them and taking a contented bite, even though—and I don't want to sound ungrateful here—they taste like sugary, crumbly cardboard.

'Thanks so much for the gummies, they'll make work this evening a *lot* more fun, but you really didn't have to, tomorrow would have been fine …'

And *shit*. We're supposed to be going to see the Christmas lights tomorrow night, we've done it every year since we became friends, but with all the trauma I forgot. I was supposed to ask Jonathan because she'd already asked Greg—her lovely boyfriend who she met at Glastonbury, 'made love to' under the stars and has been with ever since—and we were going to double date. Meet each other's partners, finally. But clearly, that won't be happening now, so I'm about to cancel, make an excuse, but then she says: 'So looking forward to it.'

My lower lip twitches. I look down at the floor. There's a heart-shaped mark on the linoleum and I stare at it, thinking, *Do not cry*. I *should* tell her that we broke up, but I'm ashamed. That I'm the unlovable one. Besides, if we get back together and she meets him, I want her to like him. And we *will* get back together.

Daphne will help me get him back.

So instead, I smile really hard, push down the tears and say, 'He said next time, he's still really busy with work. They're trying to get funding.'

'Ahh, that's a shame, still working at this time of year? Greg was so excited to meet you. But no mind, we'll have fun without them,' she says. There's something about the kindness in her voice that makes me want to cry even more.

I nod and force a smile and say, 'I'd better go. I'll be late for work.'

'Go, go,' she whispers as she opens the door.

As I get outside I glance down at my phone: 5.03 pm. And shit, now I really *am* late.

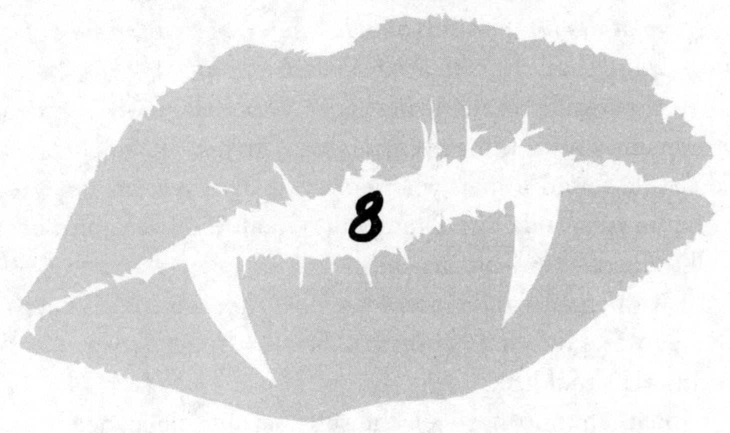

8

Just to hammer home the gravity of my situation, I should probably finish the story of how Jonathan and I first met. How I first learnt that he was my soulmate.

Two hours and two bottles of wine after Jonathan saved me from Pepperoni Guy, Daphne and I were still sitting with him and Baxter. It was dusk by now, so my energy was lifting, and all my attention was on Jonathan. I could smell that his blood was O positive, I could hear his pulse, and we were sitting close enough that I could feel his heat.

I could tell he liked me—his pupils were dilated and his heart sped up just a little when he looked at me. And not just in the way men always liked me, he was really listening to what I was saying and replying with thoughtful follow-up questions. I couldn't shake the sense that he was *special* somehow.

And then, his knee touched mine under the table, my stomach clenched, I thought, *Please, not now*, and in came one of my flashes.

Black and white and sped up, blurred at the edges and silent.

He's walking through a living room, up a staircase, pushing open a door, there's a wedding ring glinting on his finger. The door opens onto a bedroom and inside is a woman. She's sitting on the edge of the bed and brushing her hair and I can't see her face but I can see that she is wearing a wedding ring too.

Ice moved through me and I pulled away, a deep disappointment settling over me, because *just my fucking luck*. I'd finally found a man who looked at my eyes, not my arse, who was kind and considerate, but of course he was, he'd been well trained—he was married.

I wasn't going to be a homewrecker for anyone. Whatever I'd been feeling, that sense that he was 'special', was clearly nothing. I should go.

Jonathan must have felt the shift because he leaned in and asked, 'Are you okay?'

I looked up at him and nodded, our eyes met, something pinged in my chest and then his hand found mine. My stomach clenched *again*.

And now, great, just marvellous, the vision was back before I could push it away. It was exactly the same as before, except with more detail this time …

Here we go again, I thought, never guessing for a moment that my entire reality was about to change forever.

He's walking through a living room. There's a Christmas tree in the corner with small unlit candles and sugared candies hanging from the branches. Beneath it, presents are piled, the wrapping paper adorned with cherubs and birds. He passes a mirror and he looks like a completely different man …

Slight relief came over me now as I thought: *Oh, right, this is from his last life, not this one …* But that was soon replaced by a strange sense of déjà vu, a feeling of awe.

He walks past a sofa and a small oblong coffee table with a newspaper on it. The date is displayed, clear as day: December 18th, 1875.

And I was thinking: *Hang on, I think I recognise this house …*

He takes the stairs, just like he did before, he enters the bedroom. There's a bed, a wooden armoire, a free-standing wash basin, a dressing table, a brass vase, an oval mirror …

I *definitely* recognised this bedroom. It was the exact same one I'd woken up in 150 years ago, covered in blood.

The woman is there, brushing her hair with a big silver hairbrush, and then she turns to look at him. Like she's just noticed him there.

I zoomed in on her face, looking for answers, and the floor beneath me seemed to open up.

I jerked my hand away, and as the images cut to black I grabbed my glass of wine, holding it so tightly it should have shattered.

What the hell was going on?

Because that woman, the woman brushing her hair?

IT WAS ME.

And according to the newspaper in that vision, it was 1875.

The year before I was turned into a vampire.

I blinked hard, trying to control my breath, which was coming out quick and shallow as Jonathan watched me, his lips moving. The vision had played out as though in real time, but in reality, it had been only a second or two. He was none the wiser.

'Sorry, what did you say?' I asked.

He smiled gently, a soft frown on his forehead. 'I said, you feel chilly, would you like my coat?'

'I'm okay, thanks.' I smiled as I struggled to make sense of what was happening, and he turned back to Baxter and Daphne. But what the hell *was* happening? In all these years, with hundreds of unwanted visions, I'd never experienced anything like *this*. I'd seen people's past lives before, sure, but I'd never seen *myself* in them. Never met someone I'd known when I was still human.

I held the pieces in my mind, trying to put them together: this vision was coming from Jonathan, so it was his memory. It was from before I was turned so … what? We were married in his last life?

That had to be it.

I looked the same because I hadn't aged. But he had died and been reborn. He was now a different man in a different body, but with the same beautiful soul, a soul that had somehow found mine all over again.

The realisation winded me. My brain lit up as if on narcotics. A strange and unfamiliar feeling pulsed through me … hope.

This is why he feels special. He is.

As I sat there, an entire version of my future, which I'd never thought possible, unfurled before me and everything shifted into soft-focus. It was as though Tinkerbell herself had sprinkled me with fairy-dust and I would never get it off. Because what did this mean?

What else might I learn about myself if I spent more time with him? Who knew what other visions I could siphon? I could finally get the answers I'd always wanted, finally learn who I was as a human, who my parents were, what I believed in, what I liked … maybe I'd finally learn who did this to me, and why they left … the possibilities were limitless.

Did this mean I could have love? Real love? I mean, if anyone could love me despite … things … surely it would be him? Someone whose soul had loved me so much in his last life that it sought me out again?

By now, Jonathan and Baxter were telling Daphne how hard it was to get funding for an app they were developing while Daphne pretended to care. But inside, all I could hear was white noise. I traced the lines of Jonathan's face with my gaze, and my vision got all wavy and that tug in my chest tightened. Because how had I been so fortuitous? This was a once-in-ten-lifetimes occurrence. Maybe even rarer. What were the chances of our souls meeting again like this? Of my dud power firing up right when I needed it?

It was the most certain I'd ever been that there must be a god, or fate or something, after all. But I needed to hold it together, not get ahead of myself. I didn't want a repeat of Freddie.

So, I made a deal with myself. I would spend some more time with him, but my focus would be solely on trying to get a few more visions—maybe I could figure out who I was and how I had become this way. I would see how things went between us, but I would not let my heart run away.

Clearly, I failed. I fell hard and fast and I didn't care. It felt too good.

But now … well, once you've tasted hope, tasted love, tasted everything you've ever wanted, once you know that it is sweet and it exists for you—not just in books and movies, but in real life—and it can make everything better, how the hell do you go back to nothing?

It's as I pin my yellow Selfridges nametag to my polo neck and look up, willing the escalator to edge its way upwards a little faster, that I see a familiar dark head of hair around five people in front of me: *Kenny*.

Shit.

I shrink down and hide behind the man in front of me, just in case Kenny turns back.

The best parts of my job are Daphne and that I get to wear black. Black blends in. Black doesn't show blood. Black is a fair representation of my inner landscape.

The worst part of my job is *definitely* Kenny.

He's my floor manager, mediocre in every way, and, honestly, he's been the bane of my life for the entire four years I've worked here. Daphne says he has a crush on me. The girls who work at Calvin Klein say I should report him for bullying. My online friend, Sally, agrees with them both. But me? I deal with him the same way I deal with everything in life: avoidance.

He moves to the next escalator, and I slowly follow behind. I can't let him see me. He doesn't deal with lateness well. He doesn't deal with anything well.

Finally, I reach the third floor.

As Kenny continues up to the fourth floor, I relax my clenched fists, rushing towards the lingerie department.

I work at the Agent Provocateur concession. It doesn't pay that well, but that doesn't matter. If there's a silver lining to being alive for 150 years, it's savings. Investments. Compound interest. I wouldn't be considered super wealthy—not by London standards, at least—but what with my thrifty lifestyle (no groceries, no expensive clothes, hell, I don't even pay for my own internet at home) I have enough that I don't have to worry about money.

I only have this job because it gives me somewhere to go four nights a week and I like hanging out with Daphne. Besides, compared with the many other nighttime jobs I've had over the years—seamstress, dancer at Moulin Rouge, nurse (not a good fit for me, for obvious reasons), baker, telephone operator, band groupie, folk singer, etc—Selfridges, with its flexible schedules and work I never take home, suits me just fine.

Daphne is helping a customer when I get there. She's twenty-six, tall and slender, half Kenyan and even when she rolls her eyes at me behind the customer's back, she looks like she belongs in a Gucci ad. The moment I see her I relax. Soon, I will have a solid plan.

I go over to the tills and put my bag underneath the counter, but leave my phone face-up beside it. I can't risk missing a text from Jonathan.

'So …' comes Daphne's voice and I look up. 'What happened? I thought everything was good between you two.'

'He said it was getting too intense, that he thought we needed a break,' I say, my cheeks warm. And I feel almost guilty, because there, beneath the heartbreak is another feeling altogether. It's a strange and tangled sort of enjoyment I wasn't expecting. Because for once it's me who is going through something. Usually, I'm the onlooker, the shoulder to cry on while others experience their mini-earthquakes, tearful reunions, lost moments they'll never get back.

'Do you think it's better that he called it a "break" and not a "break-up"?' I add, hoping she puts my mind at ease. Tells me those are very different beasts. That I'm being negative thinking they are one and the same.

'Maybe,' she says. 'It means he wants to keep the door open. But he didn't say how long for, did he?'

I shake my head.

'And he hasn't checked on you?'

I swallow. 'No.'

'Okay, I'm just going to level with you, it's a break-up. He was probably just letting you down easy,' she says, pity in her eyes.

A wave of humiliation rolls over me.

'This is exactly why I told you not to be too intense,' she adds. 'It always freaks them out.'

'But we were both like that,' I say defensively. It was as if we were living in a bubble and the regular rules of dating didn't apply to us. Until the bubble popped for him.

'Yes, but there are two sets of rules, one for them and one for us. They lull you into a false sense of security and then judge you just for matching their enthusiasm. It's completely unfair.'

I've all but stopped breathing. Panic spurts through my veins. What does this mean? That it's really over? That there's no way to resuscitate it? She notices, and touches my arm to comfort me.

'Look, at least you found out quickly,' she says. 'You've only known him, what, a month?'

'Five weeks,' I say. 'But what do I do?'

She raises her eyebrows. 'You go out and get drunk and fuck someone else. Come out with me tonight.'

This was *not* the plan I had in mind.

'What? No …' I say.

Daphne gives me a stern look. 'Aubs, come on. Life is short, and you won't be young and hot forever. You can't just sit around mooning over some guy,' she says. 'And you always say no.'

She might be wrong about my life being short, and me not being young and hot forever, but she's right about me always saying 'no'. She's asked me out numerous times but I always opt instead for a nice, long night walk and the calm safety of my flat. However, right now I have an iron-clad excuse: there are two bags of blood in my bag that will expire in a few hours.

I shake my head.

'Well,' she says, a mischievous look on her face. 'If you want me to tell you how to get him back, you're going to have to come tonight. Those are my terms.'

My stomach twists. I do not want to go. I *really* do not want to go. But I need help. And whole blood can last eight hours at room temperature and my shift is only five …

I let out a big breath. 'Okay, maybe, just for a little bit. But you *have* to help.'

'Of course,' she says with a wink. 'He won't know what hit him. But I'm warning you, it's crucial that you listen to me this time. You won't get another shot with him if you ruin it again, okay?'

'I promise,' I say.

And then a female voice interrupts us with: 'Excuse me?'

We both plaster on our counter-smiles and look over to a woman of around forty or so, with perfectly groomed auburn hair standing by a rack of red balconette bras with cobweb-fine lace on the far wall. 'Do you have any more sizes of this out the back?' she asks, pointing to them.

Daphne goes over to help her, and I start to untangle the pile of bras on the counter, putting them on hangers, as cheerful Christmas songs play in the background, completely ambivalent to my personal problems. And then, somehow, I find myself reaching for my phone.

I stare down at it, my throat tight, thinking, *Do it, text him. Tell him everything.*

No, don't do it. Don't you dare. You don't want a repeat of Freddie, do you?

Freddie asked me to marry him in 1939, just after the Second World War broke out. He was a barman, and out all night, so it was easy to hide my secret from him in a way it wasn't from other men. I'd grown to truly care about him, and was touched that he wanted to marry me, but I knew he couldn't truly love me unless I was completely honest. And, blame the potential end of the world, blame the fact that I was only sixty-three vampire years deep, blame the fact that I hadn't been burnt by love yet, but I naively sat him down, held his hand, and … showed him my fangs.

He bolted, didn't speak to me again, acted like he'd never met me. Soon after, he voluntarily signed up to go to war. I never saw him again.

But, as much as that stung, the truth is, I never felt for Freddie half of what I do for Jonathan—that cosmic tug beneath my ribs. So I really need to do whatever I have to do to get Jonathan back. I need to listen to Daphne.

Which means I need a distraction. Any distraction. NOW.

I pull up a browser window and navigate to the VHC website, which is where I met Sally.

The Vampire Hunters' Collective.

Yes, I know, but I can explain.

I spent my first few years as a vampire laying low, doing whatever I had to do to survive and reading as much as I could without raising suspicion. I started with folklore (Portuguese, Slavic, Polish, Irish, Egyptian, Romanian, Albanian, you name it), then moved on to poems like *The Giaour* and *The Bride of Corinth,* a few short stories and then novels like *The Vampyre* and *Carmilla*, among others. It didn't take long to figure out nobody knew what the hell was going on. Stake through the heart, they said. Fire. Silver. Garlic. Bollocks.

But I just kept reading, kept thinking: *Someone must know. One of these books must hold the key. I just have to find it.*

They didn't.

Instead, the more stories I read, the more confused I became—each seemed to contradict the last. I mean, did I really bring the plague? Should I invest in a coffin? And what the fuck was up with the bats?

In fact, the only thing every story *did* agree on was vampires were really bloody hungry. It was a hunger that, in the end, would win out over everything else. A hunger I'd seen play out in real time with Hans. A hunger that made us kill; made us … bad.

I wasn't bad, was I? I'd done bad things, but I felt guilt. I had a conscience. I'd tried to save that boy. Ever since Hans, I'd lived off blood from hospitals or choked down animal blood, even though it was revolting, did very little for me, and was not without its own moral quandaries. And it's not like I'd *chosen* to be this way.

Honestly, I identified with the humans in the stories I read far more than the so-called vampires. Who the hell was writing them? And where were they getting their information?

It was like reading the worst review of yourself from all angles, some of it lies, some of it truths you don't want to rehash. And you can only hear bad things about yourself so many times before you start to accept them as truth … as inevitable.

So, I made a choice.

If I was going to be stuck here on this earth for eternity, with no god, no others like me, and no real guidance, I couldn't leave my fate up to chance. I couldn't keep looking outside of myself for answers. I would need to decide for myself.

Who did I want to be?

To be honest, it was a lot simpler to define who I *didn't* want to be. I *didn't* want to be someone who elicited the look of terror I'd seen in that boy's eyes. I *didn't* want to be a monster, like the vampires I'd read about. I didn't want to be a vampire at all.

And thus, with the aid of a circle of salt, some blood from a butcher and a candle (I don't know, I just wanted to make it feel official), I vowed that no matter how hungry I got, I would *not* do harm. I would *not* give in to my darkness. I knew I couldn't feed off humans nicely because once I started, I couldn't stop and someone always died—so I wouldn't feed off them at all.

I would find a way to accept my grim fate gracefully.

And even though I couldn't remember who I'd been as a human, I would hold on to my humanity with everything I was.

But to do that, I needed to turn away from vampires altogether.

I lost myself in human stories instead. In these, I found everything I yearned for, but was denied, in life. Hope. Warmth. Positive outcomes. Happiness. Meaning. Purpose. Fragility. The poetry of a ticking clock and moments that passed and could never be retrieved. In short, the trimmings of mortality. And most of all, love.

True love.

The kind of love that was intoxicating and fated, that while always complicated, always requiring sacrifice and a fight, and always coming with a hefty dose of pain, would *always* win out in the end. The kind of love where you are never too little and never too much, where someone sees every part of you—darkness and all—and loves you anyway. The kind of love that changes you.

I confess, I still cheated on my promise to turn away from vampire stories. I watched vampire movies, read vampire books, and woke up early to get to the library before it closed so I could pore over folklore. I'm drawn to the darkness just as much as anybody else, probably more so. And I still wanted answers. But these forays into the dark side always left me in even more despair. Even more certain that I did not, under any circumstances, want to be a vampire.

Honestly, it wasn't until the likes of *Buffy the Vampire Slayer* and *Twilight*, *The Vampire Diaries* and *True Blood* and others that came after them that I found representation of vampires … like me. Vampires who had clung to their humanity, vampires with souls, and consciences—vampires with love stories that were much like those in the human stories I adored. Vampires that were almost human. I mean, they weren't all good, but *some* of them were, and that was enough for me. They made me feel seen, less strange. Less terrified of myself. Less alone.

But in the real world, it's always been just me, alone.

Friends have always been transient. Aside from Freddie, there's been no romance to speak of. And aside from Hans, the only other vampire I've ever met was some sulking guy I happened upon by chance in the 1990s, in Berlin. But he left the bar without even saying goodbye when I told him that I only drank from the bag. Mainly, I've told myself this was a blessing in disguise, at least I'd never fall prey to the darkness through peer pressure.

But every year on the fifth of May, I have commemorated my vampire birthday with a sad little candle in a cupcake I do not eat. And, every year, without fail, there is one specific vampire I *have* yearned for, despite myself. Who am I kidding, I've thought of him daily.

My sire—the one who made me this way.

Even though it appeared that he'd abandoned me, in my more vulnerable moments I'd think: *What if* … What if I was being unfair to him? What if he'd been kept from me? Kidnapped, or buried in cement? What if he'd been looking for me this whole time? I'd let myself imagine us meeting again, that feeling of warmth, of understanding, feeling protected, like it wasn't just me against the world alone anymore—I'd imagine myself hearing the reasons for his absence, feeling the pure relief of realising I wasn't unlovable after all. But then I'd think about Hans and Count Orlok from *Nosferatu* and Lord Ruthven from *The Vampyre* or Count Dracula and that would snap me back into reality. What if my maker was a monster like them? I mean, that would be just my fucking luck.

Aside from which, where would I even find him?

For a long time, I did nothing. I just waited for the wondering, the longing, to stop. But I've watched the moon rise and set 55,016 times now and I *still* think of him, wonder about him.

So, two years ago, I decided it was finally time to look for him. Because, with the advent of the internet, I could now search anonymously from the safety of my flat, which was a lot safer than putting a 'wanted' ad in a local newspaper or anything else available to me before. If I found him, and he turned out to be bad, I would simply go on with my life and pretend I didn't know. But if he was good, like me—which was possible—I would no longer be alone.

Of course, this was all before I met Jonathan, because once he came into my life, I didn't need anyone else.

But that's how, after multiple false starts—TikTok videos by supposed vamps; Reddit threads; meet-up groups run by healthy-looking men named Craig or Geoffrey and attended by humans in latex with coloured contact lenses; weeks wrangling with Tor only to realise the dark web is bullshit—a cautious little vampire like me ended up here. On this VHC website.

Because what better way to find a vampire than to start chatting to a bunch of vampire hunters?

I look up and around to make sure nobody is watching, then quickly log in.

Welcome, Margot, it reads at the top.

While I could have chosen any screenname I wanted, it seemed a bit pointless given that anybody who tapped on my profile could see my 'real name' anyway. Well, the name that matches the ID I used to sign up to this site (more on that later).

I tap through to the VHC noticeboard and scan the most recent posts: PENNSYLVANIA COUPLE CLAIM TO DRINK BLOOD, BRONX SUBWAY STABBING ATTACK APPEARS RANDOM, BREAK-IN TURNS DEADLY …

The way this forum works is simple: members copy and paste the main information from news articles detailing crimes they suspect might have been committed by a vampire, or that reference vampires directly. Usually these involve stabbings—apparently that's how we 'vamps' cover our bite marks, at least according to the ever-growing number of members on this site.

Sometimes, when there is a particularly compelling article that everyone agrees most probably describes a vampire attack, there are IRL (in real life) events in the relevant location to 'strategise'. Members can even 'Zoom in' electronically from other locations if they want to.

I've only been to one of these—a meet-up organised by a psycho called @Riley—and *never again*.

I tap on **PENNSYLVANIA COUPLE CLAIM TO DRINK BLOOD** and scan down to the comments.

There's only one: *If they want to act like vamps let them die like vamps! Wrap them in chains, bury them with rocks in their jaws like the olden days!*

It was posted by @NancyJayne, whose avatar is a little circle with the text *Jesus Loves You* in the centre.

I tap out of it. My stomach clenches.

Comments like that are par for the course, but I won't lie, sometimes they hurt. But every time I've almost deleted my profile, I couldn't. This is the only place I've found where people actually believe vampires exist. And in a world where all I can do is stay hidden, and lie to everyone I know … that's everything.

Besides, now I *can't* leave, because I've made a friend here. Sally. Otherwise known as @Connecticuthousewife011. And even though yes, she lives in Connecticut, so we'll never get to hang out in real life, that's kind of a good thing. There's something comforting about having a screen and an ocean between us. About knowing I could delete my profile at any time.

It means I can almost be myself with her. Almost. While yes, she thinks my name is Margot, and no, I'd never tell her my biggest secret, I've told her more than anyone else. Things I'd never dare tell anyone who knew me in real life.

Like, this year on my vampire birthday, I was having a particularly bad night. I was sitting there with my stupid little cupcake, sobbing uncontrollably, certain that the ache inside me would never ease, and I just had to get it out.

I didn't know Sally that well, we'd only been messaging for a couple of months about various articles, but she'd once written that she wished a vampire would come and scare her husband out of inertia. She'd added 'LOL' like it was a joke, but I could tell there was some truth to it. A latent pain that meant she might understand. Besides, she was so far away that if I was going to be honest with anyone, she was perfect.

So I logged in and typed the thing I'd never said out loud: *I want to die sometimes*.

Then, of course, came the terror of judgement. As the typing bubbles flared, I was preparing myself for the worst, getting ready to delete my profile altogether, thinking: *Have you lost your mind?* But then she wrote back: *It's okay. Me too.*

It was the most normal I'd ever felt. And we've been friends ever since.

I'd say our friendship is thirty per cent sexy-vampire memes, thirty per cent complaining about life, twenty per cent chatting about what it might be like to actually *be* a vampire (she thinks it'd be amazing, I usually gently suggest it might be more like a holiday in hell—though obviously under the guise of surmising), ten per cent discussing articles on the site and ten per cent real talk.

For me, that real talk used to mean telling her exactly how lonely I was, how nobody ever saw beyond my surface, but maybe if they ever did, they wouldn't love me anyway. How I thought Edward from *Twilight* was the perfect man, that sort of thing.

But recently, all I've talked about is Jonathan and how I'm *so* in love with him. I have, however, been careful to dilute that with a lot of complaining about Kenny and work because I know Sally is unhappy in her marriage and I don't want to be insensitive.

Sally talks a lot about killing her husband, Frank, and making it look like a vampire did it, though she does routinely take breaks from that train of thought to 'ooh' and 'aah' over things Jonathan has said or done, or to pray for Kenny's demise and encourage me to do the same. I'm pretty sure she's joking about all of it, but who knows? I'm certainly not going to judge. And thanks to the time difference, I can talk to her late into the night while the rest of London sleeps.

But the best part is, I get to keep her.

Because I love Es and Daphne, but they have a shelf-life. In three to five years, I will have to fade out of their lives the way I always have to disappear from the lives of my friends, before they figure out I'm not ageing—there's only so much I can put down to Botox, good hydration and a nine-step skincare routine, although those things have bought me a little extra time in recent years. It meant I had a little longer before needing a new ID where the picture matched the birthdate. But online friends don't know if you're seventeen, seventy or 150, so I can keep those friends for as long as they are alive.

I tap through to my inbox and stare down at Sally's last message: *In-laws arrived today. MIL is already reorganising my cutlery drawers. FML. How's the man? How's work? Douchebag boss die of a heart attack yet? Still praying!*

She sent it yesterday, but what with the break-up and everything, I didn't get to it. And now there is no man and every part of me hurts.

Then I hear: 'Aubrey, no phones on the floor.'

That's Kenny's voice. The douchebag in question.

My stomach clenches and I look up. He's staring at me with those beady little eyes of his, shifting from foot to foot like he's brought the London marathon training he never shuts up about into work.

That marathon is why Sally thinks he might have a heart attack one day soon if we both 'pray on it'. I don't have the heart to tell her that if there is a god, he hasn't answered my prayers in a very long time. Honestly, he'd probably keep Kenny around just to spite me.

I put my phone back under the desk. 'Sorry.'

Kenny's eyes graze my chest and linger around where my nipples would be if he could see them. He licks his lips just a little and my insides recoil. I imagine myself lurching forward, my fangs exposed, going for his pasty neck. Not because I'm hungry or tempted by his blood, but because I want him to feel violated too.

Stop it Aubrey. Push it down.

'I'll put a meeting in so we can talk about your sales targets. Again,' he says, eyes to mine now. As he wanders off I think, *How have I sheltered from bombs in the London Tube, fought as a suffragette, gone to war, pushed through the Great Depression, evaded electric shock therapy in the 50s, dealt with Y2K, 9/11 and the 2008 crash (along with everything else), only to have to deal with the likes of … Kenny?*

Daphne rushes over.

'Oh my god, what is his deal?' she asks. 'Are you okay?'

I nod.

'Such a lech,' she says, sneering in Kenny's direction. Then she turns to me, her eyes on mine. 'It's okay, Aubs, stop looking so sad. Jonathan is *just* a guy. But if you want him back, we'll get him back, okay?'

And as she says it, that elusive hope is back.

12

Daphne belongs to an exclusive members club in Mayfair, right near Marble Arch—she got membership from one of her sugar daddies a while back—so that's where we go tonight. We stand on Dunraven Street in front of a relatively innocuous-looking wooden door. There's a brass intercom with a snake logo at the top, and she presses the button, stands in front of the lens and smiles. There's a click, then the door opens.

A hostess with a short black bob greets us. A big, brass *STRICTLY NO PHOTOS* sign hangs on the wall behind her, and there's an iPad in front of her. 'Welcome to Serpentine,' she says, then she nods to Daphne. 'Nice to see you again, Ms Roberts. You know the way?'

Daphne nods and strides through an open doorway to our left, into a low-lit bar, ornate lamps on every table emitting an amber glow.

As we move towards the bar I feel awkward and conspicuous; everything smells of old money and heritage. You'd think that would make me feel right at home, but I've spent my whole life on the edges of society, avoiding rooms like these. If somebody wealthy said I was a vampire, they'd probably be believed.

Daphne, on the other hand, moves like she doesn't have a care in the world, like she feels safe being noticed, and oh, how I envy it.

We sit on high stools at the bar and a barman comes over to us. He's clean-cut, late twenties, maybe early thirties.

'Two dirty martinis,' Daphne says to him as her eyes dart around the room, then she turns to me. 'Okay, I'm going to tell you this stuff, but only if you promise to cheer up,' she says, frowning at me.

I plaster on a smile. 'I promise,' I say.

'Good,' she says. The bartender begins pouring our drinks, and Daphne stops speaking, like she's worried he'll overhear her war strategy. Finally, he's done, pushing them across the bar on two napkins. Daphne goes to pay but the bartender says, 'Compliments of the two gentlemen behind you.'

We both turn to look.

One is short and sturdy looking with dark hair, while the other is tall and lanky with mousy-brown hair and a deep side part. Both mid-forties. Daphne flashes them a quick smile and a wave, and I take a sip of my drink. I like martinis—the shape of the glass, the romance of them—even if they don't really work on me.

While I *can* drink alcohol and do drugs, and they *do* affect me eventually, I'd need a LOT more than Daphne or any other human would to get a real buzz. Lord knows I've tried it all over the years, looking for something, anything, to take the edge off, even if just a little. Cigarettes are the most effective thing I've found—probably because their toxicity rivals mine. But the closest thing I've ever had to a real high in recent years was Jonathan.

'Where were we,' Daphne says, leading me to a table and taking a sip of her drink. We both put our coats on the backs of the chairs then sit down.

'Right, getting him back,' she starts. 'Well, I mean there are the standard things like not texting him, and posting pictures of yourself living your best life, blah-blah-blah. But men aren't completely stupid, and they can be a teensy bit arrogant. You just have to look at them and they think you're picking out bridesmaids' dresses. He'll automatically assume you're doing it all for him unless you're a bit … sneaky.

'So,' she says, leaning in and lowering her voice a little, 'when you post pictures, make sure you're not just posing and smiling and looking super hot. You need to look natural and be laughing, it needs to be the kind of picture where you just know someone else was there taking it. He needs to think you've totally forgotten him—that way, his ego gets involved.' She nods, as if to drill the truth of what she's saying into my head.

And I nod too, saying 'right, right,' even though I'm not sure I like the sound of this. It doesn't sound very soulmatey.

'Then,' she continues, 'when he starts watching your Instagram stories or texts you something inane, you reply with the exact same thing. He sends a fire emoji, you send a fire emoji. He sends "Hey" then you send "Hey".' She uses her fingers for air quotes. 'Nothing more, nothing less. Eventually he'll start to think he's lost his hold on you and that, my friend, is the key. When men think they have you, they stop seeing you clearly, they think you're replaceable. You need to show him you're not bothered.'

She takes another sip of her drink. 'But …' She pauses for drama, and I wonder how many other times she's imparted this wisdom. 'You only get one shot at this, so Aubs, you can't crack first. That's the mistake we always make, we give up right before they crack. And they *always* crack—they can't help themselves. You just need to wait it out. That's when the real work starts.'

'What do you mean?' I frown.

'Well,' she says, leaning in a little further, like she's just getting to the good stuff, 'that's when you have to start being *different*. Like Aubs, but version two-point-oh.' She raises her eyebrows and smiles. 'Now you're fun and elusive and unpredictable. Think mysterious, alluring … maybe a little bit dangerous.' She winks.

I recoil at the word *dangerous* … she has no idea.

'That sounds like playing games.'

She shrugs. 'Oh, it is. But they do it too. And honestly, you're doing him a favour. Men produce vasopressin when you stress them out, and that's the same chemical that makes them bond with you. It's science.' And that's typical Daphne, she'll spout all these mind games that make her seem a bit mean or manipulative and then pull out a scientific fact to back it all up. It's pretty convincing. 'Still, I don't even know why you're wasting your time with all this. It's not like he was paying your rent or something. And you could have anyone you want. I could introduce you to some others?'

I take a small sip of my drink while I think about this. My eyes meet hers. 'I just want him.'

She shrugs. 'Ah, young love. Well, then there you have it. That's how you get him back.'

She reaches for my hand and squeezes it and a warmth rolls through me. And for a single moment, I have a friend. A real friend. But then I remember that a few years from now I'll be nothing but a memory to her, that if she ever knew my secret she'd run as fast as she could. And the loneliness is back.

Her eyes move over my shoulder and her voice drops to a murmur. 'Oh god, they're coming over. You can practise being mysterious on these guys.' Then she puts on a big, beautiful, billboard-worthy smile.

I glance behind me and see the two men who bought us drinks approaching. I quickly look away from them, back down at the bar. *I shouldn't have come.*

Daphne arches her back.

'Good evening, ladies, could we join you?' the tall one asks, in one of those rah-rah British accents that indicate he's never had to work a day in his life, but probably has a job as a fund manager that his father or a 'friend from school' got him. 'I'm Timothy, and this is Ray.'

'Sure,' Daphne says, batting her eyelashes. 'I'm Jasmine and this is Harriet,' she lies. Daphne often lies about strange things, I think she gets off on it, so I just smile along.

'Hi,' I say, and they both look at me in that way men *always* look at me.

Timothy sits by Daphne and Ray sits closer to me. His blood type is B positive and there's a little white indent on his wedding ring finger where a ring should sit. *It's probably in his pocket.*

'So, what have you girls been up to tonight?' Ray asks, edging his body closer to mine. He smells sour.

'We just got off from work,' Daphne interjects, answering for me.

'Working late …' he says. 'What do you do?'

'We're in PR,' Daphne lies again with a sweet smile, taking one of the martini olives seductively in her mouth.

'Groovy,' he says, and I flinch. I remember that word. Remember it fading out of fashion and me dropping it at the same time everyone else dropped it so I wouldn't give myself away. There are many words and phrases I love but cannot use in conversation: glad rags, swell, dope, cataclysmic, petrichor, mellifluous … nothing that suggests I've read more books than my twenty-two years might allow. Or, worse still, that I was around when those words were in routine circulation. Though, conversely, I do love how I can say 'fuck' so freely these days. So, you win some, you lose some, I guess.

Daphne throws me an amused look—she noticed 'groovy' too—then spits out the olive pip and downs the rest of her drink.

'We have a place near here,' Ray says.

'Oh, that's nice,' Daphne says, not taking the bait.

Ray grins at her, his eyes narrowing like he's accepting an unspoken challenge. 'How about we get you another?'

'Sure,' Daphne answers with a shrug. 'Harriet?'

I nod and smile, even though I'm still sipping my first drink.

'I'm going to go and powder my nose,' she says, and disappears.

Ray heads to the bar and Timothy follows him, leaning in and whispering something. I tune in, curious, just in time to hear, 'Like shooting fish in a barrel.' They laugh.

My darkness gathers beneath my ribs, an anger starts to rise, but *NO*. I push it down.

This is why I don't socialise much—it's always disappointing. That, and I might slip, do something I regret.

My phone vibrates with a message and I reach for it in my pocket. It's a text from Daphne, from the loos. It reads: *OMG isn't he so fucking tedious? Like anyone cares.*

I frown down at it, a little confused, as more typing bubbles flare, then: *Beep.*

In comes an image.

It's a screenshot of Kenny's Instagram page. His profile is private but Daphne hate-follows him. It's a graphic from one of those running apps that tracks your route with a little squiggle and shares how many kilometres you've run, and all the other data nobody cares about. He posts these almost daily and Daphne, who doesn't like exercise, takes each and every post as a personal attack.

I heart the image and type back: *God I hate him.*

Typing bubbles flare, then come a series of vomiting emojis.

I laugh and look up. Timothy and Ray are still at the bar so I log in to the VHC website and tap through to Sally's last message: *In-laws arrived today. MIL is already reorganising my cutlery drawers. FML. How's the man? How's work? Douchebag boss die of a heart attack yet? Still praying!*

As I look down at it, I know I should tell her about the break-up. I've told her everything else about our relationship—it feels a bit like she's been watching a TV show, she's fully invested, and now it's been cancelled. But my thumbs just hover in space, and I can't. I don't want our love story to be over. It can't be.

So instead, I answer her other question, the one about Kenny and his potential heart attack. I send her the screenshot Daphne just forwarded me of Kenny's running track with the text: *Not yet, but it's looking promising.* Then I add an emoji with the prayer hands.

Send.

And then … comes a jolt.

The little hairs on the back of my neck stand up on end and my breath catches. *There are eyes on me*. I look up and around. Most people are sitting and talking quietly among themselves. A few men sit alone, staring down at newspapers. But I can still feel the gaze on me … there, on the other side of the room.

There's a man. He's staring right at me.

He's sitting at a table cordoned off by red rope. He's flanked by three women, and a silver ice bucket with champagne. He's not pretty, but he has a strong face, dark curls, and there's something rugged and unbothered about him that clearly his companions fancy. As I meet his gaze, another zap of electricity moves up my spine.

What the hell was that?

I look down, my shoulders tight.

Calm down. Men look at you all the time.

And so, I do what I always do when I don't want to be bothered. I start scrolling on my phone, frowning into that blue-white light like I'm doing something very important.

So … I don't *mean* to open Instagram.

I don't *mean* to check on Jonathan.

It's an accident.

But now here I am, staring at the beautiful lines around his mouth when he smiles, remembering what it felt like to be his—safe and like everything was right in the world—and now a dull ache rings out in my chest. Like there's a big empty cavern inside me.

How did we get here?

And do I really want to stay here? In this misogynist, old-money bar with the likes of Timothy and Ray and some guy staring at me from across the room? It's all so sordid. So pointless.

No. I do not. I don't want to be here at all.

I just want to be with Jonathan.

So, I know I just agreed to do what Daphne said, but what if it doesn't work? Or what if it works *too* well and I become just that girl he thought was 'the one' for a while, but who he never heard from again? Who was posting happy snaps on Instagram within a week?

That's totally what's going to happen if I do this Daphne's way. My stomach clenches, my head gets light.

Screw it.

I can't do this. I just can't.

I need to go to him.

That's what I need to do.

Once he sees me again, he'll remember everything … us. *He just needs to remember.*

I look up, just in time to see Daphne arriving back from the bathroom.

'You have to go to the loos,' she whispers in my ear. 'So lush … They have a Jo Malone candle in there.'

'I have to go, I'm so sorry,' I say, standing up and pulling on my coat.

'Babe,' she says, looking at me long and hard.

'I'm just not ready for this.'

'What are you going to do? Remember Aubs, don't crack first …' She's frowning at me.

'I won't,' I say, because I can't deal with an argument right now. 'I'm just going home. But be careful with these two. They're arseholes.'

She rolls her eyes and whispers, 'Whatever, I'm just using them for drinks. There are far hotter men in here.' She winks.

'Are you going?' asks Ray, grabbing at my sleeve.

'Yes.' I smile politely, pulling away.

Before he can protest, I'm heading through the crowd towards the door, reaching for my phone, checking the time … I trip, almost hit the floor but catch myself just before impact. I straighten, look up and around, a little embarrassed, but nobody noticed, except for one set of eyes. That man.

He's still watching me. *Glaring* is probably a better word for it.

What the hell is his problem?

Then comes the paranoia: *Does he somehow know what I am?*

But *no*, I tell myself as I rush past the hostess and out the door, into the icy night air. *Of course not. I'm too careful for that. It's just my imagination.* This feeling isn't new. Hypervigilance, a certain level of paranoia, the constant feeling that maybe I'm being watched while simultaneously feeling totally invisible? That just comes with the territory. So, I push it aside.

And as I look at the sparkling wet streets, Christmas lights reflected in the puddles, all I can think about is Jonathan and us and it's as if that little cord connecting us is pulling me towards him.

13

The first cold raindrop hits my forehead as I emerge from Archway tube station. I don't have an umbrella but I don't care. As I head up the hill towards Jonathan's street, the clouds crack open and I practise what I'm going to say: 'I'm so sorry for being so intense, I can do better, give you space, I will, I promise …'

I dodge the traffic, the red of taillights and the white of headlights reflecting off the wet tar as I run across the road and down his street, and now I'm breathless and my coat and hair are wet, and there is his house, just up ahead.

I wipe the rain from my face as I move towards it, searching the cars parked along the street for a red Kia. That's Jonathan's car. So beautifully understated, just like him. And there it is, raindrops glistening from the roof. He's home.

What will he say when he sees me?

But *ah shit*, there Baxter's white Audi, parked on the other side of the road. And he's *always* home, so this shouldn't surprise me, but I really don't want an audience tonight … But *it's okay, I can do this.*

Because now I'm here, right outside his house. My hair is so wet that it's sticking to my head but this reminds me of that scene in *The Vampire Diaries* where Damon and Elena are kissing in the rain … It's romantic.

I swallow hard, look up towards his front door, and then to the bay window to the left. There's a faint yellow glow seeping out from between the curtains. I take a deep breath, move my hair out of my face and head up the path to the front door. Butterflies flood my stomach as I reach for the doorbell, and I'm listening out for the familiar sound of his heartbeat when instead …

I hear a giggle.

A woman's giggle.

My hand freezes in midair.

That's not right.

I rush back down the stairs, step into the flowerbed in front of the window and move close to the glass. There's a thin gap between the curtains. I peer inside.

I see Baxter first. He's standing on the rug Jonathan and I slow-danced on, not far from the Christmas tree, its little lights blurred by the rain on the window. I look to the right, searching for Jonathan. And he's right there, so close, on the sofa we sat on so many times. And he's beautiful, so beautiful—but one of those men who doesn't know that he's hot, which just makes him even hotter. He's wearing the same blue jumper he wore on our first date, and I reach out as though to touch him as a warmth moves through my veins. But as my fingertips hit the glass, the world spins faster and now I'm struggling to breathe. Because there, beside him, is a woman. I can't see her face, she's sitting with her back to me, but she's wearing a bright red sweater and has dark curly hair, flowing down her back.

WHO THE FUCK IS SHE?

The rain is getting heavier, but I can't tear myself away. Instead, I watch helplessly, my heels sinking into the mud, as she reaches over and tousles his fucking hair.

Then Jonathan says something I don't quite catch because stupid Baxter is talking over him, and then the woman turns for just a moment to look at the Christmas tree, and I see a flash of her face.

Oh perfect. She's pretty.

Pretty. Tousling his hair. And on the warm side of the window.

While here I stand, in the rain, two bags of blood in my bag.

This isn't how tonight was meant to go.

I scan the scene, from Jonathan to her to Baxter to what I presume is her beige Chloe handbag on the table by the sofa. Lying beside it, with a bunch of keys is a security badge from an investment bank. I zoom in on it. Staring back at me, from just below a slightly pixelated version of her face, her long dark hair, is a name: *Olivia Coombes.*

I bristle as I mouth it silently. And I hate the way it feels in my mouth. Hate that she has a name someone gave to her, not like me.

But now they're talking again, and I focus in, seeking out clues as to why Olivia fucking Coombes is there to start with.

'He's clearly lost,' Baxter says. 'I'll go and stand outside so he can see me.' And then he moves towards the front door.

And … *oh no.*

I can't let them find me here, like this. Not with her all dry and normal in there. I'd look like a stalker.

So I turn and run back towards the gate, onto the street and jog towards the main road, my face angled down, not daring to look back in case Baxter sees me. A car with an Uber sticker drives past me, the wipers quick in the rain, and I stand at the corner of his street, hugging myself and watching as it pulls up at Jonathan's house.

An ache rings out beneath my ribs. An insane part of me wants to go back, give my little speech, do it in the rain. But another, rational part, is not so sure. Because now that I think about it, me turning up in the rain like this isn't romantic, it's positively unhinged. Daphne was right, I need to reel it in. Now. Before I make things worse.

I rush back to the station, wet to the bone, as people move past me, huddling under umbrellas. There's a little corner store beside it, a neon 'open' sign hanging in the window and I go inside and up to the counter and scan for the strongest packet of cigarettes. Because I need something right now, something to take the edge off.

'A packet of Benson and Hedges, please,' I say to the bored-looking shop clerk. 'And a lighter,' I add.

'What colour?' the clerk asks in a monotone voice, pointing to the tray of lighters behind him as he eyes my dripping hair.

I could choose pink, or blue, or yellow. But the only one I can see right now is: 'Black.'

He hands me the cigarettes and the lighter and I pay him. Then, in a daze, I go back to the station and through the turnstiles and onto the platform. And now here I am, back at Archway, putting on my sunglasses just in case I cry.

Again.

Part of me wishes I'd never met him. That I didn't know what it felt like to lie in his arms. That he'd never come to that pub on that Sunday afternoon, and I'd never looked into his blue-blue eyes …

But I'm lying now.

I don't wish any of that.

The truth is, even if I *could* stop this feeling, go back to a time before him, I don't think I would. Because he took me closer to my humanity than I have ever been. He gave me a reason to hope. And after wandering around like a shell for 150 years, with no idea who I was or what had happened to me, it was the first time I knew I wasn't just some mistake of nature. It was the first time I was sure that I … existed.

14

By the time I walk out of London Bridge station and into the brisk night air, it has stopped raining and I am numb. I walk quickly over the bridge, the Thames on one side, traffic beeping on the other, my eyes trained on the cracks in the pavement.

Soon I'm walking under the railway bridge near Pret A Manger. A train rumbles overhead, all around me people stare down at their phones, and a red London bus slowly approaches. On its side, a family is pictured sitting around a Christmas tree. The slogan beneath the image reads: *Priceless*. And now something pierces through the numbness and hits me deep in my core.

As the bus passes, I want to throw myself in front of it.

To force the world to see me. To acknowledge my pain.

I imagine the commotion, the confusion. The bags of blood tipping out of my handbag. People pulled away from their phone screens for just one moment.

But instead, I let the bus splash past me, then I rush through the cold night air until I'm heading past the bins and the pub, pulling open the flimsy black metal gate and hurrying downstairs to my door.

Cat is there in her usual spot, waiting for me. I push the key into the lock and she follows me inside with a small 'meow'.

I rush to the freezer, put a bag of blood in my spinach box and then put the other one in the Fortnum & Mason tin in the fridge. I'm not even hungry.

Then I sit down on the sofa, and as Cat jumps up and starts kneading my leg, I pull the cigarettes out of my bag. But I can't get the plastic off them and *fuck*, I don't even want to smoke, I just want Jonathan back, telling me *not* to smoke. I throw them across the room and reach for my phone instead.

As I stare at the blank screen, I'm filled with this uncontrollable urge to call him. To talk to him. To beg him to love me. But then comes the shame. Because maybe he deserves more than me.

So, I just stare down at the screen and do nothing as a heavy sadness settles over me. Resignation.

This is how it has always been for me. I guess this is how it will always be.

This is my destiny.

So, I do what I always do when I'm feeling this way. I log in to the VHC website, go to my inbox and type out a message to Sally: *He said he wanted a 'break'. I think it might be over.*

There. Now it's real.

And then I sit there, staring at it, waiting for a reply. Needing typing bubbles. Something to fill the great vacuum that has reopened within me. But nothing comes. Because she, along with everyone else, has a life, with in-laws and a husband and I have … *this*.

I look around the darkened room, at my makeshift little life that I've never really settled into because I know I'll have to leave. My novels, and the few belongings I've carried from life to life. The old fridge that hums all night and the sofa that needs replacing. There are no pictures on the walls because you just have to take them down again. I never get too attached to anywhere I live, it would just make leaving hurt more.

I let out a big, shuddering breath as I glance out the window and up the stairs to the street to the place where Jonathan first kissed me. It was just as we were all leaving the pub, that first time we met. Daphne and Baxter were standing nearby, pretending not to watch, when Jonathan leaned in and touched my face. I could feel his breath on my lips, something flipped in my stomach, and then his mouth found mine. He tasted like red wine and metal and … home. Now our entire love story to date flickers in my mind, then everything we were supposed to be, and I'm filled with warmth and hope and then … doom. Despair. A flash of *her* hand reaching for his hair and me in that garden bed … then cold, stark clarity.

Because am I really going to just give up this easily? Wave a white flag and let some other woman have my soulmate?

Am I that weak?

No. I am not. So fuck this.

FUCK THIS!

I'm very, very sorry, but this cannot just be over.

Not without a fight.

Because who is this woman?

She's not his soulmate, I know that much.

Heat pulses through me as I frantically tap through to Instagram, go to the search function and stab in: *Olivia Coombes*.

Up come five potential profiles; five tiny circular faces staring back at me.

No. No. No. No.

YES.

The bottom one is her. I'm sure of it.

I tap on it, quickly, like it might disappear if I'm not fast enough, the rest of the world blurring as I wait the quarter second for it to load.

Cat meows, probably in disapproval, but I ignore her and scroll through Olivia's grid. She's always in either athletic wear or business suits. Judging by the bars she frequents, she lives in Richmond.

I glance at her bio and my gaze catches on just one phrase: *Former Forbes 30 under 30 Europe*. And *oh joy*—she's successful, and smart too. Pretty, successful, smart, and the worst part is she looks like a really nice person. Like the kind of woman I might be friends with.

Pull it together, Aubrey. You can't like her, can't side with her, or you'll never get him back. And look, she doesn't have any pets in her pictures so she can't be that great. Right?

I scroll down a little further, drinking in the images, like maybe if I know her well enough I can make her disappear and then, out of nowhere: *Tap, tap, tap.*

I turn to look at the door.

Freeze.

Because nobody knows where I live. Not Jonathan. Not Daphne. Not Es. Not even Brendon who sells me weed gummies upstairs.

Nobody.

But then it comes again: *Tap, tap, tap.*

I hold my breath, get up and tiptoe towards the door.

I stand there, listening, not wanting to look through the peephole in case whoever is out there sees movement. But my lights are off, they can't know I'm here. Not for sure. *Maybe it's some drunk guy from the pub upstairs?*

Then, in a low, posh voice, I hear: 'I know you're in there.'

FUCK.

I creep forward and look through the peephole and—*what?*

The dark curls. The broad shoulders. The strong face.

It's the guy from the club.

The one with the champagne and the table and the red ropes and the girls … The one who was looking at me.

I was right, he somehow knows what I am.

AND WHERE I LIVE.

Then he looks right at me, like the door isn't even there, smiles and says, 'Open the door, Aubrey. It's Oscar.'

The hairs on the back of my neck stand on end.

How does he know my name? And why is he acting like I should recognise his?

I swallow hard.

'Open the door, or I will force it open.'

I'm not a fool, really I'm not, I know what I need to do right now, I need to call the police and tell them to come over and save me from this lunatic. They'll never believe anything he says anyway … I've practised what I'd do, what I'd say in this kind of situation.

But … despite myself, no matter how hard I resist, I find myself reaching for the door handle. *No*. I fight the urge, try to pull back, but it's like he's forcing me somehow. I fight harder. *No, no, no*.

And then: *Click*.

I watch with horror as the lock clicks open, the handle turns and the door swings open.

He's standing there holding a credit card, a grin on his face. 'You were taking too long.'

My ears pulse. I should run. Scream. Something. But clearly something is wrong with me. Because I don't.

I just step aside and he moves past me, closing the door behind him like he owns the place. I watch silently as he flicks on the light, walks into the middle of the living room and looks around. His eyes dart from the sofa to the bookcase, to the packet of cigarettes on the floor, to Cat, to the kitchen. Cat scurries away and hides under the sofa.

And then he looks back at me and asks, 'Do you have anything to drink?'

15

I stand dead still, barely breathing and taking him in. Up close he looks around thirty-five. He's about six foot four, his dark brown curls shine under the kitchen light, and he smells like … leather. And moss.

He's watching me, waiting for an answer, but my mind is a tangle. *What does he want? Why does it feel like I'm stuck in here, why can't I run?* And: *Hang on, I can't smell his blood … and his heart is beating veeeerrrry slowly, very faintly, just like mine.*

Is he … like me?

'Aubrey,' he says impatiently. 'I asked if you had anything to drink.'

I have lactose-free milk for Cat, water or … blood. But I need to be careful here. I've been hiding the truth about myself for 150 years, I can't just hand it over now, to someone I don't even know, because of a hunch. Even if he is like me, what if he's a bad vampire?

'I have some milk,' I say, swallowing hard as I watch his expression.

'Milk?' he replies, looking vaguely amused. 'Suit yourself.'

Then he crouches down and looks towards the sofa where Cat is hiding, and in a soothing voice calls, 'Here, kitty, kitty.'

Cat lets out a little meow, peeks her head out and starts to trot towards him. *NO!* A mad panic flies through me. My gums tingle and I feel my fangs emerge. I run forward and grab her, hold her tight to my chest.

He looks up at me. 'Jesus, Aubrey, lighten up, I'm not going to eat the fucking cat. I'm not an animal. But where is it?' His eyes glint and seem to see right through to my core.

'In the fridge,' I say, my voice small. 'The tin.'

He nods, rolls his eyes and goes over to the fridge and as he does, I lurch for my knitting project. I hold one of the thick needles—it's wooden, so kind of like a stake—out in front of me. I know I can't kill him, but I also know, from experience, that getting skewered isn't comfortable. But he doesn't even notice, he just pulls my bag of blood out of the tin, looks at it, frowns and says, 'Just as I thought, you're feeding yourself rubbish. No wonder you're so weak and clumsy. You need proper nutrition to have any power at all. Wh—'

Then he looks at me. At the knitting needle.

He calmly drops the bag of blood into the rubbish bin and then *whoosh*, my back hits the wall. A jolt of pain shoots down my spine. He's there in front of me, leaning in, his weight heavy and his big fingers tight around my throat. I can't move. I can't breathe.

He's so fast. Just like Hans was. *I was never that fast, even when I was with Hans.*

His eyes flame as he stares into mine. They're green, but there are golden rings around his irises, just like mine. Right now, they're glowing, like there's a fire inside him. Like he might burn a hole right through me. And there's this dark electricity pulsing off him. It's like nothing I've ever felt before—it makes my marrow ache.

'Don't,' he says, the 't' coming out clipped.

The knitting needle drops from my hand; it hits the floor with an empty clack.

As I look into his eyes, I feel *terror*. It rolls through me like an icy current, reaches into my chest and grabs hold of something deep inside me. But whatever power he has over me is still there, I can feel it. Even if he let go of me right now, I couldn't leave.

'Who are you?' I croak, and his thumb releases just a little.

His eyes flicker and he says, 'I told you, I'm Oscar.'

I frown. Why does he keep saying that like it should mean something to me?

And then he adds, 'Your sire.'

My ears pulse as I try to make sense of what he's saying, take in every line of his face. I've imagined this moment a thousand times, maybe more. Imagined feeling understanding and warmth and protection. I've yearned for it. But now that it's here, it feels more like standing on the edge of a cliff in an electric storm. Dizzying. Unsettling. Dangerous.

But maybe that's just what it feels like, being with your sire.

'How did you find me?' I ask, trying to pull away but he holds me still. I need him to say he's been looking for me all this time. That he was kept from me.

'Oh, please. I know where you live, Aubrey,' he says, his expression almost bored. 'I'm not completely inept.'

The space beneath my ribs contracts, aches. But no, there has to be more to the story; if he'd known where I was all this time, surely he would have come to find me sooner. Surely.

'Did something happen the night you turned me? To make you leave?'

Say yes. Say you were torn from me. That you're sorry.

But he doesn't say anything. He just stares into my eyes and I stare into his. Then his pupils flare. My stomach contracts and I get a flash.

But it's different from my normal flashes. It comes in technicolour, not black and white, and there's nothing blurry or vague about it. It feels … real, like I'm *there*. And I can hear things too—there's a soundtrack. And I realise he's doing it on purpose, like it's a memory he's willingly passing over to me, to show me something.

He's standing in a bedroom.

It's the same one I lived in with Jonathan. I look to the bed now—there's a woman lying on it. She's wearing a long pale blue dress and it's covered in blood, and I know before I even focus in on her face that it's me …

All I can hear is heavy breathing.

My gaze catches on the mirror and there, staring back from it is a face I recognise. It's the same face that's in front of me now. Oscar. But his chin, his white dinner shirt, are blackened with blood.

My blood.

It's everywhere.

Then he rushes to the door and down the stairs, leaving me there.

16

I gasp and pull away, and this time he lets go. The images cut to black. I'm just standing there in front of him, my feet stuck in place, my breath quick and shallow as I stare at him, trying to make sense of everything as that flash replays in my mind. It didn't look like *anything* made him leave. It looked like he wanted to. But that can't be right. And I still have so many questions … questions I've always wanted to ask. Questions fighting for air.

'Who was I?' I blurt out. 'What was I like?'

He stares at me, expressionless. 'How the fuck would I know what you were like?' he replies. 'I didn't know you. I was just hungry and your front door was unlocked.'

Wait … *WHAT?*

So, it was random? I was unlucky—that's why I'm a monster. That's why I can't die. That's why I'm unlovable. That's why I have abandonment issues and sent a zillion texts and lost my soulmate.

Because he needed a … snack.

My stomach fills with cement. *That means he can't tell me anything about myself. Nothing at all.*

All those years of thinking about him, wondering … believing he could finally fill in the blanks for me, for nothing.

I look back to him and he's still watching me. Silent.

'So you turned me into this thing, and then you just left me like this? Alone?' I squeak.

He rolls his eyes. 'I gave you eternal life, you should be grateful. What did you want me to do, hold your hand?' he asks, terse. 'You're a vampire, we survive. And look at you, you're fine. Besides, I've checked in on you now and then. You've coped better than others.'

He's done this to others.

His eyes move to my neck, my clavicle, my breasts. He reaches out and touches my face. I feel myself recoil. 'Besides,' he croons, 'I'm here now … and you don't seem very happy to see me.' He gives a little smirk.

Heat rises in my stomach. My lower lip shakes—not from sadness, from anger—and I clench my jaw. *I'm so naive, I should have expected this.* I mean, I've read the books, seen the movies, did I really believe that he'd done it while violins played? I think of how much I needed him when Hans left, how vulnerable and lost I was, how often I thought of him, and all the while he was right here, in London. Living his best life. That heat swells in my solar plexus, rises up my throat, hits the spot in the middle of my forehead, and whatever trance he has me under breaks for a split second. I can feel it, the moment it happens. Like a bubble has popped. I turn quickly and reach for the door handle.

My hand stops the moment before I reach it, like it's stuck. I hear him laugh.

Oh right, he made me this way, that explains the power he has over me. Perfect.

He grabs me by the shoulders and turns me to face him again. He's so strong. This is my fault, I shouldn't have gone there tonight, to that club. Then he wouldn't have seen me, and he wouldn't be here. Everything would still be normal. Bad—miserable, really—but bad in a way I understood, at least.

'I'll scream,' I say, my voice a strangled whisper.

'You can try.' His face is hard, unblinking.

I'm barely breathing. Doing my best to think straight. *How dangerous is he?*

'What do you want? Why are you here?' I seethe, staring him down.

His eyebrows raise a little. 'Such venom,' he says, and gives a little smile. 'Frankly, I don't want to be here, either. I had to leave a very cute little blonde behind. But I have a duty.'

Resentment bubbles beneath my skin. 'What duty? It's a little late for that, don't you think?'

He ignores me and keeps talking. 'I was surprised to see you tonight. It's not like you to go out on the town after work, is it?'

He's right, it's not. Usually it's just going to work, getting blood, going for long ambling walks to pass the night, then eventually sitting at home—or, more recently, seeing Jonathan whenever he had time—but where is he going with this?

'Usually, you're too sensible and controlled for that. Too safety conscious,' he continues calmly. 'You're usually quite boring. I could feel immediately that you were … different tonight … erratic, tripping all over the place. You're weak. Conspicuous.'

In drips a memory of me rushing out of that club, desperate to get to Jonathan, tripping, almost falling.

'I'm not weak or conspicuous, I just wanted to get home,' I say, heat swirling in my stomach. 'Like you said, I don't go out much, I don't like it.'

He glares at me, unflinching. 'I don't believe you.' His voice is low and hard. 'I think you're severely compromised because of your lifestyle choices.'

I frown at him.

'There are growing dangers to us out there, Aubrey. Humans are starting to believe that we exist, vampires are being found and targeted. It would be catastrophic if they got proof, you understand?' His eyes narrow. 'We have all been told to make sure our proteges are not the weak link. I thought you wouldn't be a problem, but tonight I sa—'

'What?' I ask. 'Told by whom?' Because I've only ever come across two other vampires. Is there some vampire government I don't know about?

'We all have those we answer to, Aubrey. Like you answer to me. But as I was saying,' he says, like he doesn't enjoy being interrupted, 'I didn't realise you were so bad. It's just a matter of time before you get yourself into trouble. And I have a duty to keep you safe.' He pauses. 'Besides, I can't have a protege of mine be the weak link that gets us all found out. That would reflect very badly on me.'

'I'm not some weak link,' I hiss. 'I've kept myself safe and hidden for one hundred and fifty years, with no help from you.'

'Well, Daphne begs to differ,' he says, slowly, drawing out his vowels. 'We had a little chat after you went home. About why you rushed off like that. She says you're not yourself right now.' His eyes dig deeper. 'Unless there is another reason you were in such a tizz?'

My stomach twists. *I'm sure as hell not telling him about Jonathan.*

'Did you hurt her?' My voice comes out like a strangled whisper. Because otherwise, why the hell was she talking to him about me?

But no. It was a crowded bar, he couldn't have hurt her. And Daphne does love to chat with well-heeled, affluent men like him. Mostly for the free drinks. I get the sense lots of women would love to chat to a man like him, drink his champagne, look into his eyes, full of sex and danger, never guessing *what* that danger is. But not me. I've been alive long enough to see through him. I don't care what kind of clothes he wears. He's completely dead inside, full of darkness. I want him to get away from me in case it's catching.

'Of course not. To what end?' he asks, in answer to my question. 'I wouldn't hurt her unless I had a reason.' Then he takes a deep breath like he's sick of having to explain himself. 'Meet me at the club again tomorrow night. I'll teach you what you need to know to stay safe. Should we say nine-thirty? It shou—'

'I don't need you to teach me anything,' I say. Because I seriously do not want him stepping in as my mentor now, at this late stage.

He leans in a little closer and the little hairs on the back of my neck stand up as he glares into my eyes. 'Yes, you do. To start with someone has to get you properly fed, so you have some power. I'm going to hazard a guess that you have no control over siphoning visions and couldn't hypnotise your way out of a paper bag right now, which means if you found yourself in a sticky situation you'd be royally fucked. And that means we'd *all* be fucked.' Thoughts dance behind his eyes. 'It's time you became a vampire, Aubrey.'

My stomach clenches, alarm bells sound in my head. Because I *can't*. I know what he means by 'properly fed'—he wants me to feed off the vein—and I *can't*.

As soon as I feed off a human, I can't stop, I need to feed again and again and, honestly, someone always dies.

'Sorry, I have plans tomorrow night,' I say, my voice cracking. And I *do* have plans: staring at Olivia Coombes on Instagram or anything other than going to see Oscar.

'This isn't a request, Aubrey,' he says. 'You'll do what I want, one way or another. I'll see you at nine-thirty sharp.'

Then, in a blur, so quickly I don't even see it happen, he's gone.

Now it's just me in here again. Me and Cat, who is back in hiding, safely behind the sofa, and the white noise in my head. Because: *What just happened?*

But also: *Daphne*.

With shaking hands, I scroll through to her number and call her. *Please pick up. Please pick up.* I know he said he didn't hurt her, but what if he's lying?

If anything happens to her it'll be my fault.

'Aubs,' Daphne answers, and relief swirls through my veins. 'Are you okay?' Her voice comes out croaky but concerned. I can hear the hum of other voices in the background.

'Where are you?' I ask.

'I'm home,' she says, totally relaxed. 'What's wrong? You sound super stressed.'

'No, I'm fine, I was just checking you got home okay,' I say, pushing visions of Oscar from my mind.

'Yep, home watching some shitty movie. When did movies become so bad?'

'Did you talk to anyone good after I left?'

'Not really, there were a couple of guys, but I left not long after you. Lost the whole night scrolling through social media. Total waste of a night.'

'What did you talk about? With the guys?'

'I don't know,' she says, 'nothing really. Nothing important. Are you sure you're okay? You sound freaked out.'

I need everyone to stop saying things like that. I'm perfectly in control.

'I'm fine,' I say.

'Okay, well, I'm going to go to sleep,' she says.

'Okay,' I reply.

As we hang up, I glance across at the bin in the kitchen, at the corner of the blood bag peeking out the top—right now, perfectly good blood will be seeping out of it. I rush over to it, and Cat comes running after me, meowing as I pull the bag to safety, salvaging what's left—there's still around two thirds. I pour some into a mug and put it into the microwave, then wipe off the bag with a wet wipe and put it back in the tin as Cat circles my legs, meowing a little louder. She wants milk. But we all need a bit of austerity in our lives, so instead I pull out Cat's bag of treats and put the last few into a saucer, then leave the bag on the counter to remind myself to get more. And yes, I realise she's not my cat, so I don't have to feed her, but I don't have much faith in her owner who is always locking her outside. Someone has to take care of her.

Then I just stand there, a little stunned, watching the timer on the microwave count down, as Oscar's voice echoes in my mind: *This isn't a request, Aubrey. You'll do what I want, one way or another* …

Who the hell does he think he is? What, he just gets to waltz back into my life now, after all this time, and order me around? I don't think so.

Beep.

I grab my blood and head over to the sofa, then look outside, up at the inky sky. He's gone, at least. Cat jumps up beside me and I take a sip of my perfectly fine blood—no worse for the hours it's been sitting in my bag. A sense of calm moves through me as my nerves relax. I don't know what he was complaining about.

Then I reach for my phone, and tap back through to Olivia Coombes' profile.

Because I'll be damned if I let Oscar derail me now, right as I find Jonathan and a life I actually want. So, where was I?

17

Tuesday is my night off, so I don't set my alarm, and by the time I wake up it's just before five pm and it's dark outside. *Here we go for the 55,017th time*. I had a horrible sleep. I woke up soon after I drifted off, certain I could hear someone in the flat. But it was just my imagination. Or maybe a sense of foreboding, hard to tell.

I sit up, my legs twisted in my sheets, and as I pull off my eye mask and take out my earplugs, Oscar's voice echoes in my head: *I'll see you at nine-thirty sharp*.

No, you won't. Psycho.

I reach for my phone.

No texts. No calls. Just one notification.

VHC: *You have two new messages.*

I log in and tap through to them. They're both from Sally. The first reads: *What???? Right before Christmas? I'm so sorry, but NEXT! He doesn't deserve you. Sending love.*

The second reads: *Just remember, there are far, far better things ahead than any we leave behind. Always.*

It feels like the whole world wants me to just 'get over' Jonathan, move on—like it's easy. It's not. And now I feel a little guilty. Because I've seen so many friends go through break-ups over the years, and I've always secretly thought that they should just get over it. That I'd be stronger somehow, that nobody could bring me to my knees after everything I'd gone through. That I'd be different; I'd do it *better*. But now that it's me … now that it's happening, I realise I was wrong.

It feels like a bomb has gone off in my chest and I find a new piece of shrapnel every time I breathe.

I tap through to the noticeboard and scan down through the most recent articles:

TAXI DRIVER SERIOUSLY INJURED BY STABBING IN STOCKHOLM, JOGGER STABBED WHILE RUNNING IN DULWICH PARK, NEW ORLEANS MAN CLAIMS VAMPIRISM IS REAL.

But as I stare down at them, my insides twist. I can't believe I ever signed up to this site looking for Oscar. That I ever hoped he might be good. A shiver moves through me as I think of the way he made me feel—more terrified than I've ever been. And he's wrong about me, I'm not a problem. A weak link.

Then my gaze catches on a post: IRL MEET-UP LONDON: CHRISTMAS DRINKS.

As I sit in bed, looking at it, I think: *Or am I?*

Because, I'd never admit this to Oscar, but I have almost messed up terribly before. There have been times when my hypnotism hasn't quite worked out, a very bad time on Coventry Street in 1922, a small 'incident' while I was working at the Moulin Rouge, there was Freddie and everything I told him, and a few other less than ideal moments too. But, most recently, there was that IRL meet-up for the Vampire Hunters' Collective. The one where I met @Riley.

Riley was a founding member, worked on the VHC doing tech, had a new line of VHC merch coming out (hoodies and socks)

and was certain he had found a vampire's hunting ground. He wanted to discuss it further in person, and assemble a crew of us to stake the place out. I was sceptical, but also hopeful. I'd scoured the site and not found any recent credible leads, so maybe this was it. Maybe this would lead me to my maker.

So off I went to a little bar on Carnaby Street. I was working that night so got there an hour after it had started but spotted Riley immediately. He was tall, with a weak chin, dark hair and pockmarked cheeks, a little unwashed with a slightly stooped posture—he looked a little like he himself had escaped from the set of *The Lost Boys* and the irony wasn't lost on me. But I went straight up to him to ask him what he knew.

He ushered me to a small table in the corner, and I sat with a white printer label with @Margot written on it stuck to my thin black cardigan, breathing in stale beer as he nursed a Guinness and told me everything. He'd followed up on a lead from the site that had led him to a pub in Hampstead. He'd decided to go there every night, just in case. And just last week, he had finally struck gold. As he was leaving, he passed an alleyway and witnessed a vamp mid-attack. The vamp was huge and male, and must have heard Riley approach, because he stopped and turned to look. As he did, Riley saw his bloodied fangs. Terrified, Riley pulled back and hid behind a building, frantically pulling a stake from his backpack. But by the time he stepped back into that alleyway, the vamp was gone. His female victim was sitting on the pavement, she had no recollection of the attack and—he added this bit in a particularly hushed tone—her wound had healed up. He suspected the vamp had wiped her memory then healed her with his blood. Did I want to be a part of the team that staked out the pub while we waited for this 'shitbag' to come back?

Until this point in the story, I'd been thinking, *That could be my maker*. I was allowing myself to blister with anticipation. But with the mention of blood potentially healing the victim's wound, I became dubious. Riley had clearly been watching too much TV. Because I'd bled into a human wound before and it had not healed up anything. It just made it messier. Added to which, would my centuries-old maker, someone powerful enough to turn me into this thing, really be so careless as to get seen? Especially by someone like Riley?

It was as I was weighing all this up, that I realised Riley had clearly got a whiff of my scent.

He was looking at my chest, then my mouth, like he thought it was a date and then he reached for my hand, clasped onto my fingers, and said, 'Wow, you're cold for summer …'

His eyes met mine. I didn't like what I saw. Dark thoughts, flickering. His gaze brushed across my pale skin then moved back to my mouth. Or, more specifically, my teeth. And hang on, was he just coming onto me or did he … suspect? Was he looking for fangs? His fingers slid up to my wrist … was he looking for a pulse?

Just act normal, I told myself. *It's nothing.*

But alarm bells shrieked from deep within me. Alarm bells honed over 150 years of hiding.

And so, I left. Quickly. Before things could go very wrong.

I ripped my @Margot label from my cardigan as soon as I stepped out of that bar.

It was only on the Tube ride home that I caught sight of my reflection in the window and saw my yellow Selfridges name badge still pinned to my chest: *Aubrey*. Panic pulsed through me as I thought of Riley's eyes on my chest.

And the panic wasn't just because I didn't want Riley knowing my real name or where I worked (though that too).

Because you can't just sign up to the Vampire Hunters' Collective. There's a vetting process you go through to 'protect the integrity' of the community. That process involves answering some key questions: *Do you believe in vampires? Would you die for the cause?* And like I said before, it requires an ID. More specifically, a photograph of you with said ID, proving that you are indeed a real person, a true believer, that you have nothing to hide. The ID in question needs to include your address. Thankfully, I had a fake set of IDs—passport, driver's licence—lying around. I'd had the presence of mind to have them made when I got my current one done (I have a guy, he lives in Brixton). So, I had used that. Wise move, until now. Because the name on my fake ID was Margot. Like my username. Like the name on my profile. Not Aubrey. Like my nametag.

My mind was a whir of: *Riley did tech for the VHC. What if he clocked my little white lie and it piqued his interest; what if he somehow had access to that picture I'd taken?* The site was supposed to delete those images, after verification, but I read the news, I knew data leaks happened, I knew companies didn't always delete the things they said they would—and it wasn't like anyone was governing a vampire hunting website. I didn't want him to have a photograph of me. And I certainly didn't want him to have my address—even if it was an old address. Because I'd given my old landlord a forwarding address: a P.O. Box at London Bridge Post Office. If Riley wanted to find out where I was, there were ways.

I considered deleting my profile, but what would that have achieved, other than making me look even more suspicious? It wouldn't stop him if he was planning on coming for me. I also considered leaving my current life and starting another, but that seemed a bit drastic all because of a nametag, a gut feeling and a wild hypothesis, which was probably just the result of 150 years of hiding, of controlling everything around me to stay safe. So I did nothing. But a dark cloud of paranoia followed me around for weeks as I watched his posts like a hawk. Waiting in part for news of the vamp from that bar, and in part for news of myself.

But a few weeks later Riley confirmed that his vamp had not returned to his 'hunting ground' and the bar in question was closing. Honestly, I was sad. It was the closest I'd ever come to potentially finding my sire. But thankfully, Riley never contacted me on the site. I realised I had indeed been paranoid. In any case, I learnt my lesson. No more IRL meet-ups for me. Though, I do wonder now whether it was instances like that, hunters lying in wait for vampires at bars, that landed Oscar in my living room last night. And it makes me wonder how many other groups there are like that in the world, that I don't know about.

I trudge through to the kitchen, tripping over the packet of cigarettes I threw last night. I drop them into the rubbish—to smoke them would be like admitting that Jonathan and I are over, that I don't need to give up smoking for him anymore—then glance around the room. The knitting needle is still where I dropped it while Oscar grabbed my throat. I calmly put it back with its partner under the coffee table. I should probably eat something, but I'm not hungry. And what's the weird smell? I sniff the air.

It's like … oxidised blood. And it smells sort of familiar. I get a flash of Oscar dropping my blood bag into the bin, like it was nothing. It must be the blood that seeped out of the bag before I rescued it. So I grab two bin liners, double bag the offending rubbish, head outside and drop my rubbish into the pub's bin—one can never be too safe.

I rush back inside, and as I close the door, I think of Oscar with that credit card last night. As soon as Christmas is over, I'm going to get a locksmith to come and strengthen my security.

My phone beeps and a message flashes up on my phone.

Es: *Meet you outside Covent Garden Station? Xxxxx*

Ah shit. With all the stress of last night, I forgot to cancel the Christmas lights. I stare down at the five kisses, wondering what sort of excuse I can make.

But I can't cancel now. Not two hours before we're meant to meet. That would be mean. And also, last night showed me that Oscar can't tell me *anything* about human-me, so if I don't get Jonathan back, I'll never know. And the Christmas lights seem as good a place as any to take some living-my-best-life-please-call-me-love-you shots for Instagram.

So I type back: *See you soon!*

But the smell of blood is still so strong, even though I've taken out the rubbish, and as I frown and look around the room I'm thinking *could one little trickle really—*

Then: *What's that?*

I see a T-shirt, glaring from the top of the washing hamper, a red smear on it.

I pick it up, peer down at it. There's a big red mark down the front. And that's not like me, I'm an exceptionally careful eater. I have to be.

I sniff it and immediately recoil.

That's it, that's the smell. But I don't understand … when?

A sense of uneasiness comes over me now, like I know it's bad but I don't know why.

Still, a lot has happened in the last twenty-four hours, I'm probably just frazzled. Hypervigilant. So I spray it with stain-remover, scrub it a bit in the sink, then throw it into the washing machine.

18

A voice comes over the loudspeaker: 'The next stop is Covent Garden. Please mind the gap.'

I stand and move over to the door, waiting for the carriage to pull to a stop. I can feel eyes on me, like I'm being watched. I turn. There's a greasy-haired guy of maybe seventeen smirking up at me; I glance down at his phone, which is pointed right at me. He's videoing me, probably trying to see up my skirt, but that's par for the course. Nothing to be jumpy about. Not usually, at least. But right now I have this horrible feeling that everyone can see straight through me, that everyone knows what I am. And I can't shake the unease I felt when I saw that smear of blood.

This is all Oscar's fault. For turning up last night and making me feel vulnerable. Looking at me with that smug face, telling me that I'm a weak link, that I'll get us all found out. Which is ridiculous. I needed his protection once, oh how I needed it, and he wasn't there. But I've survived 150 years all on my own. That's 150 years under the male gaze, which is more than he could survive. I'll be fine.

The screech of brakes fills the air, we pull to a stop, then the doors slide open. I get out quickly, push my hands into my pockets, then rush through the station and out into the winter air. It bites at my cheeks as I look around for Es.

She's standing nearby, looking down at her phone, huddled in a big coat and the turquoise scarf I knitted her earlier this year. Back before Jonathan, when knitting was my most recent fixation. I smile and go over to her.

'Heellllooooo,' she says in her thick Liverpool accent. 'Oh, I love this so much,' she says, looking my Afghan coat up and down. 'Is it vintage?'

'Mmhmm,' I say. And it is. Usually I wear plain clothes, whatever is currently in style—nothing to get me noticed. But I love this coat now as much as I did when I bought it new in the 70s. I can't bring myself to get rid of it.

Then she links arms with me and pulls me up the street. 'By the way, thanks again for those weed gummies. They are stroooonnng,' she says, as we weave our way through foot traffic towards the market. 'They're going to make Christmas so much more bearable.' Then her tone shifts and she looks over at me. 'Wait, have you got plans yet?'

I nod, enthusiastic about my imaginary plans. 'I'm going to do an orphan's Christmas with Daphne, my friend from work,' I lie, my voice cracking at the thought of spending another Christmas all alone with Cat. It doesn't sound like a big deal, to spend Christmas alone, I'm certainly not religious, but it stings knowing all those you love are with 'their people', and you're not. It reminds you that you have no people.

'Are you sure you don't want to come with me? My family is a bit bonkers, but Mum really wouldn't mind,' Es says, as if she can read my mind.

The truth is, I'd love to go with her. But that would come with too many questions about why I was eating so little, why I never wanted to go on lovely country walks in the day, why I was an insomniac and spent all day in bed. It would not be good for our friendship.

'I'd love to, but I can't. I have to work on Boxing Day,' I say. 'But thanks.' I squeeze her arm and she smiles back at me.

'If you're sure,' she says.

'So have you done all your Christmas shopping?' I ask, keen to change the subject.

'Yeah, finally,' she says, as we move past a bright red phone box. There's a lot of red in London: phone boxes, letter boxes, buses. It might as well be painted in blood. It's like this entire city is whispering, *I know what you are deep down, what you'd do for fun if you let yourself go*. Taunting me. Reminding me you can always hate yourself a little more.

'Which reminds me,' Es continues, 'I got you something. It's just small,' she says, pulling a weirdly shaped present out of her bag and handing it to me. It's kind of heavy.

'But I didn't get you anything …' I say, guilt rolling through me. I should have thought of it. I've been so distracted.

'Umm, you get me weed gummies all the time and never let me pay for them, I think we're good. Don't open it until Christmas, okay?'

I nod. 'Thanks, Es,' I say, then drop it into my bag, wondering what it is. Probably some kind of weapon or safety device, knowing Es. She's addicted to true-crime podcasts and is always feeding me personal safety titbits like holding my keys between my fingers as a weapon or using hairspray as makeshift mace, or never going on a date without letting a friend know the address … She tells me all these things, never guessing that I might be the problem. That I might be the worst kind of danger.

Her eyes move up. 'Ah look, isn't it magical?'

I follow her gaze to the enormous sparkly Christmas tree looming above the crowd, and I take in the scene as we walk into the piazza. It's an assault on my senses. A line of carollers singing 'Carol of the Bells' a cappella, and a thousand conversations taking place all at once, a thousand different heartbeats, accents, lives.

'Oh my god, I bet they have mulled wine. Come on,' Es says as she grabs my arm and drags me over to a little stall.

As we wait in line, I look back towards the carollers and the market building. I've watched so much of this city be built from nothing, seen trees be planted and grow to size, seen the skyline change time and again. The parts that have been here as long as I remember hold a special place in my heart—and this is one of them. If I squint, I can almost imagine women with baskets of flowers wandering around. There have been many renovations, but along with the moon, it's one of my constant touchstones. Each year it gets a little more special to me. If they ever demolish it I might totally lose my shit.

We get to the front of the line. Es orders and I pay. 'My treat,' I say.

'Thanks.' She takes a gulp.

I sip mine slowly as we stroll through the market and I try not to scrunch up my nose. Like I said before, I have sensitive taste buds and I'm drinking hot wine with substandard spices out of a cardboard cup lined with micro-plastics. And honestly, all I want is for this mulled wine to make me calm and giddy and a little numb, to take my thoughts away, just as it will for Es. But it doesn't.

We go inside and I look around and up. There's an arched Apple Market sign, and golden bells with red ribbons and big red baubles hanging from the ceiling.

'Look,' Es says, and I turn to where she's pointing. In front of us stands a red sleigh in front of a set of small Christmas trees; I can smell their pine needles. There's a couple sitting in the sleigh, taking a selfie. She's wearing a red woollen hat and as I look at them, it's as if I'm pressing a bruise on my heart.

I should be here with Jonathan.

In leaks a memory from our third date: ice-skating at Somerset House. It was the midday session, so I wore big sunglasses and claimed a hangover to explain my shakiness.

It was okay for the first five minutes, but after an hour of taking laps on the bright white ice beneath a cloudless sky, I was pretty sure this might be the path to true death I'd been looking for all along.

But then Jonathan stopped me in the middle of the ice, took the red woollen beanie off his own head and put it on mine. Then he leaned down, and there, in front of everyone, he kissed me. As he did, my stomach clenched and in came a flash: *I'm lying on the sofa, my head on his lap, I'm reading a book, laughing* … And just like that, I knew human-me liked to read too.

'Oh my lord, look at that queue,' Es says, scrunching up her face and I follow her gaze. There are eight people in line. 'Should we just get a picture from here?' she asks.

'Sure,' I say.

So we turn around and squish our faces up together and she takes a few pictures, moving her head from side to side as I do the same.

'So cute,' she says, flicking through them while I look at them over her shoulder. But now I'm thinking of Daphne's wise words about posting pictures: *You need to look natural and be laughing, it needs to be the kind of picture where you just know someone else was there taking it*.

'Can you get one of me alone for Mum? She collects them,' I say, rolling my eyes like it's an annoying habit of hers, when the truth is, I'd give anything to have a mum who did things like that.

'Of course,' she says. 'I hope they get over here soon so they can see how magical Christmas is in winter.'

I nod as I step a little closer to the sleigh. I told her my parents live in Australia. I tell everyone that. It's far enough away that it makes sense that we don't visit each other.

She aims the phone lens at me and I fake a laugh.

'Aww,' she says, taking a few pictures.

She looks down at her phone then quickly up at me again. 'I'll airdrop them to you.'

I pull my phone from my bag, and as I do, I see a missed call from Daphne. She's left a voicemail too. Usually I'd check it right away, but Es's photos are pinging onto my phone and this is important. I quickly scroll through them, trying to figure out which one to post. I choose one where I'm laughing and looking at the lens with love. I upload it as a story, add a filter and just one emoji at the bottom of it: a Christmas present. And then I post it.

Now, all I need is for Jonathan to see it. For one little sign that he's still thinking of me. Still connected to me. That there's still a chance for us.

Then I'll feel better.

19

Half an hour later, he *still* hasn't looked at it and I feel even *worse*. Es is finishing off some oozy custard-filled doughnut as I refresh my story views for the zillionth time. But still, nothing. There are twenty-seven little faces underneath my story, twenty-seven people who *have* seen it, but none of them are Jonathan.

And he *always* looks at my stories.

Panic rolls through me. What if it's actually over? What if there is nothing I can do to change that?

'I'm getting tired,' Es says, as she wipes sugar off her fingertips with a napkin and looks around for a rubbish bin. 'Should we go?'

'Sure,' I say. She spots a rubbish bin and as she goes over to it, I frantically tap through to Olivia's profile. And I don't want to be this woman—jealous, paranoid, clingy—I really don't but here we are.

Her grid loads, slowly, slowly, and then …

A calm comes over me. My thoughts slow. *It's fine.*

Olivia's last post is a selfie of her and two others—a blonde woman and a man with patchy facial hair and an ostentatious little hat with a purple feather in it. It was posted only ten minutes ago, and in good news, Jonathan is nowhere in sight. She's standing outside a black building with red ropes outside and I can make out some white lettering behind her. As I zoom in, I realise I recognise the building … *I know where she is.*

I scroll to the caption: *Going to see my talented friend Mark tonight. #spokenword #openmic #poetry #supportyourfriends*

'Are you ordering an Uber?' Es asks as she comes back over to me. 'I might do the same. It's freezing, I can't feel my toes.'

'Me neither,' I say absentmindedly, as we walk towards the exit. With each step, I'm telling myself, *I'm just going to go home*. Have some dinner. Go to bed. That's the safe, controlled thing to do. Oscar is wrong about me, I'm perfectly capable of keeping myself safe, the way I always have.

But also … Olivia is only a few minutes' drive from here. In Soho. Which is a little close to Coventry Street for comfort—and feels like a warning right now—but also I can't punish myself for everything forever.

My stomach churns. Would it be completely crazy to go and get a look at her, up close?

I mean, maybe the guy in the little hat is her boyfriend and it'll put my mind at ease—then I can stop obsessing.

So I turn to Es and say, 'How do you feel about going to a poetry open mic? There's this great one in Soho I've heard about. We could just go for a little while.'

'Eh, I don't know hon, sounds like a trek, and I'm so tired. Got to get up early to catch a train to Liverpool tomorrow.'

I nod, and we head out into the icy air surrounded by the sounds of Christmas carols and laughter. *Maybe Es is doing me a favour?* A reconnaissance mission doesn't sound very hard-to-get or Aubs 2.0 … maybe it's better I don't.

But the moment we step outside, snow flurries start to fall. It's not real snow, of course, it's the fake snow they pump out every hour on the hour at Christmas time, which means it's nine pm now. The snowflakes are all lit up by the lights outside and it feels magical, like a sign.

A sign not to give up.

And I can't very well turn up alone. *Everyone* looks at a woman alone. Aside from which, Olivia has probably seen Jonathan's Instagram page—I'm on it.

I bring the images in question to my mind's eye: I'm wearing huge sunglasses in one photo and you can barely see my face through my hair in the other. But still, I'll need to be careful.

So now I do something I'm not proud of. I turn to Es and look her deep in the eyes. I feel my pupils flare and my insides warm up, and in a calm and soothing voice I say: 'You've changed your mind, you want to go and see some poetry at an open mic night in Soho.'

I hold my breath. Watching her.

Please let this work.

I watch and wait … and then her eyes glaze over and she nods slowly. I blink and look away.

'Hey,' she says from beside me and I look over to meet her gaze. 'I've changed my mind, let's go to Soho. I feel like watching some poetry, it'll be fun'

I shrug and say, 'Sure.'

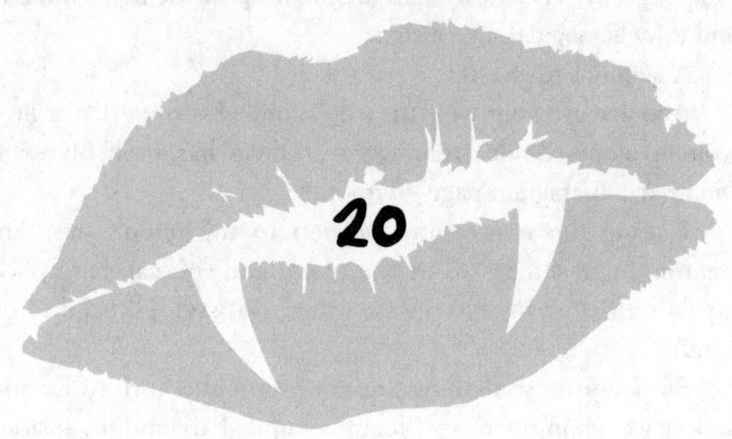

Six minutes later we're in the back of an Uber, slowly heading down Old Compton Street. I look out through a rain-streaked window, searching for the building I saw on Olivia Coombes' post. The street is bathed in pink and red light from neon signage, pedestrians wander arm in arm down the pavement, a rickshaw drives past us, then …

There it is.

A black building, with a line of maybe ten people standing outside, behind red ropes.

I check the time on my phone: 9.17 pm.

It probably starts at 9.30.

'Here's fine,' I say. The driver glances at me in the rear-view mirror then pulls over. We get out and weave our way across the road as I conduct a quick assessment. My hypnotism seems to be working tonight, the line is moving slowly and time is of the essence—we need to get inside, seated and halfway through our first drink, before my hypnotism invariably wears off and Es decides she wants to go home. I go up to the bouncer and as he looks me in the eye I feel my pupils flare and a warmth in my solar plexus. In a perky voice I say, 'You will let us in first.'

He grins. 'Will I?' Then he looks me up and down the way men always do.

Shit. It didn't work.

My cheeks get hot and doom pulses through me as I glance over at Es, who is still in a bit of a trance, but who knows how long for …

But then he says: 'I like your confidence, blondie. Sure, go in.'

I reach for Es's hand and we rush inside before he can change his mind. It smells of beer and cologne, and in the far corner, just past the bar, is a darkened staircase with a printed sign at the bottom reading: *Spoken Word Open Mic upstairs tonight! Just £7!*

'This way,' I say to Es. I lead her up the stairs.

A woman with three nose piercings and a mauve pixie cut takes our payments, stamps our hands with red stars and gives us two pink drink tickets. Then we go inside and, keeping my head angled down, I surreptitiously scan the room for *her*.

I see dark blue sofas and low tables, a small bar with one bartender behind it, a stage area at the front with a mic and a small red rug for the performer to stand on. There are maybe twenty people in the audience, all seated with drinks, chatting and laughing.

And then I see her. At a table right at the front. Olivia Coombes.

Her back is to us but I know it's her immediately, I recognise her long curly dark hair from Jonathan's living room last night. She's sitting flanked by the same two friends I saw in her Instagram post: the blonde woman and the guy in the small ostentatious hat.

'There's one over there,' I say to Es and she follows me vacantly over to a table against the wall, far enough away from Olivia and her two friends that they won't notice me, but at the perfect angle for them to be in my direct eyeline.

We put our coats on the backs of the chairs, and as Es takes off her scarf and goes to sit down I say, 'I'll get us some drinks,' holding up the pink drink tickets.

Then I leave her there, staring blankly at the stage.

As I wait for the bartender, I glance back at Olivia's table. She tosses her hair back as she laughs, and as she looks around the room, I take her in. In real life, without the softness of Instagram filters or the glass of a rainy window between us, I can see that objectively, I'm prettier than she is, but even so, all I can think as I trace her features is: *She's so perfect.* Because her nose may be a bit bigger than we're told a nose is meant to be, bigger than the images of women in magazines, and her face is self-consciously sculpted by bronzer and highlighter, but she's so *normal*. So human. And that wins out over everything, because *that* is something I will never be.

I look at her with envy as I home in on her conversation. 'Well, I think it's very telling that he still hasn't posted a photo of you online after three months,' she says, and her friends nod. 'It's like you don't exist.'

'I know,' says her blonde friend in a sad voice—*they must be talking about some guy she's dating*. 'But he al—'

Then the bartender's voice distracts me; draws me back. 'What can I get you?'

I turn back to him, annoyed by the interruption. 'Two glasses of house red,' I say.

He takes my drink tickets and heads off and I turn back to Olivia's table. 'Babe, no guy is *that* private …' That's Olivia speaking again.

'I know,' says the blonde. 'You're both so right.' Then she looks at Olivia. 'So what's the latest with you and Jonathan? You've been spending a lot of time together recently.'

Time all but stands still. Because: *What? They've been spending time together? And her friends know about him?*

Already? This isn't putting my mind at ease at all. It's worse than I thought.

I mean, does he … like her?

Could he?

If he *does* like her, then what am I doing here? I'm being so selfish. I should just leave them alone. Let him be happy. Let him choose whomever he wants. That would be the right thing to do. Abort the mission. Go home right now. I *want* to do the right thing.

But I *really, really, really* want Jonathan.

'Here you go,' the bartender interrupts again and I take the drinks back to Es. I sit down, putting my phone on the table and obscure my face with my hair.

'Thank you,' Es says, then takes a big gulp. 'But should we skol this and leave?' she asks, looking back towards the door. 'Quickly, before it starts?'

Her eyes are clear now, and so is her mind. I guess my little trick has worn off. But at least it worked for long enough to get us here.

I smile and say, 'We're here now, let's stay for a little bit.' Then I crinkle my nose like it might be fun, take a gulp of my drink and glance back over at Olivia.

She's holding up her phone, taking another selfie of the three of them.

Then the blonde woman says, 'You must be making some progress, how did the other night go?'

'It was okay, but Baxter was hanging around *again*. God I wish he'd get a girlfriend or something, he's just always *there*. I mean, I know we all work together, but I'm never going to get to the next stage with Jonathan if Baxter doesn't leave us alone.'

That syrupy hope is back and pulsing thickly through my veins as I cling onto the phrases *next stage* and *work together*. Never have I been so grateful for Baxter's homebody ways. Because this is good. It means the only reason Olivia was in

Jonathan's living room, the only reason they've been 'spending time' together is because they work together. It's not his fault that she fancies him. He can't control that. And it sounds like maybe nothing has happened yet.

'You have such patience,' says the guy in the hat. 'Hope he's worth it. I mean if it didn't turn into anything when you hooked up last time, maybe it's not meant to be.'

'That was two years ago,' Olivia replies, terse. 'I've grown since then, so has he. Besides, "meant to be" is so juvenile. What matters most is that we make a good team. We have similar life goals. I mean, I'm almost thirty now and he's thirty-three. We both know what's out there, and you can't hold out for butterflies forever. Eventually, you make the sensible choice.' She shrugs. 'I just need him to see that and stop focusing entirely on work for a moment.'

My vision gets all wavy and this is *all wrong*.

She doesn't love Jonathan. Not even a little bit. He doesn't even give her butterflies. And I bet she absolutely knows about me—it sounds like she's had her sights on him the whole time we were together—but she doesn't care. She's awful. He deserves so much more.

She shrugs. 'Eventually he'll figure it out. We just make sense. Men are always slower with these things.'

'You're so wise,' says her blonde friend. 'I wish I could focus on men who made sense.'

'I know, I'm an old soul … it has its drawbacks,' Olivia says and my gums tingle because *this is so unjust!* She doesn't know the first thing about what it is to be an old soul. The torment.

Stay calm, Aubrey. I can't afford to have my fangs pop out right now.

Besides, this is all good.

It sounds like she has her sights on Jonathan but he hasn't reciprocated. Not yet, at least. But also, she sounds pretty determined. *I need to get him back before he falls for her trap.*

My phone lights up with a text message and I reach for it. Daphne: *Did you get my voicemail???*

I'm frowning down at my phone, wondering what she means, what's so urgent, when *one, two, three, one, two, three* comes over the mic, and I look up. It's a man with a buzz cut, readjusting the mic stand to be a bit higher. 'Good evening,' he says. 'I'm Karem and I'm your host for tonight. I ask that you all put away your devices and give your full attention to the talented poets we have gracing our stage this evening.'

I put my phone in my bag and Es tugs on my sleeve. 'We could still sneak out,' she whispers.

I smile over at her and say, 'We'll leave after the first set.' Because now that I'm here, I know exactly what I need to do.

I have to put Olivia off Jonathan somehow. I imagine myself following her to the bathroom, giving my hypnotism another shot, telling her to block Jonathan's number and never see him again. Maybe she could put in a good word for me while she's at it.

But then … a dizziness falls over me.

My ears start to ring. Loudly. So loudly it hurts. So loudly that I can't hear what Karem is saying. It's like the worst kind of speaker feedback. I press my hands over them and look around, but nobody else is flinching. And that's when I realise the sound is coming from *inside* my head. I'm struggling to breathe. The first poet—a woman in a long purple dress—gets up on stage and speaks into the mic, but I can't hear what she's saying, all I can hear is Oscar's voice in my head.

He's whispering, but it's loud, so loud.

'It's nine-thirty, Aubrey, where are you?'

I swallow hard and try to ignore it, try to focus on Olivia instead. But the ringing gets louder and louder. And I know what I have to do, I can feel it in my chest, it's like a magnet, pulling me towards him … I know where it wants to take me, but I don't want to go.

Because Olivia is right there, and when else am I going to get this chance? I need to talk to her. I need to do something. But my eardrums feel like they're going to explode.

So I stand up, my hands still over my ears, and rush to the back door. Es watches me go, frowning and worried, but I just run.

My vision stutters as traffic, lights and cold air swirl around me. I spy a cab just up ahead, pulling up on the corner of Greek Street, and run towards it. A man in a grey suit gets out as I lean into the cabbie's half-open window.

'Dunraven Street in Mayfair, please,' I say as calmly as I can, while my ears scream and pulse.

He nods and I get in, slamming the door after me.

'Careful,' he says into the rear-view mirror.

'Sorry,' I say.

He just nods, and starts to drive. We edge forward, the cars bumper to bumper, horns beeping, and my ears keep ringing and that pull towards him is even stronger now. *Maybe I should just get out and run there*. But I won't make it, I'm too dizzy, I'll fall over.

At least Oscar's voice has shut up now.

I frantically tap through Google Maps—*how long until we get there?*—and that's when my phone starts ringing: *Es*.

I send the call to voicemail and type *Dunraven Street* into the search bar. Eleven minutes. We should be there in eleven minutes.

A text flashes up on my screen.

Es: *Are you in the loo? Everything okay??? xx*

I go to text back but I can't think, I can barely breathe right now, and besides, how could I possibly explain *this* to her? I just need to get through it. We're on Charing Cross Road now, and the traffic has thinned. We're moving faster.

I sink back into the seat and close my eyes and try to conjure Jonathan's face in my mind's eye. But I can't think of anything other than the ringing in my ears and the searing pain in the centre of my head. All I can do is grit my teeth and get through it.

'You all right, love?' comes the cabbie's voice and my eyes flick open. He's watching me in the rear-view mirror. 'Tell me if you're going to be sick, right?'

I nod and look out the window—we're almost there, we're slowing down. And then: relief. I can see the door to the club up ahead. We pull to a stop outside.

I pay the driver, then tumble out into the cold air and rush up to the door, press the doorbell just like Daphne did, and as soon as the door clicks open, I pull on it and go inside.

The very moment I step beyond the threshold, the ringing, the dizziness, it all stops. My ears throb with the silence, the aftershock, and I'm shaking a little. *I'm okay, I made it*.

And I'm done with this. It won't be happening anymore. I don't care who Oscar is or even that he made me, or that he thinks I'm weak. If I don't want to be a regular vampire, I don't have to be. He lost the right to an opinion on that a long time ago.

The same hostess from last night, with the short black bob, is standing behind the console, looking me up and down. 'Name?' she asks, glancing down at her iPad.

'Sorry, I'm Aubrey, I'm here for—'

She looks up. 'Oscar,' she finishes for me. 'He's waiting for you. This way.'

As I follow her up a long hallway, her heels clicking on the floorboards, I frown, thinking: *She's human—I can smell her blood, hear her heartbeat—and she works with Oscar. Does she know what he is?*

We stop outside a door and she knocks.

'Come in,' calls Oscar, and something clenches in my stomach.

She twists the handle and I get a flash of last night, how he was entirely in control, how I couldn't leave, and then that ringing in my ears tonight, and I want to tell him this has to stop. But as we go inside, it's not anger I feel, even though I want it to be. It's … fear.

The office we step into is lit by several lamps emitting an orange glow. The air smells of old wood and cigar smoke. And Oscar is sitting behind a huge desk, wearing a crisp white shirt, the light reflecting off his silver cufflinks as he raises a lit cigar to his lips. I can feel the latent threat pulsing off him.

'Thanks, Kimberly,' he says, polite and cold. The hostess nods, then scampers out of the room like he makes her nervous and closes the door behind her. It's just us in here now.

I swallow hard and stand there, watching him as he watches me. He takes a drag and blows a smoke ring, like he's enjoying his control. Like he knows that with each moment he makes me wait, I'll get a little more anxious. A little more unsure of myself.

'You're late,' he says, his eyes still on mine. He's giving me the same hypnotic look I know probably wins human women over. But it makes my skin crawl and it's slightly irritating that he thinks he can boss me around like this.

'I was busy,' I say, crossing my arms over my chest.

He gives a small smile, like I've amused him, then he stands, stubs out his cigar in an amber glass ashtray, just like one I had in the 70s, and walks past me towards the door. 'Come.'

I don't follow him.

Because I can't. He told me last night he wants me to feed off the vein. I know where that leads: once I start, I can't stop. Then someone dies. Or a few someones.

I *won't* do it.

'No,' I say, trying to be strong, but my voice cracks, betraying me. And then I add, 'I'm sorry.' *Why am I apologising? He's the arsehole.* But he's frowning now and there's something I can't read in his eyes. Panic spurts through me. 'I know you're trying to help me,' I add, not wanting to appease him, but knowing I have to. 'I've always been careful, even you said so. I'll stay careful, I promise. But I need to live on my own terms. Please, I've never let anyone find out who I am, I'm not going to start now.'

This is a lie, of course—I told Freddie—but minor details.

He stares at me and says nothing. But it doesn't feel like he's forcing me to stay, not like last night, so I take a step towards the door, then another. Soon I'm standing right by him, I can smell the leather of his cologne. But the moment before I step outside, he grabs onto my upper arm. I look up and our eyes meet.

'Aubrey,' he says calmly, looking down at me, 'I don't have time for this. I said *come*.'

I have a split second to make a choice. Do I force my way out of here and see what he does? Even though my ears still feel like they're full of cotton wool from whatever the hell he did before? Even though I know he won't let me go? Or do I appear compliant, try to win him over to my way of thinking?

I choose the second option.

I nod slowly.

'Good,' he says.

He waits as I step through the doorway. But as I make my way down that hallway, his footsteps echoing on the wooden floor behind me, my stomach churns. Because I'm pretty sure I just made a big mistake.

22

'Stop here,' he says as I reach a door. I can feel him behind me, and a shiver runs up my spine. I do as he says, and he steps in front of me and reaches for the handle. But the moment before he turns it, he lifts his forefinger to his lips. 'Shh …'

He pushes the door open and we go inside.

The first thing I notice is the amber and spice of perfume. Then I see some flimsy, barely opaque red curtains hanging across a separate room. He closes the door gently and we move towards the curtains.

As we draw closer, I can make out what's on the other side. There's a room, windowless, and empty aside from some bookshelves against the walls and a huge red chaise in the middle. Two women sit on it, talking. One has ash-blonde hair and is wearing a lime-green camisole, while the other has a short chestnut bob and is wearing a strapless black dress.

They're both sitting with their legs crossed, hunched over their phones, little handbags beside them. What do they think they're waiting for? Why are they so calm?

Is he going to kill them? How can I stop him?

A voice in my head is screaming, *RUN!* But Oscar senses it, and his hands find my shoulders. He grabs me, stares deep into my eyes and I'm thinking, *I should never have looked for him. I should never have gone to that club. I should never have stepped outside the safety of my carefully built little life.*

'Relax,' Oscar whispers, but there's nothing in his tone to make me relax. Then he adds, 'They will both walk out of here alive … unless you do something stupid.'

'I can't do it,' I whisper back, my insides twisting. Then in a small voice I beg, 'Please don't make me.'

He frowns. 'They're for *me*, Aubrey. Just watch and learn.'

Then he leaves me there by the curtain and I watch helplessly as he strides towards them. I can see their faces as they gaze up at him.

'You will both sit still, you will stay calm,' he says in a soothing voice, looking from one to the other. Their eyes glaze over and they nod and he sits down between them. Dread settles over me and I press my hand to my mouth in case I yelp.

He turns to the chestnut-haired one, cups her face in his hands and murmurs, 'Aren't you beautiful?' And I can see her face, she's looking deep into his eyes and just letting it happen.

And then one of his hands finds her breast, and she arches her back and leans in and he kisses her. First on the mouth, then on the jawline, then his mouth moves to her neck …

And he bites.

She flinches, lets out a small cry, but she doesn't fight. She just stays there, growing limp, while he keeps feeding. The blonde one gazes out at the room vacantly. Oscar pulls away and the chestnut-haired woman flops forward like a rag doll, then he turns to the other woman. He doesn't even bother kissing her, he just leans in and bites her neck immediately. My other hand comes to my mouth now.

Oscar's eyes move up and meet mine, and something electric moves between us. I look down. Away.

All I want is to leave. But if I do, what's he going to do to them? At least if I'm here, there's a witness, not that I could take this to the police.

He pulls away and the blonde one's head leans against his chest.

Are they okay? The first woman's fingers are twitching and neither of them have collapsed, so they're definitely still alive …

Then I watch as he bites his own wrist, and with an expression I can only describe as boredom, he moves it to the wound on the first woman's neck, pressing his own blood into the bite. Then he does the same to the second woman's wound. And before my very eyes I watch them heal.

And … *what?*

I've seen this trick performed in TV shows, but always thought it was just lazy scriptwriting, because I never saw Hans heal anyone with his blood—though granted, that wasn't really his personality type. Plus, like I said before, I've bled into a human's wound—not on purpose, but still—and it did *nothing* to heal them.

It just made an even bigger mess.

So why is it working for him? Because it's undeniable: their wounds have vanished.

The first woman is moving, coming back to life. He turns to her, lifts her face to look at his and whispers something I don't hear. She nods. Then he turns to the second woman, sits her up, looks her dead in the eye, and this time I catch it: 'You came here tonight, but you and your friend got bored, so you went home early. We never met. This never happened. You spent a couple of hours scrolling through social media before bed, which is why most of the night is a blur … a big black hole …'

This is how he gets away with it.

He must have hypnotised Daphne last night too, I realise. Because that's exactly what she said about her night. Now anxiety brews inside me because: *What exactly did she tell him?*

Woman number two nods. They get up, sling their little handbags over their shoulders and then Oscar leads them to a door on the other side of the room. They walk through it without even looking back.

And then they're gone. And still alive.

Relief pulses through me. *It's okay. That wasn't so bad.* He just wanted me to see how it was done.

He comes over to me now, and he looks well, healthy. His fangs have retracted and there's not even a drop of blood on his expensive-looking shirt, nothing on his teeth, on his face. You'd never guess he was a monster. But at least it's done. I've watched his demonstration, now I want to go home, thanks.

'Thank you,' I say. 'That was really helpful. I should probably be going though, I have things I have to do before work tom—'

'Absolutely not,' he says. My breath catches and the room swells with silence.

And then: *Creak*. The door on the far side of the room opens, and another woman comes inside. She has strawberry-blonde hair and is wearing a short silver sequined dress and stilettos.

Oscar looks at me. 'Now it's your turn.'

I stare at the woman and an icy terror fills my veins. I can hear her pulse from all the way over here, I can smell her—B positive—but *no*. I can't do this.

He can do whatever he wants to me, but I'm *not* feeding on her or anyone else.

I need to get out of here before he tries to force me. So, I nod and give a tight smile, and he starts to lead the way towards her, but as soon as his back is turned, I run for the door.

I'm two steps away, reaching for the handle, when I bang into his chest.

He glares down at me and I get a little dizzy. The muscle on the side of his jaw clenches.

Uh-oh.

I glance at the door and then back up at him, and maybe I should fight, force my way out. What's he going to do? Kill me?

But then, slowly, calmly, he says, 'I'm not going to force you to do anything you don't want to do, Aubrey.' My insides unclench. 'In fact,' he continues, 'from this moment on I can promise you that unless it is vital for your own protection, your choices are your own. Happy?'

I nod, even though that sounds like a loophole he can abuse, but still, at least he's being reasonable. 'Really? Thank you,' I say. 'And look, maybe one day, but right now I just want to go home,' I add, glancing across at the woman again.

He lets out a big breath. Shrugs. Thoughts move behind his eyes. 'Of course. Like I said, it's your choice. But let me know if you change your mind after you talk to Daphne ...'

A little jolt of terror rolls up my spine.

Because now I'm thinking of the missed call from Daphne. Of the voicemail she apparently left.

'What did you do?' I ask, my voice coming out as a whisper as I fumble through my bag for my phone. Frantically, I tap through to my voicemails. As I wait for Daphne's message to play, I look up at him and I can tell he's enjoying this, he finds it ... funny.

I push my fingertip against my ear so I can focus on Daphne's words, even though it's basically silent in here.

'Aubs,' she whispers, like she's on the sales floor, or in one of the dressing rooms, calling in secret. 'Oh my god, Kenny is dead. He was mugged this morning, while he was out on his run, they took everything he had on him. This is why I don't exercise,' she says. 'Anyway, they've offered us free counselling, so I for one will be calling in sick tomorrow. Wanted to let you know. Call me when you get this.'

My head gets light, my vision tunnels. And as I drop my phone into my bag, all I can think about is the smear of blood on that T-shirt. How it smelt icky, but familiar.

No. Please no.

'You killed Kenny,' I say, needing to be wrong. Because I didn't like Kenny, but he was a human being with a life and a future and you can't just *kill* people.

Now, that mild amusement morphs into an actual smirk. 'Well, that's a matter for the authorities, isn't it, Aubrey? Given what's in your flat right now, and the fact that Daphne will corroborate anything I want her to, I'd say maybe *you* killed him. Everyone knew you didn't like him very much.'

The room tilts.

A flash of his running track in the message from Daphne. And my reply: *God I hate him*.

'I found that T-shirt,' I say, searching for disappointment in his eyes. I need that T-shirt to be all there is. But the look doesn't come.

'Tampering with evidence, tut-tut. That won't look good when they find the rest.'

My throat tightens, then my stomach. He's insane. To him, this is all just a game. But what the hell does he mean by *the rest*?

'Be a shame if someone tipped off the police about it. He was such a loathsome fellow, wasn't he? But Aubrey, just in case, you might want to think about how you could account for your whereabouts in the early hours of this morning …'

I want to hit him. To bare my fangs. To scream. To tell him that I hate him, that I wish he'd never found me. That I was better off without him. But I get the sense he'd like that, so I don't. I push it down. I need to think.

Because I know he's telling the truth. I saw with my own eyes how easily he let himself into my flat. And also … that noise that woke me up. *That wasn't my imagination*. He must have killed Kenny on his five am run, then broken in and planted the evidence in my flat, like a total psychopath.

I stand there, mute, desperately searching for a way out.

I could try to talk to Daphne, maybe hypnotise her myself, get her to side with me. But it's very clear that Oscar's skills are far superior to mine.

'But if I'm arrested for Kenny's death, they'll figure out I'm a vampire. And that's exactly what you *don't* want,' I say.

Ha!

'True,' he says. 'Which is why I made sure to leave some

evidence in Daphne's flat too as a backup. I'll simply hypnotise her and get her to confess. I didn't want to do that to her, but as that seems to be your preference … I'm happy to oblige.'

I stare at him, my breath lodged in my throat. *I'm not going to win this. He's thought of everything.*

His eyes are hard, and he looks straight through me. 'So, do you still want to go home?'

I hate him. I truly hate him.

The world spins double time. *I can't let him do that to Daphne.* Or me. I look behind him, to those red gauzy curtains. I can hear that woman's heartbeat in the other room and I can't do *that* either. I have to buy myself some time, so I can figure this out.

My eyes snap back to his, and I nod. 'Okay, I'll do what you ask, but I can't do it now. I need to get myself emotionally ready.'

He clenches his jaw. 'You must think I'm as thick as a brick. It's a yes or no question, Aubrey. You don't get to *emotionally prepare*. This isn't a theatre class.'

My throat tightens. I look back at the woman, then up at Oscar again.

'Surely I get to at least think about it?'

He narrows his eyes. 'Fine. But think fast.' Then he adds, as he bites his own wrist, 'But until you learn to protect yourself, you're going to have to let me protect you.'

He holds his wrist in front of my lips.

And these are the moments when I really, really, really wish I could die.

'Drink,' he says.

'But you're a vampire.'

'Thanks, Aubrey, that's so helpful. Just drink.'

'Why?'

'It'll give you some of my powers for a while—twenty-four hours, give or take, depending on how quickly you metabolise it. That way you can at least protect yourself while you "think". And who knows, maybe once you get a taste of what life could be like, you'll enjoy it.'

I look at him, wary, thinking of how in TV shows, when someone drinks a vampire's blood it means the vampire can find them. That must be what's going on here …

'Is this … so you can track me?' I ask, suspicion dripping from my voice.

He frowns at me. 'It's not GPS, Aubrey, it's blood. Just do it,' he snaps, exasperated. And honestly, I just want to get away from here before he tries to make me feed on that poor woman.

So I drink. His blood tastes different from human blood, cold and bitter and it makes me a bit woozy.

I pull away and my fangs retract.

'You're extremely weak, so it might take a couple of hours to kick in, but I think you'll enjoy yourself.' He motions to my bag. 'Now, give me your phone,' he says.

I don't want to, but he'll just take it, so I unlock it and hand it over. I watch helplessly as he scrolls and taps.

'I'm putting my number in here. You text me when you've made a decision. Now go, I have company to deal with … Oh, and Aubrey?'

I turn towards him.

'Don't make me wait.'

24

Cat is waiting for me like usual when I get home. I let her in, close the door, drop my bag and coat on the sofa and look around. I take in my bookshelf, all those self-help books—where is the chapter on something like this? Then the washing machine, the light blinking to tell me it's done. I go over and pull out the T-shirt, inspecting the offending mark.

There's still a faint brown stain. I toss it in the bin—no point taking the risk—then I look around.

My gaze travels from the sofa to the humming fridge, to the bathroom, the TV, my bedroom. Whatever is in here, it could be anywhere, but *I'm going to find it*.

So I flick on the light and sniff the air, seeking a direction.

It's still there, the smell of old blood, and now that I know who it belongs to it's so damned obvious. Of course it's Kenny. But I can't tell where it's coming from.

Cat watches from the sofa as I rush over to the bookshelf and start feeling around behind the books—nothing. I look behind the bookshelf. In the fridge. In the freezer. Above the washing machine. I check the kitchen cupboards, reaching into the dark corners, examining all the drawers. I look under my bed, beneath my mattress, in my closet, in every shoebox, in my laundry hamper. Under the sofa, the cushions, the coffee table. But I don't find anything.

I can't find it, but I can still smell it. It's like it's coming from *everywhere.*

FUCK.

I flop down beside Cat and she lets out a little meow. How the hell has Oscar wandered back into my life and blown up 150 years of caution in just twenty-four hours? How bad will it be in thirty-six? Forty-eight? All of sudden, a volcanic heat erupts beneath my ribs, and before I know what I'm doing, I pick up the knitting needles from under the coffee table and fling them at the wall as hard as I can.

I watch them fly across the room. I wait for the clickety-clack as they hit the floor.

But Cat and I both watch in horror as they lodge themselves deep into the plaster.

I sit there, staring at them.

How did I do that?

I look down at my hands, and now Oscar's voice filters back to me: *It'll give you some of my powers for a while—twenty-four hours, give or take* ... Is that what this is? Am I super strong now? What if I break something important?

Maybe it'll fade in my sleep.

And so I let Cat out and she doesn't even meow, not once. It's like she knows it's for her own safety, just in case. I strip off my clothes and leave them in a trail on the floor on my way to the shower. I want to wash tonight off me. Then I put on some pyjamas and get into bed. It's too early to sleep, but it feels safe in here. Like if I cocoon myself in the covers, I can't make anything worse.

As I lie there, I reach for my phone and go to my messages.

There's still nothing from Jonathan, but five from Es. I go

to her last one and type back: *I'm so sorry. Jonathan broke up with me in a text. I was in shock. Love you xxxx*

Then I tap on Daphne's last message, bite down gently on my lower lip and start to type: *WHAT? That's terrible. His poor family! Hope you're not too upset. Xx*

Send.

There. Now if anyone reads that, we'll both look sort of innocent … Or like a couple of masterminds covering up a murder.

And then I tap through to Instagram. But as I navigate to my profile, I'm filled with a sense of doom. Maybe I've really done it, maybe I've really lost Jonathan forever.

I tap on my story and glance down once again at the little faces to check who's viewed it, yearning to see his.

My breath catches.

Because … is that him?

It is.

His little circular profile picture is staring back at me, second from the top.

He hasn't forgotten me.

My brain lights up as if on narcotics, and hope sparkles in my veins. I knew it! He still cares about me. I let out a big sigh of pure relief.

Then reality comes flooding in, ice cold and full of debris.

This *isn't* good. Not at all. Because Jonathan won't be safe if he's back in my life. Tonight showed me that.

If Oscar killed Kenny to get control of me, and threatened Daphne to motivate me, what would he do to Jonathan if he found out how much I care for him? Who we are to each other? Oscar would probably kill him. I can't put Jonathan in danger like that. I just can't.

Which means I have no choice. I need to walk away, before he can get hurt.

I have to.

But also, if I do walk away, then what?

It might be a millennium before we cross paths again. It might *never* happen. Maybe he'll be lost to me forever. A dark and lonely eternity unfurls before me, everything in greyscale, each night harder to get through than the last—like it was before we met. Where I knew nobody would ever be truly close to me, where I had to keep everyone at a certain distance, control what they knew about me. Where love was for everyone except me. And I can't even turn him into a vampire like me, because I don't know how to do that—not that I'd want to inflict that on him. I just want this one life with him. One measly human life. Eighty years. Sixty. Ten. Five. Hell, even two months. Anything.

There has to be a way to get him back without Oscar hurting him.

And then it hits me: *There is.*

I just really don't want to do it.

Because I'm going to need to do what Oscar asks. To do exactly what he wants, so he has no reason to harm anyone I love.

I need to do this for Daphne. For Jonathan and Es, if Oscar ever finds out about them. This isn't just about *me* anymore.

I can do this. I *have* to do this.

I scroll through my phone and find Oscar's contact and then I stare at it for a moment, my mind whirring, searching for another way out. Another solution. But there isn't one.

And so slowly, with a tight knot in my stomach, I type back four little letters: *FINE*.

I hit send, and Oscar's reply comes in almost immediately: *Splendid. Chat soon.*

All I can think as I stare at it is: *What have I done?*

25

I wake with a jolt, my insides wired and jangly, my alarm roaring from my phone. *Here we go, for the 55,018th time*. I pull out my earplugs, take off my eye mask, and reach for my phone to turn off the noise. As I do, I catch a glimpse of the back of my hand, the entrance stamp from the open mic night still smudged across it. Then everything else comes tumbling back too, but I push it away and search the screen for Jonathan's name.

Because he looked at my story … so *maybe*.

But it's not there.

In its place are two other text notifications.

Daphne: *WHATEVER! Like you're sad he's gone??? PARTY TIME!!!! Xx*

Great. Now we both look even more guilty of Kenny's demise.

The second is a text from Es: *Oh babe. I'm so sorry. LOVE YOU TOO!!! Call if you want to chat. xxxxxx*

I think of us, standing in the fake snow, me hypnotising her so I could go and stalk Olivia. Then the Christmas present she gave me, still sitting in my bag. I'm an awful person.

I stand up. My limbs are heavy and my mouth tastes weird and bitter and I'm hungry, so hungry. I'm thinking about the blood in the tin in my fridge and how I want it NOW, and then … *whoosh* … I'm there.

Standing right in front of the fridge.

WHAT IS GOING ON?

I stand dead still and look around. How did I just do that? I can *never* do that. I've tried, many times.

And then … a memory. I swivel to look at the knitting needles, still lodged in the plaster where I threw them last night. *Oh god.*

Oscar's blood.

Well, that explains the bitterness in my mouth.

I can hear his words in my head: *It'll give you some of my powers for a while—twenty-four hours, give or take …*

I can't be like this for twenty-four hours. I have to go to work.

So now, carefully, intentionally, slowly testing whether I can control my movements, I reach into the tin, pull out my blood and pour some into a mug. Then, equally carefully, I put it in the microwave and press 'Start'.

So far, so good.

I just stand there like a statue, watching the mug spin, thinking: *See, you're fine, nothing odd is happening*.

Beeeeeppp.

I open the microwave, reach for my mug and take a sip, then wait for the calm to hit. But I don't know whether Oscar's blood is messing me up, or if it's something else—the calm I usually get from bagged blood isn't there. I'm still jangly, a bit wired.

I sip again, but again, nothing. *Shit*.

I take my phone and mug over to the sofa by the window and open the blinds. The sun is just setting outside, the sky settling into dusty mauve twilight and as I glance over at my bag, I can see the corner of Es's present: little red and white Santas on green paper. I pull it out, setting it down on the coffee table, then stare at it, wondering what it is. It feels like an emblem of the boring, greyscale life I've always resented. But now I'm not so sure. Not if what Oscar wants for me is the alternative. Suddenly boring seems enormously appealing—at least I could predict what was coming next. Because how the hell am I going to get through my shift tonight with his blood in my veins?

But if Daphne isn't going into work, I'm not either … I call in sick.

Then I sit there, staring at the wall, Oscar's blood pumping through me, my foot tapping on the floor. And all I want is to be close to Jonathan right now. For him to calm me down. So I pull up his Instagram profile and go to his posts to see his face. But as I look down at the picture of us laughing in the movie theatre, I can almost feel the worn velvet of the seats beneath my fingertips, and every part of me aches, even my palms.

I can still remember the feeling—like we were invincible—as we left the cinema that night. We were giggling and rushing out the doors and as we went to cross the street he reached for my hand. His was so big and warm and as I took it, my stomach clenched and I got another flash. Black and white. Sped up. Silent.

We're in a small church and I'm walking down the aisle, a small bunch of flowers in my hands, people are in the pews on either side of me. My wedding dress is off the shoulder, and I'm wearing a small crown of flowers on my head, connected to a long tulle veil. I'm smiling and my eyes are filled with clear, human tears, as I walk down the aisle, towards Jonathan and into my future …

What am I going to do if I never get him back? If I lose my soulmate, I also lose every link to my human-self. I want to know her. I want to get back to her.

I glance across at the image of him and Baxter at rock climbing from Wednesday last week, when everything was still good, and my insides pang.

But then: *Hang on. It's Wednesday.*

My blood races as I pull up a browser and navigate to his rock climbing gym's website and then their contact page and before I know it, I'm looking down through their holiday hours.

They're open tonight.

Jonathan is probably there. During the five weeks we dated, he never missed a session. Said it 'cleared his mind'.

Now all the pieces of a plan fall together in an instant. Because what other powers might Oscar's blood have given me? Siphoning visions with greater control, perhaps? And while I can't go and grab onto Jonathan and get them that way, if he's out of the house, I could go past and see if I could get any visions from things he owns. It could be possible. It could also be batshit crazy, I know that, but rational argument doesn't sound so enticing right now. I have to give it a shot.

And I have do it NOW.

Because I've only got around three hours—the time he spent at rock climbing every other time he went—before he gets home. I don't plan on ingesting Oscar's blood again anytime soon. It's now or never. I can't afford to hesitate.

26

The cold winter air bites into my cheeks as I make my way up the hill to Jonathan's street, doing my best to walk a normal speed. I figured out—through trial and error—that whatever 'powers' I have right now, courtesy of Oscar's blood, only work when I want something really badly or feel something too much. Like, it was intense hunger that zoomed me over to the fridge. It was fury that had me hurl those knitting needles into the wall. Otherwise, it seems, all good. A little aggressive, a little jangly, but otherwise fine.

And I'm wearing my lucky earrings—the ones I wore the afternoon we met—they *have* to bring me luck.

As I head towards his house, I scan the street for his red Kia, just in case I'm wrong. But I can't see his car, and I can't see Baxter's car either.

I glance behind me as I walk, making sure nobody is following me.

Now that I've agreed to Oscar's terms, there's no need for him to kill anyone else to 'motivate' me, but I don't want him knowing about Jonathan all the same.

But there's nobody there, nobody is following me. And now I'm standing in front of Jonathan's townhouse, scanning it: all the lights are off, except for the blinking of Christmas tree lights through the crack in the living room curtain, and a faint glow upstairs.

I move up the pathway, duck through the side gate to the back of the house, then stand still, listening for movement: the beating of a heart. A breath. A TV. Any sign of danger.

But all I can hear is the rustle of the wind in the trees, traffic in the distance and the faint sound of chatter floating in from the neighbours.

I scan the back door—locked—the kitchen window—closed and locked—then look up to the second floor …

Jonathan's bedroom window is ajar.

The light is on inside, but I know he leaves it on to deter burglars, and as I look up at it, all I want right now is to be inside his room. I *want* it. An energy zips through me then *whoooooosh*, my hands find the drainpipes, and I'm pulling myself up, feet hitting bricks, hands moving one above the other as I scale the wall. Until I'm there, and now my fingers are clasping onto his windowsill, the paint cold and peeling, and I'm peeking inside.

I hold my breath. The coast is entirely clear, so I pull myself through the window.

As I step onto the carpet, I can feel Jonathan everywhere, smell him—cedarwood and bergamot—mingled with his laundry detergent and that other musky scent that was always just him. Everything is just the same as the last time I was here. The room is large and minimalist, decorated in slate grey, black and white, and well ordered. The only messy part is his desk. His laptop sits on top of it, with a bunch of papers scattered around it, and in the corner stands a picture of him and his parents, staring out at the room.

A dull throb rings out in my chest as I go over to it and pick it up, looking down at his parents' faces, wondering if they'd like me if they met me. Or if they'd instinctively know that there was something wrong with me.

But maybe I can get a vision from this.

I close my eyes and try to focus, I *want* to see something, I *really, really want to*. I wait for my stomach to clench, for images to stream in. I want to see something about us. Something about me. Anything at all.

But … nothing comes.

Shit. This needs to work.

I put the picture back down on the desk and look around. *Maybe I need something that's meaningful for the two of us?* My gaze moves to the closet across the room, just beyond his free weights and stretch bands. And then *zoooooom*, within a millisecond, I'm there, opening the doors and tracing Jonathan's jumpers with my fingertips.

The mustard jumper he wore the day we met is on the top of the pile. I reach for it, hugging it to me. I take a deep breath, clench my eyes shut, breathe in his scent and try to conjure everything he made me feel: warmth flooding my veins whenever he laughed, his hand reaching for mine as we crossed the road, the feeling of him inside me when we made love, our eyes locked …

But nothing. Just blankness.

COME ON!

I clench my jaw and turn around and face his room. Is there anything else I could try to use? But there's a little voice inside me saying: *This isn't going to work.*

Disappointment settles heavy in my stomach.

I put Jonathan's jumper back in his closet, close the closet door and head back to the window. But halfway there, I spy The Doors T-shirt I used to sleep in, right there, still folded on the chair near his desk. And I always wanted to tell Jonathan that I'd met Jim Morrison backstage at The Roundhouse in

1968, I kept thinking one day I could tell him everything. But if I don't get him back, I can't tell him *anything*.

And how is any of this fair? Why did fate or the gods or that string connecting us bring us back together just to pull us apart again?

So much for my lucky earrings helping me out …

But then I have an idea.

I could do something, I realise. *Give him a little nudge*.

I mean, I'm already here. So I reach for one of my lucky earrings, pull it off, go over to his desk and drop it underneath. From the bed he should see it. Surely, when he sees it, he'll call me.

I look around, in case there is something, anything else I can do to tip the scales in my favour. His pillow. I *zoooooom* over to it and rub my wrist then my hair onto it, trying to transfer onto it whatever scent I carry that men always pick up on. He'll miss me, when he smells it … But also, have I lost my mind?

I really should get out of here.

I move over to the window and get ready to climb out, but just before I do, movement flickers on the other side of the fence. His neighbours—two women in big coats—are coming outside. *No, please no*. *Go back inside*. *GO!*

I squint at them. I see the flicker of a flame; a lighter. I stick my head out and take a few deep breaths, focusing in, assessing the risk. And *great, just great*. They're smoking … weed.

They'll be out there for a while.

And I can't very well climb out now—what if they see me, scaling my way down the guttering?

Still, there are perfectly good doors downstairs.

I whoosh down the stairs and enter the living room, looking around, taking it all in. The same Christmas tree blinks with the same little lights as last time I was here, watching through the bay window. The same sofa we lay on, him stroking my hair, the rug we danced on … all of it just the same.

Except now there's a big pile of cardboard boxes in the corner of the room, and as I notice them, reality hits me afresh: Jonathan's life is going on without me, he's building furniture I might never see. A life I won't be a part of.

And then … rattle, rattle, rattle.

My gaze snaps to the front door. My vision tunnels.

They're home. Early.

If Jonathan catches me here, I will never get him back. Ever.

I will forever be the psycho ex who broke into his house while he was out.

I rush through to the kitchen and there, on the dining table, is a small pile of mail. And on the top is a blue square envelope. It's upside down so I can see the return address: *Olivia Coombes*.

And of course she's the kind of woman who sends Christmas cards while I'm the kind of woman who breaks into her ex's house.

But the door is still rattling and I need to get out of here.

So I grab the card and zoom out the back door just as the lights flick on. I can hear chatter inside, movement, someone is calling to someone else, but I'm running through the side gate, looking around, and then bolting towards the main road.

But as I turn towards Archway tube station, a shudder moves through me. I've spent so much time building this safe little life where I don't take risks and I never let my feelings get the best of me and now I'm … what? Breaking and entering? Do I want to get caught? Am I *looking* for a repeat of Coventry Street?

27

When you never die and reinvent yourself every five to seven years, you wind up living in a lot of places. In my 150 years, I've lived in East London, West London, a wash of English villages, various arrondissements in Paris (yes, I speak French along with a smattering of Russian, Italian and Japanese), Berlin for three months just after the wall came down, and a few stints travelling. Most of these lives have blurred together, like a watercolour painting left out in the rain, each forgotten as soon as I've moved on to the next, but there are some nights in some lives that brand you forever. Nights you wear like a tattoo from then on.

Mine was 16 April 1922. And it is second only to what happened with Hans.

London was still recovering from the impact of the First World War and the Spanish flu, Princess Mary had just had her wedding, and there was a sense of optimism in the air, a feeling that things were on the way up. I'd only been a vampire for forty-six years—so I was still young enough to believe that might be true.

I was living in a small apartment not far from Coventry Street that I told people my father rented for me—the fewer questions, the better. This was still seven years before women were allowed to work night shifts as telephone operators in London, a job I would come to have in time, so I was still working as a hostess at a nightclub in the West End—think jazz music and dancing, sticky floors, and the smells of cigarette smoke, aldehyde perfumes and brandy—the kind of place where you could get a drink (and many other things) until the wee hours, despite the laws prohibiting such behaviour. The kind of place where a girl like me was routinely propositioned, sex for money. I said no, though I didn't judge the women who said yes—we do what we need to, to survive. But I couldn't help but watch the men who fed on their desperation with a certain level of disgust. They had plenty of money. They could have simply helped. Been kind.

Early one morning, after work, I was on my way home. Sometimes, in the darker months, I'd go for breakfast with the other women. The aromas of cigarettes and fried eggs and bacon would fill the air as we swapped gossip about the clientele until our eyelids were heavy. Then we'd go home and sleep through the day. But it was mid-spring by then, so by five am dawn was coming; soon the streetlights would switch off. And I was starving, I needed to get home to the little blood I had stashed away in the icebox.

I was halfway home when I heard the first cry.

My insides froze. I listened harder.

Then came a thud, another cry.

I moved quickly towards the sound, then stood at the corner of the street and peeked around it. Not far from me stood a man, holding up his fist. There was a woman in front of him, cowering, her arms covering her head. From her lack of shawl and bonnet, her low-cut neckline, I suspected she was a sex worker, though I didn't recognise her. Then she moved her arms aside and looked up at him, and said, 'Please …' And her face was sheer terror. I recognised the look from the little boy Hans had killed …

My gums tingled, darkness swirled, but *no, no, no*. I tried to push it down, control it. I almost managed.

But then the bastard struck her again.

My ears rang, my vision blanched, my fangs came out, and a volcanic rage rushed through me.

I lurched towards them, attacking him from behind. I grabbed his shoulders and pulled him backwards, and as he hit the ground, she ran away. Instinctively, I dropped to my knees and my teeth sank into his neck.

As soon as his blood started to run onto my tongue, bliss sparked from my veins, my vision snapped to high definition and the entire world sounded like an orchestra. After forty-six years of feeling half-dead inside, of never letting myself go, of pushing down the darkness and holding myself in chains, I felt ... alive.

And I wanted more.

But then—*ow*. Something sharp plunged into my stomach. I pulled away, looked down—the man was lying limp beneath me, but he was holding a bloodied knife and I was bleeding all over him. His chest, his neck. His face. My blood mixing with his.

And then I heard voices coming towards us.

The rage turned to panic.

What am I doing?

But also, I felt fucking fantastic. I wanted to laugh, even though nothing was funny. But I needed to go.

So I left him lying on the ground, and ran home, light on my feet and hidden by shadows.

I was healed by the time I got home, washed the blood off me, got into bed, and tried to go to sleep.

The problem was, now that I'd tasted blood from the vein again, I didn't just want more. I *needed* more. And I needed it NOW. It had awoken something inside me, something I couldn't lull back to sleep any more than I could lull myself to sleep.

I got up and paced the floorboards, need gurgling in my stomach as I watched the sun rise, thinking *I should sleep, I should sleep*. But I didn't want to sleep. I wanted to eat. I was no longer scared of the darkness; now, I wanted to swim in it. The strangest thing was, as the sun rose in the sky, I didn't feel the same intense sluggishness I usually felt during the day.

I was certainly a little weaker than I had been just two hours before when it was dark, but not as weak as I'd usually be. And … I had the munchies. Bad.

Maybe I *could* just get one more little taste … I felt like with my increase in strength, I could do it.

I'd be careful this time. Only have a little bit.

I fed twice more before a velvet night descended. And as I sat in the bath afterwards, completely unslept, I remember thinking that maybe I'd found a new way forward, maybe I'd been wrong all along. Because, I reasoned, I wasn't really that bad. The first guy had deserved it, and the other two hadn't been hurt. Not really. Just a little puncture wound. Sure, I might have gone too far if I hadn't been interrupted both times, but that didn't matter. They'd be fine. So, maybe I could live like this forever … I could be strong and alive, light and razor-sharp …

Life could be *liveable*.

I was still thinking about that as I climbed out of the bath and got ready for work.

As I made my way back to the club, I was grinning, congratulating myself. I thought I'd found the elusive answer, the holy grail I'd been looking for. Everything would be better from now on. The pain of living was finally over.

But then I passed a newspaper vendor. The headline screamed: *VAMPIRE ATTACKS ON COVENTRY STREET!*

Everything inside me froze. But I kept putting one foot in front of the other.

Act normal. It'll pass. Maybe nobody will believe it.

I mean, who believed in vampires?

Lots of people, apparently.

When I got to work, *everyone* was talking about it. Apparently, the woman I'd saved now remembered me as a huge shadow in the dark who'd come forth and attacked them both. She'd sold her story to the papers. It didn't help matters that all three men—one dead, two in hospital—shared the same puncture wounds on their necks. My only saving grace was that according to the survivor descriptions, I was all sorts of horrifying things. I was a monster, grotesque, terrifying, huge! But I *wasn't* a mere woman. A woman could never have brought them to their knees.

Hearing myself described that way reminded me of all the books and legends that had made me decide never to do this. Never to become this way. Because they were right. Two of my victims had been entirely innocent. What sort of monster would I become if I left my hunger unchecked?

How much worse would I get?

Guilt pulsed through me, followed quickly by pure revulsion. How had I slipped?

How had I been so reckless, so lacking in control? What would I do if one of my victims saw me one day, recognised me, remembered the true turn of events? Was I going to get caught? I mean, they'd hired a vampire hunter! What if whatever Professor Van Helsing they'd entrusted with the task actually found me?

The public hysteria just got worse over the next two days, the effects of the blood I'd fed on quickly dwindled, and soon it was four days later, I hadn't left the house, I was starving and weak, and the full gravity of what I had done was hitting with full force—I was sickened. I hated all that I was, all over again. How had I let this happen? All I could think as I stared into the mirror, loathing everything I saw, was NEVER AGAIN.

I quit my job, moved to Paris, and stayed there until the end of 1928, when I cautiously ventured back to London. But I was extra careful, and I always avoided the West End, even though I loved and still love the theatre … just in case.

Every time I caught a Tube that passed by Piccadilly Circus or Leicester Square, I'd renew my vow: *Never again.*

I would always be good. No matter what. And I would be careful too, even more careful than before. And aside from that one weak moment when I told Freddie things I shouldn't have, I *have* been careful.

But tonight, I wasn't careful. Cautious. Measured. Or safe. I was reckless. And I can blame Oscar's blood, or pin it on my need to know who I was as a human. But that wouldn't have saved me if someone had seen me scaling that wall.

Still, who am I kidding? All of that is still far less of a threat than Oscar's *Chat soon*.

Because here's what I know about darkness: it feels good. Really good. It sucks you in. Once you start to feed on the vein, it's almost impossible to stop—the books and movies got that much right. I've been lucky thus far—each time I've slipped, something has pulled me out and stopped me in my tracks: the terror in that little boy's eyes, ending up in the papers, hearing myself described as a monster … something to ignite my humanity before it was lost to me completely. But what if I'm not so lucky this time? What if this time, nothing stops me, and I can't stop myself? What if, this time, the darkness pulls me in and never lets me go?

What will I become?

I wake to daylight leaking in around the edges of the blinds, those church bells ringing full throttle, announcing with joy that it's Christmas Eve. Selfridges closes early, so I have until Boxing Day off from work. Which should be a good thing, and I want it to be a good thing, but instead my head throbs, my mouth is dry and I've never felt so alone.

Because I'm always alone on Christmas Eve, but *this* one was meant to be different.

I was meant to be with Jonathan.

I put my eye mask and earplugs on the table by the bed and reach for my phone. It's only 11 am, but there's no way I'll fall back asleep now, not with everything.

There's one new text, but it's not from Jonathan.

It's from Daphne, a picture of her at some party with lots of beautiful people with glowing skin and life in their eyes.

I heart the photo, and as I do, her words come floating back: *Aubs, you can't crack first. That's the mistake we always make, we give up right before they crack …*

A flash of me last night, rubbing my scent on Jonathan's pillow, leaving my earring under his desk …

I'd say I've well and truly cracked first.

As I get up, I feel even worse than I usually do in the daytime, my limbs are heavy, and Oscar's blood has completely worn off. I make myself a cup of warm blood then sit on the sofa and reach into my bag for that blue envelope from last night and peel it open.

I pull out the card—a silver-glitter snowman with *Merry Christmas* in cursive beneath it in the same glitter.

Inside, in loopy handwriting it reads: *Merry Christmas J, can't wait to see where the new year takes us, Love, Liv xx.*

She calls him J …

Does he like it when she says that? Does he like *her*? With her cookbooks and her air fryer and her face creams in the bathroom—all the other normal things I'm sure she has, while I sit here with my warm mug of blood?

Is she why he hasn't texted me yet? Because he can somehow sense that while she's normal, I'm defective. Broken. Even if he doesn't know why?

God, imagine if he ever found out what I did last night?

Shame pulses through me as I move the blind aside and glance up at the sky. It's overcast and glary, like my mood. And those bells just keep on ringing like they couldn't care less about me and my heart.

A flash of Jonathan and me, just three weeks ago, lying in bed, my head on his chest. Listening to the heartbeat I'd recognise anywhere, as I stared at the moon out the window.

'Are you okay?' he asked. 'You seem sad.' And usually I was happy with him, but right then I *was* sad, because I knew one day he would get old and die and I'd be without him again.

'No, I'm just thinking,' I said, extra cheerfully, because I've learnt the hard way that people don't always respond well to my melancholic churn.

But he didn't falter. 'You don't need to fake anything with me, Aubrey,' he said. 'You're allowed to feel whatever you feel. I love that you're so sensitive.' He held me a little tighter. 'Nothing could ever change my feelings for you.'

It felt in that moment as though he could see into my soul and it was terrifying ... but also, it wasn't. Because I'd shown him something real, and he hadn't recoiled. Instead, he'd said 'love'. It wasn't 'I love you' but it was on the way there. And you don't say things unless you mean them—not when you're Jonathan, a guy who freaks out over too many texts. He meant it.

And he might still come around, it has only been what, four nights since we broke up? He's probably been thinking about us, and tomorrow is Christmas.

That's a perfect excuse for him to text me: *Merry Christmas.*

I close my eyes. *Please god, if you're up there, if you have any affection for me at all, please just get him to text me Merry Christmas. Please? I will make him happy, I promise.*

My eyes open slowly, and as I refocus, I see the empty bag of cat treats still sitting on the counter, reminding me to get more. And that's something I can do, something I can succeed at. Then at least I'll have Cat with me on Christmas Day—assuming her neglectful owner leaves her outside again.

I get up, pull on my coat, grab my keys and bag, put on a cap and sunglasses and head up the stairs into the daylight. Even through my sunglasses, the glare makes my head throb. But I keep moving, past the bins outside the pub, across the road and towards Borough Market.

I walk slowly, like someone recovering from an illness. I'm almost at that pub from *Bridget Jones* and now I'm thinking about how Bridget and Mark Darcy also had problems. *It's normal.*

As I enter the market I'm hit by a swirl of laughter and chatter, a flurry of last-minute Christmas shoppers. And it's almost nice being out, among people, even if it is daylight. It's nice to forget myself for a moment. And at least the market is undercover.

I move through the stalls, the aromas of bread and doughnuts and dates and vegan brownies all mingling together until I'm in the fresh food section. I peruse brightly coloured clementines and pears that I won't buy and then walk towards the stall with artisan pet treats up ahead.

I get in line and buy a new bag of treats, turn to leave, and as I do, one single face stands out in the crowd.

Is that … it can't be …

My breath catches and I step to the side, peering through my sunglasses, squinting to get a better look: tall, weak chin, pockmarks, long dark *Underworld* coat, slightly stooped posture.

And it is. You've got to be kidding me.

There, standing by the fruit stalls, next to a stack of cranberries, is Riley.

That creepy guy from the vampire hunters' meet-up.

Fuck.

Fuck. Fuck. Fuck.

My throat tightens. *Am I hallucinating?* Is this some horrible come-down effect from Oscar's blood? Because it definitely looks like him. Exactly like him. He's talking to some guy with blond hair, showing him something on his phone.

And shit, it really *is* Riley.

A flash of the way he looked at me the night we met in that bar on Carnaby Street, his hand on my wrist like maybe he was checking for a pulse, his eyes on my mouth, his voice saying, 'Wow, you're cold for summer …'

And the last thing I want right now is to have him see me and remember I exist. Especially while I'm standing here, in sunglasses, looking like death warmed up, like I don't do well in the daylight. So I turn around, doing my very best to blend into the crowd, and rush home.

My breath is quick as I get inside and close the door behind me. I rush to the fridge and put Cat's treats inside, then go and sit silently on the sofa.

That was close.

I close my eyes and take a few deep breaths. I feel my blood slow to its usual crawl, my stress levels lower, and then: *Ping*. My eyes flick open. I glare at my phone.

One new notification.

VHC: You have one new message.

WHAT IF IT'S RILEY?

What if he saw me there and wants to catch up?

I tap through to the Vampire Hunters' Collective and log in, then go to my messages.

But there, sitting waiting, is just a message from Sally. My shoulders relax as I tap on it.

And then, I'm a lot less relaxed. Because it reads: *OMFG have you seen this? Didn't you know him??? Have you heard anything?*

Beneath her message is a link.

29

The headline reads: JOGGER STABBED WHILE RUNNING IN DULWICH PARK.

As I stare at it, taking in the meaning of each word, it feels as though my perfectly constructed little world—my imperfect world, sure, but *my* world all the same—folds in on me in earnest. And it occurs to me just how flimsy it's always been. A house of cards. One little breeze and *poooffff*.

Title: JOGGER STABBED WHILE RUNNING IN DULWICH PARK

Location: London

Posted by: @Viciousdelicious

A JOGGER has been stabbed to death while running in Dulwich Park in what police have described as a random and unprovoked act of violence.

The 37-year-old victim, Kenneth Brawley, died at the scene.

The alleged attack took place just after 5 am on Tuesday. The victim was found at 8 am by a dog walker.

There have been no arrests.

'Our first priority is keeping the community safe,' said Detective Sergeant Jon Cairns, who is leading the investigation. 'We are doing everything we can to find the perpetrator. However, we need the community's help. If you witnessed anything suspicious at all on the morning in question in the Dulwich Park area, please let us know as soon as possible.'

While this appears to be an isolated incident, nearby residents have been warned to stay vigilant and avoid the park after dark. The victim's family was not available for comment, but a work colleague at Selfridges has said: 'Kenny was such a light, always smiling, such an important part of our team. Our thoughts are with his family and friends, especially this close to Christmas.'

Anyone with information is asked to call police on ...

My vision blurs.

The room melts around me—the sofa becomes the coffee table becomes the wall—and *what the hell is going on?*

But *it's okay, it's okay, it's okay* ...

Of course this ended up on this site. Kenny's death was murder, a stabbing, and those always end up on the VHC. Stab marks are how we, the vamps, supposedly cover our bite marks. And it seems Oscar, with his plan to plunge a knife into Kenny so he had a murder weapon to plant, which he could then use to frame me or Daphne, has played right into that belief.

I quickly scroll down to the comments, chewing gently on my cheek as I assess the damage.

@Eric22: Another vamp attack for sure, London is getting out of control. And a guy from Selfridges? I shop there. It could have been me. We need to do something.

@Connecticuthousewife011: Dawn. A stabbing. Seems like a strong maybe.

@HenryD: Dulwich Park has all those bats! Worth a closer look.

@Vampitup: Just spoke to my police contact. He said there were genuine bite wounds on neck as well as stab wounds! Said it was probably a fox or a dog but my gut says this is IT. Will try to find out more. Stay tuned!

Fuck. Fuck. FUCK.

That last comment glares back at me and then it winks.

Because those bite marks probably *were* from foxes. Dulwich Park does have a fox problem. But that doesn't matter … the people on this site will grab onto that with both hands. I know they will.

And this is bad. Very, very bad.

My mind races as I think of all the ways this can come back on me.

I complained about Kenny to Sally by name, many, many times. She knew I hated him—I was very vocal about it—*so* vocal that she was praying for his demise. She knows I work at Selfridges because I've told her. And … oh my god. I sent her a picture of his running track from his app. I did that just the other night. The night before he was killed.

What was I thinking?

How did I ever let my guard down this far?

But I know what I was thinking: Sally lives on the other side of a big-arsed ocean, we've never met, we were never going to meet and, most importantly, Kenny was not meant to die. I wasn't going to kill him. I just half-heartedly wished him dead. This should never have been a problem. If it was even a teensy problem, I should have been able to delete my profile and disappear, added to which, to everyone on that site I would always have been Margot. Untraceable. Unfindable.

Except … Riley knows I lied about my name.

And he was just at Borough Market.

Did he see this post? Kenny? Selfridges? The vamp attack? Think of me and my cold skin and my yellow Selfridges nametag and suspect me? Come looking for me? I wouldn't be the first vampire he'd stalked down. What if he *did* somehow find out my forwarding address … What if—

Aubrey, that's crazy talk. Be rational. It's Christmas Eve, and Borough Market is a famous market. He has every right to be there. It has nothing to do with you. A coincidence. That's all.

But still, there's something about Riley skulking around so close to my home that makes me itch. Has alarm bells ringing loud in my ears and I can't turn them off.

This is bullshit. I shouldn't even be in this predicament. And every part of this is Oscar's fault. Killing Kenny. Abandoning me so I had to sign up to this website to find him.

God, when I signed up, it never, in a million years, occurred to me that I'd end up hunting *myself*.

That's what's going to happen here though, if I'm not careful. I can feel it, gnawing at my insides.

I have an impulse to just pack up my life and leave, the way I have so many times before. Move somewhere else. Never get onto the internet ever again. But that would mean giving up on Jonathan, on *us*, forever. I don't want that. There has to be another way.

Think, Aubrey, think. You can deal with this.

So I tap back to Sally's message and stare at it: *OMFG have you seen this? Didn't you know him??? Have you heard anything?*

The world spins faster than it ever has as my thumbs sit frozen in place. I look around the room, horribly aware that somewhere in here are other pieces of evidence implicating me in Kenny's death. I don't know if I'm more frightened of the police, or the people on the VHC finding me right now. Option one ends in me being hooked up to machines for eternity in some government testing facility, possibly the subject of multiple classified documents. Option two ends in me potentially being buried in chains with a stone shoved in my jaw by @NancyJayne. Or worse.

Trust no one, Aubrey …

I could just deny it. Pretend she misunderstood. That I'd never met a Kenny. But she won't fall for that.

So what would I say if I *wasn't* a vampire? If I wasn't scared that I'd get blamed? Found out.

I start to type. *OMG! Yes, that's the guy, the one I told you about, Kenny! I can't believe he's dead!*

Good, good, good.

I'll def ask around as soon as I'm back at work!

I wait for a reply, my hands shaking.

Beep.

Sally: *Well keep me posted on anything you find out, okay? How are you doing otherwise? Are you away for Christmas? In-laws here FML …*

I stare at it, not sure what to reply but knowing it'll look really suspicious if I type nothing. So what would I say if I really believed this was all good news?

I decide on: *Of course, I'll let you know the moment I hear anything!*

And then, I sign off and put myself back to bed.

I'm woken by someone banging on the door. Adrenaline sparks in my veins and I pull the covers to my chest as I stare towards it. The sky outside is dark now, no light seeping in around the edges of the blinds.

Is it Riley? The police? Something worse?

I want to escape, but I can't. This flat only has one window—*that's why I bloody rented it*—and that's right by the front door. I'm stuck.

I tiptoe over to the door, then carefully look through the peephole and … just great. Just when I think things can't get any worse.

Because it's Oscar, his eyes glowing green and gold as he frowns at me through the peephole.

A heat boils within me. He is the reason Kenny is on that noticeboard. He is the reason Sally or Riley might get suspicious and figure out what I am. He is like a grenade that has rolled into my life and I can't find the pin to put it back in.

I want to ignore him. Tell him to go away. But he'll just open the door himself.

So I reach for the latch and pull open the door.

'Aubrey, I don't like waiting,' he says, irritation in his voice as he looks me up and down. His gaze lands on my tangled hair and he frowns. 'Were you still sleeping? It's well past dusk. You really are lethargic, aren't you?' Then he pushes his way inside. 'Come on. You need to pack some things.'

'Wh-where are we going?' I ask, my insides clenching as I throw a glance up the stairs to the road—*no Riley*. I close the door quickly.

'My place in the countryside.'

Panic sparks in my veins. 'What for?'

He shrugs. 'You need a few nights without distraction to get well fed and focus. By the time you leave, you'll be a real vampire. Think of it as a wellness retreat,' he gives another little smirk, like he's amused by his own joke and I want to hit him. 'Besides, it's Christmas Eve. Do you *want* to be here, alone?' His eyes bore into me, my insides twist. 'But hurry up. I'm having a little soiree tonight and we can't be late.'

I don't want to go anywhere with him. Not now, when tomorrow is Christmas and Jonathan might find my earring and call, wanting me to go over there. And especially not to some undisclosed location in the countryside. What if he pushes me too far and I'm trapped there? So I'm about to state all the reasons why I *can't* go with him, sorry—work, Cat, life.

But then I stop myself.

Because I hate to admit it, but in this one instance Oscar might be right. It doesn't matter how much I try to 'logic' myself out of it, seeing Riley so close to my home earlier, has me spooked. I could use a little space from it all. Then I can watch the VHC noticeboard from a distance while I try to glean how big my problems are.

So instead I say, 'Okay, but I'm supposed to work on Boxing Day. I'll have to call and—'

His expression shifts, like he's pleased. Like he wasn't expecting me to be so compliant.

'I've already called them. They were very accommodating,' he continues. *Of course they were: Kenny, grief, counselling … Oscar's hypnotic ways.* 'You're off until January second. Now please, hurry, the traffic is going to be a nightmare.'

That's just over a week. My stomach twists. But I don't see any other choice right now.

So I nod and in a flat tone I say, 'Okay, sure. But you can wait in the car. I need to change and pack.'

'Suit yourself,' he says, then he goes over to one of the walls, pulls open a ventilation duct and grabs a man's wallet—Kenny's? Then to another duct, on the other side of the room, and pulls out a phone. No wonder I didn't know where the smell was coming from. But as I watch him put them in his pocket, I wonder what he left in Daphne's flat. A driver's licence? A few strands of Kenny's hair? The knife?

'I'll get the rest from Daphne's place when we're done,' he says. 'But you might want to change your toothbrush head too, just to be safe.'

I feel myself gag and he smirks. 'Just joking.'

Then he goes back outside, the door shutting behind him with a click.

I grab Es's present from the coffee table, rush through to my bedroom and pull my suitcase out from under the bed and open it up. But before I pack, I rush back through to the kitchen.

First I grab a cooler bag and fill it with ice packs, and then I reach into that spinach box in my freezer, retrieve my final bag of blood, put it in the cooler and zip it up. I don't know how long it'll last without proper refrigeration, but I can't go into this with nothing. I need a backup plan, just in case. I know I need to appease Oscar and appear to be compliant. I know he's going to make me feed off a human—he has said as much. There's nothing I can do to avoid that. But even so, I can't allow myself to descend into the darkness, give in to the hunger, the desire, the way I have every other time I've fed off the vein. I'm going to have to find a way to control myself, to stop. Because I simply cannot kill anyone else. So this bag of blood might be a flimsy backup plan, but it's all I've got, and at least it'll give me a chance—some way to pull myself back from the edge. To regain my equilibrium. And as long as I don't kill anyone, my soul can get through until the new year unscathed. At least, I think it can.

31

Oscar has a black Aston Martin and he's driving fast, his eyes trained on the narrow, curling country lane ahead as he speeds around the corners, his headlights illuminating the little mounds of dirty snow either side of the lane. Rap music blasts from the speakers and we haven't spoken the entire journey. I've just sat here, looking out through tinted windows, at paddocks with cows and sheep, watching the stars glow brighter and brighter in the dark purple sky the further we get from the lights of London.

I glance down at the blue-white light of my phone screen, holding it against my side so Oscar doesn't ask what I'm doing, then scan the VHC board for the tenth time. Nothing more about Kenny. No comments from Riley.

Yet.

We take a sharp turn, my breath catches and I look up at the road ahead, if indeed it can even be called a road. It's getting narrower and more precarious the further we get. If someone comes at us from the other direction we'll have a head-on collision—I don't fancy a car crash right now, they don't kill me, no, but they're not a good time. And what if we kill someone else? That doesn't seem to bother Oscar.

'Be careful,' I say.

Oscar ignores me, and I watch the speedometer go up even more. All the while the rapper keeps rapping about hoes and drugs and *how the hell did I end up here?*

I sit back and close my eyes and tell myself, *It's just until the new year. That's only eight nights, how bad can it get in eight little nights? The problem is, I've seen what can happen in just one night: you can lose your soul, you can meet your soulmate, you can be turned into a motherfucking vampire.*

Finally, we slow down and my eyes flick open.

In front of us stands an old cast-iron gate. On either side are high hedges.

Oscar presses a button on his keys and the gate staggers open. We drive in and up a driveway with rolling lawns on either side and trees in the distance. As we get to the top of the hill, I can see where we're going. The driveway dips again, into another valley, and then there, standing high on the next hill is … I'm not really sure what to call it. *House* doesn't seem grand enough.

Because it's HUGE.

It's like one of those enormous manor homes you see in period dramas. There's a large fountain out the front, the driveway curling around it. And the closer we get, gravel crunching under the tyres, the bigger it seems. It's made of grey stone, with creepers on some of the walls and so many windows … how many rooms must there be? As I take it in, irritation simmers beneath my skin—while I've been working night jobs and staying invisible, hustling for blood, pushing down my feelings, all alone and confused, he's been here, living like *this*.

I get a flash of what my last 150 years might have been like if he hadn't abandoned me.

Although … then maybe I wouldn't have held on to my humanity. Maybe I'd have turned out just like him, seeing others as mere pawns to get what I want. Maybe I too would be a ruthless killer, the human part of me extinguished long ago. Then Jonathan and I would never have had a chance.

Maybe Oscar did me a favour.

As we park near a hedge, I sneak a quick final look at the VHC board—still nothing new about Kenny—and am about to lock my phone when, so quickly that I can't react, Oscar grabs it.

'What are you so fascinated by?' he asks, peering down at the screen.

I watch him, helpless, getting a little dizzy. The VHC noticeboard reflects in his eyes.

'What the fuck is this?' He seethes as he scrolls through the posts, then his eyes dart to the top, to the banner that reads *Vampire Hunters' Collective* and then to the top right, to the icons for my settings and inbox. He glares at me. 'You're a member?'

I swallow. 'I … I only went on that site looking for you,' I say, defensive. And there's part of me that hopes this will make him feel guilty, but … it doesn't. It seems to piss him off even more. He stares in front of him, through the glass of the windscreen, like he's trying to calm himself down.

And I dare not say anything else. If he knew about the bits of information I'd let slip, that I'd gone to a meet-up, how all that might genuinely get me found out, he'd completely lose his shit. And I don't know what he'd do, or to whom.

Then he takes a deep breath, opens the glove compartment, drops my phone inside and slams it closed. 'You're fucking confounding,' he says under his breath, getting out of the car and slamming the door after him.

I stare at the glove compartment, needing my phone back. I need to know what's happening. With Jonathan. With the VHC. Dare I take it back? But before I can do anything, Oscar opens my door.

'Come on, it's already seven,' he says through his teeth, clearly still pissed off. 'We've only got an hour before everyone arrives. And you need to get changed.'

So I get out of the car and follow him up the stairs to the front door—thin arched windows on either side—and go inside.

The entry hall is tiled in black and white, with two huge wooden staircases winding up to the upper level on either side and a large chandelier sparkling above us. It smells like furniture polish and fireplaces and roses, which makes sense, there's an enormous bouquet of red roses sitting in the middle of a big circular table. They, like me, are stuck in their prime, unable to see the natural cycle of life through …

I watch as Oscar goes over to a side table and drops his keys into a big silver bowl. Then I look to my left; it's a hive of activity, lots of people dressed in black and white bustling around.

'Mr Parker will show you to your room,' Oscar says, and I turn. Beside him stands a man of around fifty-five with greying hair, holding my suitcase. Then Oscar adds, 'There is an outfit for you in the closet. Put it on.'

Then Mr Parker starts heading up the stairs to our right, and I don't know what else to do, so I follow him.

We move past large oil paintings—landscapes and still lifes—on the wallpapered walls, past a suit of armour. And I can hear Mr Parker's heart beating faster as we take the stairs, smell his B-positive blood. *He's human*. Does he know what Oscar is? What I am? He opens a door and ushers me inside.

To my right is a wall with a bookcase, and to my left, centred against the wall behind us, is a huge, dark wood, four-poster bed with crisp white sheets. The room has three large windows, each boasting heavy navy curtains held aside with thick golden rope, looking out onto a vast garden. Beneath the central window is a writing desk with an antique porcelain vase, holding an array of fragrant red roses, just like the ones downstairs. There's a dressing table with a mirror, then a doorway to what I assume is the bathroom, and against the far wall stands a big, wooden Narnia-style wardrobe.

Mr Parker nods, puts my suitcase by the door, then leaves the room without another word, closing the door behind him.

I lift my suitcase onto the bed, take out my toothbrush, toiletries and make-up, then push the case under the bed. I'll unpack later, once I know the lay of the land. The last thing I need is somebody seeing that cooler bag, discovering I've come prepared. Taking it off me.

I take my things into the bathroom—white marble, gold fixtures, a big mirror and a huge freestanding bath, then return to the bedroom.

I look over towards the wardrobe again.

The doors have ornate carvings of flowers all around the edges and an old-school key in the lock. As I move towards it, my stomach churns because what exactly did Oscar mean by *an outfit*?

As I pull open the doors, the smell of potpourri and old wood filters out.

There are multiple hangers on the rail, but only a few in use, holding up the various layers of an old-style Victorian ball gown—the corset and petticoat, the bustle, and then the dress itself.

I reach for it and trace the fabric with my fingertips. It's silk, and a deep, blood red—which feels a bit on the nose—and long, the hem sweeping the ground. I study it, imagining how it will all look once it's on: it's off the shoulder with a trail behind it that's gathered at the base of the spine in a bustle.

Something twists in my gut.

A flash of that first night, when I woke up this way. Me looking around, opening my wardrobe, trying to figure out who I was, what I was, and what the hell was going on. Amid the more plain cotton dresses, there were also gowns like this. Ornate and expensive; rich colours and textures. The kind I've only seen since behind glass cages in fashion exhibitions at the Royal Victoria and Albert Museum in South Kensington … the exhibitions I've wandered through over the years, hoping something would spark a memory, remind me of everything I've lost. Everything I've forgotten.

My gaze moves down, to the base of the wardrobe, where some matching dancing slippers sit.

I smile as I reach down for them and warmth moves through me; I haven't seen anything like these in a long time, not since just after I was turned. I sit on the bed and put them on, nostalgia flowing through me as I tie the ribbons. I get a flash back to my early years, when these were commonplace for balls … I bought some for myself once, wore them at home, pretending.

But then the warmth turns to heat.

Because I never went to balls. It always seemed too high risk. If I allowed myself to become a part of society, people might notice when I was forced to fade out and move on. All I could do was stand at the edges, watching, imagining what it might be like to dance in a crowded room without fear of being noticed.

Who the hell does Oscar think he is?

He abandoned me when I needed him most and now, what? He's back and ordering me around, treating me like some vampire-Barbie he can dress up?

I think not.

I imagine myself storming out of the bedroom, down the stairs, and demanding answers. Letting *everyone* know our secret. Letting him deal with the mess he's made.

But 150 years of being cautious can't be undone that quickly. I can't predict what he'd do. For all I know, he'd kill Mr Parker the way he killed Kenny, and then I'd have two lots of blood on my hands.

So I don't do any of that. But the churning in my stomach continues, and there is no damned way I'm going to Oscar's silly little soiree tonight. I'll learn what he has to teach me, but I will *not* be dressing up for him.

I will not be wearing the dress that he picked out like he's the boss of me … even if I do like the dress.

Tap, tap, tap.

I look towards the door.

'Come in,' I say, ready to tell Oscar I'm not going.

But it's not Oscar. Instead, a small woman pokes her head inside.

'I'm Mrs Parker. Mr Carmichael has requested that you wear this in your hair,' she says, coming over to me. *She's human too, just like her husband.*

She hands me a hairpin. It's crimson and gold, with little stones reflecting the light. 'And you'd better hurry up and get your make-up done. People will be arriving soon.'

'I'm not putting on make-up, because I'm not going,' I say, folding my arms over my chest.

'Miss, you need to go,' she says gently. 'Mr Carmichael won't respond well if you refuse. And it's a party, you'll have fun. We do it every year, everyone dresses up.' She smiles hard, like she's hoping that will convince me. 'Here,' she says, reaching into my wardrobe and pulling out the ornate dress. 'Let's get you dressed.'

I want to say 'no', stand my ground. But I can see the fear in her eyes, hear her heart speeding up at the very idea of me defying Oscar, and after Kenny, I don't want to find out why. So I'll do it. I'll wear the silly dress, smile and get through it. Let him believe he's in control of me.

I nod. 'Fine, but I'm not putting on make-up.'

She helps me into my dress, putting on the many layers and lacing up the corset tight.

'There,' she says, as we study my reflection in the mirror. 'You look beautiful. So young and fresh. I think you're even more lovely without make-up.'

And I hate to admit it, but she's right. I do look lovely.

33

My waist looks even smaller thanks to the corset and the bustle over my hips. The off-the-shoulder detailing highlights the line of my collarbones, and the dress fits perfectly, like it was tailor made. Oscar may be a psychopath, but even I have to admit he has very good taste.

'Take a seat so I can do your hair,' Mrs Parker says, patting the chair by the dressing table. 'Where is your hairbrush?' I get a flash of that silver hairbrush from Jonathan's memory of me, and resentment simmers. Because if Oscar had just chosen a different house to enter the night he turned me, Jonathan and I would have lived out our lives together, and I wouldn't be here right now. Like this.

I reach into my handbag and pull out my brush, hand it to her then carefully sit down, so as not to damage the wire of the bustle. She expertly twists my hair up into a low knot at the base of my neck, securing it there with the ornate hairpin. As she moves, I wonder how many other women she has done this for. How many other vampires like me Oscar has made. Abandoned. Then waltzed back into their lives on a whim to mess it all up.

Where are they now? Could we form a club? Could we take him down?

'There,' she says, and I look back to the mirror, turning my head from side to side, the stones of the hairpin sparkling in the light.

'One more thing,' Mrs Parker says, reaching for a small velvet bag in her pocket. She pulls out two small clip-on pearl-drop earrings. And of course they are clip-ons—I can't pierce my ears, they just close up, no matter how long I leave the earrings in for. Control-freak Oscar has thought of everything.

'They're beautiful,' I say. As I put them on, the sound of music floats in through the door and I look towards it. Someone is playing a piano. And there are stringed instruments playing too.

'Right, it's time,' Mrs Parker says.

I nod and stand up.

'I can go myself,' I say.

'You might find the stairs a bit hard to navigate in that dress,' she says as she opens the door, and I'm hit by the full swell of music and chatter coming from downstairs. A wave of nerves bubbles up in my stomach. We head out into the hallway and I glance down over the banister. I can see people arriving and moving through the opened-up rooms, all dressed up like me.

We move towards the stairs and I realise Mrs Parker was right. I could probably get *up* the stairs okay if I picked up the bottom of my dress with one hand and held the banister with the other, but going down I might well trip on the fabric of the train. There is a loop on it for dancing, that I could put around my wrist, but it's been a long time, I don't trust myself. I imagine myself tumbling down the stairs in front of all these people and grip the banister tightly with my right hand. I pick up my dress with the left, and Mrs Parker holds on to my elbow, offering extra support.

We move down the wooden staircase slowly, watching more and more people filter in from outside as I try not to trip. When Oscar said, *a little soiree*, I didn't realise he meant … this. It's not little at all.

When we reach the bottom of the stairs, Mrs Parker lets go of my elbow and I drop my dress and follow her towards the music, the chatter, the laughter.

We walk through a long, narrow room, towards another set of double doors. 'This is the gallery,' Mrs Parker says, like a practised tour guide. How many other women has she said these exact words to? We step into a huge and opulent room. 'And this is the ballroom.'

I look around. It has white marble floors and glittery chandeliers hanging from the ceilings, oil paintings on the ornately wallpapered walls, off-white pillars, and a series of chairs upholstered in stone-coloured fabric along the walls. A few people are sitting on them, but most people are milling around what I suspect is a dance floor in the centre, chatting happily while the trio, consisting of piano, violin and cello, play.

I scan the crowd. There are around 200 people here, all dressed in ball gowns and suits, while waiters circle bearing silver trays of champagne and tiny hors d'oeuvres. Up close, most of the outfits are cheap-looking, and from differing eras—some dresses are Victorian, some come from the Edwardian period, others from the 1920s. It's like everyone shopped on Amazon but nobody was entirely clear on the brief. That said, everyone has made a huge effort. It's like being surrounded by the ghosts of fashions past, and I'm filled with a nostalgia for how things might have been if I'd never become what I am. I would have had a family. I don't know what kind of life I would have lived, or exactly what I'm missing; I just know I didn't get to live it. And instead, I'm here, among all these people who get to be *alive*. I listen to their hearts beating and smell their blood, hating myself for everything I am.

'There he is,' says Mrs Parker and I follow her gaze towards the edge of the room.

Oscar.

He's leaning up against a wall, wearing a crisp white shirt and a black jacket, talking to a woman dressed in a pale yellow, Edwardian-style dress that drops from under the breast and skims the floor. Her hair is the same colour as her dress, half up and decorated with some sort of feather clip, and she's standing on her toes, whispering into Oscar's ear. I should just ignore them, but I can't help myself. I home in on them, wondering what she's saying … wondering if she's like me. In fact, is anyone here like me? Or is this lesson number one? Is this about to turn into some sort of feeding frenzy, like in *From Dusk Till Dawn*. A vampire smorgasbord?

'Tell me something real … about you …' Yellow Dress says.

He puts his hand on her waist and leans in to whisper back.

'Emma, I want to do very, *very* bad things to you …'

My insides recoil.

She giggles and Oscar stands up straight and then, like he can sense I'm there, he turns to look right at me.

Our eyes meet. A shiver rolls down my spine.

He turns back to his companion and says, 'I'll see you later on,' then he smiles at me and moves my way.

Shit.

'Aubrey,' he says, offering me his forearm to hold onto. Mrs Parker leaves us to it, and as we walk through the crowd, I'm intensely aware of eyes on me. Suddenly, I'm not sure what to do with my free hand and I need to concentrate on every step.

One of the waiters moves past us and Oscar grabs a glass of champagne off their tray and hands it to me.

'Thanks,' I say, glad to have something to hold onto. I take a sip and try to ignore the curious glances. I'm anxious. I don't like not knowing what's coming next.

'Smile,' he mutters under his breath. 'I hold this ball every year for the village. We put all proceeds towards town maintenance projects. There's even a reporter here doing a nice write-up about it for the local paper, so at least pretend you're happy to be here.'

Phew. No feeding frenzy then. It's just a dance. A big, elaborate dance to make everyone think he's a good guy.

Then, out of nowhere, a raven-haired woman appears before us, stopping us in our tracks. Her skin is so pale that it's almost translucent, she's wearing a cream dress and she's flanked by two men. One has dark skin, short dark hair, blue shimmering eyeshadow above big doe-eyes and a necklace of sparkling teal sapphires and a matching ring. The other has blond hair, wild and curly, and his skin is greyish and waxy, like he does too much cocaine. He's wearing a white shirt just like Oscar, but with a charcoal jacket, and there's something about the way he's looking at me that makes my skin crawl. Even more than Oscar's gaze does.

'Oscar,' she says in a posh voice, 'who's your friend?' The woman eyes me up and down. My gaze moves from her to her companions, and that's when it hits me: I can barely hear their hearts beating. I can't smell their blood either, and they all have the same golden rings around their irises.

They're like me.

And there are three of them.

That makes five vampires in this one room alone. How have I only found two in 150 years? Maybe vampires usually flock together, unless they're cast out, like me.

'This is Aubrey,' Oscar says, 'my protege.' He adds that last bit in a tone I can't quite decipher. 'Aubrey, this is Carmilla,' he says, motioning to the raven-haired woman, 'Rupert,' he indicates the darker skinned man with the eyeshadow, 'and Felix,' he finishes, motioning to the blond man.

Carmilla nods at me, gives a little tight smile that doesn't reach her eyes, and I wonder if Carmilla is her real name or if she changed it to be like that vampire novella by Le Fanu. Rupert is scanning the room like he's looking for someone more interesting, while Felix grins at me, then looks at Oscar. 'A protege, nice. Nothing like a bit of youth to keep things exciting.'

Oscar's jaw clenches. A tense moment passes between them and I can't figure out what's going on, but then the other guy—*Rupert?*—the one with the necklace, says, 'Lovely to meet you, Baby-V.'

The chandeliers dim just a little and the music stops. A new song starts up and I recognise it, though I haven't heard it played in a public setting in a *very* long time. It's a waltz, 'The Blue Danube'. Oscar turns to me. 'Time to dance,' he says, taking my hand and leading me over to the empty dance floor.

And now I can *really* feel everyone looking at me. My insides twist as I reach for the loop on the train of my dress, and thread my wrist through it.

In one quick manoeuvre that tells me he's done this hundreds—maybe thousands—of times, one of his hands holds mine tightly while the other is on my midback. My hand lands on his shoulder, and now we're moving and I know the steps, even if I am a bit rusty. They're from a long, long time ago, before Gangnam Style, before the Twist, before the Foxtrot. Oscar's movements are strong and sure and I follow his lead, scanning the room as others follow us onto the dance floor until it's full.

Oscar twirls me, and as he pulls me towards him again, all I can think about is Jonathan, and that rug in his living room, and how we slow-danced on it and I was so sure we'd be together forever.

We still will …

'Aubrey,' comes Oscar's voice and I turn to look at him. His eyes have narrowed. 'Stop frowning,' he says under his breath as his hand tightens around mine. He twirls me again.

I swallow hard, plaster on the kind of smile I use at work, and look away, back to the crowd as we do a side step. And there are Carmilla and Felix, she's nuzzling into his neck—*are they a couple?*—while Rupert looks a bit bored. I wonder if they live here too?

I've seen that on TV shows, where vampires all live together in nests, and bring out each other's darkness. I'm going to have to work really hard not to let them bring mine out while I'm stuck here.

The music stops, and Oscar's grip lessens. As the next song begins, I say, 'I'm going to take a little break. My feet are tired.' He shrugs, like he's bored of me anyway, and releases his grip.

I drop the loop on my dress, walk over to one of the seats near the entrance and watch as Oscar strides up to the woman in the pale yellow dress—*Emma?*—and then leads her onto the dance floor. Unlike me, her eyes don't move from his, and her cheeks are getting rosier every time he speaks. I feel this need to protect her. There's no way she knows what he is, what she's in for. But what can I do?

And also, *hang on* ...

Oscar is preoccupied, and Mrs Parker is nowhere to be seen. Oscar's car is parked right outside, my phone in it ... Dare I? I need to know what's going on and besides, I might not get another chance.

I glance behind me, to the doors I came in through, and take a step towards them. But then a hand touches my arm and a high-pitched voice says: 'Do you know Mr Carmichael well?'

Shit.

There's a woman with bright pink cheeks and mousy hair smiling at me. She's wearing a black flapper dress and long fake pearls, holding a fake cigarette holder in one hand and a champagne glass in the other. She's with another woman—also in a flapper dress, though hers is silver—who could be her sister. They look around thirty-ish.

'Not really.' I smile, looking away, keen to shut the conversation down quickly so I can get back to the plan that is quickly forming in my mind.

'He's lush,' says the other one, who is slurring a bit. 'And so very rich.'

'We *all* fancy him,' says the first woman, leaning in like she's telling me a secret. 'But he's so mysterious, isn't he? Are you from the village?' There's interest in her expression, young and naive. But there's a hardness in her eyes, too, like she's sizing me up as competition. And this is the one thing that saddens me most about the modern world. After everything women's lib has done for us, we are still taught to view each other as competition. Honestly, if I'm stuck on this earth for eternity, I truly hope that one day I get to see us band together, stand up and change that. But from the look in her eyes, it's safe to say that today is not that day.

So, I put her mind at ease. 'No, I'm from London, just visiting. We're old family friends.' I'd love to warn her off him, but that would probably only make her want him more. And besides, I need them to leave me alone. 'But I hear he's single,' I add. 'Why don't you ask him to dance?'

They both let out a nervous giggle and I watch them head across the room to watch Oscar as he begins another dance with Emma.

Screw it.

I pick up my skirt and move quickly through the double doors, across the gallery and back into the entrance hall, trying not to look suspicious as I glance back over my shoulder. But nobody is watching me. I rush over to the silver bowl and pull out Oscar's keys, then creep out into the cold night.

There are so many cars parked out here now, neatly lining the driveway. But there's nobody around; they're all inside. So I stand tall, like I'm not doing anything wrong, and walk briskly over to Oscar's car.

34

The taillights flash as I get to it, like the car can sense the keys nearby. I glance back at the front door—nobody's there, nobody's watching—then pull open the passenger door, gather up the bottom of my dress and do my best to manoeuvre the bustle inside. I slam the door shut, then duck down a little and reach forward, opening the glove compartment. My phone is right there, on top of the leather-bound manual.

I hold my breath as I check the screen, willing there to be a *Merry Christmas* message from Jonathan.

There isn't one.

Disappointment settles in my stomach. *But it's only Christmas Eve, he might send it tomorrow.*

And so I push thoughts of Jonathan aside and tap through to the VHC website, my stomach churning, then glance down through recent posts, scanning for Kenny's name. There's an article from Poland: TEEN CLAIMS TO HAVE BEEN TURNED INTO A VAMPIRE, a nothing article about a home invasion in Kentucky, something about putting vampire bats on treadmills … but nothing more about Kenny.

Which *should* calm me down but doesn't.

Instead, it seems to fuel the gnawing in my gut; the pending sense of doom. The sense that more is coming, I just can't see what it is yet. That I'm standing in the eye of the storm.

Stay calm. Act normal.

And there is a little red 'one' on my inbox so I tap on it.

It's from Sally, and it's a picture of a turkey. The turkey she didn't want to cook. The text reads: *Hope your heart is healing and you're not alone. Let me know you're okay?*

See? All fine.

I let out a big breath and type back: *Away in countryside. It's … interesting.*

Send.

I glance back at the house. It's still just me out here, so I tap through to Instagram and navigate to Jonathan's profile. He hasn't posted anything new. Not even a story. Which I suppose is better than posting things and not texting me.

Still, here I am, dressed in a beautiful vintage red dress, and red is my colour. As I look around at the luxe interior of Oscar's car, I think: *I need to remind him.* I pull up the selfie camera, angle it down at my face slightly, trying to capture the manor through the window behind me, hold up my fingers in a peace sign, smile and take a picture.

And then I upload it to my Instagram stories captioned #christmaseve.

A reply comes in immediately from Es: *WOO HOO! Jonathan who???? Where are you? Looks DREAMY! Xxx*

Now all I need is for Jonathan to think that too.

I send her a love heart then lock my phone and put it back in the glove compartment, then reach for the door handle to get out, glancing briefly through the window as I do.

I catch a flicker of movement.

There, over by the door.

I duck down a little further and watch a figure hover by the stairs, partially obscured by the potted plants. What if it's Oscar, looking for me?

But then the figure goes back inside. So I sneak out of the car, pick up the bottom of my dress and take a step towards the front door. And I'm going to go back inside, but then the figure appears again. *Shit.* It's just a silhouette against the light behind it, but I can tell from the height, the breadth of the shoulders, that the person is probably male. He seems to be looking around.

Oscar … I bet it's him.

I get a flash of the fire in his eyes. Then the way he killed Kenny, just on a whim. He won't be pleased if he discovers I snuck out with his car keys. It's better I avoid him. So I turn around and run behind the hedge.

Behind the hedge is a French-style garden, with paths weaving through more manicured hedges and flowerbeds full of red roses, all covered in snow. Beyond them I can see an arched greenhouse enclosure, so I rush towards it, struggling not to slip on the ice. I can hide in there.

I reach it and look around; there's no door, and only three glass walls. I step undercover and hide in the corner, listening. I can hear footsteps, but I can't tell if they're coming towards me or moving away, so I just stand still and close my eyes, pushing my fingers against my ears. Fear is heightening my senses; I can hear everything from the music in the manor to frogs croaking in the distance and it's *too much*. I need to stay calm.

And then, in the darkness, muffled by my hands over my ears, I hear, 'Aubrey, what are you doing?'

My eyes flick open and I get ready to make my excuses, but when my eyes focus, they're not looking at Oscar.

It's that other guy, Felix. The one with the curly blond hair and the greyish skin.

'Does Oscar know you're out here?' he asks, coming towards me.

Great. Oscar sent him to spy on me.

'I just needed some air,' I say, smiling as I step towards him. 'It's a beautiful night and it's lovely out here. But I was about to go back inside.'

I go to walk past him, to leave the greenhouse, but as I get to the threshold, he grabs onto my arm.

I turn to look at him; what's he doing? There's something in his eyes. Something I've seen in human males before. My insides recoil, and panic floods my veins. Then comes fear. Because I don't know what he wants from me.

But I do know that he's a vampire, like me, so if he hurts me, I can't even kill him. Besides, he's bigger than me; older and stronger, too, I suspect. I'm no match.

My gaze darts to the glass wall behind him and then to my left, to the path back through the hedges and back to the house. I pull my arm away with all my strength and fake a laugh. I don't want to anger him. But he doesn't let go; he tightens his grip.

'Let go,' I say, my voice high-pitched. I want to feel heat, I want to feel fury, anger. But all I feel is … terror.

And then he grins like he's enjoying my fear, and I watch as his fangs emerge. What's going on? He knows I'm a vampire, Oscar told him. He knows he can't feed off me.

Oscar's keys are still in my hand and I think of Es, of all the self-defence advice she's dealt out, so I swipe at him with the keys. I get his cheek, but it's barely a scratch. His eyes flame orange, like lava, and his pupils get huge, and I watch as the scratch heals instantly. And then he grins at me again, like me fighting back is exciting him.

I go to scream, to run, but he lurches forward, so quickly that I don't know what's happening—*whoosh*. He's so fast and so strong, just like Oscar. He covers my mouth with his hand

and pulls me back into the greenhouse, yanking my head to the side. He's got me pinned; I can't move. He leans forward and his fangs sink into my neck; a sting, an ache. I have an impulse to hit, to scream, to kick, but then a dizziness comes over me, like he's draining me of any power I might have. I'm stunned, unable to move.

All the fight leaves my body, and I go limp. I can smell his hair—like rancid citrus, limes—and pine needles, and hear the music in the distance and *why did I come out here?* My vision is getting blurry now, and I can feel tears dripping down my cheeks. My hand droops by my side, my grip weakens, and the keys fall to the ground, landing with a muffled thud.

A sound rings out in the distance, some kind of loud bird call.

Felix hears it and pulls away, and through blurred vision I see blood—my blood—dripping from his chin, staining his shirt, and I want to run but I'm so weak. He pushes me to the ground, rough and cold beneath me, then he's lifting up the layers of my dress. That bird call sounds again, closer now, and it feels like a bird of prey because he's heavy on top of me and I can feel the freezing air on my bare legs, I can feel tears rolling down my temples towards my hair, towards the ground.

This horrible sense of the inevitable comes over me, like some kind of déjà vu—like I've been here before, even though I haven't. I'm thinking: *Just don't make it worse.* And then I'm thinking: *Move! Do something! Why are you so weak? Why are you letting this happen?*

There's a flicker of movement, right behind him.

Followed by a loud and gruesome ripping sound.

His body falls heavy onto me, and it's wet and hot near my face. He's not moving. I roll him off and crawl away, glancing back frantically in case he's coming after me.

But he's not coming after me. He's just lying there, and as I struggle to catch my breath and my vision clears I can see that yes, he's lying there, but not all of him. Because there, right behind him, is Oscar.

And in his hand, he's holding Felix's head.

36

Oscar drops Felix's head into the snow behind him and steps inside the greenhouse. I'm holding my breath, scared to move. And he looks *furious*—his chest is heaving, his eyes glowing gold in the night, blood all over his shirt. I just stare down at Felix's body, waiting for him to come back to life.

But he doesn't.

Oscar rushes over to me, and I panic, thinking *how pissed off will he be?* But he crouches down beside me and reaches for my face. 'Did he feed off you?' he asks through his teeth as he cradles my face in his hands.

I nod. My words won't come. I just swipe at my tears with the back of my hand, then wipe my hand on my dress—the tears meld in with the red fabric and lace.

He moves my head slightly to the side, his touch gentle, and I can feel his breath as he inspects my neck. Then he lets go and I straighten up and look at him.

'Did he hurt you?' he asks, his voice cracking as he searches my gaze. 'In any other way?'

I shake my head. 'He tried.'

My gaze moves to Felix now and fixes on his severed head, which is still lying there, leaking blood into the snow, eyes vacant and staring right at me. It looks like that scene from *Let the Right One In*. Red blood. White snow.

'Why isn't he moving?' I whisper.

'Because he's fucking dead, Aubrey,' Oscar snaps, standing, and reaching for my hand to help me up. 'Look at him.'

'But … how?' I ask. Because how can Felix be dead when I've never been able to die?

'What do you mean, *how*?' Oscar asks, all tenderness gone now. 'I killed him.' He looks back to the manor, probably wondering if anyone knows we're out here. Then his eyes move back to me. 'What were you doing out here?'

'I needed air,' I lie. My eyes move back to Felix, avoiding Oscar's gaze. 'But I've *tried* to die,' I say. 'And it never works.'

A flash of that time I went shark diving in Cape Town without a cage, but even the sharks could smell I was toxic and wouldn't go for me. Or the week I spent lying on a beach in Spain, certain that it was the shitty UK sun that was standing between me and oblivion, only to return without even a tan. Or the time I covered myself in silver crosses, forcing down a whole bag of communion breads I'd bought off eBay. All for nought.

'Well you can't kill yourself, you morbid little minx,' he says, looking around, though I'm not sure what for. 'It wouldn't be much of an eternal curse if it was that easy to break.'

'Oh,' I say, my face very still, as if reality as I know it isn't fracturing before my eyes. As if a million questions aren't crowding my head and I don't know which one to ask first. 'Does it have to be like that? With, you know, the head? And … do we come back again?'

He frowns. 'Have you never seen a vampire film, Aubrey? There are lots of ways to kill us. Stake. Beheading, obviously. And no, we don't come back. We're not human. When we die the second time, we're *dead*.'

Screw him and his condescending tone.

'Well maybe you should have stuck around and told me all that,' I spit out.

He shoots me a look. 'Well,' he says slowly, deliberately, 'I'm telling you now.' As he says this, his eyes latch on to something just over my shoulder. I turn to follow his gaze: his keys on the ground. My insides contract.

But he doesn't say anything, he walks over to them, picks them up and puts them in his pocket, then pulls his hands through his hair and takes a deep breath, saying, 'Right.'

We're interrupted by a voice, distant and female. 'Felix, are you out here?' It sounds like Carmilla. Did she see Felix leave the party?

Oscar stands dead still, his forefinger to his lips. I dare not even breathe.

The voice stops and he closes his eyes as if listening very intently for something else, maybe footsteps, or breathing. Then his eyes flick open. 'It's safe,' he says.

He bites his wrist, his eyes still on mine, then smears some of his blood on my wound—I'm not sure why, I've always healed quickly by myself. *It must be different when a vampire bites me*. He takes his thumb, wets it with his tongue and traces it over my cheeks and hairline, my neck, presumably clearing the red of my tears, of his blood. He frowns as he glances at my neck. 'It has healed as best as I can manage, but it's going to leave a mark for a while, I'm afraid.' Then he takes off his jacket and says, 'Put this on.'

'I'm not cold,' I say, momentarily confused. But he throws me a look, so I put the jacket on. He leans in towards me and lifts up the collar, covering whatever is left of my wound.

'Go back to the house and straight upstairs. You understand?' he says. 'Don't talk to anybody.'

I nod.

'I'll deal with this. And Aubrey? We'll never speak of it again.'

My breath is quick, and the world is spinning triple time, but I nod and stumble back towards the house.

The sounds of merriment—glasses clinking, chatter and music—assail me as I lift my dress with one shaky hand and grab the banister with the other. I'm halfway up the stairs when I hear a posh voice say, 'Aubrey, have you seen Felix?'

Icicles seem to form in my veins.

I look down at Carmilla and shake my head. 'No, sorry. Um, I'm not feeling well, I'm going to bed. Lovely to meet you.'

She shrugs. 'Lovely to meet you too. I'm here for Christmas so we'll have plenty of time to get to know each other. Hope you feel better.'

I make my way up the stairs to my room. As soon as the door is safely closed behind me, I shrug off Oscar's jacket and go into the bathroom and inspect my neck in the mirror. The wound is still there—*why isn't it healing*? A flash of Felix's fangs, sinking into my neck. The hard ground beneath me. My breath speeds up, and now the dress is too tight, too hot, I can't breathe.

I reach back and try to untie it, pulling at the laces, but it won't budge. What do I do?

Unless I want to go back downstairs and find Mrs Parker, I'm stuck this way.

Panic spurts through me. I need to get it off me; get *him* off me.

My make-up bag is right there by the sink. I unzip it, scrabble around and pull out my nail scissors. Then, standing with my back to the mirror in the bathroom, straining to see, I reach behind me and snip at the dress until finally the ribbons give way and I can breathe. The dress falls to the floor and I step out of it, strip off my underwear and shoes and take the hairpin out of my hair. Then I turn on the taps, get under the water and cry.

Blood tears mingle with the water and swirl down the drain.

By the time I'm out of the shower and in my pyjamas I'm numb. I don't know what to think about *anything* anymore.

As the sounds of the festivities continue to swirl up from downstairs, I go over to the window and look up at the night sky. Even though it's the same stars and shimmering moon I've seen 55,019 times now since I became this way, it all looks different tonight.

More fragile somehow—or maybe it's *me* that's more fragile. Because everything changed tonight, and I don't just mean I saw another, deeper—dare I say it, softer—side to Oscar. I mean, because Felix *died* tonight.

And apparently, I can die too. And I don't know how I feel about that.

37

When I wake up, I'm lying on my side, my mouth full of hair. Birds chatter, announcing dusk and a memory of the birdcall I heard last night leaks in. My eyes flick open, and I look towards the big heavy curtains. The evening sky glows a dusty blue-grey between them, and the glass rattles with the wind outside. Oscar's jacket is still there, at the end of the bed. The image of Felix's head, dripping with blood as it hung from Oscar's hand, flickers through my mind.

I sit up, breathless, then walk over to the bathroom, where my dress lies in a crumpled pile on the floor. I lean into the mirror and inspect my neck. Oscar was right, the bite is still there and it looks like … exactly like what it is: a vampire bite. Like I've been making out with Count Dracula. To make matters worse, a strawberry-like mark has formed around the area, like a bright pink highlighter.

How long will it be there? What am I going to say if someone asks what happened? I can't tell them the truth, then they'll ask where Felix is now …

I grab my make-up bag and cover the mark with concealer as best I can. Then I grab Oscar's jacket and head out into the hallway, looking for Mrs Parker. I want to tell her about the dress. Oscar was so kind to me last night—we had a moment, I know we did. Maybe now, he won't make me do anything I don't want to do. Certainly, he'll go easier on me. So I can't go and piss him off again—the dress looked expensive. It's just the ribbon laces that need replacing, and while it has been a long time since I worked as a seamstress, I could probably mend it. Maybe Mrs Parker has a needle and thread in the right colour.

I glance left and right, but it's just me up here. I look over the banister. Everyone has gone, the big wooden doors that opened onto the gallery and then the ballroom are closed again, and the cleaning staff must have been here all day because the house is now sparkling clean, nothing out of place, the air smelling of bleach and citrus.

I turn and walk down the hallway, passing paintings and light fixtures, looking into the rooms. They're all bedrooms and bathrooms. Where would she be?

But then faint murmuring floats up from downstairs, so I rush down towards it.

A shriek of laughter emanates from my left, so I rush in that direction, under the stairs I just came down, and into a wide hallway.

There are a few doors here, some open, some closed, but the one in front of me is ajar, and that's where the voices are coming from. I can hear Oscar and Rupert; Carmilla is probably there too. But I can't talk to Oscar in front of them, not about last night and why I might have ripped my dress off. And where the hell is Mrs Parker?

To my right, there's a room that's dominated by a billiards table. To my left is what looks like a library—a tall shelf of leather-bound books stands against the wall—and even though I doubt Mrs Parker is in there, something pulls me towards it. I gently step through the doorway, still clutching Oscar's jacket. The door brushes the ground with a gentle *whoosh*, and before I can step inside, I hear: 'Aubrey, is that you?'

Shit.

I step back into the hallway.

'We're in here,' Oscar calls, and I go over to the correct door, push it all the way open and step inside.

It's a dining room, with multiple arched windows looking out onto the back garden. There's a long, rectangular table in the centre, and sitting at the head of it, with a newspaper splayed out in front of him and a glass of amber liquid in his hand, is Oscar. He's wearing a dark green silk bathrobe, his chest visible beneath it. And … is that a silver cross around his neck?

A flash of his hands cupping my face, the way he protected me last night.

Carmilla and Rupert are to his right, in pyjamas like me, smoking cigarettes, and there are two unoccupied places set to Oscar's left. They look towards me, all at once.

'Merry Christmas,' Oscar says, his eyes looking straight into me.

'Merry Christmas,' I respond as I search his gaze for the kindness, the softness I saw last night—for some hint of understanding—but it's not there. There's nothing but ice. *He's probably just trying to cover up last night.*

'I was looking for Mrs Parker,' I continue, looking away from him and to the others. Because I should try to cover it up too. Rupert takes a drag of his cigarette and Carmilla frowns at me.

'The Parkers were only here to help with the party. They'll be off until New Year's,' Oscar says. 'Sit.' I look back to him and he's nodding to the seat beside him. 'Is that my jacket?'

I nod and hand it to him, wishing I hadn't brought it with me, knowing Carmilla and Rupert are probably wondering why I have it. Hoping Oscar isn't pissed off. But nobody asks. Carmilla stares down at her phone and Rupert lets out a big puff of smoke.

I take the seat furthest from Oscar, leaving a place between us.

'Anyway, like I was saying, is there nothing you can do about the peacocks? They were right outside my room most of the day,' Rupert says, clearly continuing the conversation they were having when I arrived.

Oscar turns his attention away from me and back to Rupert. 'Just be grateful it's not mating season,' he says, taking a sip of his drink. 'Anyway, they'll calm down. Last night probably upset them, so many people. They're very territorial, you know—better than watchdogs if you ask me. And they're awake all day, while we sleep.'

Rupert takes a final drag of his cigarette and then stubs it out in an ashtray. He throws me a kind smile. 'What do you think, Baby-V, did those big fucking birds keep you awake too?'

A flash of the bird call last night. *It was a peacock. Is that what alerted Oscar?*

'I wear earplugs,' I say, trying to not take sides. But inside I'm thinking: *I've never loved a bird more.*

'Well, lucky you,' he says. 'Have you met *any* of Oscar's pets yet? What abo—'

Oscar shoots him a look and Rupert stops mid-sentence, then Carmilla looks up and says to the entire table: 'This is so messed up, the last time he stopped sharing his location with me he came back married to someone else.'

'You haven't seen Felix this evening have you?' Oscar asks me, all seriousness. He's frowning as he nods to the other set place. 'We can't find him anywhere.'

I shake my head. 'Sorry.' I'm going for nonchalant, but I'm all too aware of Carmilla's eyes, which are trained right on me now. On my neck, to be specific.

'No matter,' Oscar says with a shrug, 'he'll turn up.' *What did he do with his body?* He finishes his drink, which I think might be whisky.

'What's that on your neck?' Carmilla asks in her posh voice, and my throat tightens.

Oscar starts to laugh. 'You know me, Carmilla,' he says, throwing her a look. 'I couldn't help myself.'

'Ah, that's why she had your jacket,' Carmilla says, and Oscar gives a small smile, like yes, that's absolutely why I had his jacket. And I realise to Oscar, life is a game of chess and he's always winning. Always in control. But it feels like we have a secret now, like we've bonded. And *this* is what I thought it would be like to find my sire. Or at least, closer to it.

'You be careful of him,' Rupert says to me. 'He'll break your heart.'

'He's right,' Oscar says to me, then he stands up. 'Let's retire to the winter drawing room. It's time for presents.'

38

The drawing room walls are covered in blue and white wallpaper yellowed with time. There are huge arched windows letting in the darkening sky, and a series of Persian rugs covering the vast hardwood floors. The room smells of the fireplace that crackles to my left, mingled with the leather and furniture polish of the dark brown sofas and matching chairs all arranged to face it, the glow of the flames flickering in their brass studs. And in the far corner, in front of one of the windows, stands a floor to ceiling Christmas tree. Tiny lights blink from the branches, and beneath it lie an array of gifts wrapped in matching thick cream paper and tied up with golden ribbons. I try to imagine Oscar wrapping them all himself, sticky tape in one hand, scissors in the other. It makes me smile.

Across the room I spy a beautiful, old looking cello that has a slight cherry hue to it, and a dark wood baby grand piano. Beside them stands an enormous set of shelves, full of vinyl records and CDs and what look like cassette tapes, together with a record player, and a CD player and tape deck I recognise from the 90s. All the bits of my own history I've had to discard over the years, in favour of invisibility and travelling light. In the centre of all that sits a huge flat-screen TV with another leather sofa set randomly in front of it, like it's not used very often.

Carmilla sighs loudly and I look towards her, watching as she plonks herself down on one of the sofas in front of the fireplace, then stubs her cigarette out in the silver ashtray beside it before immediately lighting another. Rupert sits down quietly on the rug by the fire and gazes into the flames. None of us need the warmth, but it's pretty and mesmerising.

While Oscar goes over to the tree and starts picking up presents, I sit on one of the chairs and neatly fold my hands in my lap.

'Carmilla,' Oscar says as he hands her a strangely shaped present. 'Rupert,' he says, handing one to him. And then he turns to me. 'Aubrey.'

He hands me a flat, square gift.

'You'll have to take Felix's to him,' he says to Carmilla, handing her another gift.

'Maybe. If he ever answers me,' she says as she angrily tears open her present, clearly pissed off. I can't help but wonder if she knew what Felix was really like, if he'd ever done that to her. To anybody else.

I look down at my present, at its careful wrapping, the ribbon that's curled just so. And this is what I've always wanted: to belong, to not be alone on Christmas night when I woke up. But now that it's happening, I'm anxious. Because what's inside this box he's just handed me? Some sort of weird vampire paraphernalia? Something he's going to make me wear or use? So, I don't open it. I just turn it over in my hands, half-heartedly tugging at the ribbon.

'Oh wow, is this a first edition?' asks Rupert, and I look over at him. He's holding up an old leather-bound book.

'Of course it is,' Oscar says and looks towards Carmilla who is still ripping at her gift.

I watch as she starts to laugh and says, 'Very naughty, Oscar, but thank you,' and pulls out an old-school whip and a pair of ancient-looking handcuffs.

'Come on, Aubrey,' Oscar snaps, looking straight at me now. 'Hurry up.'

I set my jaw and tear open the paper to reveal a black velvet box inside.

And after seeing Carmilla's present, I'm even more worried. But everyone is watching me now, so I hold my breath, tell myself *don't react, no matter what it is*, and open the box.

Inside is a piece of jewellery. It's clearly very old—a cameo necklace with a woman on the front. I take it out and inspect it.

'Put it on,' Oscar says, and I look up at him.

'Now?' I ask. Because I'm wearing pyjamas.

'Yes, now. So everyone knows you're mine.' And then he sits down and lights a cigar and watches me. Disappointment rolls through me. I shouldn't be disappointed, I shouldn't even be surprised, but he seemed almost normal last night. Tender. Kind. Now his voice filters back from when he introduced me to Carmilla and Felix and Rupert: 'This is Aubrey, my protege.'

Ah, I think, realisation dawning.

He gives these to all his 'proteges' … like a kind of branding. So everyone knows I'm off limits.

The events of last night are quickly recontextualising. The ice in his gaze this evening is not a cover. And his fury—eyes flaming, chest heaving—at Felix last night was *not* because he has some hidden empathy or softness. It was simply because he thinks I'm his possession. He didn't like Felix playing with his toys.

As I realise all this, my hope that maybe he'll go easy on me, won't make me do things I don't want to, dissolves like the smoke from Carmilla's cigarette. Anxiety takes its place.

'What about you, Oscar?' Carmilla asks as I struggle with the latch on my necklace. 'We didn't get you anything.'

'Aubrey has a present for me,' he says, looking at me. 'Don't you?'

My stomach twists. He stares at me, his gaze boring through me like he's challenging me to defy him.

And it's then that I finally manage to make the necklace catch. But right as I do, I hear the doorbell ring. Then Oscar says, 'Here's my present now.'

39

I don't want to do this, I don't want to do this, I don't want to do this … That's what I'm thinking as Oscar gets up to answer the door.

'Just relax, Baby-V,' Rupert says, and Carmilla goes back to scrolling on her phone.

But how can I relax?

I hear chatter in the distance, laughing, footsteps, and then Oscar is back, and he's brought company. It's the same woman he was talking to, dancing with, last night, the one in the yellow dress.

Except now she's in jeans and a black top, and there's a dazed look in her eyes, like she's vacant, not there.

He's hypnotised her.

'Inside,' Oscar says in a honeyed tone, and she moves between the sofas.

Rupert and Carmilla both clap their hands as she stands there on the rug, waiting like a robot.

'Sit there on the sofa,' he tells her soothingly, like she's in a dark slumber he wants to draw her deeper into, then points at the space beside me. She does exactly as he says, she sits down right next to me and I instinctively shift a little away. And then Oscar says, 'Aubrey, a promise is a promise.'

I swallow hard; he's not going to let me get out of this.

I look at him. 'Not with everyone here,' I say.

'Leave us alone,' Oscar tells the other two, his eyes still on me.

They silently get up. Carmilla winks at me and says, 'Have fun,' in a sing-song voice as they leave.

Now it's just me, Oscar and poor Emma sitting in here.

All I can hear is the crackling fire and Emma's heart. At least she's not scared; her heartbeat is regular and there's a small, docile smile on her lips. She wouldn't be smiling if she knew what was coming.

'Emma,' Oscar says in his velvet voice. 'Aubrey's going to feed off you. Are you okay with that?'

She looks into his eyes and nods. But it's not like she has a choice. She's in some kind of trance. Panic rolls through me. *I can't do this.*

I need to buy myself time, so I ask a question. 'Your voice, when you talk to her, you use that specific voice. Like you're trying to keep her entranced. Does that matter?'

He smiles, like he's mildly impressed. 'Yes, your voice is the most important part. Our eyes hold their attention, but our voices hypnotise. Now feed.'

I stare at Emma.

'I can't,' I whisper, looking back at him. 'I'm sorry'.

'Of course you can,' he says, frowning at me. Then he turns to Emma and in that same voice says, 'Now, lean your head over to the side.'

'I really can't,' I repeat. A flash of how every time I feed once, that's it, game over, the seal is broken and I can't stop. 'Please don't make me, I'm still shaken after …' I lower my voice to a whisper, 'last night.'

He throws me a twisted look that clearly says, *Do not talk about that. Ever.* Then, so quietly he's almost mouthing it, he says, 'Aubrey, think. What would have happened if I hadn't been there? Last night is a perfect example of why you *have* to do this.'

My insides clench, because … he's right. If he hadn't been there, I wouldn't have been able to fight Felix off. Now comes a flash of Riley's hand on my wrist, his eyes scanning my mouth that night we met. If he, or anyone else from the VHC, ever gets hold of me again, it would be nice to be able to get myself out of the situation.

But also … in comes a flash of those first nights with Hans. My face in the mirror, the face of a monster. The terror in that child's eyes.

I shake my head. 'You can teach me the other things. Like I'd *love* to learn to hypnotise properly, I'd *love* to be able to control the visions I get sometimes.' And I would. Then I could maybe get some more intel from Jonathan, if he ever wants to see me again. 'I'm totally cool with learning to be faster and stronger. And I'm happy to drink blood, I just need it to be from the bag,' I say, my voice small.

He shakes his head slowly. 'Blood loses its essence, its life force, once it's out of the vein. That's why you're so weak. Feeding from the vein is the only way for you to be properly nourished, and until you feed properly I can't teach you anything else. You won't have the life force to do it. This is the first step, Aubrey. I, for one, don't want this to take any longer than it has to. So just drink.'

As his words swirl around me, I know he's telling the truth. While bagged blood has kept me functional, it never made me feel alive the way feeding from the vein did.

But this is the exact kind of information I needed him to tell me a long time ago. These are the exact lessons he should have already given me. If he'd just done his job properly, maybe I wouldn't have done any of the bad things I've done. I would never have met Hans. Maybe I wouldn't have so much baggage. Maybe I would have learnt to control myself when I feed. But the damage is done, I am 150 years old now, my issues are my issues, I am how I am.

I shake my head. Hard. 'I can't. You don't understand, when I start, I can't stop. I have no self-control.'

'That's why you're practising,' he says, clearly irritated. 'Just lean forward, smell her skin, her blood, hear where the vein is.'

I just sit there. Staring at her.

'Aubrey,' he snaps, 'stop being so fucking vexing. You made a deal, now feed. Or I'll go back on my part too.'

There is no give in his voice. He's not going to back down.

I think of Daphne. Of that knife that killed Kenny probably somewhere in her flat. Then I think of Felix and how helpless I felt last night. Then of Riley and how badly that might all go.

I look at Emma's neck.

I can see her pulse, tapping just beneath the skin of her jugular. I can smell her sweet, sweet, blood—AB negative, which is delicious—and my choices are either run out of here and have Oscar pull me back, force me to do this, or to do the thing I said I'd never do again.

I lean in and her pulse gets louder, and I hate myself for it but my gums tingle, my saliva starts to flow, and I feel my fangs pop out.

I'll just have a little taste.

Oscar's hand pushes gently on the back of my head. I open my jaw, and I bite. As soon as her blood hits my tongue I'm hit by a RUSH through my veins. She tastes like night and glitter all mixed up—euphoria and sex and hope—and *holy fuck, I forgot*. Life force sparks in my veins, swirls in my solar plexus and her heartbeat sounds like a drum, beating out the rhythm to my favourite song. My breath gets quick, I hold on a little harder, bite a little deeper. My vision snaps to high definition and my skin is warm and Oscar is saying something but it's hazy, his voice sounds like music, like an oboe, and there's a hunger inside me that's so much bigger than I can control … now she tastes sweet, like iron, hot chocolate, and—

'That's enough,' Oscar says, prying me away from her. *I'm not done!* I sit still, my lungs heaving as I look at her neck, and I can still taste her blood on my lips.

I'm still hungry. I want more.

I grab onto her arm, go to bite again. Oscar holds me back, but my hand is still on her arm and my stomach clenches as a silent black and white movie fills my mind. It's of a small pale dog swimming across a kidney-shaped pool.

He pulls me away a little harder and as I let go, the images cut to black.

'Stay,' Oscar says to me as he comes back into focus.

I watch as he calmly bites into his own wrist and puts a few drops of blood on Emma's wound.

'What are the visions for?' I ask, as her wound starts to heal before my eyes. 'When I touch people,' I continue, 'why do I see things?'

'The visions give us common ground to talk about and create trust. They help us bond with our prey,' he says, monotone.

But I feel fantastic now, colours are brighter, the world more exciting. And I'm full of thoughts and questions and good will. I haven't been this high in forever. 'Why does your blood heal her but mine doesn't heal anyone?'

'I told you, until you're well fed, you're essentially useless. This will help, but it's just a start. You need to be consistent. You need to feed every night to have power, Aubrey. Think of yourself like a battery you have to charge.'

'When will I be fast?' I ask.

'Not for a long while,' he says. 'That comes last.'

He reaches over to a side table and pulls a wet-wipe from a box. Then he turns back to Emma and I watch as he gently cleans his blood off the spot where her wound was. It's completely gone now, no trace of what just happened. She's fine.

'There,' he says. 'Good as new.'

And I'm still hungry, I still want more, but he's like a safety catch on a gun—he'll stop me.

I reach for his arm now, because this wasn't so bad. And he saved me last night; I misjudged him. In this moment, I forgive it all, I love the world and I love him too and we can all get on.

He turns to look at me, frowning.

'Thanks for last night,' I gush, my voice a whisper.

'No problem,' he says, his voice icy. 'It's my job.' But then something shifts behind his gaze, something I can't decipher. Then he grins and he says, 'Lesson over. But screw it, my turn.'

And before I know what's happening, he turns back to Emma and his teeth sink into her neck. She doesn't move. Doesn't fight. She's stunned. I'm torn between the smell of her blood, the feeling of it running through my veins, the vaguely chocolatey taste of it on my lips, the wooziness I still feel, and this instinctual need to help her. But then her eyes are rolling back in her head and he's hurting her! He's going to kill her!

My ears ring, my vision blanches white, a heat—a fiery rage—rushes to my head. A dizziness I haven't felt in a long time comes over me, a fury courses through my veins. I lurch forward, swiping at Oscar. He grabs me by the throat and holds me there as he feeds and feeds and feeds. I don't stand a chance against his strength.

All I can do is hold my breath and watch as Emma's eyes close, then she slumps like a deflated balloon, her hair in front of her eyes. Blood seeping from her neck. And that does it.

It's as though I've been doused in ice water. The hunger is gone. Stopped dead by self-loathing.

This is why I can't feed from the vein.

Oscar's hand is still tight around my throat, but then comes a knock on the door. He looks towards it as Carmilla's voice rings out. 'Oscar,' she whines coyly. 'Pleeeease, can we use my presents?'

'Just a moment,' Oscar calls out, nonchalant. Then he lets go of Emma, and she falls to his lap. He turns to me, my neck still in his grasp.

'Don't do anything stupid, I'm not in the mood,' he whispers to me, and then he lets me go.

I reach for my throat to soothe it.

'Oscar?' comes Carmilla's whine again.

'I said just a moment,' Oscar yells back, his eyes still on mine. Then he gently puts Emma on the floor—no thud, no sound at all—and pushes her under the sofa. Far under the sofa. He throws me one more threatening look. And then he calmly calls out, 'You can come in.'

The door flings open and Carmilla strides inside, two women and one man trailing behind her. I recognise the women, they're the ones who were wearing flapper dresses last night, the ones who were asking me about Oscar ... But now they're just in their bras and knickers.

'Aubrey, which one would you like?' Carmilla asks, a challenge in her eyes, like she wants to make me uncomfortable. Feel out of my depth. But Oscar beat her to it.

'I'm okay,' I say, a little numb, my breath quick. 'I just ate.'

'We're not going to eat, silly,' she says, unzipping the man's pants. 'We're going to do other things.'

I look over to Oscar—the two women are sitting on either side of him. One of them is pulling out a small mirror and cutting a line of cocaine on it on her lap. She thinks this is a party. She has no idea what's beneath the sofa she's sitting on, but these people don't have that trance-like look in their eyes. They're all very much awake and willing. I feel sick. *Is this what this week is going to be like?*

Oscar's eyes are narrowed as he watches me, watching them. He reaches out and undoes two bras at once like it's a party trick, then grins at me, and my throat tightens. 'Aubrey, don't be so pedestrian and judgy. A little depravity is good for the spirits.'

A panic rises within me, as I think of Emma lying there while all this goes on.

I look away from him and back towards Carmilla.

'Where's Rupert?' I ask.

Carmilla rolls her eyes. 'Reading, being boring …'

I see my out. 'I'm going to go and read too. Have fun.'

40

As I reach the top of the stairs, I can hear moans coming from the drawing room. I close the door behind me to shut them out. I can still taste Emma's blood—sweet, light, with dark chocolate overtones—and I hate Oscar but I think I hate myself more. For liking it. I rush over to the bathroom and shake as I rinse out my mouth, brush my teeth. I spit, rinse again, and splash my face with water. And then I reach back for the clasp on the necklace and take it off, banging it down on the marble countertop.

I will *never* be like him.

I take back anything good I ever thought about him—he's just as bad as I believed. No, he's worse.

I go over to my bed, glancing out the window as I pass. I can see Emma's car there. Waiting for her. But she won't be coming back. All because she was a good little girl, just as she was told. Just like me. I pull my suitcase out from beneath the bed, find the cooler bag and check my backup bag of blood is still there. Now terrified Oscar might have somehow sniffed it out and taken it. I wouldn't put it past him. But it's still there. Still cool. And a calm comes over me as I see it.

Because who knows how many times he's going to make me do this, how bad it'll get? At least I have a safety blanket.

Then my gaze shifts to just beside it, to Es's Christmas present. A flash of the night she gave it to me—the same night I agreed to Oscar's terms. I reach for it, trace the wrapping paper with my fingertip. *It's Christmas.*

I push my suitcase back under the bed and sit down on the mattress. There's a tiny card stuck to the paper with sticky tape. *MERRY XMAS!!! LOVE YOU!!! Xxxxx*

My insides ache as I rip off the paper, revealing … a snow globe. It's of Covent Garden market. There's a tree with baubles and little carollers all in a line and the entrance to the market with a tiny green wreath above it. I shake it up and watch as snowflakes swirl and fall.

And all I want right now is Cat and Es and Daphne and my work and Jonathan and to be e-stalking Olivia from my sofa like any other heartbroken woman. I don't want to be here. Feeding on people. Fighting the worst parts of myself.

I shake up Es's snow globe once more, leave it on the writing table and get into bed, pulling the covers up to my chin. I can still hear Carmilla and Oscar and their guests downstairs, and Oscar is wrong, I'm not judgy. People can have whatever kind of sex they want—hell, wear a gimp suit if you fancy. I certainly tried it all when I was first turned, so desperate for anything that could take the edge off existence. But it didn't work. Not for me at least. It just left me feeling emptier and more alone—more aware of the fact that it didn't matter how many sets of sheets twisted around my legs, I would never be able to let anyone close enough that it could turn into real love.

I look across at the window, through the space between the curtains, and the moon is right there, staring back at me from an inky sky. It's bright and almost full—55,020 moons now—and as I look at it, I think about Jonathan. I can still remember the exact rhythm of his heartbeat. Still conjure the feeling of his stubble beneath my fingertips. The exact shade of his eyes. The way he bites his lip when he's trying not to laugh. And that tug on my ribs is back, just as strong as ever, and I need him. I really need him. I need the version of me he can tether me to. Human-me.

By the time dawn comes, its apricot glow seeping through the gap in the curtains, the moans have stopped, the guests have left and the whole house is silent. I've been lying here all night, awake and thinking, and now my eyes are finally fluttering closed. But I can't sleep, not yet.

Because everyone else is asleep and it's dawn on Boxing Day. And I need to check my phone. Anything could have happened.

Jonathan might have texted me *Merry Christmas*, the VHC board might have another post about Kenny. I have no idea how I used to wait for letters to arrive or the blinking light of an answering machine back in the day.

I get up, pull on my dressing gown and tiptoe to the bedroom door in my socks. I slowly open the door, creep over to the banister and gently make my way down the stairs, staying to the side so the steps don't creak. When I get to the bottom, I go over to the silver bowl and slowly, carefully, reach for Oscar's keys, holding them tight in my palm so they don't jangle. Then I edge open the front door and, under a sky that's quickly turning baby blue, streaks of cloud tinted pink and apricot at the rims, I run over to Oscar's car. The gravel cuts into my socked feet as I look around. Emma's car has gone. He must have moved it. Covered his tracks like he did with Felix.

Where did he put her?

All around me the world is waking up: birds singing, a thin morning mist clinging to the air, and winter frost sparkling on the grass. And even though my head is thick with the fog that daybreak brings and I'm squinting in the low light, there's an awe-inspiring beauty to it all. A world I long to be a part of again—a world of sunshine, warm on my skin; a world that cares about the smell of cinnamon and newspapers, not blood—is rousing. But I need to hurry before the sun gets any higher, before I feel any worse.

The taillights flash red as I get to the car. I hear the doors click open, and I quickly get inside.

I look back at the manor; nobody is coming. Then I duck down and reach for the glove compartment. But when I open it and reach inside for my phone, all I feel is the leather of the car's manual.

My phone is gone.

I tossed and turned all day, dreaming of Emma and Count Orlok and sinister organ music, waking in fits of self-loathing, too scared to go back to sleep. I got up before dusk, unpacking my clothes into the wardrobe just for something to do while the sun was still glowing like an orange laceration along the horizon.

And now I'm standing in front of the bathroom mirror inspecting the mark on my neck and dabbing concealer on it—it's fading, but still there, still looking very much like a vampire bite—and going over my plan of action.

It is clear to me that Oscar doesn't have any of the boundaries others have. He's kind one moment, cruel the next, ruthless and sadistic, and with no decipherable conscience—he's not morally grey, he's morally corrupt. But he's also stronger than me in every way; there is no point in fighting him. I need to get him onside. To play along. To learn what he wants to teach me as quickly as possible and then get the hell out of here. Give him no reason to force me any further than he did last night.

No reason to escalate things.

The plan is simple: to go with the flow and not be a problem; nod and smile and wear his necklace like I am right now; make him think I *want* to be a vampire. I will do what I've been doing for 150 years: I will fake it. And then I'll go back to my life. And provided I've played my role well enough, learnt what he wants to teach me, I'll leave knowing he has no reason to harm Daphne or anyone else I love.

Because after last night, I *know* he'd do it. I know it in my gut.

I look at my reflection, look myself in the eye. *It's all going to be okay. You can do this.*

That's when I hear a woman's voice, high enough to shatter glass. *Is that … opera?* I move to the bedroom door, edging it open. *Yep, opera.* It's coming from downstairs. As I descend the stairs in my pyjamas to see what's going on, I think: *Please don't let Oscar be having another get together*. I'm not used to all this socialising, I just want to do whatever I have to do then go home. Never see him again.

I move towards the music; the woman is in the middle of some high-pitched trill, and it's coming from the same room we were in last night, the drawing room. Carmilla is in there, lying on the sofa, moving her cigarette around as if she is personally conducting the orchestra. Rupert is putting logs onto the fire.

'Hey Baby-V,' he says to me over the music. 'Come to join the mental breakdown?' He nods towards Carmilla.

I look at her; she just keeps on with her conducting.

Then I hear, 'What the hell is going on?' from behind me. I turn to look as Oscar storms across the room. His green silk dressing gown is hanging open, revealing his well-formed villain torso: the obligatory six-pack, pectorals you could crack an egg on, and the shoulders and arms of an underwear model. He looks as though he's made of the same hard and impervious material as his heart. He stomps over to Carmilla, grabs a remote control from beside her and presses a couple of buttons. The music turns off.

'It's only four pm, you animal,' he seethes.

'I'm upset, I couldn't sleep,' Carmilla says, sitting up. She's pouting.

'Felix still isn't answering her texts,' Rupert says, standing up and crossing his arms.

Oscar does up his dressing gown, and again I notice that little silver cross on a chain around his neck, catching the light. He sees me looking and reaches for it, but I look away. I'm scared he'll see how much I hate him in my eyes.

Then he says, 'Well, I have to go into London to deal with something at the club tonight, so you two can take care of Aubrey. She needs a bit of training out in the wild anyway.' He looks from Carmilla to Rupert, then back to Carmilla.

'But we're going into town,' Carmilla whines. 'Some of the shops are open late for Boxing Day sales … retail therapy. We can't babysit.'

Oscar just looks at her, his jaw set.

She rolls her eyes. 'Fine, she can come.' Then she looks over at me and says, 'But hurry up and get dressed.'

The town is quaint and adorable, Christmas lights still strung up across the cobbled street. The buildings are made of uneven stone, shop windows adorned with tinsel and small plastic reindeer. Something about it feels familiar, but I can't put my finger on it. The sky is clear tonight, the air freezing, and we're walking arm in arm down the street, Carmilla, then Rupert, then me.

'What shall we do first?' Rupert asks, and I wonder if anyone walking past will notice that none of us is breathing fog.

'I'd say get Aubrey a scarf so nobody wonders about … that,' Carmilla says, nodding to my neck. 'You'll need to get better at concealing marks if you're going to keep letting Oscar feed off you.'

I self-consciously reach for my neck. I'd thought my turned-up coat collar was hiding it.

'What's the deal with you and Oscar, anyway?' Rupert asks.

I can feel them both looking at me. I shrug. 'It's nothing,' I say. 'He's just, you know …'

'Nothing?' Carmilla asks, her eyes searing me. I swallow hard.

'Well, not nothing,' I say, backtracking. Because if it's nothing, that means Oscar didn't bite me and someone else did, and why do I get the feeling she'd love to piece it all together? And that she'd blame me, not Felix, or even Oscar, if she knew what had happened. 'But nothing serious.'

'So … it's not serious but you let him bite you? Sharing blood is the most intimate thing two vampires can do. And to let him do that after he abandoned you …' She says something else under her breath that sounds like 'desperate much', but I let it go. I want to change the subject.

Rupert, on the other hand, does not want to let it go.

'Oh my god, stop being such a judgemental bitch,' he says.

'I'm just warning her. We both know what Oscar's like. I don't want her getting her hopes up.' Then she looks me dead in the eye. 'Oscar doesn't care about you, he just wanted to get high on your blood.' She tosses her dark hair.

I'm confused. Do vampires get high off each other? When I drank Oscar's blood, I didn't get high. There was no euphoria, no bliss. I just got kind of aggressive and agile and strong.

'How would it make him high?' I ask, frowning.

Rupert squeezes me gently and, in a kind, teacherly voice, says, 'Oh, Baby-V, so much to learn. Young blood gets you high, old blood gives you power.'

'I'm not that young …' I say.

'Compared to us, you are,' he says, and we keep walking for a bit as his words tumble around in my brain. I think of the glitter in my veins as I fed on Emma, how hard it was to stop. How hard it *always* is to stop.

'But I do get kind of high on human blood,' I say softly to him.

'No, you don't,' he whispers back. 'Not like new-vampire blood. Whole other circus.' He winks at me.

'All I'm saying,' Carmilla cuts in, 'is that I hope you're not expecting some big commitment. All Oscar ever gives is heartbreak and despair.' Carmilla scoffs. 'He'll chew you up and spit you out, even if you wear some necklace he gave you every day for the rest of your life,' she gives a mean little laugh. 'I've seen him do it again and again.'

My cheeks get hot. What kind of idiot does she think I am? I see straight through him. But also, I need to be careful here. I can't let her think for a moment it wasn't Oscar who bit me. Can't have her suspect the truth.

'I don't care,' I say. 'I'm …' I almost say I'm in love with someone else, but I stop myself. I don't want any of them to know about Jonathan—they might mention him to Oscar. I want him safe. 'I'm just in it for sex.'

'Classy,' Carmilla says.

'Wait,' says Rupert with a laugh, 'are you of all people seriously slut-shaming her now?' And then he stops dead in front of a clothing store. 'Ooh,' he says, staring at a mannequin wearing a frilly, open-chested pirate shirt. 'I *need* that.'

'I'm going to take a lap,' Carmilla says, looking down at her phone. 'I'll be back in a few.'

'Don't worry about her,' Rupert says as we watch her stride away. 'She's just being a bitch because Felix is gone. He does this. Disappears, screws around on her, then comes back all apologetic. It's totally toxic, but it's their thing.' Guilt pulses through me because I know Felix will *not* be coming back, not this time.

'But she's had sex with someone else too, at the house …'

'Yeah, revenge for not texting her back. Carmilla has two sets of rules: one for everyone else and one for her. Typical fucking Leo,' he says as he goes to pull open the shop door but it's locked. There's a woman in there, at the counter, pretending not to see us. But Rupert isn't having any of it. He bangs loudly on the glass and grins at her as he says to me. 'But Carmilla *is* right about one thing, Baby-V. You be careful with Oscar. He's alluring, but he's got a … dark side. And you seem like the kind of girl who wants love. He can't give you that.'

The shop woman glares at us, comes over and opens the door. 'We're closed, sorry,' she says, flashing a fake grin.

'No problem,' Rupert says, his eyes latching on to hers. Then in a honeyed tone says, 'I'd like to try on the shirt in the window, please.'

'Of course,' she says, a familiar daze in her eyes. 'What size are you?'

'A large.'

'Of course,' she says, going over to a rail of white clothing. We go inside and the door closes after us, and as she finds Rupert's size, he inspects the other racks.

'Here you go,' she says with a smile, handing him his size. He's already got five more pieces from the racks hanging over his arm.

'Change rooms are over there,' she says pleasantly.

'Lovely,' he says, looking her dead in the eye again. 'Now leave us. You can come back in twenty minutes.'

She nods and walks out the door and Rupert flits over to the changing cubicle and disappears behind the curtain. I hear drums, a bass—a song start to play; I'm guessing it's coming from his phone. I recognise it immediately: 'Bloodletting (The Vampire Song)' by Concrete Blood. I take a seat on a large pink velvet chair and wait, watching his feet move under the curtain.

The curtain swishes and Rupert steps out in the white shirt from the window, striking a pose in front of the long mirror.

'What do we think?' he asks, looking at me and then back to his reflection and turning side-on. 'Do I look fabulous, like Lord Byron?'

I give a little laugh. 'I love it.'

'Me too,' he says with a grin.

He disappears behind the curtain again as the song ends and 'vampire' by Olivia Rodrigo starts to play. And I don't know whether it's because I'm here, among them, or if it's because I only found out I could die two nights ago, and honestly, I should have known that before, but now I want to know the rest of it. All the things Oscar never explained to me. And Rupert seems like the most sensitive of the bunch, so, as the song changes, I say, 'Hey, Rupert …'

'Mm?' he replies, from the other side of the curtain.

'Have you ever met a human … again?' I ask, thinking of Jonathan. 'Like, someone you met and then they died and came back and then you met them again, in a new body?'

The curtain swishes open. 'Did Carmilla tell you something?'

'What? No. Why?'

'Well, yes I have,' he says, coming out in a teal shirt with frills around the collar and sleeves. He poses in front of the mirror, one knee bent, then the other. 'I didn't realise at first, of course, but once I did, I kept my distance. Thankfully he didn't know,' he says, lifting his hands to his hips.

'Who was he? How did you meet him the first time?'

'Just some guy I knew,' he says, shrugging. 'I guess we had unfinished business or something.'

That makes sense, I think. *I was torn from Jonathan, and we have unfinished business, a love that was interrupted.*

Rupert looks at me. 'Sometimes that happens, our souls are tied to those we knew before. Destined to find each other again and again. Why? You meet someone you knew before?'

I shake my head. 'No, but sometimes I see past-life visions and it occurred to me that it could happen, so I was just wondering …'

'Argh, those mess with your head, don't they? But they are a nice little reminder that no matter how shit the world gets, at least it's not the fifteen hundreds anymore,' he says, turning back to the mirror and tilting his head. 'What do you think of this one?'

It suits him; it's the same colour as his necklace, as his ring. 'It's perfect,' I say. 'Do you ever wonder who you were, you know, before? When you were human?' I know I'm being a bit intense, but this is the closest I've ever got to getting answers of any kind.

He crosses his arms and frowns. 'Hell no. Whoever that fool was, he wasn't as hot and fabulous as I am.' His eyes bore into me. 'What's going on, Baby-V? Why are you asking all of this?'

I look down. 'I just want to know. Nobody ever told me.'

'Ah. Yeah, Oscar was a right shit for doing that to you,' he says. 'But you're looking at this all wrong. You are a motherfucking vampire, Baby-V. We have everything everyone wants. Stop taking everything so seriously—have some fun with it, okay? The night is ours …'

I nod, and he smiles and heads back behind the curtain.

As 'Bela Lugosi's Dead' by Bauhaus plays, then 'Vampire Blues' by Neil Young, then 'Closer' by Kings of Leon, he tries on three more outfits, and I think about what he just said. I can see the appeal, the fun, of living like this. Doing what you want, when you want—having total agency. Wading into the darkness and letting it swallow you whole. Just letting go.

But now comes a flash of my face in that mirror, hair tangled and covered in blood. That little boy in my arms. Emma, last night.

And I think: *At what cost?*

Fifteen minutes later, the shop woman is back and then Carmilla comes in too.

She flops down on the chair beside me and immediately starts looking at her phone. Rupert comes out of the change room with the clothes he wants on one arm and those he doesn't on the other, and goes to pay.

As we step out into the night air, Carmilla puts her phone in her pocket and says, 'You know what? I'm done with this.' She looks at Rupert and me in turn, and there's something dangerous in her eyes. 'Could you eat? I saw a pub on the corner. I could eat …'

42

I'm anxious as we walk into the pub, because I'm guessing we're not here for the burgers. Carmilla and Rupert wander over to a high bar table against the wall, a tea light and a folded over newspaper in the centre. We all sit down on bar stools and they look around, perusing the options like they're scanning the freezer section of a supermarket. I, on the other hand, lean forward and dip my fingertip in the wax of the candle, then start anxiously peeling it off, thinking: *How do I get out of this?*

Because I know the plan was to go with the flow, and I know if I don't comply it'll get back to Oscar, but also, the only reason I could stop feeding last night was because Oscar was there. Stopping me. The only reason the hunger abated was because he hurt Emma and that snapped me out of it.

Tonight I'd be all alone. With nobody to stop me. Nothing to snap me out of it.

I can't do it.

I take a deep breath and look up, ready to make my case, just as Rupert and Carmilla lean in towards the centre of the table.

'Green shirt, edge of bar,' Rupert whispers.

We all glance over. It's a guy, standing alone.

Carmilla nods. 'I'm going black leather jacket, opposite side of the room.'

I turn to look. 'But he's with a woman,' I say.

'She can join …' Carmilla says with a shrug. 'Or not.' She smiles and flashes her fangs like she doesn't care who sees. Then she retracts them and gives me a knowing look.

'What about you, Aubrey?' she asks, and her voice is laced with something I can't quite place. Challenge, maybe.

'I … I don't know,' I say, my stomach clenching.

'Remember what we spoke about,' Rupert says kindly, putting his hand on mine. And even though his hand is cool, it's still comforting. 'Have some fun. What about the hot one in the red flannel shirt? He's been watching you since we came in.'

I glance around the room to see who he's talking about.

Red Flannel is sitting alone, at the end of the bar, and Rupert is right, he's looking at me. 'I might just sit this one out,' I say to Rupert, anxiety bubbling under my skin. 'I don't think I should. Oscar said I need to make sure I don't get us all found out.'

Solid excuse.

Carmilla gives a sigh of annoyance. 'I knew she wouldn't even try,' she says, then stands up. 'I'm going for it,' she says and strides over to her prey.

'Oscar told us to teach you some things, Baby-V. We're right here if something goes wrong,' Rupert says, reaching for my hand reassuringly. 'Nothing bad is going to happen to you, as long as you use your head.'

'You don't understand, my hypnotism skills are seriously bad, I can't control my visions yet so I can't bond with—'

'Oh, you don't *need-need* those visions,' Rupert says, leaning in and tucking my hair behind my ear. 'Humans are dead easy to manipulate, even without them. You just pretend they're the most special person you've ever met. Hold eye contact. Look right into their soul. And you don't show your fangs until you're somewhere safe,' he adds, giving a little chuckle at his own joke.

I swallow hard. Shake my head, trying to show him that he doesn't understand.

'I don't have a lot of self-control … I find it almost impossible to stop,' I whisper. 'So, that's why I think it's better I don't. Not yet.'

He lets out a sigh. 'Suit yourself, nobody is going to force you. But the more you feed, the more control you'll have, the more you *will* be able to stop. And in a fix, all you need is a handbrake. For me, I imagine I'm sucking on roadkill. It's so revolting it jolts me out of it every time. Anyway, do as you will, but I'll be right here if you run into trouble.' He winks and says, 'Wish me luck,' and then he's up and heading over to green shirt and I'm alone, and I don't even have my phone to scroll through.

So I just sit there, listening to hearts beating around me, frowning at that tea light flame and thinking: *This is fine.*

I reach for the newspaper and start to flip through it. It's the local paper, and there on page three is an article about the charity ball at Mr Oscar Carmichael's abode. I fold the paper over, frown down at it and start to read.

'It's not that bad,' a male voice interrupts me, and I look up. It's Red Flannel. 'I saw you were alone. Can I get you a drink?'

I'm about to say *no thank you*. I can smell his blood—whisky, Coke, O positive—and hear his heart beating and I don't need the temptation. Not after the trauma of last night. But then my gaze snaps to the phone in his hand and a lightness moves through me. Who knows when I'll get my phone back? While I can't check the VHC board from his phone, I could go through to Instagram and look up Jonathan's profile, to see his face, see if he's posted anything new. Maybe something to make me think he's missing me—that I'm not just delusional. His profile is public. It would be easy.

So I nod. 'Sure.'

He heads to the bar and I finish reading the article—a glowing account of both Oscar and the ball—and then Red Flannel is back and sliding into Carmilla's seat. I put down the paper and glance over his shoulder—Carmilla is heading for the door with her couple, but Rupert is still here, standing by the bar with Green Shirt.

'What's your name? You from here?' asks Red Flannel, and I recoil a little. He has that look, the one men always get around me, his gaze moving down to my neck, my chest, then up to my mouth. And I'm thinking how easy it would be to ask him to go for a walk right now. Go back to his place.

How easy to do the bad thing.

He puts his phone on the table.

'Harriet,' I lie. 'And no, I'm from London. What's your name?'

'Jeff.' And there's something about the way he says it that makes me wonder if he's lying too. But why?

'Can I borrow your phone for a second, Jeff?' I ask. 'I just want to check on a friend.'

'Sure,' he says, shrugging and unlocking it, then handing it to me, but the moment before I take it, he stops. 'For a kiss.'

Argh. But I smile coyly, then lean in and kiss his cheek and he lets the phone go. I tap quickly through to Instagram, type Jonathan's handle into the search function, and hold my breath as I wait.

Helium fills my veins as it loads, anticipation coursing through me.

But then: doom.

Pure undiluted doom.

Because Jonathan's profile … is now private.

Every part of me gets hot, then cold, then hot again. When did he turn his profile to private? It wasn't private when we met, when I added him and he added me. Why would he do that unless he knew I'd be watching his page?

And if he made his page private so I couldn't see anything … did he block me too?

Remove me as a follower?

My breath speeds up as I stare at the screen.

I can't know the answer to any of these questions without logging into my account right here, right now, and I know it's a bit extreme but who knows when I'll find my phone again so … should I?

But then big hands come forward and prise the phone from my hands, and all I can do is watch that box with all the answers in it disappear into his pocket.

'That's enough,' Jeff/Red Flannel/Whatever says, threading his big fingers through mine. 'Whoa, your hands are cold. You should drink your drink,' he says, 'it'll warm you up.'

Don't freak out, Aubrey. It's just a private Instagram account, it might mean nothing. *Maybe he changed it to private ages ago. How would you know, you follow him?*

I reach for my drink and take a sip. It tastes like whisky and Coke—just like his blood smells—and I don't like either of those things, but then … *hang on* … There's something else in there too.

Something not right.

My taste buds tingle and my gaze snaps to my glass. My nostrils flare. I look up at him, look him in the face—his expression is self-satisfied and smarmy. 'That's a good girl,' he says with a grin, and realisation hits. Drugs might not really work on me, but this dipshit doesn't know that.

He's trying to roofie me.

And damn … it's kind of strong.

43

My gums tingle, a familiar heat glows beneath my ribs, my vision snaps to high definition and rage rolls through me. Solar plexus. Fingers. Head. I push it down—*I'm in a public place, NOT NOW, NOT NOW*—but shit, I know this feeling. There's no use fighting it. It's too strong. *I should run out of here, before I do something I can't undo*. But also … *should I?*

Because all I'm thinking as I take another sip is: *He planned this, he came here looking for a victim*. How many others has he done this to? I doubt I'm the first. Or that I'll be the last. And I know I'm extra upset right now because of Jonathan's Instagram page, and the memory of Felix's attack, and Oscar killing Emma, and me being helpless, and 150 years of guys like Red Flannel Jeff trying to finger-bang me while wives waited at home, but suddenly, I don't want to fight it. I don't want to run. This thing they want me to do? It doesn't seem like such a bad idea.

It's almost poetic. Funny. I'd be performing a public service.

But more than that: I *want* to.

I take another gulp of my drink, then another, and I get a little buzz—it really is strong, he really wanted to make sure I went down—but not enough to have me lean against the exposed brick wall like I am right now. Not enough to have my eyelids heavy and fluttering closed as he watches me, chatting inanely and staring at my lips. I take another gulp, put my hand on his well-muscled leg and let my eyelids close a little more, let my words slur. And soon, he helps me to my feet.

He's big and he's basically carrying me out, but nobody stops him. I catch Rupert's eye and wink at him, and he gives me a little smile.

We go outside and Red Flannel Jeff is talking in a cheery voice as he helps me, saying, 'We'll be home soon, baby,' presumably for the benefit of passers-by. I can smell his sweat—sour and musky like day-old deodorant—and hear his heart beating fast as we move across the car park. It's speeding up. *The thrill—he gets off on the thrill.* And now we're at his car. He has one of those tinted window SUVs and it's parked in a dark corner, facing a wall. I know why he parked there: he didn't want witnesses or lighting or CCTV. He didn't want anyone to see him put me in the passenger seat and then hurry around to his side, like he's doing right now.

But … fine with me.

My gums tingle as he gets into the car and slams his door. His keys jangle as he puts the car key into the ignition. But the moment before he turns it, he looks over at me. Reaches across, puts his hand on my knee and traces it up my leg, towards my thigh, slipping under the hem of my skirt.

'Nice legs you have there,' he says in a gross whisper as his hand slides a little higher.

Fuck this.

My vision blanches, my fangs come out and that volcanic rage rolls through me. I grab his hair with one hand, his shoulder with the other and stare at the vein on his neck. And then I bite.

He struggles for a moment then goes limp, and I drink and drink and drink. His blood is laced with whisky but he must eat well because it's sweet, nourishing, and I want to drink forever. My vision snaps to high definition; his low and lumbered breath is like a melodic whisper, and I dig in deeper and suck a little harder. For a moment I forget about Jonathan and his private Instagram profile, and all is well in the world and I AM A GOD!

I drink and I drink and I drink and I drink and—

Beeeeep.

A horn sounds in the distance.

I should stop, I know I should.

But also, fuck it, I don't want to stop. I can't stop.

I won't stop.

I close my eyes and drink some more …

And then voices … just outside. *But that's okay, they're not that close.* It's not like they're tapping on the window and it's dark outside. *I have to stop.*

But how? HOW?

My eyes flick open.

I think of roadkill, like Rupert said. Really revolting roadkill. Intestines and gall bladders and fur. I imagine sucking on it. My stomach turns, and I gag, but I keep on drinking and then … I think of that little boy's eyes.

The terror mirrored back at me.

The rage turns to ice. I pull away and sit dead still. Staring at him. His blood is bright red and all over his neck, dripping down to his shirt.

This is how it happens, I think. *This is how you end up stuck in the darkness!*

Still, I reason, *he kind of deserved it.*

But the voices are still out there. I glance in the rear-view mirror and see a couple getting into their car. The doors slam, taillights flash red. As they drive away, I look back at Red Flannel Jeff as I wipe his blood from my face with the back of my hand.

Panic swirls through me as I take in his pale face. *What have I done?* I can't just leave him here like this: unconscious with fang marks on his neck.

Rupert was wrong, he's not here when I need him. And neither is Carmilla. And I don't have my phone so I can't call Oscar. Besides, what would he do anyway? He's in London.

It's just me. Alone.

Fuck.

FUCK. FUCK. FUCK.

Now my heart is beating even faster than his was. I didn't think this through.

Okay, I can do this. I've fed twice. I must be stronger. And Oscar said once I'd fed from the vein a few times, I'd get some power.

So I quickly bite my wrist. I put some of my blood on his wound like I've seen Oscar do. Then I stare at it, willing it to work. Work! Work!

But what if it doesn't work?

And then, as if by magic, I watch as the puncture marks slowly disappear.

Yes!

Oscar was right.

I lick my fingers, wiping away my blood from his neck as best I can, but his blood is still there, dripping; smeared. There's a half empty bottle of water on the floor by my feet, so I reach for it, slosh it all over his neck.

Now the blood is gone but he's starting to regain consciousness, so I lock my eyes on his and in the most velvety voice I can muster, I say, 'You won't remember any of this. You will only remember going out to a bar, and realising you never want to harm another woman again.'

But screw it, that's not enough.

'If you ever want to do this again, you will pee yourself, no matter where you are. And … you will take your bag of roofies to the police and confess to every assault you have ever committed.'

He nods.

'Good boy,' I say, feeling my fangs retract.

I get out of the car and practically skip back to the pub. Because Rupert was right, this IS fun. It feels good to be the hunter, not the hunted for a moment, the predator, not the prey. To have some sort of agency. Power.

And I'm still good, right? Surely this doesn't count.

Red Flannel Jeff was bad, and he started it, and I didn't even kill him …

Oh wow. Have I found a moral loophole?

Or is this just how it starts? The descent into darkness, the loosening of morals.

I can't tell. Right now, I don't care. I just know that I feel AMAZING. I've probably saved countless other women from that dirtbag. I just want to revel in this moment because for the first time, possibly ever, I *like* being a vampire …

Scrap that. Right now, *I love it.*

I want to print it on a T-shirt, sky-write it, etch it in stone somewhere … maybe buy a car and put on personalised number plates.

Rupert is standing outside the pub, smoking a cigarette with Green Shirt. 'Back already?' he asks, frowning and looking behind me for my guy. Adrenaline pulses through me.

I nod, pirouette and give a little curtsy, then reach for his cigarette and take a deep drag, then hand it back to him. 'I'm tired, I need to go home. Can I have the key?'

'Carmilla wants you to wait,' he says. But then he pulls the key out of his pocket and hands it to me with a grin. 'Just leave the gate open and the door unlocked.' As I take the key, a cab pulls up and someone gets out, and it feels like the cosmos has aligned for me at last.

'See you later,' I say to Rupert,

'Ciao,' he says, and blows me a kiss.

I run to the cab, lean into the open window and say, 'Umm ...'

Because that's when I realise I don't know Oscar's address. But buoyed by my accomplishments, I improvise. 'I'm going that way, just out of town,' I say, pointing to the left, the way we came in. 'It's at the very top of the hill.'

'Mr Carmichael's place?' the driver asks, looking impressed, and I nod.

'Get in,' he says.

And *ah shit*, all I can smell is his A-negative blood. *NO, AUBREY*. But that hunger is there, growling like a pet I have to feed.

'You a friend of Mr Carmichael's?' the driver asks as we head out of the village.

'Yes,' I say, taking deep breaths. 'I'm just staying for Christmas.'

I can see his neck from where I'm sitting, hear the gentle tapping of his pulse ... I focus on roadkill, sucking it dry.

'Wild parties he throws, yeah? Never been myself, always working. But I read about it in the paper. He does it every year, they say. Both Christmas Eve and New Year's Eve. Driven a few friends home for him, they say he's a nice chap?'

He's glancing back at me now in the rear-view mirror and I can tell from the inflection of his voice that he's wants me to weigh in. But I don't want to talk, I'm too busy focusing on locking my jaw. 'He's lovely, very kind,' I lie.

'Charitable, too. He paid for the school to be repaired after it flooded three years back. Imagine that?'

I smile and nod and take slow, deep breaths, thinking, *Well of course he did, he didn't want anyone to believe one of his victims if they said something bad about him*. I think of Emma. On Christmas. *What does her family think happened to her?* But kudos to Oscar, he's creating the perfect cover. Far easier to hide in plain sight.

'So how do you know Mr Carmichael?'

I swallow, pray my fangs don't pop out and say, 'I'm … I work with him in London.'

'Oh, nice.'

And Oscar's gates are just up ahead, FINALLY, so I press the button on the key and they open and we drive inside. The cab driver pulls to a stop and says, 'That'll be nine pound, love.'

That's when I realise I don't have my phone. Or money. Or any way to pay.

'I … I don't have my wallet,' I say, my voice small. *Please don't kick up a fuss, please be understanding. I'm really trying here. I don't want to bite you (although I do, I REALLY DO).*

He smiles calmly, clearly unaware of my mental turmoil, and says, 'No worries, I'll put it on Mr Carmichael's tab.'

I nod, relieved, and as I watch him drive away, I finally exhale properly. But as I look around, scanning the grounds, lit up by some outside lights, I realise I'm here alone. Just me and the howling wind.

Oscar's car is still gone and Rupert and Carmilla aren't here. I have the house all to myself, and the life-force blood sparkling through my veins is telling me that if ever there was a time to look for my phone, this is it.

44

I don't have a floor plan, and I haven't had that much time to snoop, but I *do* know that upstairs consists entirely of bedrooms and bathrooms—on my side at least—so I stay on the ground floor and head under the stairs, towards the dining room and the drawing room … because there were other rooms there too.

All the doors are closed now. I pull open the one beside the dining room and find a sitting room with a couple of pale yellow sofas on either side of a coffee table. But the fireplace is immaculate and clean, and there are no papers or books strewn around; I focus in on the floors. With Red Flannel Jeff's blood pulsing through me, my vision is razor sharp, even sharper than normal, and I can see a thin layer of dust with no footprints on it. Nobody has been in here for at least a week or so.

I rush out again, closing the door behind me so nobody knows I've been in there, and stride across the hallway towards the room I saw yesterday, when I was looking for Mrs Parker to fix my dress—the one I thought looked like a library. And now that I think about it, it was as I pushed the door open that Oscar called for me.

That must be it. *It's in there. I just know it.*

The walls creak. The little hairs on the back of my neck stand up on end.

I stand dead still and listen for a moment. *What if I'm wrong, what if someone* is *home?* But then comes the howl of wind outside, and the rattle of windows. Other than that, it's silent.

I twist the doorknob and go inside.

The room is huge and smells like dust and old cigars, with dark wood panelling and ornate cornicing. Even without Oscar in here, I can feel his energy swirling, warning me of consequences I dare not even imagine. This must be his office. The walls are filled with books, most old, some modern, there are two spiral staircases that lead up to the second level of books, and there's a large spinning world globe in the corner that looks like it's from another time entirely. On the far right, is a solid timber desk with a laptop charging in the middle of it.

I bet it's in there.

I rush towards the desk. Where would he have hidden it? I pull the drawers open, one by one, rifling through cigars and paperclips and expensive-looking pens and a Rubik's cube that's half solved, but it's not in any of these.

Maybe I'm wrong.

Maybe it's in one of the other rooms. Maybe in that big set of shelves in the drawing room with the Christmas tree? I'm about to give up, leave, search another room, but then I see … a box. It's dark wood and sitting on his desk. My pulse speeds up a tiny bit and I reach for the latch, pull it up and open it.

Inside sits an old brass kaleidoscope, the kind I haven't seen in a very long time. The kind where you twist it and the sands shift, creating new and beautiful patterns.

But there, beneath it, is my phone.

A lightness moves through me—I found it! I really found it! I'm hit by relief, hope … and then a massive wave of fear.

What if Jonathan really did it? Really turned his profile to private and blocked me?

Frantically, I reach down, touch the screen and wait for it to glow to life.

But it's out of charge.

Great.

I've got a charger upstairs, I could go and get that, but then I see one. Right there by Oscar's laptop, threading down the back of the desk. With shaky hands, I plug it in, then stand shifting from foot to foot, waiting for that little white Apple logo to flash up at me and put me out of my misery.

It's just Instagram, I tell myself.

But it doesn't feel like *just Instagram*. It feels like this one moment will define me forever. Like it'll confirm whether I am in fact completely and utterly unlovable, whether even my soulmate could just delete me with the click of a button and walk away, without so much as a backward glance.

Finally, my phone turns on.

The screen lights up; it sees my face and unlocks. And then quickly, breathlessly, ignoring the notifications on the screen, I tap straight through to Instagram. My stomach churns as I navigate to Jonathan's profile.

As it loads the room around me gets fuzzy, and I'm holding my breath. *Please don't have done this. Please!*

But then … his profile loads, and it's all okay.

He hasn't blocked me and he hasn't posted anything new either. Not to his stories and not to his posts.

I flop down on the chair by the desk and start to laugh. *Of course* he wouldn't block me. Why would he?

So I move through to my texts now. Maybe he sent me a *Merry Christmas* text ...

Nothing.

An ache rings out beneath my ribs, that little string tugs. *It's okay*, I tell myself. *He will, just give it time*.

I tap on the one message that is there instead.

Daphne: *WORST BOXING DAY EVER! I SWEAR KENNY IS STILL HAUNTING ME. WHERE ARE YOU???* She's sent a photo showing a mangled tangle of bras from a change room.

I type back: *Home soon. Miss you!*

But I really should get out of here, so quickly I tap through to the VHC website, and go straight to the posting board, hungrily scrolling, scanning for Kenny's name. There's a post entitled PARIS METRO ATTACK and one called WOMAN INJURED AFTER BIZARRE ATTACK … But it looks like I'm in the clear.

So I'm about to log out before someone comes home and catches me in here. But then: *FUUUUUUCK.*

There, glowing back at me like the Grim Reaper's eyes beneath his hood, is exactly what I don't want to see.

URGENT LONDON MEET-UP. RE: KENNETH BRAWLEY

My vision gets wavy as I tap on it and speed-read the full post.

Title: URGENT LONDON MEET-UP. RE: KENNETH BRAWLEY

Location: London

Posted by: @Vampitup

Calling all London members. We are organising an urgent meet-up to discuss the death of Kenneth Brawley. I have important information to share from my police contact. There were indeed bite marks on the victim's neck, I saw the photos and took copies. While these could be attributed to foxes, I'd say it's worthy of further investigation. Especially since we might have a lead. There is CCTV footage of a black Aston Martin pulling up and parking near where the attack took place. I have more information that I will share with you on the night. BUT THIS IS IT. OUR MOMENT. Come and meet with us so we can strategise and find the vamp who did this! We will be meeting tomorrow night at the usual place in Carnaby Street at–

Oh god.

It's happening.

Every part of me gets ice cold.

And not just because of Oscar's black Aston Martin, which will soon be parked outside again. Not just because @Vampitup said he has more information and what more could there possibly be?

But because: a meeting.

Sally has a vested interest in this case because of me, she'll Zoom in for sure.

And what if Sally and Riley *both* join the meeting?

Then I truly will be fucked.

Because the information they each have about me individually is a little compromising but combined … it could be catastrophic. The room sways as I imagine how it might play out.

First, Sally would excitedly mention that one of our members worked with Kenny, that I knew him personally, he was my boss. Then everyone would ask her who I was. Sally would tell them that my name is Margot, and Riley would pipe up and say, 'Hang on, I've met her. You say she knew him personally? Interesting. She might be a suspect.

'Because her name isn't Margot, it's actually Aubrey. I always suspected she was hiding something, otherwise why lie? She was really cold to the touch, even in summer. Had pale skin and golden rings around her irises and I could barely feel her pulse.'

He'd ham it up, of course. He'd make me sound like a monster.

Everything would go downhill from there.

Sally would be so hurt that I'd lied to her about my name, her trust would evaporate. She'd start wondering about what else I'd lied about. She'd think about all the times I messaged her through the night, how I was empathetic to vampires, how I hated Kenny—HATED HIM—that I'd wished him dead and sent her a screenshot of exactly where he ran, the very night he died.

She'd tell the whole lot of them this.

They'd think I killed Kenny, for sure. Even I think I sound guilty.

I'm spiralling, I have to stop.

Because it's also possible that neither of them will join the meeting. That all this threat is in my head. But I can barely breathe and it feels like the entire world is closing in on me.

I sit forward and clench my eyes shut and bang down on the desk. It rattles and thuds from the weight of my fists—*ah shit, I forgot blood from the vein makes me stronger*.

And then, I hear the clink of something small and light falling to the floor.

What was that? Have I broken something?

I look down, under the desk.

And there, lying on the floor, is an old-looking box. It's small, like a match box, and wrapped in very old, faded wrapping paper. I pick it up; it feels light. I shake it, but there's no sound from within. The edges have been worn down by time, the paper now delicate and fading, has little cherubs and birds on it and I vaguely recognise the pattern. There's a tiny card attached to it, made from the same wrapping paper that's covering the box. I open the card.

Darling Oscar,

This is a box of my love. Never open it, just carry it with you knowing that I will always love you.

Yours forever, Aubrey.

45

The floor spins beneath me as I read the words again. I don't remember writing that card, but it's definitely my handwriting. The way I sign my name. And that wrapping paper … I recognise it. From Jonathan's vision: the presents under the tree.

My pulse speeds up to an almost human rate as I struggle to make sense of this. Because right now, as I hold this box, it feels like some distant part of me *does* remember. That I can feel that love. It's there, lodged beneath my ribs, winding me. As if through finding this, I've opened some portal to a memory I don't want to access. Panic floods my veins.

How do I shut it off?

I swallow hard; I don't like the picture forming in my mind. *Because … hang on … does this mean I … cheated on Jonathan?*

What does this mean?

Am I a bad person?

All this time I've wanted to know more about my human-self, been trying to get back to her, and now it turns out I was … a cheater?

No. That can't be right. If that were true, surely I'd know it?

Oscar must have seduced me the way he does so many women. He must have had me fall in love with him, turned me into this … monster … and then abandoned me …

That makes so much more sense.

Now his words come floating back: *I was just hungry and your front door was unlocked.*

Well, that was clearly a lie.

Screw him for lying to me about something so important.

But now, every part of me aches in a way I've ached many times over the past 150 years. I think of how miserable I've been. How lonely, how separate from the world. Always having to stay hidden, having to move through life alone year after year. Pushing down my hunger, hating myself and all that I was.

My breath is quick and I can feel my lower lip quivering, but I bite back the tears.

Because human-me must have really trusted him. For me, this would have been a token of true love, but I know Oscar.

To him, it would have been nothing more than a trophy. I was just another one of his 'girls'.

I look around the room, wondering how many other trophies of broken hearts, broken lives, he has hidden in here.

And then I think about the sound of that box dropping to the ground.

It dropped from *somewhere.*

I crouch down to find where it was hidden.

He probably keeps all his trophies together. Pulls them out and thinks about his conquests. *He's worse than any vampire in any book, any movie, any TV show.*

I peer into the darkness beneath the desk, and at the very back, I can just make out a small hidden shelf.

I squint at it, crawl deeper under the desk and put my little box back, then feel around to see what else is there. There's something large and flat; an envelope. I tug on it, feel its thickness between my fingertips; it's full of something—papers maybe. I pull it down and scramble back out from under the desk. And then, sitting on the floor in that darkened old library, I open the envelope and pull out the contents.

Pictures.

Lots and lots of photographs.

They must be of us, his victims. His 'proteges'.

I scatter them on the floor, scanning through them, not sure what to think. Some are black and white, some are colour. Some are square, some are rectangular—depending on the camera, I suppose. But as I leaf through them, looking for the others, others like me, other women he's done this to … there are none.

Every single photograph is of me.

The room stutters around me and I blink rapidly, trying to make sense of what I'm seeing. My gaze jumps from picture to picture.

It's like staring down at some weird time-lapse montage of myself. There's me in a 1940s blue military suit with cork-soled platforms. Me in a black 1950s dress nipped in at the waist, a beaded cashmere sweater around my shoulders. Me, smoking a cigarette and walking down Kingly Street past Bag O'Nails in the mid-60s—I'm in the white knee-high boots I loved and a high-necked, sleeveless black dress … I had accrued enough assets by then to be a lady of leisure if I so pleased, but instead, I was living in a small flat in The World's End. Blending in. Always blending in. Oh look, me marching on Grosvenor Square in 1968, protesting against the Vietnam War. I only narrowly escaped arrest. There's me in dark wash flares, me in shoulder pads, me in a slip dress, then low-rise jeans and high-rise jeans. Me, through the windows of a flat I had in Battersea, another one in Greenwich, a couple in small country villages that all blur into one another. Oh my god, there's a picture of me in Paris, when I danced at the Moulin Rouge in the mid-1920s. It's black and white and grainy, and looks like it was taken on one of those Leica cameras everyone lusted after when they first came out.

I lean in to study my never-changing face. The costumes change, as do the streets, the buildings, the windows, the make-up trends, but I never do. It's like the world kept on spinning for everyone else, but for me the clocks stood still. Even when I'm smiling, even when I'm faking it, I can see the sadness, the despair, in my eyes. And it's jarring to see myself so clearly, so objectively.

And *oh look*, there I am through a window, me and a cupcake with a single sad candle.

He was there while I was missing him. Watching me.

And then I find a newspaper article. It's one of the ones that came out after the attacks on Coventry Street.

Oscar knew about that.

He'd said he'd checked on me *now and then* over the years, that I'd always seemed … how did he put it? An echo of his voice comes floating back: *Sensible … controlled … safety conscious … quite boring*. But looking at these now, I'd say, *miserable beyond comprehension and always, utterly alone* might have been a better way to put it. And he let me stay that way. Maybe he *liked* me that way.

But there are so many pictures here. At least one for every year. This is a lot more than *now and then*.

And hang on … there are a couple of old bits of paper in there, scattered between the pictures. I reach for one. It's worn at the edges, and as I frown down at it, recognition tugs at me. *My bank details.* From that bank in Lombard Street where Hans helped me set up an account.

Why would Oscar have these?

HOW would Oscar have these?

I reach for the other piece of paper—thick stock, turned yellow and brittle with age—and glance at the cursive writing and blotted ink.

It reads: *Sir, I did as you asked, she will be fine. But I think I'm more hindrance than help now. I suggest I take my leave of her. Please advise.*

Hans.

My breath sticks in my throat as the pieces fall together: in comes a flash of me sitting in that garden, that first night I woke up.

I didn't just happen upon Hans in that garden. Oscar sent him to help me.

My gaze skips across the contents of the envelope, all laid out before me.

It's too much. I can't make sense of it.

Because it sounds insane, but it's almost as though he ... cares for me. If he didn't, why keep all this? Why keep that box of love? And so many photographs?

Is that possible? Can someone like him even feel love?

Don't even think about that, Aubrey. It would be a terrible thing if Oscar cared about you. Because it's Oscar we're talking about. OSCAR! He kills people for sport, he manipulates and lies and forces you to do things you don't want to do.

Besides, of course he doesn't care about me. If he did, he wouldn't have watched me suffer for all that time and never made himself known to me. That's cruel.

And then my gaze catches on one very specific picture in the middle of the mess. It's relatively recent, taken about four years ago. I'm outside Selfridges and I know exactly when it was taken because I'm standing with Daphne and it was my first week working there—I know this because she still had hair extensions from a modelling job and she hasn't had them since.

The floor beneath me ripples.

Realisation hits.

Oscar already knew about Daphne before I went to Serpentine with her that night. And now that I think about it, it does seem somewhat coincidental that Daphne would be a member of a private members' club that my vampire-maker owns, doesn't it? It seems more likely that he sought her out and gave her membership and told her to remember it came from one of her sugar daddies instead.

He's been using her to get information about me …

I feel sick. Like my whole life has been a farce.

Like I've been play-acting for an audience I didn't even know I had.

And then I realise, if Oscar hadn't seen me that night at the club with Daphne, if he hadn't been told to make sure I wasn't a weak link, if he hadn't decided I was a risk, and might get us all found out, then I'd *still* be all alone. I still wouldn't know who turned me. Or how I died. I'd still be yearning for him.

I want to be angry about that. I should be angry. But actually, I'm just so sad.

What am I meant to do with all this?

Hang on, if he's been watching me, and he's been talking to Daphne all this time, does he know about Jonathan? *He can't know. He'd have used it against me by now.*

The sound of tyres on gravel cuts through the wind.

Someone is home.

My hands shake as I put the pictures back into the envelope, crawl under the desk and put them back on the secret shelf at the back, with the box of love. My love. Then I put my phone back where I found it in that box under the kaleidoscope, and I run out into the hallway, under the staircase and back into the entrance hall.

I can see headlights shining in through the windows on either side of the front door as I run upstairs. It's as I get to the top that the front door opens. I peek over the banister.

It's Oscar.

I tiptoe back into my bedroom. As I close my bedroom door, the look in Oscar's eyes the night he saved me from Felix flickers in my mind. The tenderness he showed me. And after all that I found tonight, that makes sense.

But nothing else does.

I almost wish he was just like the vampire villains on TV. Pure evil. No soul. That he really had just abandoned me completely, never sent me Hans, never checked on me. It would be simpler. But he's more complex than that. There are hidden depths, and now I don't know what to think—how good or bad is he? But worse than not knowing what to think, now I'm feeling things I don't want to feel. It's like everything I found tonight has reopened Pandora's box and I need to slam it shut again.

I just don't know how.

46

I wake up breathless. *What did I do?*

Because last night I fed on a man. Willingly. I can still smell his deodorant in my hair, taste the whisky of his blood on my tongue. *He wasn't a good man though, and I didn't kill him,* I tell myself. But still, *I liked it*. A lot. *And* I loved Oscar once. *And* I cheated on Jonathan.

Argh.

I pull the covers over my head and clench my eyes shut to make it all go away, but now all I can see is: URGENT LONDON MEET-UP. RE: KENNETH BRAWLEY … It's flashing in neon lights in my mind.

They'll be meeting tonight.

I throw the covers off and go over to the bathroom to check the mark on my neck.

It's gone. Finally healed. One good thing.

But Oscar's necklace is still there on the dressing table. And so is the memory of everything I found last night. I don't want it. Don't want whatever feeling reignited inside me as I held that little box. But it doesn't matter what I want, it's there now. A little ember burning deep inside me that I need to stamp out before it turns into anything bigger.

I turn on the water and splash my face, thinking: *Snap the hell out of it. Just forget.*

Because this is just like when Eric got amnesia in *True Blood* season four, and for a moment it looked like he was cute and not evil at all. It's confusing, but it's not real. Jonathan is real. And that's who I love. Things might not be great between us right now, but he's my soulmate, we'll get through it.

I pull open the bedroom door and hear voices downstairs. I move into the hallway and over to the banister, then look down. Oscar, Carmilla and Rupert are standing just outside the open front door, chatting. There's something on the ground near Rupert, I can just see the edge of it—grey, scalloped.

Umm … is that a suitcase?

I quickly pull on my robe and slippers and go downstairs to see what's going on. But as I step into the grey dusk light, I see Oscar. As he looks up at me my breath catches and I look away; I focus on Carmilla and Rupert instead.

What are they doing?

They're standing by Carmilla's black BMW and … *oh no.* It *was* a suitcase that I saw. Two suitcases, in fact, and they're putting them into the boot. I plaster on the counter-smile I use at work and rush over to them.

'Are you going somewhere?' I ask, struggling to hide the panic in my voice. Because I don't want to be left alone with *him.*

'Back to London, to see if Felix has been at his place,' Carmilla says.

NO. PLEASE NO.

'But we'll be back for New Year's,' Rupert adds. 'You did good last night, Baby-V,' he tells me with a wink.

I watch helplessly as they both get into the car and the engine turns over. As I watch them drive away, their red taillights flaring in the dusk light, Oscar is right there beside me, the air charged between us. My head is full of static; I can't think straight. I don't know what to say to him. It's like there's this enormous elephant in the room now, so many questions I want to ask, but how will I explain knowing about those photographs? He won't be pleased that I went through his study. What do I say?

But then he speaks first. 'Right, well, have a good night, Aubrey. I have plans but we'll start lessons again tomorrow. You can watch a film in the winter drawing room if you get bored. The remotes are all there.' He looks at me the same way he's always looked at me, with no hint that he's been secretly stalking me for 150 years.

I sit in the drawing room for a while, watching the fire crackle and the Christmas tree lights flicker, expecting Oscar to come out of his study looking annoyed and saying something cruel or sarcastic at any moment, and wondering how I might broach things.

I have to ask him somehow.

But he doesn't emerge. And every time I go to check, his library door is still closed.

I've been trying to find a movie to watch, but I can't focus. How does one watch a movie when there is so much drama going on in their own life? Jonathan. Oscar. And tonight is the VHC meet-up.

I let out a big breath, press pause and look out of the misted-up windows. It's not raining, not snowing.

I'll go for a walk. Clear my head. That will help.

The air is icy and smells of pine needles and moss, and I hear the faint buzz of insects as I look around. It's like stepping into a melancholic postcard: bare trees, probably even older than me, set against a dark and starry sky. I look to the right, but memories of Felix lie that way. Instead, I go left, around the side of the house, to the garden I've only seen through the windows. In the distance, I can see the silhouettes of trees and what looks like a guest cottage.

But as I walk through the manicured garden with its well-trimmed lawns and immaculately shaped hedges in huge, ornate pots, beneath a sky so dark I can see every single star, and a moon that for the longest time was my only confidante, everything is so beautiful, beautiful in a way I don't recall it being before. Like I'm seeing it for the very first time.

Is this because of the blood I've been drinking?

Or is it because I know I can die now? That all this could disappear? And everything is always most beautiful when you know you can lose it—cities, centuries, people. Is it because I finally have what humans have: the poetry of a ticking clock and moments that pass and can never be retrieved, the trimmings of mortality?

I can feel that changing me in ways I didn't expect.

I could feel it last night with Red Flannel Jeff. If I hadn't known that I could die—that the consequences, whatever they might be, could end—I would have rushed out of that pub, too scared to see where it led. But it seems there is a lightness, a boldness that comes with mortality. I finally understand what carpe diem means, why humans say *life is short* and then do something reckless. It's the ultimate freedom.

But I fear this shift inside me is from something else entirely. Someone else.

Oscar.

Because I can deny it as much as I want, force myself not to feel whatever it is that sparked within me last night, but something profound changed when I found those pictures and my box of love.

It was as if I'd been looking into that kaleidoscope on Oscar's desk my whole life, certain that the pattern I was seeing was the only pattern, the right one. With one little click, it all shifted. The sands stayed the same but a new pattern emerged. And everything was different.

Suddenly, I hadn't spent 150 years all alone, abandoned, unlovable. Suddenly Oscar was there all along, helping me, albeit from a distance.

And I think that's what's confusing my heart.

Because Oscar is everything I loathe. He's cruel and a killer and manipulative and he lies. He's as close to pure evil as I've ever met.

But also, he knows me. All of me.

He knew me as a human, and he's watched me the whole time that I've been a vampire. He's seen me at my saddest, when I wasn't performing for the world; he knows my deepest, darkest, most shameful parts, and to him they aren't shameful at all. There's something healing in that.

That's what I've always dreamed of.

For someone to know me—all of me—and love me anyway.

I just don't want it to be *him*.

Because while Jonathan could tether me to my humanity, my light, keep me good, Oscar could only take me deeper into the darkness.

Besides, could I really call whatever it is he feels for me love? Or is it merely a sense of ownership? Possession? Why am I even allowing myself to think these things? It can't lead anywhere good.

Now I'm standing by a bed of roses, the same ones as those near the greenhouse. Winter roses, the kind which can survive in snow when every other flower might wilt. They're the same ones I saw in my room and in the entry hall. I go over to them, wondering what this garden looks like in spring, when all the other flowers are out, and none of the trees are bare. I bend down to one of the roses, smelling it. It's so rich and deep and sweet; like roses used to smell before genetic modification created the bland versions you get in supermarkets.

The beds look well tended. I glance across at the bed beside the roses, and there are tiny little plants in there, like they've only just been sown. The earthy scent of mulch in the air. Like someone has been gardening despite the ill weather.

Oh god.

Is this where Oscar buried Felix?

I step away from the roses and head back to the house, quickly.

When I walk inside, the library door is still closed, so I go upstairs. I go over to the bookshelf and pull out a copy of *Wuthering Heights*—it's dusty, like it hasn't been read in years—then I lie down and read.

But half an hour later, I'm barely ten pages in. I've been reading and re-reading the same line fifty times and *this is ridiculous*.

I put the book down, grab my eye mask and earplugs and try to sleep, even though it's far too early.

I toss and I turn.

After about an hour of that, I let out a big breath and sit up and think: *I'm going to ask. About all of it.*

I have to.

So I pull on my dressing gown and slippers and edge open my bedroom door. A faint murmur floats across the entrance hall—from the floor above the left-hand staircase. I tiptoe down the stairs and up the ones on the other side of the foyer, my heart a little quicker than usual in my chest. I've never been up here before. I look around and see light spilling out of a room towards the end of the hallway.

I move towards it. That must be where he is.

I'm just going to knock, have a quick chat, and ask him.

I'm almost at his door when I hear a slight moan.

I creep forward until I'm standing at the door. It's ajar, and I can just see inside.

Oscar is on his bed, with two women. When did they get here? While I was on my walk?

One of them is sitting against pillows, giggling. The other lies with her head just off the end of the end of the bed, her light brown hair flowing down to the floor. Her legs are splayed, Oscar's face between them. Her eyes are clenched shut, her little button nose scrunched up as she moans ...

Is he hurting her?

But then he lifts his face and there's no blood on it.

Right. He's just having sex with them.

I roll my eyes—*of course he is*.

And I almost laugh at the absurdity of it all. Me, standing in this hallway, full of questions, and him in there not giving a shit.

How can I be looking for answers from *him*?

A man—a vampire—who has committed his entire eternity to such pointless pursuits? No real love. No real connection. No meaning at all, just pure hedonism. Selfishness.

While I've been tying myself up in knots, desperately needing some deep answer to make it all make sense, he's been happily fucking away. Oblivious. Unconcerned. Standing here, it hits me that it really doesn't matter why I loved him once, or if he cared for me too. Or even if he cares for me still, in some strange little way.

He left me. Let me suffer alone.

If it was love—real love—he would never have done that.

I'm hit by a familiar ache. It acts as a warning of all the pain that could be to come.

And I realise I have a choice to make. Either I ask my questions, and risk reopening the wound, deepening it, risk feeling whatever I felt for him before all over again—because

I know it's there, simmering deep inside me even now, threatening all I am—or I let it go.

And what is there to gain, really? Aside from satisfying my curiosity. I don't want his affections, and even if he answered truthfully this time, am I sure I want to know what he could tell me? What if it's horrible? Makes everything even more confusing? He only knew the version of me who cheated; not the version I was before. The good version. Only Jonathan can take me back to her.

So, as I stand, frozen to the spot in the darkened hallway, I make a decision.

I will not ask questions. I will pretend I know nothing.

I step back, creep over to the staircase and down to the ground floor.

But … Oscar is otherwise indisposed, and his office is right there, and my phone is there too. And the VHC had their meet-up tonight.

As scared as I am to check, I need to know.

If I go to log on and am blocked, I'll know for sure that I am now officially suspect number one.

I rush through to the office, knowing I must be quick, because Oscar is here this time, and his hearing is better than a canine's.

My phone is still right there in the kaleidoscope box, so I grab it and plug it into his charger, waiting for it to turn on.

As soon as it flashes to life, I frantically move through to the VHC website and … I log in.

It works. I'm in! A calm comes over me as I scan for an update. There's nothing new. No new messages either.

I let out a big breath and tap through to my text messages. Still nothing from Jonathan. The space beneath my ribs shrivels. I really thought I'd hear from him by now. I let out a big breath and tap through to his Instagram page, but there's nothing new there. And then I tap through to Olivia's page.

Just in case.

She's posted one new story.

I tap on it, and watch as it loads. And then comes utter doom. Because it's a picture of her and Jonathan together on his sofa. Jonathan looks happy, there's a light in his eyes. And the caption reads: *The future has never looked this bright! Bring on the new year!*

My throat tightens up and every part of me hurts.

And then, *beep*.

My phone pings with a message. The sound bounces off the walls, echoing loudly in the silence of the study.

My ears roar. My heart flares.

I turn and stare at the door, listening for footsteps, the whoosh of Oscar coming down here to check what the hell is going on … but nothing comes. He's too busy. I turn my phone to silent and, as I do, I see the preview on the screen.

Es: *Hey, hope this doesn't wake you but something happened at work this evening and I can't sleep. Some guy came in and asked about you. Seemed kind of creepy* …

I quickly tap on it and read the rest: *Tall, dark hair, shitty skin? Do you know him? Xxxxx*

The walls sway. The earth spins a little sideways.

FUUUUUUUUCK.

Riley. That sounds exactly like Riley.

Which means I was right. I'm not paranoid. He absolutely *does* suspect me. Why else would he go and ask my blood connection about me? On the very same night as the VHC meet-up? He wanted to present as much information as he could about me. It wasn't enough that I had cold hands, golden rings around my irises, a weak heartbeat, lied about my name and worked with Kenny … he wanted to tell the group about my friend the phlebotomist. Which really does clinch the deal. Even without what Sally knows.

And this means he probably *was* at Borough Market looking for me. That he probably did figure out my forwarding address was London Bridge Post Office. A flash of him showing that blond guy by the cranberries something on his phone. Was he showing him that picture of me with my licence? Asking if they had seen me?

But hang on, if that's what happened, then why hasn't the VHC blocked me? Kicked me off the site?

Did they not believe him?

Or … are they planning something?

Now my breath speeds up. If he knows about Es, and he knows whereabouts I live, how much more does he know about me?

And what did Es tell him?

Fuck.

I quickly text her back: *He's just some creep who likes me. What did you tell him?*

The walls creak with the wind and my insides clench. I need to get out of here. I stand up, put my phone back in that wooden box, and tiptoe out the door, through the entrance hall and quickly back upstairs to my room.

I lie down, put on my eye mask, put in my earplugs and do everything I can not to think about that message or Riley looking for me or … any of it. I grasp for images of Cat and Daphne and Es and Jonathan and my sofa and that window I loved to look out of instead. But with each moment that ticks by, it feels like the life I knew is crumbling around me, like the more I grab for it, the more it disintegrates.

All I can think about as I lie here is that picture of Olivia and Jonathan together. And how his life is going on without me. There are new year's plans being made that I'm not a part of. While I'm here. Doing all this. For the first time since the break-up, I think: *Maybe I should let him go. Maybe we aren't going to make it after all.*

Because he hasn't texted me even once.

He looked happy, hopeful in that photograph with her.

Isn't that what you do when you love someone? Set them free? Do what's best for them? How am I best for anyone?

Then my mind moves back to Riley. How he went into Es's work, looking for me. He's out of control.

And the worst part is Oscar could help me with that, but his version of 'help' would be to kill Riley, and as much as he's not my favourite human, he's still a human. Even if there was another way, it would come at a steep cost. Oscar would use it against me, as proof of my erraticism, and who knows how long he'd want to keep tabs on me after that? I can't let that happen. Whatever that life looks like when I get back to it, at least it will be mine. With my choices.

So as the sounds of laughter and pleasure float through the walls, echoing in emptiness, I tell myself I'll deal with this alone. The way I always have. Then I cover my ears and force myself to go to sleep.

The sun is still high in the sky when the sound of the peacocks rings out. I know that without even taking off my eye mask. I can tell because my head is throbbing and I'm dizzy and tired and my thoughts feel like decades-old molasses. In comes a flash of Olivia and Jonathan together. I bury my face in the pillow.

And then the doorbell rings—a loud, shrill sound.

I pull off my eye mask, take out my earplugs and then lie there, squinting at the light leaking in through the middle of the curtains thinking: *It must be one of the women Oscar has been seducing, popping past for a daytime visit. Serves him right.*

The doorbell rings again.

A moment later, I hear footsteps.

Then chatter.

I lie in bed, my head aching, willing them to go away. But then, hang on, the voices sound male.

And serious.

I sit up.

Something is wrong.

I pull on my robe and slippers, gently open my door and

creep over to the banister, then look downstairs into the grand entrance hall.

Oscar is up, wearing jeans and a white shirt, sunglasses on, looking like some sort of doomed romantic rock-and-roll dream, and there are two men down there with him. Men in uniform.

The police.

The police are here.

The world dissolves into soup around me.

Why are they here?

Is it about Emma?

Or is it about Red Flannel Jeff?

Ah fuck. I bet that's it. It's far more likely that I'd get caught than Oscar. That's just how my life goes.

Red Flannel Jeff must have done what I said, gone in and confessed, and then … remembered me. What I did to him. Is that it? Or did the taxi driver figure something out? Was there still blood on me? Or did someone film me? Those people outside the car, did they see something?

How could I have been so reckless?

'Aubrey, darling,' comes Oscar's voice as he looks up at me calmly. Our eyes meet and I'm thinking, *Yours forever, Aubrey*, then of those pictures of me in his office, then of Emma's body under the sofa, then those women he was in bed with last night. 'Would you put on some clothes and come down here? The police have some questions.'

My throat tightens. My vision blurs for a moment.

I nod. 'I'll just get dressed.' Then I retreat to my room and fling open my wardrobe, looking through the clothes I brought with me.

I pull on a demure-looking cream dress, a no-sir-I'd-never-eat-someone dress, rinse my mouth out with mouthwash and run a brush through my hair. I slip on a cardigan and some thick socks, and as I go downstairs I think: *Or maybe this is about Kenny?*

Maybe the police are following up on all the black Aston Martin owners. Maybe there's something else Oscar left linking me to Kenny, something I don't know about?

But no matter what the answer, none of it is good.

As I go downstairs, I realise how far into the darkness I've fallen. The three dead bodies, Riley looking for me, the people we've fed off … how much I enjoyed Red Flannel Jeff. This is exactly like every vampire book and TV show and movie I've ever watched. Exactly who I was never going to be … Maybe I deserve this.

By the time I get to the door of the sitting room, and take a deep breath before entering, I'm thinking: *I'm done for*. I'm imagining myself being put in the back of a paddy wagon. Trying to explain why I can't eat their prison food … I mean, Oscar won't go down for it, will he? He'll do whatever he needs to slither out of it. He'll probably just move somewhere dark, like that nickel town that gets almost no sunshine—Norilsk, in Russia—and wait till it passes. It'll be me who takes the fall.

Unless he helps me. And I loathe that I have to rely on him for that.

I smile as I walk into the room.

The police are perched on a lemon-yellow sofa. Oscar is on the other sofa, his sunglasses still on, and there is a pot of tea, some cups and a plate of biscuits on the coffee table.

'Big night last night?' one of the officers asks with a cheery grin, nodding at Oscar's sunglasses, and probably the fact that according to the grandfather clock in the corner of this room it is one pm, and we've clearly just woken up.

He's around thirty-five with pale blond hair, pink cheeks and a northern accent just like Jonathan's. And now I'm thinking of that post of him and Olivia last night again. My insides shrivel, the world takes on a greyish hue, and I suspect I have officially entered the depression stage of grief.

'Yes, it's that time of year, I'm afraid,' Oscar says as I sit down next to him.

'I hear you.' Cheery Cop smiles as he bites into a biscuit. The other one, dark-haired, more serious, is frowning and pulling out his pad and a pen. I can hear both their hearts beating. Both are calm.

'So,' starts the serious one, who isn't eating any biscuits, 'tell us about the party you had here that Felix Anderson came to.'

Felix. This is about Felix.

Relief flows through me—this has nothing to do with me—but it's short-lived. Because now I'm thinking about that garden bed. About how I bet Felix is buried in there. Surely the police are well versed in this sort of thing. What if they notice that the beds are newly dug up? What if they look closer? Instinctively, I look out the window to check if I can see the bed from here, and instead see one of the peacocks wandering around.

'I do it every year,' Oscar says, lifting his sunglasses onto his head and looking concerned. 'It's a nice thing for the people of the town, brings us all together. Gives us a reason to dress up.'

'But Felix is from London, not here?'

'That's right, he's a dear friend,' Oscar says, frowning. 'You said you were investigating his whereabouts, but what exactly do you think happened to him? Because he seemed fine. Didn't he, darling?' he asks me, reaching for my hand.

I want to pull my hand away, Oscar is the reason I'm in this situation, everything was fine-ish before he appeared. But he holds my hand still.

'Yes, in very good spirits,' I say, doing my best to play along.

'Strange situation,' says Serious Cop as his pen scrawls across the page, and the other one takes a big slurp of tea. 'He hasn't been seen since the night of your party. Not on CCTV at the train station. Nothing.'

'Right, right,' Oscar says. 'I think he would have driven, though. I can't be certain, but Felix doesn't like public transport.'

'Hmm,' says Serious Cop, his mouth distorting, like maybe he's chewing on his cheek. He turns to me now. 'So how did you know him?' he asks me.

A flash of his teeth sinking into my neck. The cold air on my legs. Then Oscar, with Felix's head in his hand … dripping blood.

'I only met him that night,' I say with a small, innocent smile. 'But he seemed nice.'

'And you're from London too?' he asks me.

'Mmhmm,' I say. *Please don't ask where I work. Please don't look it up. Please don't be too interested.*

'Look,' Oscar says, letting go of my hand and leaning in towards them like he's about to tell them a secret, his legs splayed and his elbows on his knees. 'I don't want to speak out of school, but Felix is known for going off on … let's call them benders. Sometimes he's gone for a couple of weeks,' Oscar says. 'You should probably talk to his girlfriend, Carmilla. She'll tell you all about it.'

Something shifts in the policeman's energy. 'Yes, she did say that, when she came in.'

Carmilla went to the police.

'But then she got extra worried because while it looked like maybe he'd gone somewhere—he'd packed a bag and taken his passport, and his car was gone too—he hadn't taken his toothbrush or his phone charger. She said that he was a meticulous packer and had never forgotten those things before.'

Now something almost imperceptible in Oscar's energy shifts too.

That's where Oscar went on Boxing Day night. He wasn't at the club, he went to Felix's place. Of course, he would have had Felix's keys from his body. He must have packed a bag with his passport to make it look like he'd gone somewhere.

I sit dead still, trying to control my expression; I'm going for a calm smile.

Cheery Cop wipes the sugar from the biscuit on his trousers and Serious Cop jots down a few more notes.

'Well, that's it for now,' Serious Cop says. 'Thank you for your time. But if you hear from him, please do let us know.'

'Of course,' Oscar says, and we all stand up. Oscar stands close to me, his hand on my lower back.

We go outside to see them off. Their car is parked right by the entrance. And Oscar's Aston Martin is right there beside it, and I'm staring at them, willing them not to look at it, not to notice a dent or something and link any of us to Kenny. Because if that happens, I just know they'll end up buried next to Felix. And then I'll be five bodies deep.

'Okay, you have a nice rest of your day,' Serious Cop says and then they both get into the car.

Oscar smiles as we watch it drive off, but as soon as they're through the gate the smile is gone. 'Fucking Carmilla,' he says. Then he turns to me. 'Get some sleep, I'll see you later on.'

48

By the time the sky is jet black outside, I'm in the winter drawing room again, rose-coloured tears blurring *Dirty Dancing*, which is playing on the TV. I'm at the end when they're doing their final dance. '(I've Had) The Time of My Life' is playing and I keep thinking about the night Jonathan and I went to see this, and how happy we were, how close I was to everything I wanted. Jennifer Grey nods at Patrick Swayze, and she runs and jumps, and he holds her in that lift.

I let out a small sob, reach for a tissue beside the sofa and dab my eyes.

'What's wrong with you?' comes Oscar's voice and I turn to look at him. He's standing there in jeans and a black jumper. He looks at the TV screen and I press pause and he comes and sits down next to me.

'Nothing,' I say. I'd give anything to be able to talk to someone about this, but Oscar wouldn't understand.

So instead, I look at him with sad eyes and try to smile, but then something softens behind his.

'Come on, it's not so bad,' he says gently. 'So, are you ready for our next lesson?'

I shrug. 'Sure,' I say. *Why not.*

He turns to face me on the sofa, bending one knee. I do the same. Our eyes meet and I think of all those pictures and that box and how I loved him and how he was having sex with two other women last night. I look away.

'You asked about siphoning those images,' he says. I look back at him. 'How about I teach you that?'

'Okay,' I say, wary. Because why is he being nice? It's almost like he's trying to make me feel better.

'In the absence of anyone else, you can practise on me,' he says. 'But I can control what I give you access to, Aubrey, so don't try anything on.'

I give a half laugh. 'I wouldn't even want to see into the darkest corners of your mind,' I say.

'Wise woman,' he says, reaching out with his big hands and taking mine. 'Close your eyes.'

And I'm a little scared. It takes trust to close your eyes with someone.

But he's watching, so my eyelids flutter shut.

'First,' he says, in a voice so seductive I wonder if he's trying to hypnotise me, 'imagine there are a thousand holes poking into you, and through each one of these holes you are leaking light.'

I nod and frown. I can imagine it. Most of my life feels like that. Like I'm drained and leaking into the world.

'Pull all that light back inside of you and close those holes up. That light needs to stay within you.'

I nod again and actively try to pull back the streams of light then close the holes. I can see it in my mind's eyes. Feel it, too.

'That's your life force, Aubrey. It should feel like heat. You generate a little of your own, but you replenish it every time you feed,' he explains. 'Now, gather it in your solar plexus, hold it there, and imagine your mind as a blank screen.'

I focus and do as he says, his hands still holding mine. But now there's a warmth, an energy moving between us, and it's disconcerting. What am I feeling?

My eyes flick open. He's watching me.

'Keep your eyes closed, Aubrey.'

I close them again and his hands are still on mine but the longer he holds them the more I feel things I don't want to feel. My breath is caught somewhere between my lungs and my mouth.

'Empty your mind. You need to *want* to see something. That's the key. You have to truly desire it.'

I nod. Focus.

'That's your biggest problem, you're always turning away from your desire, your hunger. Don't.'

And then, from somewhere, images stream in. They're colourful and there's sound too. *I can hear laughter and footsteps and see a ball. He's in the ballroom of this house looking out at a crowd of people. On the table behind him are rows and rows of dark green bottles. I zoom in on the labels: Vin Mariani … That coca wine that used to have cocaine in it. I haven't seen those in over a hundred years. Oscar is looking around, frowning—*

He inhales sharply and lets go of my hands. 'Can't let you probe around too much,' he jokes.

But I'm filled with this feeling of accomplishment. I did it. I did it on purpose. For the first time ever.

'I saw something,' I say, nodding. 'It was here, there was a ball, but I could tell from the hair and make-up it was a long time ago.'

'Good,' he says.

And this is the first time since that night when he saved me from Felix that I've felt good with him again. As I look at his face, I find myself searching for the parts of him I must have loved.

'Thank you for saving me from Felix,' I say.

He frowns, pain comes over his face. 'Don't even mention it. What he did was inexcusable. Grotesque. He deserved everything he got.' And then he looks to the frozen image on the screen.

'We could do that lift, you know. Maybe that's the way to make you actually like being a vampire.' He raises his eyebrows.

'Really?' I ask, with a small laugh. Is he joking? Is this a trap?

'Sure, come, I'll show you.'

I put on some shoes and follow him to the garden. We walk onto the lawn, and then he stops and says. 'Okay, you ready?'

I smile, shrug.

He walks a little further then turns back to me.

'Go for it. I'll catch you,' he says, his fingers moving in anticipation.

'Are you sure?' I ask.

'Fuck, Aubrey, stop thinking so hard. Just live.'

'Okay,' I say. I run at him, fast, but the moment before I get to him I panic. I stop.

His hands are already on my hips, he's already lifting me a bit, but he puts me down. 'What's the problem?' he asks. 'Don't you trust me?' He looks almost hurt.

'I'll try again,' I say.

I walk back to my starting position, my heart a little quicker than normal. I take a deep breath and run. And I don't want to jump, I really don't … but I do it anyway. With everything I have, I leap. His hands are on my hipbones, and he holds me overhead and I'm high above and can see everything. I start to laugh, my arms out to the sides, and this must be it, this must be what I fell in love with as a human, this side of Oscar.

He lowers me down and my feet hit the ground.

Our eyes meet and *zap*.

Something stronger than I've ever felt—lightning striking—moves between us. It hits me square in the chest and I can see it hits him too. He gasps for breath, and his face softens. But then just as quickly, it's gone. He looks away, clenches his jaw.

'Okay, enough of that,' he says, stepping away from me. 'We still have more to do tonight. He starts walking and all I can do is follow him, but what the hell was that? Was it similar to the other night when I found that box? Those pictures? That feeling I got?

'Where are we going?' I ask.

We're moving towards the garden bed where I'm pretty sure Felix is buried. But we pass it and now we're heading to that little cottage I noticed the other night. I'm two steps behind him.

'What are you going to teach me?' I ask. Because why is he suddenly being cold again? So quiet. What did I do wrong?

He reaches for a key and opens the door to the cottage then turns to me and says, 'Come inside.'

49

As soon as I'm inside, he locks the door.

'What is this place?' I ask as my gaze shifts from one part of the little cottage to another. There is no furniture. No kitchen. No fridge. It's a bare carcass of a building. The windows are covered in newspaper. Then there is the smell, like straw or earth or an animal. 'What are we doing here?'

I look over at him and he's watching me, but the kindness I saw in the drawing room, or just a moment ago in the garden, is gone. Now he's cruel Oscar again. It makes my stomach twist.

'You're strong enough, you just showed me that. It's time for you to learn to control your prey.'

'You mean hypnotise?' I ask, struggling to keep up with him.

'Yes,' he says. 'Rupert mentioned you were worried about that. In my experience, if a vampire is fed and still has trouble with their power, it is a question of will.'

I hear a sound on the other side of a wall, and look over to it. And there, wandering in from an adjoining room, is something big and orange and black.

My breath catches … a tiger.

A TIGER.

I stare at it, the room around me blurring, as I try to make sense of what's going on. I look back to Oscar but he's already closed himself off in a small room to my left. Through a Perspex door with a small hole in it, I can hear him when he says, 'Aubrey, meet Tina.'

You've got to be fucking kidding me.

I stare into the animal's eyes—they're amber, like mine—trying to gauge how much danger I'm in. Her pupils are still small, so at least she's not angry. That's good. I look around for a weapon, because there's no damned way I can hypnotise her, I can't even hypnotise humans half the time. But I don't see a weapon. No pots, pans, light fixtures. Instead, as I look up, I see a bloodied, charcoal piece of fabric. My heart thuds against my ribs in a way it never does. *Was that Felix's jacket? Did Oscar bring his body here first and then bury what was left in the garden?*

'Get me out of here,' I say to Oscar, under my breath, not looking away from the animal.

'Like I was saying, in my experience,' comes Oscar's voice from behind the safety of the Perspex, 'it's usually a question of will. And the best way to access will is through fear.'

'What do you want me to do?' I ask, my voice shaking now. Because I think he's actually serious. And I could die here. This tiger could rip my head off. Like Oscar did to Felix. He knows this and yet he's put me in here.

A hot fury rises within me. *First he pretends to be kind with that bullshit* Dirty Dancing *move and then he does this. I am simply his plaything.*

'I want you to hypnotise the cat,' Oscar says, nonchalant.

'This is not a cat. This is a tiger,' I say, my voice small and desperate. I turn around and pull on the door, even though I know it's locked, but it doesn't budge. I turn back to the animal, my breath stuck in my lungs. It moves before me carefully, eyeing me. Placing its feet carefully as it assesses me.

'Hypnotise it to do what?' I spit out.

'To lie down. Sit,' comes Oscar's low voice. 'She doesn't listen to anyone but me, so if you can get her not to attack you, you will have passed the test.'

My vision gets wavy.

'Oscar, this isn't funny,' I say, as I start to shake. Because I can see the animal's teeth now, and they look dirty. I know I've always wanted to die, but not like this, not when it wasn't my choice. And certainly not for Oscar's amusement.

'You're a psychopath,' I seethe as I stare at the tiger. 'Sit,' I say, trying to calm my voice, trying to access the soothing quality I know I need. But I'm terrified, paralysed in place, and it comes out crackly.

The tiger takes another step towards me and it's crouching down now …

'Sit,' I try again, my heart beating in my throat and my breath is so shallow I feel like I might pass out.

I take a step backwards, my back hits the door. Tina crouches a little lower; she's about to pounce.

'Don't be scared, Aubrey,' Oscar's voice croons. 'Use your anger, harness it.'

Arsehole.

I stare at the tiger, eye to eye, and in the most velvety voice I can muster, I manage to say, 'Tina, sit.'

I watch as the tiger's eyes glaze over. She … sits.

She fucking sits!

I am filled with joy, elation. *I did it. I did it. I won. Fuck Oscar and his mind games. I did it!*

I look towards him, and he's grinning at me. But then something shifts in the animal's stance, and I look back. So quickly, so fluidly that I barely register what's happening, she lunges at me. Like she has springs in her joints.

I could fight. I could scream. But … I don't.

That split second stretches like it's in slow motion and all I can think about is my blank phone screen, how Jonathan has moved on, and how without him there's nothing to hold me in the light. I can feel myself slipping into the darkness, becoming a monster. And my sire, who I longed for, is cruel and has put me in this room for his amusement. The world isn't that great anyway; I've seen the moon enough times, thanks. *There is nothing to live for. Nothing to hope for. Nobody will miss me, not really.*

I don't fight it. I clench my eyes shut. Wait for impact. Wait for the inevitable oblivion like I have so many times before.

This is it.

Finally.

But first comes a swooping noise, then the bang of a door closing, then big arms holding me. My eyes flick open.

Oscar's face is right there, his eyes stare into mine, his arms hold onto me. I can't read what's in his eyes but it's violent and furious and hurt all at once.

He reaches for my face, and I'm not sure if he's going to stroke it or rip it off, so I flinch, pull away, my eyes still on his. He frowns, like he's wounded.

'I'm not going to hurt you, Aubrey, I'd never do that,' he says, his voice a whisper. His eyes bore into mine.

Which is fucking rich. He just put me in a room with a tiger. I sit up, looking behind him for the cat. The door to the adjoining room is closed now. She must be in there. My breath is quick as I stare him down. I'm shaking. I don't know what's happening. Why he saved me when he clearly hates me in some way.

'Why didn't you fight to live?' he asks, his voice shaking. 'You just stood there.'

As I look at him, all I can think about is how many times I've tried to die. And why.

'I've *never* fought to live,' I whisper, looking straight at him. 'I want to die because of what you made me. Because I hate myself and I don't trust myself. And because you are cruel and you do things like *this* to me. I yearned for you, Oscar, for years. But every kindness you show me is a lie.'

And for a splinter of a moment, it feels like he understands, like he's moved. But then his eyes are hard and blank again. He just walks over to the door and unlocks it and says, 'You can go now.'

I think of those photographs I found and that box of love and 150 years of yearning for him and the tiger in the next room and I whisper, 'Fuck you.'

Then on shaky legs, I leave the cottage. The moment I hear the door close, I run. From him. From that tiger. But mainly, from me. From whatever part of me ever loved someone like him.

It's starting to snow; tiny flakes hit my nose, my forehead. I look behind me but he's not coming. I get inside and take the stairs two at a time, my lungs heaving, my heart bruised and then *whoooosh* he moves past me.

When I get to the top he's already there.

He grabs me by the throat and my back hits the wall and his face is so close to mine. I can feel a heat rising within me and all I can hear is static. He's got me trapped, is staring me down. His pupils are huge, the gold around them flaming like molten lava, and he's letting out short, sharp breaths. I've never seen him this angry, not even that night with Felix. All the softness in his eyes from earlier tonight is gone again, like it's been leached out. Like I imagined it all along, like it was never there. And so much for never hurting me.

'Let me go,' I say. But he just holds me still and now every part of me flames. 'Let me go!' I yell, my eyes on his, and I don't look away, not for a moment.

He glares back, unblinking, like he's trying to burn a hole right through me. 'Be careful how you speak to me,' he says slowly, threat in his voice.

'Or what?' I challenge. 'I know you won't actually hurt me and even if you do I don't care.' The air around us rings with silence.

He gives a small smile, and calmly says: 'No? What about if I hurt ... Jonathan?'

The walls pulse in towards me. I can't breathe.

How long has he known about Jonathan?

He gives a small smirk, like he knows he's winning. And now that familiar heat is boiling in my solar plexus, it's moving to my throat. Gathering there. Swirling. I'm not even scared anymore, I'm just fucking furious.

'Right,' I say, my voice cracking. 'That's what you want, isn't it, for me to be as alone and messed up as you? What, should we both live here in this miserable house?'

A small part of me is telling me to stop. To shut up. Am I insane? Why am I yelling at this man—this vampire—who I've witnessed *killing* two others? Who has a pet tiger he could feed me to? But I can't stop now, to not say it all would be to let him win. And no. Just no.

'I saw your pictures of me, Oscar,' I spit. 'That little box I gave you. I loved you. I trusted you. You should be ashamed of how you abandoned me. Of what you did to me last night. Of how you're treating me right now. Because I know I'm the only one, that you don't have any other proteges. I know in some way you care. Otherwise, you wouldn't have sent me Hans, you wouldn't have been watching me all these years. I see the way you look at me. But you can't even admit it, can you? Which means you're nothing but a coward.'

Thoughts dance behind his eyes.

I can hear my own breath.

'Aubrey,' he says calmly, letting go of my neck. 'Don't embarrass yourself. I have those pictures because I had to check on you to make sure you weren't going to compromise any of us. I kept that box because I'm not a complete arsehole, no matter what you might think of me. No, I don't have any other proteges, but that's because I learn from my mistakes. But please be clear on one point: I don't care about you. I'm just protecting myself, and all this,' he says, looking around at his high ceilings and ornaments, 'from you and your uselessness. When we're done here and I am certain you won't be a problem for the rest of us, you'll never see me again. I can promise you that.'

And then he's gone, and something deep in my chest throbs.

I run into my room and slam the door. I sit on the floor, hugging my knees as my lower lip quivers. I smell rust. Once the tears start, they won't stop. I can feel them streaking my face, gathering on my neck, my face contorting as I sob. I can't tell if I'm crying from fear or from still being here or because of Jonathan and Olivia or the fact that I don't want another new year alone, pretending to be happy … Or if I'm sobbing for every night I've spent alone for 150 years, for every dream I had of Oscar, or for the vampire who I thought I'd find, the one who could have made everything better.

And even though Oscar can surely hear me sobbing through the walls, he leaves me here alone. Like always.

The next night, I'm lying in bed, staring out the window, when I hear tyres, then murmurs, then footsteps on the stairs and then a knock at my bedroom door.

I don't want to answer it. *It'll be Oscar.*

I'm done with him and his casual cruelty, his mind games. Maybe he could blow hot and cold with me when I was a human but not anymore.

The knock comes again so I stomp over to it, pull the door open and glare out.

But it's not Oscar standing there.

It's a young woman of about twenty-four, dark hair to her shoulders and that tell-tale glazed-over look in her eyes.

'You are to feed off me,' she says.

Oh.

I move aside so she can come in and note that she smells of citrus perfume and AB-negative blood. My gums are tingling and I'm starving as I close the door and leave her standing there. I need to feed. I haven't eaten since Red Flannel Jeff three nights ago. But there's nobody here to stop me and this isn't the same thing—she is smaller, weaker, more innocent.

If I couldn't stop, if I killed her, Oscar would have won. And that's what would happen. I can feel that hunger growing inside me even now, I know how powerful it is once I start. I need to fight it. *Roadkill, roadkill, roadkill*.

I look her dead in the eye and in the most velvety voice I have, I say, 'Go downstairs and tell Oscar I fed.'

She nods, her eyes still blank. I lead her out of the room and close the door behind her.

It feels like that's one small step back towards the light, my humanity.

The next night I'm sitting on the floor and drinking from the bag of blood I brought with me.

If this isn't an 'emergency', I don't know what is.

The blood has been somewhat preserved by the weather and the lack of central heating, even though the ice packs aren't cold anymore. But, and I hate to admit this, it tastes bland and chalky compared with Emma or Red Flannel Jeff. I've drunk the whole bloody bag in one sitting and I still feel dead inside. Okay yes, I *am* dead, but whatever. The levity, the strength, the jangly life force from live blood—it's all missing.

It was better before I remembered that.

Still, I'd better get used to it again if I ever want my old life back. If I don't want to end up heartless like the psychopath downstairs.

So I take another sip and look out through the window as it rattles. The sky is the colour of navy ink outside and it's maybe eleven pm. There's no clock in my room, so it's hard to tell. I reach up for the snow globe Es gave me and shake it, then watch the snowflakes fall again and again and again.

But then … the sound of music floats up from downstairs.

I turn to stare at my door.

It's some sort of stringed instrument, low and soulful … I think it's a cello. I frown, listening.

What is that?

Because there's something about the piece; a strange sense of déjà vu that tugs at my insides. A sense that it's important somehow—vital, even—but I don't know why. It pulls at a memory somewhere deep beneath my ribs. I don't know what it is, it's like a phrase on the tip of my tongue that I just can't recall …

I go over to the door, edging it open so I can hear it better.

It's coming from downstairs.

But the more I hear of the song, the more I feel it in my bones, like there's a memory in my marrow. Like I *know* it. Like it's going to bring me to tears.

I tiptoe down the stairs, drawn towards it, all the while knowing it could be the Pied Piper, leading the rats to drown.

It's coming from the drawing room. The door is ajar and I can see inside, through the space between the hinge and the door. I move my eye in closer.

It's Oscar.

He's stooped over a cello, playing, his hair falling forward over his face as he moves with the music. His entire body sways as his hands move. He's playing like a man who has had many lifetimes to perfect his technique.

I stand there, transfixed, watching the muscles on his arms flexing as he moves.

It's mesmerising.

And then my lower lip quivers and I can smell the rust of tears, feel them dripping down my cheeks and *what's going on?* Why does this hurt so much? There's a twisting in my chest, like the music is wringing out my heart.

Yet I've never heard this song; not that I recall.

I wipe away my tears silently.

And then, the music stops. Mid-phrase.

Oscar sits there, bent over his cello like he's sadder than anyone has ever been. I watch his shoulders heave as he lets out a huge breath. And I know I shouldn't be watching this, it feels like a violation.

I take a step backwards, but the floorboard squeaks beneath my foot.

SHIIIIIIITTT.

His stance stiffens just a little, like he knows I'm here.

A flash of two nights ago. His hand around my throat. His eyes flaming.

I hold my breath and stand dead still. *What's he going to do?*

Then he says, 'Aubrey, come inside.'

His voice is hoarse, not like it usually is. I move into the doorway and his eyes meet mine; he notices my tears and looks away. I watch as his jaw clenches, and I can hear him swallow.

'I do care, of course I care,' he says, his voice a bit stronger now. 'But Aubrey,' he says slowly, his eyes on mine again, 'I care the way a maker cares about the one he makes. I am bound to protect you, to make sure you are safe. But that's as far as it goes. Similarly, any feelings you have for me are not real; they're purely because you're sired to me. Which is why it's forbidden that we be together. Vampire lore cannot be broken. So whatever you feel, forget it. Okay?' And he's saying it in a way that tells me he *needs* me to understand.

I think of that moment that passed between us in the garden, that electric jolt that I could feel in my core. This is what that was.

I nod. Shrug, as though it's fine. Nothing.

But there's a flare beneath my ribs, like by him saying that, acknowledging that this thing between us is there and real, forbidden or not, he's given that little ember I've been fighting since the night I saw those photographs a good dose of oxygen.

He swallows, like he's about to say something else. 'I won't hurt Jonathan or do anything bad to Daphne. I'll get the evidence from her flat the next time I'm in London. I'm sorry, I shouldn't have threatened that. All I want is to make sure you can protect yourself. Because I can't be there for you. I want you to be happy. But Aubrey, be careful getting involved with a human. It never ends well.'

'Okay,' I say. 'Oscar ...'

He looks at me.

'Can you tell me about myself, as a human?' I ask.

He lets out a sigh. 'Not really,' he says. 'I didn't know you that well. I'm sorry, I wish I could tell you more.' Sadness swirls in my stomach.

'But ... I loved you?' I ask, as I think of that little box of love I gave him.

He nods slowly. 'I seduced you, and you thought it was love, but it wasn't. None of this is your fault, Aubrey. I shouldn't have turned you. I'm sorry. I was reckless that night. But what's done is done.'

I give a little nod.

He takes a deep breath. 'But I know you didn't feed off Tiffany last night,' he says. 'You really are going to have to eat something soon,' he continues, changing tack abruptly. 'I can get you someone to feed o—'

'I ... I brought a bag with me,' I say, unsure of how he'll react.

He gives me a sad little smile and nods; he doesn't fight me on it. And I realise we've come to a new understanding. Which should be a good thing, I'll get to live on my own terms, but it feels cold and isolating.

He turns back to his cello and starts to play another song, so I go back upstairs and get into bed and tell myself *everything is fine*.

But everything is not fine.

Every part of me is ... missing him. That's what it feels like, missing him. Which is all wrong.

I put in my earplugs and pull on my eye mask and lie there in the dark, trying my hardest to think about Jonathan, to conjure his face, and erase whatever just happened. But he's … not there. I search for his heartbeat, the warmth of his breath on my ear, the smell of his cologne. I can't make out the lines of his face. I can't hear his voice. I try to imagine him reaching forward to touch my face … Then he's there, fuzzy, but there. I think of him saying, *I love that you're so sensitive*. But then Jonathan changes before my eyes. My feelings are still there, but now I see … Oscar. His eyes. His face.

My breath catches and my eyes flick open. As I stare at the ceiling in the dark my heart speeds up faster than it should and I'm shaking.

This is all wrong. What is happening to me?

Whatever it is, it's dangerous. And it feels like the longer I stay in Oscar's orbit, the more I lose myself to the murkiness. Because that invisible cord that has always linked me to Jonathan has loosened. Now, in its place is another. Whether I like it or not, whether I understand it or not, it is tying me to Oscar …

I could leave.

He said he wouldn't hurt Jonathan or Daphne. I could get up and walk out the door, never look back. But the most confusing part is that I don't want to go. And that's all wrong, I should *want* to get away from him. But I don't.

Besides, it's just one more night here. What could happen in one more night?

51

I'm reading *Wuthering Heights* in bed, or trying to, doing everything I can to avoid going downstairs and facing Oscar. Because whatever is going on inside me is scaring me. I'd rather just avoid him altogether until I have to see him later. Then I'll deal with it. Because tonight is New Year's Eve.

Oscar is hosting another damned party.

And so I focus on reading. Or try to.

But then a familiar voice floats up the stairs: 'Baby-V?'

Rupert.

They're back. *Finally.*

Something to ease the tension. A cushion.

So I go over to the door, push it open and rush over to the banister.

Carmilla and Rupert are standing in the entrance hall with their bags; Mr Parker and Oscar are helping them. Rupert looks up and blows me a kiss. I wave back and Oscar glances quickly up at me, then turns to Carmilla.

'Did you find Felix?' Oscar asks. 'The police came to ask about him. Do they think something happened to him?'

'Nobody knows,' she says. 'His bags and passport were gone though. Arsehole.'

'Yes, Aubrey and I had to get up in the middle of the day to deal with them, didn't we Aubrey?' Oscar says, looking up at me like nothing has happened in their absence. Our eyes meet and my breath catches—has he always been this beautiful? Did I just not notice?

I look away, to Carmilla instead. 'Yes. I hope Felix is okay.'

She stares at me, thoughts I can't read moving behind her eyes.

And then blessed Mrs Parker comes in from outside and heads up the stairs. She's carrying a black garment bag.

'Hello, Miss,' she says as she gets to me. 'I have your dress for tonight.'

We step into my room, and I relax as soon as I'm out of Oscar's orbit. I must be insane to be staying here by choice. *I'll leave tomorrow*. I'll go back to London and my life. Although now an anxiety courses through my veins. Because that's not without its own problems.

Mrs Parker is over by the wardrobe, unzipping the bag. She hangs up my dress cheerfully, asking, 'Did you have a lovely Christmas?'

'Yes. And you?'

She turns to me with a grin. 'Yes, ours was wonderful,' she says. 'Lots of grandchildren running around. Mr Parker dressed up like Santa Claus and everything.' She's giggling at the memory, and that makes me laugh too, even though that familiar sadness is back. I can feel it in every part of my body. 'You'll need to get ready soon,' she continues. 'Everyone is arriving in an hour and a half.'

I nod. 'Thanks.'

Her eyes catch on the red dress, crumpled on a chair. She picks it up. 'What happened here?'

'I'm so sorry, I couldn't get it off and I panicked.'

'No mind.' She smiles. 'We'll fix it.' As she heads to the door, she says, 'I'll be back in half an hour to help you dress.'

As soon as she's gone, I go over to look in the wardrobe. The dress is long and soft gold with detailed embroidery—even more beautiful than the last. Of course it is, everything about Oscar is an illusion. A beautiful, alluring illusion. I touch the fabric and I tell myself it's not real. This connection I feel to him is nothing. It's just because he's my sire.

But, even so, as I wait for Mrs Parker to come back, I put on make-up.

Half an hour later I'm dressed, sitting in front of the mirror while Mrs Parker puts up my hair.

As she escorts me down the stairs, people are streaming in and moving through to the ballroom, just like that first night on Christmas Eve, all in period costume again. It occurs to me that everything looks just the same, but it *feels* different.

We walk through to the ballroom then I turn to Mrs Parker and say, 'I'm okay, thank you.' She nods and leaves me there and I scan the crowd.

Tonight, the strings and piano of the Christmas party have been replaced by a DJ who is playing songs from the 80s, 90s and 00s. It's jarring against the period costumes, but nobody seems to care. Everyone is smiling and chatting, and I spot Carmilla and Rupert nearby. But as I scour the room, despite my best intentions, I'm only looking for Oscar.

He's leaning against the far wall, wearing his habitual white shirt, talking to a young woman with light brown hair. I recognise her—a flash of her scrunched up little button nose, the sound of her moans, Oscar's face between her legs. She looks plenty happy to be here. He doesn't force these women to have sex with him, that much I'm sure of. And as she looks up at him and smiles, something sears me. Her hand is on his arm and he's looking down at her intently, and here I am standing on the other side of the room, watching him as he touches her face with the back of his hand, his eyes on hers.

But this is good. It's better this way. It's not real.

And then I hear, 'So what happened while we were gone?'

It's Rupert's voice and I turn to look at him and smile, thankful for the interruption.

'Not much,' I say, and his face crumples up in some weird smile-frown configuration.

'*Something* happened,' he says, swirling his glass and then taking a sip, his eyes trained on me. 'You could cut the tension between you two with a knife.'

I shrug, grab a glass of champagne from a passing tray and take a gulp. *Is it that obvious?*

'Is Carmilla okay?' I ask, needing to change the subject.

'Oh, fine,' Rupert says, 'but still pissed off. She got a text from Felix this evening. He's apparently in Portugal. Felix will be Felix …'

'Oh,' I say. *Oscar must have sent it from Felix's phone*. 'Good.'

Then Rupert leans in towards me, his eyes over my shoulder, and whispers, 'Incoming.'

I turn to follow his gaze.

'Aubrey,' Oscar says, reaching for my arm but not meeting my eye. 'We have to dance the first dance.'

He's still not looking at me, but I let him lead me onto the dance floor.

His hand finds my midback and a jolt runs down my spine; his other hand folds over mine and we start to move. And even though it's modern music, he's dancing like it's 1880. And I can feel a charge between us, in the space between our chests. Or is it just me? Am I imagining it? His grip on my hand softens just slightly, becomes tender. I can feel myself melting forward into him, my heart is beating in a way a vampire heart shouldn't beat, and I'm barely breathing as I let myself look up at his face for just a moment. His jawline, his stubble, his mouth, and then … his deep-green eyes.

He's looking right at me, the amber around his irises glowing, and as I meet his gaze, my throat catches. It feels like he can see straight to my core. Then he looks away, over my shoulder. I try to read his expression, but I can't—is that vulnerability, boredom, nothingness? We don't speak. Not once. It feels uncomfortable even swallowing. As he twirls me around the room in seemingly slow motion, all I want is for this dance to end. And then, at last, it does. The music fades.

In a cold voice, without looking at me, Oscar says, 'Have a good night.'

He heads back to the woman he was talking to earlier. Another song starts up and I watch as he leads her onto the dance floor.

I want to look away, but I can't. I watch as he twirls her, and she shrieks with laughter. Then he pulls her close and his mouth finds hers and something inside me cracks. The world tilts off its axis, reality stutters and slurs.

'Just breathe,' Rupert says.

'I'm fine,' I say.

'No, you're not. I told you to be careful of him. Love is a motherfucker, even if it's not with bloody Oscar.'

'I don't love him,' I snap, frowning at him. 'He's just my maker. Of course I have feelings for him, but they're not real.' I say this as much for my sake as his, grabbing another glass of champagne and downing it, even though it does almost nothing to numb me. 'That's why it's forbidden,' I add.

Rupert frowns. 'What's forbidden?'

An unease rises within me. 'Being with your maker,' I say, my voice small.

'Huh? No, it's not,' he says, gulping his drink.

'It is,' I say.

'Baby-V, I have a maker too,' he says, 'and I do NOT want to fuck that guy. I *have* to see him sometimes, but what you've got going on with Oscar is not the same.'

My lip quivers, but I clench my jaw so I don't cry.

Right. Okay. I get it.

It all makes sense. Oscar told me that so I'd let it go.

Intense humiliation washes over me; I'm so stupid.

I need to get away from here.

'I'm going to do a quick lap,' I say.

Rupert nods and I turn around, push my feelings down, and walk towards the door. When I get to the gallery, I start to jog.

Because there are moments in life where you have to choose which version of yourself you want to become: the light or the dark. And I don't want to become what Oscar will make me. What I'm already becoming. Or at least that's what I'm telling myself, that's the reason I'm giving for why I need to get away. But beneath that is something else. Something I can't quite name. Because what the hell happened? When did he start to win? When did I become like every other woman under his spell? I'm just like all the others to him. Because Rupert is right.

I *do* love him.

I hate it, but I do.

Oh god … how could I? He's slept with half this room. Probably *more* than half. He lies all the time. He kills people. And … he doesn't love me back.

NO MORE.

I need to leave. Now.

When I get to the library, my phone is still there in the kaleidoscope box. I reach for it with shaky hands and frantically plug it into the charger. As soon as it's on, I check my messages. I've never needed a message from Jonathan as much as I need one right now. To tell me it's me, that someone loves ME.

There are a bunch of notifications, but none are from him.

I scroll through them, needing to be wrong. But I'm not wrong. At least Es has replied about Riley: *Well, I told him you were in Australia seeing your mum and I didn't know when you'd be back! WEIRDOS! Btw, have you heard from Jonathan over the holidays?*

And no, I have not. Because it seems my soulmate doesn't want me and my maker doesn't want me, and clearly I was right all along: I *am* entirely unlovable.

I run upstairs with my phone, go into my room and close the door. As I look around, breath heaving in my lungs, I think, *Don't feel it, don't feel any of it, just do what you have to do*.

I pull out my suitcase, find my phone charger, plug my phone into a wall socket, and then fling open the wardrobe and, with trembling hands, I start to pack.

52

I throw my clothes in first, then I grab the snow globe Es gave me, wrap it in two jumpers and put that in next. I take off Oscar's necklace and leave it on the writing desk. But as I put it down, there's something pulsing through me, something that burns: it's agony and ecstasy and love and hate and yearning and bitterness and hope and despair, all mixed up together. Like razorblades and candyfloss. And I want it to stop, but I can't. All I can do is clench my jaw to stop the tears.

Why would I ever have wanted to feel all this?

Love is … balls.

I rush through to the bathroom and grab my toiletries. As I check I haven't left anything behind I catch sight of myself in the mirror. I wash my face, cleaning off the make-up I put on for Oscar, then dry it with a hand towel. And that's when my gaze moves down and I realise I'm still wearing the dress. But screw it, I'll post it to him. Because I will not stay here one moment longer.

I rush back to my suitcase, gathering belongings on my way, and throw everything haphazardly inside. Then I close it up and frantically pull at the zipper. It gets stuck on some fabric, so I pull it back, pack it tighter, and try again. This time it closes …

I grab my phone and the charger, and even though it's only got seven per cent, I drop them into my handbag, sling it over my shoulder and grab my suitcase. And that's when my door opens.

I look up, expecting it to be Rupert or Mrs Parker, checking on me.

But it's not.

It's Oscar.

A dizziness comes over me as I take him in. That static starts up in my head again, like his very being disrupts my circuitry. I can barely breathe.

'What are you doing?' Oscar asks, frowning, his eyes moving to the suitcase then back to me.

'I'm leaving,' I say, my voice steady.

'You can leave tomorrow, we've already discussed this.'

'I'm leaving *now*, Oscar,' I say. Because he doesn't get to tell me what to do anymore. I'm not his toy.

He looks at me, clenches his jaw and looks down at my suitcase again. I go to pick it up, to carry it, but I'm too weak right now, so instead I roll it towards him. There's a part of me that thinks he's going to stop me, that wants him to, but he doesn't. He simply moves aside so I can go out into the hall, and it feels like he's tearing my heart apart.

Then he reaches for my suitcase, to help me carry it down the stairs, and as he does, our fingertips touch. I look up, our eyes meet, and something moves between us, something wild and electric. My head gets light, my breath uneven.

He pauses for a moment, and his lips part like he's about to tell me not to go.

And then he says: 'Fuck it.'

He reaches his hands into my hair and pulls me close. I can feel his breath on my lips, and as we kiss, all the noise, the static, the questions, the confusion, it all fades to silence. He tastes like champagne and cigarettes. He walks me back inside, closes the door behind us. Our eyes meet.

'I …' I start. Because I should go. But it's like there's something inside me, pulling me towards him, and before I know what I'm doing, it's *me* leaning in, *me* kissing him again, and now my hands are in his hair as he walks me back towards the bed. The world spins around us and my breath is so quick. *What the hell am I doing?* He reaches around to the back of my dress, I feel him tugging at the laces, trying to untie it …

'I forgot how annoying these were.' He laughs, then he gives up and rips it open and it falls to the ground.

The air is cool on my skin and as he looks into my eyes, a rush moves through me, a rush greater than any blood I've ever drunk. It's like terror and yearning all mingled together. But even so, I reach up for the top button of his shirt, and as I undo it, he smiles. And there it is, that look, that softness, that part of him I recognise—*I really do recognise him*. I remember this love. I undo the next button too. Then he quickly does the rest and takes it off and then reaches for the edges of my underwear.

I can feel my heartbeat everywhere as he pulls them down to my ankles and I step out of them. Then I sit down on the bed and watch as he takes off the rest of his clothes. He takes a step towards me, my breath gets quick, then he slowly lies down on top of me. I reach my hand into his hair, searching his eyes for answers to questions I haven't asked.

'Are you sure you want to do this?' he whispers, his mouth so close to mine that I can feel his breath on my lips. And yes I want to do this. I'm dizzy I want him so much.

'Yes,' I gasp.

He leans forward and kisses me again, gentler this time, but his stubble is rough against my mouth. I wrap my legs around his waist. He pulls back just a little, his eyes lock on to mine. A jolt moves through me, it hits me square in the chest, and I can tell he feels it too—his pupils flare. And it feels like I am a part of him, like I am his and he is mine and … and if this is why people fall into the darkness, I understand it.

Something cracks behind his eyes.

I can see it the moment it happens. It's like a door slamming closed. His whole face hardens.

What's happening?

I reach for his cheek, his stubble, I want to open the door again.

But he's frowning now … he looks away. Down. He stands up, steps backwards, his breath quick. Then he looks up, and his face is serious, his eyes and jaw set. He whispers, 'We can't do this. Sorry. Fuck.'

Then he turns away from me, pulls his hands through his hair, then dresses. All I can do is reach for my dress to cover me and watch him. Then his shoes are on and he's walking right back out that door. Just before he leaves, he looks back, and says, 'I'll see you downstairs.' Then he does what he does best: he walks away.

And a final part of me, a part I didn't know was still there, breaks.

53

I sit there, clutching the lace of my dress, the cool air on my bare back, staring at my packed suitcase as the same sounds of laughter and glasses clinking and music drift up from downstairs. What just happened? How could he do this to me? How could I *let* this happen? Let him draw me in again? Abandon me again? What the hell is wrong with me? I'm such a fool. I look around, my breath quick and heat swirling through me.

What am I doing just sitting here?

I could just leave. I *should* leave.

Be free of all this. For once and for all.

I go over to my handbag, pull out my phone, plug it into the wall, and sit beside it on the floor thinking: *I'll just catch an Uber back to London.*

But when I look down at the screen, my breath catches. Because there, floating on the screen, is a notification. A text notification. And not just any text. The room spins as I take it in.

Jonathan: *I'm a mess. I'm so sorry for everything. Please can I see you? Xx*

I blink hard.

I read the message again, checking it's not some hallucination. But it's not, it's real. He really texted.

And now that I think about it, even though it has felt like forever, it's only been eleven nights since the break-up.

Daphne was right. All I needed to do was ignore him. Wait it out.

But now guilt oozes through me. Because I was about to sleep with Oscar. Why was I so weak?

I could go to him. Now.

I glance at the time on my screen: it's 9.24 pm. My mind begins to whir.

The train will take an hour, maybe an hour and a half to get to London Paddington, then add another twenty minutes for a cab or maybe the Tube. It'll be tight, but it's possible that I could be at Jonathan's door by midnight.

And then we could see the New Year in together.

It'd be the perfect way to start our new life. Our future.

Because I want all of it. I want so many great memories with him that Oscar is nothing more than a distant blip. I want so much love and contentment that even after Jonathan dies, memories of him sustain me for a century. Maybe two. I want everything I know we could be. Hell, maybe I'll find him again in his next life, too … We can do this over and over again, ad infinitum.

But I can't spook him. Not like last time. I need to be chill. Mysterious. Alluring. What was it that Daphne said? *Aubs two-point-oh*.

I type back: *Hey! HNY. What are you doing tonight? x*

Typing bubbles …

They stop. Then they start again …

Jonathan: *Honestly? I'm at home. I miss you. I found this. Xx*

Then *beep*, in comes another message.

It's a picture of my earring. The one I left under his desk.

I write back quickly: *Oh wow, thank you! I've been looking for that! x*

And in a single instant, the haze clears and I know exactly what I need to do.

Go to him. Right now. While I still have some shred of my soul left.

I pull open my suitcase. What to wear, what to wear? I grab a pair of jeans and a pink fluffy jumper and quickly get dressed. I google the closest train station and order an Uber, then I put on my coat, slide my suitcase down the stairs. With the noise of the music, nobody even hears it bang to the bottom.

I wait outside in a badly lit area behind a row of parked cars and slouch a little, just in case Oscar looks outside.

My app flashes: *Monroe is six minutes away*.

And then I do the thing I'm most scared to do. I log into the VHC website.

Nothing could stop me going to Jonathan right now, but still, I need to know what's going on. I anxiously scroll through the posts.

The title **KENNETH BRAWLEY, WHO IS WITH ME?** screams back at me and I tap on it. It was posted by **@Vampitup** and it's another call to action.

I scroll down to the comments, bracing myself.

But this … isn't so bad. Dare I say, it's *good*.

Because the tide has turned.

@Bloodygood: Man, I'm sorry I just don't think you're right about this one. I googled and those do look like fox bites. I vote just a regular stabbing.

@Victor: Second that. Too bad. Next time.

I scan down, searching for names I recognise in the comments. Nothing from Sally …

And then I see Riley's name.

@Riley: Sorry I couldn't make it.

Relief pulses through me. Riley didn't even bother to go to the meeting. He believed Es. That I was in Australia. I couldn't have killed Kenny if I wasn't here.

There's one message from Sally in my inbox: *In-laws finally left, thank god. Btw turns out Kenny really was a stabbing, hope my prayers didn't do it. I feel bad. Are you back in London? xx*

I type back: *Oh really? I thought we'd definitely found a vamp! Def not your prayers, just a bad thing. I'm on my way back to London now. Can't wait to get back to routine. Xx*

And just like that, my life is going back to normal. It might not be lavish and exciting, I may not routinely go to balls or do *Dirty Dancing* lifts in the moonlight, but I also don't end up in a room with a tiger, or battle feelings for the prince of fucking darkness. I can't wait to have 'normal' back.

Then my phone flashes with a notification: *Monroe is arriving now.*

I look up as headlights snake towards me, past the parked cars. Monroe pulls up, pops the boot and gets out.

'Aubrey?' he asks.

'Yes,' I say. As he loads my suitcase, I look back to the manor one last time. And who should I see walking in a little late? Emma.

Alive and well. In the same yellow dress she was wearing the night of the Christmas Eve party.

He pretended to kill her, so I'd be scared and do what he said. No more. Never again.

I get into the car quickly, keen to leave before Oscar checks on me.

'You going to the station?' asks Monroe as we drive towards the gates, his eyes on mine in the rear-view mirror.

I nod. 'Yes.' Then I plug my phone into the charging cable he has sitting over the console.

'Looks like a fun party, why are you leaving before midnight?' he asks.

'It *was* fun,' I say. 'But I'm going to London to see my boyfriend. I want to be there by midnight.'

'Nice,' he says, and then returns his focus to the driveway.

I sit back, and as gravel crunches beneath our tyres, I think about everything that's happened over this last week.

Felix and Red Flannel Jeff and Oscar and those pictures Oscar has of me. The box, the necklace he gave me, the tiger, the dancing. Tonight. I push away the thoughts. It's like I'm running away from the circus.

Instead, I focus on the good. Because even through it all, good *has* come of it. Now I know I can die, for one. That's pretty important information. I learnt to control those visions—even if I'm not perfect at it yet. I learnt how to hypnotise. I even learnt how to feed off the vein without killing, not that I'll be doing that once I'm home. It'll be bagged blood for me again. But being away from Jonathan, almost losing him, has made me even more sure of him. It's like Oscar just made it clear to me why I need Jonathan so much.

We pass through the gate, and now that big house and Oscar are small in the distance. And I know—*I know*—I'm finally headed to where I am really meant to be. Somewhere I can be good and human and never even think of this past week again. Because, while I can still feel that gentle tug at my ribs, I know that the further I get from here, the more that will fade.

I fought the darkness, and I won.

Oscar promised that he wouldn't harm Daphne or Jonathan. He may be severely flawed, but there does seem to be a nobility about him. Some tiny thread of decency, no matter how deeply hidden. He'll keep his word, I know he will.

But me? I'm done. I pull up a browser window, and buy a train ticket to London Paddington.

54

It's 9.38 pm by the time I get to Kemble train station and tumble out of the Uber. I rush up to the platform, struggling to lug my suitcase up the stairs. *Have I always been this weak?* But I have to hurry—it's New Year's Eve, there's a limited service. If I don't catch the 9.49 pm train, there won't be another one until morning.

By the time I'm standing on the platform, I'm breathless but have three minutes to spare. It's just me, a drunk guy sitting by himself, slurring into a FaceTime call as he stares down at his phone, and a couple who are French kissing up the other end of the platform, his coat enveloping her.

I feel the rumble first, reverberating through the platform. Then I see the glow of lights as the train approaches.

My stomach fills with butterflies and I move towards the edge of the platform—a swirl of cold air, dust—and wait as it screeches to a halt. The doors open and I get on and find a seat towards the back of the carriage.

The window is misted up, and as we pull away from the station, I can't help myself. I reach up, and without anyone seeing me, I draw a little love heart in the fog with my fingertip. It makes me smile.

I reach for my phone to text Jonathan, to tell him that I'm coming—then stop myself.

Because no, that will spoil it. I want to see his face. His unfiltered reaction when he sees me there at his door after all this time. I want that. I want all of it.

So I plug my phone in to charge, pull up the first *Twilight* movie, the one where they meet—I'll only be consuming soft and fuzzy vampires from now on, thanks—put in my earbuds and let it play, the volume down low, as I head back to the city and my future.

55

Everything always feels different from what you expect, especially when it's something you've wanted for so long. I'm finally here, in the back of a cab, driving down Jonathan's dark street towards his house, a single light in the dark. And I thought I'd just be happy, but I'm really nervous. The cab pulls to a stop and I get out and check the time. It's only seven minutes to midnight. I made it.

I stand there for a moment, holding my hair to the side as the wind whips around me, looking at the bay window and just soaking in this feeling. The curtains are drawn, but there's a yellow light emanating from within. I can almost see myself there, standing in the rain, looking in through that small space between the curtains …

My phone lights up with a message from Es: *Hey are you back in London yet? Greg had to go away for business last minute and now I have nothing to do for NY. Had two weed gummies but still so bored. Where are you? Xxx*

I don't want to jinx it, but I can't hold it inside either. I have to share this with someone. So I hold my phone up and take a quick video of myself, spinning around slowly, grinning at the lens. Then I type: *Guess? xxx*

Typing bubbles …

Beep: *I don't know, suburbia? Please let's do something? xxx*

I text back: *Jonathan asked me over! I think we're getting back together! xxx*

Typing bubbles …

WHHHATTTT???? Let me know how it goes! Good luck!!! Xxxxxx

I type back: *Will do. Double date soon! HNY! xx*

Then I stride up to Jonathan's door, running my fingers through my hair, take a deep breath, and press the doorbell.

And then butterflies swarm in my stomach. I'm pretty sure some of them get into my head too, because I'm dizzy now.

I hear footsteps on the floorboards inside, then shadows dance under the door.

The door handle rattles and turns, and the door opens and …

It's Baxter. Of course Baxter is here. He's always here. But I will not let anything ruin this for me.

'Hey,' he says, frowning at me. 'Aubrey. Umm … come inside. It's freezing out there.' He looks at my suitcase but doesn't say anything, just rolls it in and closes the door. At last, I'm on the right side of the door again, back in the warmth, back in the fold. Almost like the last eleven nights never happened. He turns around and yells, 'Jonathan, Aubrey's here.'

I hold my breath and then I hear footsteps and Jonathan comes through from the kitchen.

His eyes get a little bigger, his mouth drops open, and then … a smile. A huge, warm smile. He rushes over, grabs me and hugs me and I can smell his laundry detergent, his cologne. And I want to say something memorable right now. Something love-story worthy. But nothing comes.

Instead, my lips hover in a half-opened shape for a moment and then I awkwardly say: 'Hi.'

But that's clearly the *right* thing because his grin widens and he pulls me in close and kisses me. But then he looks at my suitcase and frowns. I don't want him to freak out, think I'm moving in, or moving too fast … Daphne's advice comes floating back: *Fun and elusive and unpredictable. Think mysterious, alluring.* I can't wait to tell her that it worked …

'I came straight from the airport,' I explain.

'Of course,' he says. 'Come, let me get you a drink.'

He disappears into the kitchen while I take off my coat, leave it on top of my suitcase and take a seat on the sofa. I hear cupboard doors opening and closing, and then he's back with two glasses of wine.

He hands me one and I take a sip, and it's like nothing exists in this entire world aside from him and me. I can't hear the traffic outside—hell, I can barely hear the music playing from the speakers; it's just us. Even the clocks have stopped ticking.

'God, it's just so great to see you again,' he says, moving a cushion aside and sitting down beside me.

As I search Jonathan's blue-as-blue-can-be eyes, I want to tell him everything. About our past, about the last week, but I know I can't. At least not yet.

All in good time.

So, I keep quiet, and I let myself bask in the fact that I am here, against all odds, that we're spending New Year's Eve together.

'I'm sorry,' he says, reaching for my hand. 'For everything. I don't know what the hell I was thinking.'

And then Baxter wanders back into the room, nursing a glass of something that looks like Coke but from the pink of his cheeks I'm guessing has rum or something in it.

'I was going to watch a movie, if you guys want to join?' he says, sitting down next to Jonathan and reaching for the remote control.

Jonathan looks at me, then back at Baxter. 'Thanks, but I think we'll go to my room.' Then he stands up and offers me his hand. I take it, and let him lead me up the stairs. It must be almost midnight by now. But halfway up, my phone starts ringing. I glance at the screen: *Oscar*.

He must have realised I'd left; that I'd taken my phone.

I turn it to silent and drop it into my bag.

Jonathan pushes open his bedroom door and we step inside and I'm looking at his profile, at his jaw, his lips, and all I want to do is kiss him. It's like we're back on the night of the break-up, and now we get to rewrite the story, change the ending.

The door shuts with a gentle click, and for one perfect moment, I am giddy with happiness. It's like everything in the world is exactly as it should be.

But then everything gets bright. Really fucking sickly bright. And I realise, no, I'm not giddy with happiness, I'm just … giddy.

What's going on?

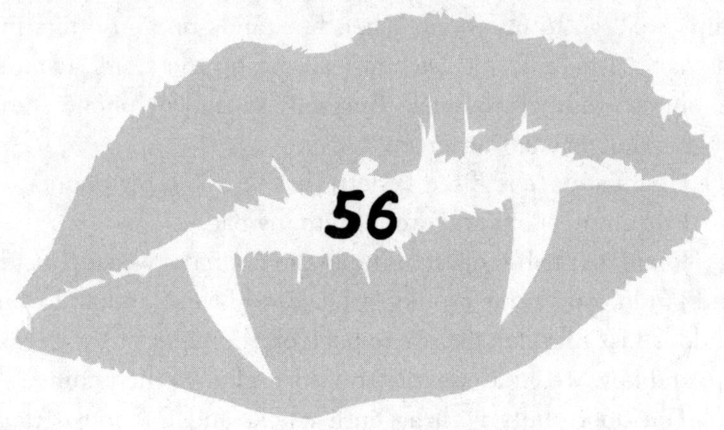

56

Every single capillary contracts simultaneously, my mouth goes dry and I'm dizzy and tired. It's bright. So bright. Like standing under multiple suns. I crumple to the floor and look up at the ceiling. It's covered in blinding strip lights—but strip lights don't usually do this to me. It's daylight that's dangerous.

Then it hits me: they're not strip lights, THEY'RE GROW LIGHTS.

Panic rises in my stomach and I start to crawl for the door but I'm slow, and Jonathan moves in front of me, blocking the way. He's not saying anything, he's just staring down at me. I turn my head desperately, looking for the window. An escape.

And that's when I see the cage.

It's right there by the window, where Jonathan's bed usually is. His bed has been moved in front of the wardrobe. My gaze moves back to the window … if I could just get there, maybe I could jump out. But the curtains are drawn, and in the crack between them, I can see the swirl of wood. *It's boarded up.*

Now I smell rust but *don't cry, don't cry, DON'T FUCKING CRY!* Because he clearly suspects what I am—why else would he have grow lights on the ceiling and a cage in his room?—

and if I cry he'll know for sure, and then he'll *really* freak out. Like Freddie did.

I look up at him, needing him to see that I'm not dangerous, I'm still me.

Because that must be why he's doing this: he's scared of me.

But he won't be scared if I tell him everything, if I confide in him about our history.

'Jonathan,' I say, my head throbbing.

But his face is cold. And now I'm shaking. I reach for my phone, get it out of my bag, but I'm slow, too slow to call Oscar. I'm getting weaker by the moment.

Jonathan says nothing. He just reaches down and takes my phone, puts it in his pocket, then grabs my handbag and throws it behind him. Then he reaches under my arms, drags me to the cage and pushes me inside. He closes the door and I hear the heavy lock click.

'Jonathan, what are you doing?' I try again as he walks to the door, but he doesn't even turn to look at me.

He just leaves the room, closing the door behind him.

My breath is quick as I squint against the grow lights, examining the steel bars, the welded corners, the cold, metal base. It's about two by two metres wide, and only a metre and a half high—I won't even be able to stand up in here. *Where the fuck did he get a* cage? IKEA? Amazon? And then I think of those cardboard boxes that were piled up in the kitchen when I broke in. Is that what those boxes were? This cage?

This is why I hate the modern world. It should be *hard* to get a cage!

I'm straining to hear what's happening on the other side of the far wall. I'm doing my best to tune in, but I haven't eaten from the vein since Red Flannel Jeff and that was five nights ago—all I've had since then is one bag of blood—and the grow lights are dampening all my senses. I clench my eyes shut and as my head throbs, I really, really focus, and I think I hear

Jonathan say, 'Here's her phone …' The voices are muffled, I struggle to hear. 'Code is zero five one eight seven six …'

When did he figure out my passcode? I guess I never tried to hide it when we were together. But that means he was already suspicious back then. He suspected I was a vampire even then.

That's why he broke up with me.

And then, from somewhere out there, I hear a chorus of voices yelling, 'Ten … nine … eight …'

It must be almost midnight. I can hear a party going on nearby, music playing—I imagine people getting ready to kiss, resolutions being made.

'Seven … six … five …'

My breath catches as I look around and clench my jaw.

'Four … three … two … one … Happy New Year!' Then comes a swell of cheering.

I imagine fireworks outside and I swear I can hear a distant boom-boom-boom as they go off. They're so vivid in my mind's eye, it's almost like I'm watching them, the way I *should* be. It feels as if my life has split off in two: there's the version of me that's out there and happy and watching the fireworks, about to head off into my future with Jonathan. And then there's *this* one. The one sitting in a cage in his bedroom under grow lights.

How am I going to get him to understand, to not be scared of me?

Because that's what it's going to take. Maybe this is my fault. If I'd been honest up front, if I'd just told him everything instead of letting him discover it for himself, he wouldn't be so terrified. None of this would be happening.

As I look around, my eyes land on his desk. I can see my earring, sitting there, on top of it, catching the light. Right beside it is a champagne glass.

But it's not just any champagne glass, there's pink lipstick on the rim.

And … that's not right.

I crawl over to the corner of the cage near Jonathan's desk, and stare at that glass. I must be wrong. It can't be lipstick. *It's fine, Aubrey, you'll just talk to Jonathan when he comes back in here … it'll be fine.*

He can't just leave me in here forever, he wouldn't do that. When he comes back in, I'll explain, and he'll let me out of here … *He will, he will, he will* … I repeat this over to myself, like if I say it enough times, it'll be true.

But now I'm thinking about Baxter, downstairs, watching a movie.

Surely he knew Jonathan was building this cage in here. He must have heard him drilling, moving his furniture around … Hooking up the grow lights. Baxter must know about this. About me.

I bet they built this cage together.

I bet this was all Baxter's idea.

My stomach knots and I swallow hard as I move over to the bars and shake them. But this is not some flimsy cage they bought on a whim. They must have really planned this.

And then, before I can think anything else, the bedroom door flings open.

And it's not just Jonathan standing there now, and not just Baxter either. There are four of them.

I squint against the bright light, scanning from face to face: Jonathan, then Baxter, then Olivia and then—*oh my god*. Riley. The walls pulse in towards me, pushing all the air from my lungs. He's wearing a black hoodie with red text that reads *Vampires are real! Join the fight!*

What the hell is going on?

How would Riley know Jonathan or any of the others? And why … why is Olivia here?

I struggle to piece any of it together, my mind fuzzy under the grow lights. So I decide to just ask. Seems like a fair question. I look straight at Jonathan and say: 'What's he doing here? He's some crazy guy with a crush on me.'

But nobody replies.

It's like I don't exist, like I'm some exhibit in a zoo. They just stand there, sipping their drinks and crowding around the cage and peering in.

It feels like I'm standing on quicksand. My mouth is so dry and I'm so hungry. I'd love to bite Olivia or Riley right now, but I'm so tired and drained, there's no way I could take down anyone, even if I wasn't in this stupid cage. Besides, if I did that, if I even *tried*, they'd know for sure they were right about me. The only way I'm getting out of here is if I make them think they're wrong. That I'm not a vampire at all. That I'm normal.

'I can't believe we did it,' Baxter says, gulping down the rest of whatever was in his glass.

Riley starts to laugh and says, 'I told you so! Man, I knew she wasn't in Australia! Can't outsmart me, bitch.'

I'm waiting for Jonathan to do something, say something, but he just stands there, watching me, like he's never met me. Like he's never loved me.

How can this be happening?

So what would a human girl do right now? She'd probably cry, clear, human tears, but that's not an option for me.

'Jonathan?' I ask, my voice shaking as I try to meet his gaze. Because of all of them, he's the one most likely to help me. He knows me. He's my soulmate.

But he ignores me.

They all ignore me.

'Well, happy new year to us,' Olivia says. And then she grabs the glass of champagne behind her on the desk and takes a sip. I look from face to face, scanning for answers.

Why am I here? What do they want with me? My gaze lands on Riley, and I'm thinking of that meet-up where we first met. Then Es's message about a creepy guy asking about me. *This must have something to do with the VHC website … Something to do with that meet-up and Kenny. They must think I did it.*

What are they going to do to me?

But surely Jonathan can stop them, whatever they're planning, if I can just get through to him. Remind him of what we have. His hand is right there, not far from the cage, just dangling by his side. So with the little energy I have, I slowly reach through the bars …

'Jonathan, what's going on?' I ask. Our fingertips almost meet. But he recoils and pulls away, and as he looks over at me, there's something in his gaze, but it's definitely *not* love.

Then Baxter says, 'Well, I for one need another drink before we get this show on the road.'

And then they all go downstairs, leaving me alone.

58

I grab onto the bars of the cage and shake them, but they don't budge; I scan the joins, desperately looking for a weak spot. But I can't see any, so I shift my gaze outside the cage, looking for a weapon. I glance at my handbag by the door, not that there's anything helpful in there, then the boarded-up window. I think of the people I saw in the garden across the fence the last time I was here. They'll come home at some point. Would they hear me if I screamed? I don't know. But everyone downstairs definitely would. Then what would they do to me?

I'm trapped.

And Jonathan seems to believe whatever Riley must have told him about me.

I need to talk to him, alone. To tell him that no matter what, I love him. That there is an invisible thread linking our souls, a thread so strong that it brought us together again in this life, despite all odds …

I open my mouth and call to him: 'Jonathan …' but it comes out so small, so weak, I barely recognise my own voice. I look out at the room, at the bed we've made love in, pushed up against the far wall, at the bedside table wedged in beside it. The desk … His black leather planner, some random papers and at the edge, a bound document. I stand up to get a better view, hold onto the bars of the cage and zoom in as best I can under these lights. The front cover reads: *Business proposal: Eternex Enterprises.*

That must be for that app they're creating.

And then my ears start to ring and throb and my insides twist. And in the echo chamber of my mind, I hear Oscar's voice: '*Aubrey, get back here right fucking now …*'

I clench my eyes shut and clutch my head in my hands.

Oscar must have given up calling me on the phone, and now he's trying to force me back. There's a tug in my chest that pulls me forward; I push against the cage bars, trying to get out, to get to him. My body knows what he wants from me and my ears feel like they might explode. '*Aubrey*,' comes his voice again.

The ringing gets even louder.

That pull towards him gets even stronger.

And as I squish against the cage bars I think, *Maybe they'll break*. But they don't. My head feels like it's going to blow off. As I bite down hard and clear my mind and try to think of nothingness, I hear: '*Aubrey, I mean it …*'

And I'm thinking: *I need this to stop, I need this to stop, I need this to stop.*

And then, somehow … it does.

My ears pulse. It feels like they're full of cotton wool, but the relief is immense, and I'm still shaking. I crumple to the floor, curl up in the foetal position and hug my knees in tight.

I stay like that, rocking back and forth, for a few minutes.

And then the door opens. And there, standing before me with a canvas bag over his shoulder, is the love of my life.

Jonathan.

59

Everything inside me softens as I take in the lines of his face. He closes the door, comes over and sits on the carpet by the edge of the cage, not far from me. Then he reaches into the canvas bag, pulls something out and pushes it through the bars. I look towards it, frowning.

Blood.

He's brought me a bag of blood.

My gums tingle as I stare at it. I'm desperate to drink it, but I know—*I know*—I can't.

If I do that, I'll never get a chance to explain. He'll side with Riley, and who knows what will happen next? I ignore the blood, swallow hard and inch a little closer to Jonathan instead. And I can feel his heat, smell his shampoo and his laundry detergent and the bergamot of his cologne and okay yes, fine, his blood too. But I will not focus on that.

'Jonathan,' I say, my voice small, holding onto the bars. 'What's going on?'

'You should eat something,' he says, nodding to the bag of blood.

'What is *that*?' I ask, frowning at it, trying to pretend my mouth isn't watering.

'You know *exactly* what it is, Aubrey,' he says, his eyes meeting mine. And this is good, he's not scared to look into my eyes even though I know he must have seen vampire movies or I wouldn't be in this fix; he must fear being entranced or hypnotised or whatever. But I never did that to him while we were together, so I guess he either thinks I can't do it (which, right now, I probably couldn't) or somewhere deep down inside, he trusts me.

'No, I don't. I don't understand what's going on, why are you doing this to me?' I ask. 'I love you, Jonathan, and I know you love me too.'

He frowns at me, gives a little smirk, and panic moves through me.

'You really are fucking stupid,' he seethes.

Alarm bells ring in my ears. What is going on? This isn't Jonathan. He doesn't talk to me like this.

'Anyway, look, just drink the blood, okay?' he continues. Even his voice sounds different, his northern accent stronger.

Those alarm bells start to ring a little louder.

Because hang on, if he knows I'm a vampire, why would he *want* me to feed? Why would he want me stronger? Unless he's still not sure? Maybe he wants me to drink it so there is no debate. Which means I can still convince him I'm *not*.

So obviously, I *don't* drink it.

'I don't understand why you want me to do that,' I say, in a fragile, confused voice. 'What is going on with you?'

'Cut the crap, Aubrey,' he snaps. His eyes meet mine and there's something hard in them which is … all wrong. 'I know what you are.'

All the air leaves my lungs; the walls pulse towards me.

I knew this conversation would happen one day, and I always knew it would be tricky, but this is not how I saw it rolling out. There's meant to be candlelight, for one. But now, here we are, at the moment of truth. And I'm not ready.

'What do you mean?' I ask. 'What am I?'

'You're a vampire,' he says, completely emotionless.

As he says it, I know I need to deny it. But there's this little part inside of me, the part that has been hiding for 150 years, that wants to say, *Yes, I am*. Because once Jonathan knows my deepest, darkest, most shameful secret, if he can get past what I am, and I can get past what he's doing to me right now, then we can truly love each other. Darkness and all.

This could be a breakthrough moment for us.

I mean, I know it looks bad, but he's scared, people do stupid things when they're scared. And I'm not perfect. I almost had sex with Oscar tonight. We all slip up.

But then in comes a flash of Freddie, the way he reacted. He went to *war* to get away from me. Not everyone can deal with the truth … And from the look in Jonathan's eyes, I'm not sure he's ready for it.

So I say, 'What? Vampires aren't real.'

'Let me show you something,' he says, reaching for his phone and tapping on the screen.

There's a picture on it. It's of Olivia and her two friends at the place in Soho, where the open mic night was. He uses his fingers to zoom in and my insides almost jump out of my body. Because there I am in the background, glaring at Olivia.

I stare at Jonathan, searching for an excuse that might make sense. Coincidence. Heartbreak. There has to be one.

But he's not even looking at me, he's tapping through to some video now. He presses play and I squint at it, trying to work out what I'm watching. It looks like a video of this room, but the way it was before … before the cage. When the bed was where I'm sitting right now.

But then … *what's that?*

My gaze catches on movement at the window, and my insides clench.

It's me. Climbing in.

I all but stop breathing. How the hell do I get out of this one? How do I explain being able to climb through a second-storey window? No wonder he's scared of me. I didn't know there was a nanny cam in here ... *Is it still here?* I look around, scanning the room, because it is taking in *the whole room*.

But there's nothing. No camera I can see, at least.

'Keep watching, Aubrey,' he says, and I look back at the screen, just in time to see myself seemingly pick up the camera and look right into it. Or near to it. Something. I close my eyes and frown and scrunch up my face. *What am I doing?*

And then ... the pieces all fall into place.

The picture frame. Of him and his parents. I picked that up the night I came here.

I turn to look at it quickly. *Ah, shit ...* There was a camera in it.

That's why they came home so quickly that night. They knew I was here.

A dizziness comes over me as I look back to the screen and now I watch in horror as I zoom so fast that I'm a blur, and then reappear by his closet. I want to reach in and stop myself. Yell: *Don't*. But I can't. I just have to watch, helplessly, as I reach in for his mustard jumper, then hold it close, and stand there for a bit. Swaying.

As I watch the rest—leaving my earring under his desk, then zooming over to his bedside, rubbing my wrist, my hair, on his pillow, I'm thinking: *How the hell do I explain this?*

Then the screen goes dark. My stomach drops as I look to him. There's something awful in his eyes. Something dark, something that's not meant to be there.

'What were you doing here? Did you come to kill me like you did that poor chap Kenny you were always complaining about? What were you doing to my jumper? Or my pillow?'

'I—'

'Save it, Aubrey,' he snaps. 'Just drink the fucking blood.' He moves to his desk. 'But just so you know, we're watching you.' He grabs the framed photograph of his parents. The one facing out into the room. As he holds it up, I can see a little lens, obscured by the black frame. 'So don't try anything stupid.'

My breath catches, and it feels like the grow lights have upped their wattage. He's staring at me with such loathing and everything is escalating and this is not how tonight was meant to go. There is only one way to turn this around. It might not work, but it's now or never.

'Jonathan, there's something you should know,' I start, my voice fragile. I look up and my eyes meet his. He puts the frame down and comes back over to me.

'Go on,' he says.

'You're my soulmate,' I say, my voice cracking. 'We were married in your past life.'

Silence swims around us as I watch his face for recognition.

First, he smiles.

And then he starts to laugh, but it's not a laugh I recognise, it's a horrible laugh. 'Jesus, Riley was right about you, you are an evil little bitch …'

And … that's not how Jonathan talks to me *at all* … he's gentle. Loving. Even when he broke up with me he was kind.

'I'm telling you the truth,' I say.

He's shaking his head. 'That sexy shit of yours might have worked on Riley, but it won't work on me. Besides, you should be careful—look where flirting with him got you,' he adds, looking right at me now.

I did not flirt with Riley!

'If he hadn't been so hot for you, he wouldn't have got all obsessed. He wouldn't have checked out your IP address and figured out you went to that pub so often.'

Wait … what?

'Or found a blood bag wrapped in a nappy in the bin outside that pub. Or figured out when you worked, waited for you at the Tube one day and saw you go to the blood bank to see your little friend Es. He wouldn't have noticed any of that, and then he wouldn't have harped on about you being a vampire to us and we wouldn't be here right now, so I'd say it kind of backfired on you, you little slut.' He gives a smirk.

I stare at him, needing him to morph back into the Jonathan I know. But he doesn't, he just keeps on talking.

'Fuck, when I think about how close we came to believing you were just some girl who worked at Selfridges. To losing yet another lead. I mean, we've been looking for one of you ever since we joined that site, that's *why* we joined. And we've come close, a couple of times, but it's never quite worked out.'

He's frowning now, like he's imparting something important that I might actually want to hear. Like I'm interested in the nitty-gritty of how I ended up here.

'But wow, Aubrey, you hid it well. Even when we were "dating"'—he puts 'dating' in air quotes, like it was a fabrication, and it feels like he has stabbed me—'you seemed … normal. You have a heartbeat. You don't need an invitation to go inside. You sleep through the night—you slept next to me. We went to Brighton for a whole twenty-four hours and you seemed normal, ate regular food. I've seen you eat Italian food—you ate garlic, for fuck's sake!' A flash of that Italian restaurant we went to. *Is that why he took me there?*

'You're weak as all hell,' he continues. 'Kind of depressed-like. And then I found tampons in your bag and I was like, Riley is just dead wrong, there is no way she is a vampire. I hate to admit it, but I was thinking what everyone else thinks about him, that he was just some crazy Uber driver with too much time on his hands. That he'd made up half the shit he'd said about you. So yeah, that was the night we broke up.'

That's why we broke up. It wasn't that he thought I *was* a vampire, it was that he thought I *wasn't*.

Now an echo of his voice, as I stood outside his door that night, trickles back in: *Fuck, I really thought she was the one.* That's what he meant.

'I was so disappointed,' he continues. 'I thought I'd wasted five weeks of my life on nothing … and we'd already ordered this cage. That shit is bespoke.' He pauses. 'But then,' his voice gets a little higher, like he's excited, like this is where the story takes a happy turn, 'Olivia saw you in her photograph and, sure, that could have been a coincidence or maybe you were a stalker, but then came the video of the break-in. That's when we knew for sure. Then we just had to figure out where you were.' He's grinning now, like he's pleased with himself.

My mind whirs as I piece together everything he's saying.

Riley worked on the site doing tech. He had access to my IP address. Which was either my 5G when I was out and sometimes when I was home—not so easy to trace—or the pub's IP address when my 5G wasn't working.

Now I think of that Uber, driving up to Jonathan's house in the rain that night I peered in the window. *That was Riley. They were probably all meeting to talk about how I'd been a dead end.*

But hang on … if that's true about the pub's IP address, then I'm guessing Jonathan didn't just happen to be at Bunch of Grapes on the afternoon we met. A flash of me sitting there waiting for Daphne, messaging with Sally on the VHC website.

My breath speeds up and everything crumbles around me.

Jonathan's eyes lock on to mine and he leans in, holding onto the bars of the cage. 'I did like fucking you though … I might have kept you around just for that if you weren't so intense, blowing up my phone every three seconds like a psycho. Then where would I be right now, huh? What would you have done to me?'

'Nothing,' I say.

He gives a dark laugh. 'Fucking liar.'

As I look at his eyes, so full of hate, all I know for sure is he'll never love me. It doesn't matter what I say.

And if this really is the end of the line for me, I need something happy to hold on to, another memory from our past life when he did love me. I reach forward and grab his finger as hard as I can, pulling his hand through the bars and hanging on for dear life.

Then I do what Oscar taught me. I pull in all my energy and focus on that blank screen in my mind … a warmth, a spark, starts up in my solar plexus.

I must really, really want it, just like he said I had to, because even here, unfed, beneath grow lights, it works.

My stomach cramps and the images flood in: *He's sitting at his desk, looking down at his phone screen. He looks over at his planner then looks down again, and I watch as he types:* Just remember, there are far, far better things ahead than any we leave behind. Always.

The images cut to black and I'm back here, caged, under grow lights, staring at him, still holding onto his hand as he writhes against my grip, and I don't know what the hell that was but I don't want *that* vision, I want a good one, from his past life, when we were happy. I clench my eyes shut, squeeze him even harder, using all my body weight to keep him still, then I focus and try again.

He walks into the living room and I can see myself there …

This is what I need. This is it. When we were happy. When I was human.

I'm lying reading on the sofa. I see him and I smile, stand up and—wait, why am I frowning like that? I look scared. I lift my arms up to protect myself, but his hand comes down hard on my face. I stare at him, terror in my eyes. The same terror I saw in that child's eyes.

What is he doing?

He punches me now, and my mouth starts to bleed. And I'm crying. I run upstairs, grabbing onto the banister to pull myself up, and he follows. I run into the bedroom and slam the door but he grabs it and wedges it open. I'm pushing back, trying to stop him, but he's stronger than me. He forces the door open and comes inside.

He looks towards the mirror and I see his face, contorted and furious. Then he throws himself forward and his hands find my throat … He pushes me down on the bed. He's straddling me, his thumbs pushing into my windpipe. And I'm trying to breathe, clawing at his hands, but he's too strong. My eyes are huge, I'm staring at him, terrified, and struggling to breathe as I try to push him away. But he keeps squeezing.

My eyes roll back in my head, but I'm still fighting. He grabs the brass vase from the dressing table, pulls his arm back, and hits me over the head. Hard. Blood starts to seep from my temple. He stands up, wipes the vase off, puts it back on the dressing table and leaves me there, bleeding, walks back down the stairs and—

His hand slips free, the images disappear and I'm left breathless, shaking. Reaching for my throat and gasping for breath like he's strangling me right now.

The room spins around me and I clench my eyes shut because this can't be what I think it is. Jonathan *cannot* have killed me. Oscar did that …

Didn't he?

But now that kaleidoscope shifts again, the sands reconfigure and a new pattern emerges. A new truth.

Or did Oscar just find me there, at death's door, and turn me into a vampire …

My eyes flick open. I stare at Jonathan; his face is all contorted, just like in the flash. He's looking down at his hand, his wrist.

'What the fuck, Aubrey,' he hisses. And I know if anyone is watching the nanny cam they'll have seen what I just did. But I don't care. I'm just empty now. An empty vessel. Nothing left to lose.

Because I've been wrong, so wrong … about it all.

Jonathan might have been my husband when I was human, but he wasn't my soulmate. He killed me. If there is something tying our souls together, an invisible string bringing us together life after life, it's not love, it's this. Trauma. *This* is our unfinished business. Because look at me, in this cage, at his mercy. He's about to do it all again.

A numbness descends on me now. So what, I'm just going to let him do this to me again? Kill me for real this time?

And then I think of that first vision I got. And even though I think I already know what I will see, I glance over to his desk and zoom in on his black leather planner. And I'm right. There, on the cover, embossed in small cursive type at the bottom, is a quote: *There are far, far better things ahead than any we leave behind. C.S. Lewis.*

He was pretending to be Sally. My only true confidante, who I'd message late into the night. Which explains why she kept asking where I was over Christmas, why she was testing me over Kenny. They wanted to find me. A flash of all the times I told her how lonely I was, how nobody ever saw beneath my surface, but how I feared that they might not love me if they did. How I thought Edward from *Twilight*—protective, charming, polite—was the perfect man. I wrote to her all about Jonathan and our dates; he was getting a blow by blow account of exactly how well he was manipulating me. And it was easy—I'd given him the blueprints for how to win me over. He would have known I'd never be able to resist a love story of my own.

But to deceive me like that, with this as his end goal? That's just pure evil …

And just like that I realise if anyone is the monster here, it's him.

I was right all along, he was like a fog. A toxic fog. I never had a chance in hell of seeing the truth.

That's when I feel the first tear fall.

60

It happens without me knowing it's happening, without a quiver of my lip, without the smell of rust. But now tears are rolling down my cheeks and I can't stop them.

Panic washes over me like a wave as he stares at me, his face a little pale now, his heart beating fast. And I know what he's seeing: a monster crying blood.

His eyes are wide, his feet fixed to the spot. I stare back at him, frantically wiping the blood from my face. Because I don't know what happens now, but I know it'll be bad. How can it not be? That nanny cam is probably still recording. Watching me cry blood.

All I can do is try to reason with him.

'But Jonathan,' I say quickly, sniffing and wiping the blood off my hands, onto my jeans, 'you dated me. You're linked to me ... If something happens to me, people will know it was you.'

His voice comes out monotone, like he's in shock, like even though he suspected this, now that I'm here before him, crying blood, it's a bit much. 'We had a brief fling and broke up,' he says.

'No. I didn't tell anyone we broke up,' I say. 'I said we were on a break. And I told my friend Es I was coming here tonight,' I continue.

He swallows hard, shaking his head. And then it's like he snaps out of it, whatever shock-trance he was in. 'I have your phone,' he says, blinking hard. 'I've read your messages. I know you told *everyone* we broke up. Yes, your friend Es is an issue, but I've dealt with it.' He turns and rushes to the door and I can't let him go, what happens to me then?

'Well, what about your Instagram? You have pictures of me up there. I follow you. And what about the messages you sent me,' I say through a tight throat, 'you clearly wanted to see me. People will figure out where I went missing if you do anything to me ...'

He looks back at me, holding onto the door frame, and with the same contempt I've seen in the mirror many times, he says, 'That Instagram was bogus, just for you. Mainly paid bots follow it. I never contacted you with my real number. Besides, I have three witnesses who will swear that I was here all night with them, that we never saw you. That I did nothing wrong. In the morning, Riley will Uber around town with your phone. Drop "you" off somewhere—maybe a train station, maybe in someone's bag. But Aubrey, nobody is coming for you. Nobody will even care when you're gone. So just relax and give into it. It'll all be over soon.' And there is this look on his face, like he's proud of himself. Like he wants me to know that he won. Again. Like even if he doesn't remember what he did to me in his past life, his soul knows, and it wants to do it again.

Like a circle that needs to complete itself.

Then he rushes outside and I hear him say to the others, 'Where were you guys, sleeping? She tried to motherfucking eat me ... did you see? Did you see? Let's watch the clip back.'

The bag of blood is still right there near me, and I'm never getting out of here, I know that now. They're going to kill me.

I crawl over to it, and as I lift it up, my gums tingle and my little fangs come out and I don't even use the straw. I bite right into it. I do it even though I know that camera is still watching me. And there, despite the grow lights, as I drink, there's heat in my stomach—a shimmering fury—a sensation I've felt many times and always feared, always pushed down. But not this time. This time, I let it pulse and burn. Because I think I finally understand. I understand why my darkness wins whenever a child, a woman, anyone vulnerable is being harmed. Why a rage takes hold that I can't push down. It's because *I* was hurt. *I* was murdered.

My mind might not remember, but my soul does. My soul remembers *everything*. It wants to protect others, the way nobody protected me.

As I drain the bag and look around at the cage I'm stuck in, it almost seems funny.

Because I've spent my whole life trying to be good, putting *myself* in a cage. Watching the world through screens and the bars of windows. Closeting myself away. Pushing down my rage, my darkness, telling myself to never-ever-ever lose control, because then I'd be a monster.

I've spent my whole life wanting to die.

Because that was better than being *me*.

But now, now that I'm most likely *going* to die soon—at the hand of the same man who killed me last time—all I want is to live. To get out of here and see the moon another 55,026 times; to feel the breeze on my skin; to see the world as it really is. Because sure, it's cruel and unfair and lonely as fuck at times, but it's *also* beautiful and poetic and surprising. This last week showed me that—it was chaotic and unpredictable and ugly and messy, and full of big emotions I couldn't push down and people I couldn't control. But it was the first time that I knew I could die at any moment, and it was magic. I felt … alive.

And I could have lived the last 150 years like that.

I could have danced all night and slept all day and worn beautiful clothes and watched the years come and go and met a million people and smoked cigarettes with breakfast and fallen in and out of love. I could have lived by my own rules. But more than that, I might not have always *been* good, but I could have *done* good. I could have dealt with guys like Red Flannel Jeff years ago. I could have been so much more than I was if I'd just hated myself a little less. Stopped trying so hard to be everything I wasn't, stopped pushing down that darkness. Stopped trying so hard to stay human, to be the complete opposite of who I am, and let myself just … be.

Now that I think about it, why have I been so desperate to become human-me again? She clearly wasn't perfect. She cheated. She probably did other bad things too. And humans aren't exactly angelic. I mean, I love Daphne and Es and they're good, but not *every* human is good … look at the ones in this house. I've always thought that deep down, despite their fallibility, humans were better than vampires. But I'm starting to realise we're all monsters, in our own way.

So maybe I've had it wrong all along.

Maybe my darkness isn't so bad. Maybe I'm fine, as I am.

For all the pain Oscar brought me, he showed me that. He lied and manipulated and was brutal and callous, but he was also unapologetically real. And he let me be real too. He showed me that life didn't have to be perfect and in soft-focus to be worth something. It just had to be lived. Really lived. I see that now. He did a lot wrong, but he did *that* right.

I finish the bag of blood and look around. I'm still tired and weak from the grow lights, but there is something inside me now, and it whispers, *I need to get out of here.*

And I don't want to do it for Jonathan or Oscar, or anyone else.

I want to do it for me.

I want to live for *me*.

I want to fight for *me*. The me I am now, the me that Jonathan murdered, *and* the me I haven't become yet.

So, when the door handle begins to turn again, I think, *Bring it on*.

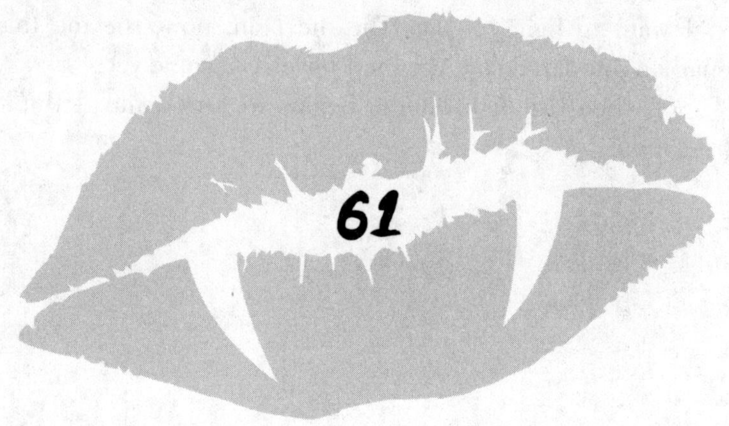

61

I drop the bag of blood quickly, hide it behind my back even though I know they would have seen me, and wipe my mouth with the back of my hand. I expect to see Jonathan, back to try again.

But it's not him.

It's Baxter. The canvas bag Jonathan had earlier is slung over his shoulder.

He's holding a drink and his cheeks are pink, and he's swaying a little.

He pulls the chair from behind Jonathan's desk, puts it in front of the cage and sits on it, his legs parted. He smiles. 'So, Aubrey,' he slurs, 'it's my turn to take a crack. Are you going to make it easy or hard? I mean, after me comes Riley, and I wouldn't want to deal with him if I were you …' He gives a little chuckle.

His eyes move to the bag of blood, now empty.

'Well, now that you've drunk that,' he says, 'we get to move on to phase two.'

'What's phase two?'

He reaches into the bag and pulls out a syringe.

I squint at it under the lights, trying to make sense of things.

'What are you going to do with that?' I ask.

'I just need a little sample,' he says.

'What for?' My voice cracks.

'Just trying to figure out what makes you tick, that's all.'

'And then you'll let me go?'

'Of course we will,' he says. But his heart speeds up when he says it. *He's lying*. It's beating so fast he might as well have just said: 'No, we're going to take your blood and *then* we're going to kill you. In the worst way we can.' And now I'm thinking about Jonathan and his heart beating faster so many times, wondering how often I should have noticed that he was lying too.

How blinded I was by everything I *wanted* to see.

I look at the syringe, and … soon we will have a problem. He won't find a vein in my arm no matter how hard he looks. If he really, really wants my blood, how else will he get it? Now I'm thinking of Felix's head, dripping blood, the night he died. I can't have Baxter get my blood that way. I need to keep him talking while I figure out what to do.

'What are you going to do with my blood?' I ask.

'Does it matter?'

I nod. 'If you want me to let you get close enough to take it, I want to know what you're going to do with it.'

'Make shit,' he says, with a gleeful laugh.

My gaze shifts to Jonathan's desk behind him. To the *Eternex Enterprises* business plan.

'Is that what your app is for?' I ask.

He smiles, or smirks rather, like he's pleased with himself. 'Nah, that was all lies, we had to tell you something. Our business is so much more visionary than some app. So much smarter than the plebs on that vampire hunting site.'

I know I'm probably still too weak to hypnotise him, but I'm desperate, and I did feed a little … maybe it *could* work?

It has in the past, with just bagged blood. And what else do I have? So, I meet his eyes and in a velvety voice, I ask, 'Is that where you met the others?' I'm testing it out, I can't go straight to telling him to let me out of the cage. I watch his eyes, needing them to glaze over.

But he's entirely unaffected.

'Sort of.' He shrugs. 'Liv, me and Jonathan knew each other from business school. We met Riley on the site and he was sick of all the red tape, keen to break off with us and form our own group.'

I nod, like that's really interesting, as Riley's comment under that post about the IRL meet-up for Kenny comes flooding back.

@Riley: Sorry I couldn't make it.

And now that makes perfect sense. Of course he didn't turn up to the meet-up to tell them what he knew. They needed everyone else to give up, so they could get to me first.

'Well, what are you going to make?' I ask in honeyed tones, my eyes boring into him, trying again. *Work. Work. Please work.* I just need some sign that he's mesmerised. Then I can get him to let me out.

'Face cream, longevity elixirs, maybe even pheromones for perfume—you do smell good—or like … a better version of Viagra.' Then his face gets serious, like he's just remembered he's a proper business person with a proper business plan, not some arsehole with a woman in a cage. 'I mean, regenerative medicine is the way of the future. First there was PRP then polynucleotides and then …. you. We just need to be the first to market.'

A flash of Olivia's Instagram profile and *Former Forbes 30 Under 30*. I bet she wrote that business plan.

'But,' Baxter continues, 'we need to see what's going on with you on a molecular level before we can figure out the exact details.' He lifts the syringe.

That explains why they needed me to feed. They wanted my blood to behave in the way it should. It wouldn't work if I was hungry—and they couldn't exactly offer me a human sacrifice.

But my hypnotism isn't working at all. I struggle to think, but I *have* to think—my life depends on it. Now Rupert's words come floating back: *Humans are dead easy to manipulate … You just pretend they're the most special person you've ever met.*

'But what *then*?' I ask, trying to sound genuinely interested. 'So, you figure it out, you give everyone eternal life, or eternal youth or whatever, then … they won't need you anymore.'

'We're not dumb, Aubrey,' he snaps, swaying a bit. And *this* is good. A bit tipsy is good. 'We've thought of that. They'll have to drink it every single day, buy more and more and more, and we can inflate the shit out of it. If that doesn't work, maybe we'll set up an OnlyFans with you, who knows? But we have options. World is our oyster. And you'll always be young and hot. Maybe I'll have a go at you next time.'

Horror moves through me. Surely they wouldn't do *that*.

'Yeah, great idea,' I say, sarcasm leaking into my voice.

He looks at me in this awful way and then says, 'You want to see the videos we already have?' Then he pulls out his phone.

My head pulses. 'What?'

He taps on his phone, then turns it so I can see the screen. There I am. With Jonathan. I'm naked and straddling him and we're moving slowly, our hands clasped. I get a flash of his face, what it felt like to have him inside me. Then he looks over towards the camera. The angle is the same as the video Jonathan showed me earlier.

That picture frame.

And it hits me: it was *always* recording. Even when he wasn't sure I was a vampire.

Even while we were having sex.

Was Baxter watching?

The heat in my solar plexus is wild now, it's rising to my throat. My ears roar and my vision tunnels and I can see Baxter's pulse, tapping on his neck. And I'm no longer interested in him letting me out. No. Now I have another plan.

I *need* him to come closer ...

'What do I have to do?' I ask. All innocence.

'Give me just a little blood. For now.'

'Okay,' I say sweetly. 'I just want to go home, so if that's what it takes ...' I need to seem hesitant, but I can smell the rum pulsing from his skin. I can feel my gums tingling.

'Come here,' he says, and I stumble forward, to the edge of the cage, like I'm still just as weak as I was before the bag of blood. I scan him. I sense everything. The slightly greying stubble on his chin, his quickening heartbeat, his shallow breath, a small bulge in his front pants pocket—is that a key?—and then another bulge beside it.

'Put your arm through the bars,' he says.

I do what he says. As he comes towards me, watching me, I look down at his lips, then up to his eyes. He clenches his jaw as he assesses my arm without touching it, just out of reach. I glance down at his pants, and the bulge is even bigger now. Good. What with the booze and the erection, he's vulnerable. Just like I was. All those times they must have videoed me having sex. All those times they planned to capture me. All those times they pretended to be Sally. I imagine them sitting around a laptop, gleefully tapping in credit card details, buying this fucking cage.

'My veins can be tricky to find,' I say, my voice like smoke and honey. He's squinting down at my arm.

'Tricky to find' is an understatement.

Impossible would be a better word for it.

'It can help to tie something around the area above the elbow,' I say. Helpful. 'Let me show you.'

He nods and looks around, then goes over to the dumbbells near Jonathan's closet and reaches for a stretch band.

He brings it over and fastens it around my arm, but he remains just out of reach. 'Stay still,' he warns me, ice in his voice.

I nod. 'There's one,' I say, motioning to a phantom vein as my fangs pop out.

He leans in towards my arm to get a better look. 'Where?'

'There,' I say.

He leans in and grabs onto my wrist.

I grab back.

My vision blanches, and white-hot rage shoots through me as I pull his arm through the bars and, in full sight of the nanny cam, I bite.

Hard.

Because if they want my blood, if they want to kill me, let them do it while I'm well fed.

I hear him yelp and his blood tastes acidic, but I drink anyway. I drink and drink and drink. Soon, that glitter is back. That levity. My vision snaps to high definition, and he sinks heavy to the ground, so I sink with him. And then he's limp, and drained, and his heart has stopped beating, so I let go.

I look over to the picture frame, my breath quick. The others will have been watching, so I have no time, I need to get out of here. Fuck getting the key.

I reach for two bars and with every ounce of my new strength, I pull them apart.

I manage to make just enough space to climb through.

I step over Baxter's body—pale and not moving—then turn off those grow lights. I leave him there. I choose darkness.

I choose me.

Then I wipe his blood from my mouth, take my earring from the desk and put it in my pocket, and walk right out of that door … I need to deal with Jonathan.

62

The lights are on downstairs, but the music that was playing when I arrived is off. As I tiptoe down the stairs, I scan for movement, for the sound of footsteps, breathing, heartbeats. But all I can hear is the wind outside noisily rattling the window panes, howling through the trees, muddying the soundwaves. Either they've run away, or they're hiding.

Because they would have seen what just happened, what I did to Baxter. They'll know I'm coming. They'll be prepared.

And I know I can die now. But it's strangely exhilarating.

I get to the base of the stairs and scan the room afresh. That Christmas tree is still there by the bay window, its little lights flashing sadly by the rug we slow-danced on … but where are *they*?

I step into the living room and swivel, alert for threat. But it's just me here.

Shit.

Because they know what I am. They have proof of it. Which part would people find most compelling? Me zooming around his room, me climbing through a second-floor window, me feeding on Baxter, or me crying blood? Hard to say.

This could ruin everything for all of us.

There's an open laptop on the coffee table and I quickly move towards it. I focus in on the screen.

A video image. The nanny cam upstairs. I can see the cage and the outline of Baxter's body even though it's dark now.

And then I hear … a heartbeat. A heartbeat I'd recognise anywhere.

It's coming from my right. The kitchen.

I pivot to look, and there stands Jonathan.

I shudder when I see him and my head fills with white noise.

His hands are up in a gesture of surrender, and his eyes are so blue, so beautiful.

'I'm so sorry, Aubrey,' he says, his voice shaking. 'I fucked up. I listened to them. I should have been stronger. I didn't even know how much I loved you until I saw you kill Baxter and I was,' his voice drops to a whisper, like he's ashamed, 'relieved.'

'Where are the others?' I ask, looking around.

'They left. But I had to come back for you. We need to get out of here.'

A flash of Pepperoni Guy, then *true fucking love* and a smile, then a red beanie and ice skates and Brighton Beach and *you don't need to fake anything with me, Aubrey*.

My ribs throb. He could have run away, but he didn't. He stayed. To save me …

I take a step towards him, not sure what I'm going to do because also, *his hands around my neck, my eyes rolling back* …

And then: a sharp pain rings out in my back.

I look down and see a wooden point emerging from my ribs. *I can't breathe.*

I've been staked. From behind. It only just missed my heart.

I stagger forward and look up, towards Jonathan. 'Help,' I cry out, my voice a whisper.

But he just looks at me, in the same cold way he was looking at me in the cage. And now comes a flash of me fighting for my life. Him hitting me over the head with that vase …

Something heavy is being put around me now. I look to my left: Olivia. To my right: Riley. They're wrapping me in silver chains. And nobody is looking into my eyes, and I couldn't hypnotise three at once anyway. With these chains around me, and this stake in my back, I couldn't fight them all either. Now I'm scared. Because silver might not kill me, but the chains are heavy and if I fall on this stake and it moves just a quarter of a centimetre and pierces my heart, what then? According to Oscar, that should do it. That should kill me.

I don't even fight, I just listen to the chains rattling and the wind outside while they give each other instructions, because I know what comes next and I know I can't change it. So, I succumb. I fall to my knees and bow my head.

Olivia says, 'Good, now let's go and get the cage ready again, see if we can do something about those bent bars. They sent spares, right? Are the tools up there?'

'I'll watch her,' Jonathan says as they head upstairs.

Jonathan kneels beside me and whispers, 'You stupid bitch, did you really think you'd win?'

But what he doesn't know is that this stupid bitch may have been staked, these chains may be heavy, but they're not *that* heavy. Not when I've just fed on Baxter. And my soul has known Jonathan's for a very long time—I just knew he'd want a moment alone to gloat.

And I needed him alone.

My ears roar, my fangs ache, and then a volcanic rage, stronger than I've ever felt, erupts.

I extend my arms either side of me and hear the chains break. He has a split second to respond. I grab his hair with one hand, while the other grabs his shoulder and I don't think, I don't hesitate, I just … bite.

My fangs sink in. He tastes sweet, like everything I thought I wanted, needed. Like my last chance at humanity. But bitter too, like sadness and hate. And it hurts, I'm aching and I can't tell if it's my heart breaking all over again or this stake in my back. I let go of him and he falls to the ground, then I reach behind me and pull the stake out. I wince as it leaves my body, but as soon as it's out, the wound starts to heal.

Jonathan looks up at me with such loathing, saying something but I can't make it out. I lean in slightly; his voice is a whisper. 'You're still a monster,' he spits.

I lean forward and whisper back, 'See you in the next life.' But I really, really hope I don't. That this is it. The circle, broken.

And then he's gone, a dark pool of blood gathering around him, his eyes vacant and his heart silent … then I hear footsteps on the stairs.

Olivia and Riley.

I run over to the wall between the stairs and the living room and wait for them to pass.

Olivia sounds annoyed. 'How would *I* know how to weld things?'

They're getting closer.

Closer.

'Jonathan,' calls Olivia, as they take the corner.

But instead of Jonathan, they're met with *me*.

I reach for both their necks at once, and I see the shock in their eyes. I bite Riley first. He tastes like metal and microplastics and too much fast food, and as I drink, the night we met flickers in my mind. Then him at Borough Market. The way he tracked me down. As soon as his heart slurs to an almost stop, I drop him and turn to Olivia. Her mouth is open like she's in shock and her eyes are wide but all I can see in them is the way she looked at me in that cage. Like I was some sort of zoo animal. No empathy for me at all. *Well, let me be an animal then.*

She smells like Jo Malone and tastes like Cadbury's, and I feed until she's limp and heavy, then I let her fall to the ground beside Riley. Soon their hearts have both stopped and it's just me here, and the rage is receding and even through the blur of my blood high, anxiety is bubbling up. Danger swirling. Because as I glance from Jonathan to Olivia and Riley, I think: *What am I going to do with all these bodies?*

I'm not ready for this.

Think, Aubrey ... what signs are there that you were here?

My suitcase is still sitting by the door. My coat on top of it. My fingerprints are probably everywhere—but that's fine, I'm not in any database. My handbag is upstairs, I'll need to get that. But also, again, my phone. *Where is my phone?*

WHERE IS MY FUCKING PHONE?

I look at Riley, then Olivia, then Jonathan. There, in his front pocket is a rectangular, phone-sized bulge. I grit my teeth and reach into it—his body is still warm as I pull it out.

But it's almost out of battery now, the little icon reads five per cent. There is one new message on the screen. It's from Es. I tap on it, frantically: *Okay. HNY then.*

No kisses. Not even one.

What did Jonathan send her? I tap through to the message thread and read the ones from tonight, the ones Jonathan must have sent to Es, pretending to be me.

Es: *Any updates on the looooovvers? Xxx*

Es: *Are you too busy to reply? HAHAHA xxx*

Es: *Babe? Please just shoot me a quick reply.*

Then came a missed call.

Then I (Jonathan) replied: *Leave me alone. I'm fine.*

Oh god ...

Es: *Well, how is Jonathan???? Babe you sound upset. What's going on? xxxxx*

Me: *I'm fine. He wasn't home so I went to a party in Hackney instead.*

Es: *Well where is it? I'll come!!!! Is there food? I have the munchies xxxx*

Me: *I think I'd rather be alone.*

No wonder she's not sending any kisses.

I tap through to Es's number and dial immediately. I need her to know that I'm still me, that I'm not some mega-bitch all of a sudden. I'll need my friends now more than ever. I'll also need some sort of alibi for tonight. I'll just tell her I went to a party and wasn't feeling like myself, but I still love her. Maybe we can meet up now.

It rings … and rings …

And then a phone starts ringing from just outside the window.

The world shrinks to a pinprick. My heart stops. I swivel to look towards the sound.

There's a tapping on the window and I hear Es say, 'Aubrey? Is that you in there? What's going on?'

OH.

MY.

FUCKING.

GOD.

I wipe my face and try to hide out of view. *Maybe she'll just go away. Maybe she didn't see me properly.*

But it's dark out there and light inside and there's a thin space between the curtains.

'Aubrey, open up, are you okay?' she calls frantically. 'What did they do to you? Is that blood? Should I call the police?'

FUUUUUUCKKKKKK.

Because not only am I covered in blood, but there are three dead bodies in here with me. Four, if you count Baxter upstairs.

Go away. Go away.

But this is Es we're talking about, true-crime Es, Es who loves me, so she doesn't go away. Instead, I watch in seemingly slow motion as she climbs through the fucking window. She steps out from behind the curtain, looking scared, holding a small can of hairspray as makeshift mace.

'Thank god you're okay,' she says, running towards me. 'What did they do to you, why is there so much blood?'

She hugs me and I hug her back.

'I knew it,' she babbles. 'I knew that wasn't you texting me back. I had such a bad feeling. Was it one of those weirdo online man-groups? I thought there was something not right with Jonathan when he didn't want to meet your friends … and then that guy coming in to my work to look for you. Thank god you sent me that video.' I remember the video I sent her outside. Me, spinning around. I bring it into my mind's eye. The street signs would have been visible if she paused it. 'Are they still here?' she whispers as she looks around behind me. 'We need to get out of here.'

Her gaze catches on Riley first.

Then it snaps to Jonathan. Olivia.

Her eyes widen, her breath stops. She's frowning. In shock. Trying to make sense of the blood. The bodies. The stake.

Me.

Her pulse is fast, like a rabbit, and her eyes are filled with terror. A terror I *never* wanted to see in anyone's eyes, let alone hers. She lets out a little yelp, thoughts flickering behind her gaze. But she stands dead still and her breathing gets really slow, like she's frozen from fear.

'It's okay,' I say. But then her gaze catches on my fangs.

She lets out another yelp and her hand moves to her mouth.

'It's okay,' I repeat in a gentle voice. 'I promise.'

'What's going on?' she squeaks. 'What … are you?'

But I can tell from the look in her eyes that she already knows. She's just struggling to wrap her mind around everything.

'I'm not going to hurt you,' I say, feeling my fangs finally retract. 'I'd *never* hurt you.'

She nods. Tears are streaming down her face, but she tries to smile.

'Are you a vampire?' she asks.

'Yes, but I'm not bad. You've seen *Twilight* … *The Vampire Diaries*? I'm a good one,' I say, even though I know all evidence is to the contrary right now.

'Wait …' she says, thoughts moving quickly behind her eyes. 'Is this why you're my friend?' She starts to sob even harder. 'It is … oh my god, I thought I was going crazy when those bags of blood kept disappearing, thought I couldn't count. Does that mean you don't really love me?'

'Of course I love you, Es,' I say, looking into her eyes. And I realise I'm not a total monster. I've stopped my hunger mid-frenzy. I'm not biting her. I didn't even need to think of roadkill—I would *never* hurt her.

'I love you too,' she says, sniffing back tears, her pupils huge with terror.

There is part of me that is so relieved. Now I have a friend who knows me. Knows all of me. I could keep her until she dies. Not have to be alone, no matter how many men come or go.

'I can't tell if I'm really, really high or having a psychotic break,' she says to me in a very rational, very stable voice. 'Please would you take me to the hospital?'

My lower lip quivers, and I can smell rust, but I hold back the tears. I know what I have to do. This is too much. She can't live with this, the weight of it will crush her. I can't do that to her.

I reach forward, hold onto her warm shoulders and, as much as I don't want to, in a honeyed tone I say: 'Es, you were never here tonight.' Her eyes get vacant. A sadness rolls through me, but this is the right thing. 'We went to a bad party in Hackney and then we both went home early. You just went to bed and lost a few hours to social media and then you went to sleep,' I finish, doing just as Oscar taught me. 'Now go straight home.'

She nods, smiles, wipes her tears away. And then she turns around, unlocks the front door and walks out. It closes with a quiet click behind her.

And it's just me now.

I sit down on the floor and pull my knees into my chest. I'm back to square one, where nobody knows me. I have no Jonathan. No soulmate. No maker worth speaking of. Es and Daphne are back to being shelf-life friends. And Sally never existed in the first place.

I drop my head to my knees, and I let myself weep.

I weep because I'm all alone again. I weep because there are four bodies in this house, and *how am I going to cover this up?*

I weep because I'm confused and scared and there is blood all over my pink jumper. Some of it mine. Some of it theirs. How am I going to get out of this?

I weep for it all.

And then, beyond my own sobs and the wind outside, I hear the door open.

'Well, what the fuck happened here?'

I look up.

And there, standing in the doorway, is Oscar.

I stare at him and he stares back at me. He's wearing the same white dinner shirt he was wearing when I left tonight, the same shirt he put on again right before he walked out of my bedroom. And that tug in my chest is back. It aches. It pulls me towards him, but I will not be the one to move. Not this time. He closes the door, turns off the lights and comes over to me. As he squats down beside me, all I can do is sob.

'Aubrey,' he says, holding my face in his hands. 'We have to get out of here.'

I nod, but the tears keep rolling. I'm all out of fight. He reaches forward and wipes away my tears with his thumbs.

'Wait here,' he says under his breath, and then he starts zooming around.

Thirty seconds later he's stepping over Riley's body, looking down at his *Vampires are real! Join the fight!* hoodie and frowning. Then he's next to me, helping me into my coat to cover the blood on my jumper. He hands me my bag, tucks the business plan, that picture frame camera and the laptop from the coffee table under his arm and reaches for my suitcase. 'Come,' he says, then we head out the back door and through the side gate to the street.

'What are we going to do if people find the cage? Or something that leads them to me, to us?' I ask as we move along a side street. My teeth are chattering from fear.

But then he looks at me and says, 'Nobody's going to find anything.' He says it with such certainty that I believe him. We move through shadows. Past darkened windows and well-tended lawns and people stumbling home from their night out.

And then we're at his car and the taillights flash red. He opens the door and helps me in, then he puts my suitcase and everything else in the boot and gets in beside me.

I put on my seatbelt and gaze out the tinted windows, numbness settling over me.

He turns the key in the ignition, puts his foot on the accelerator and pulls away, and as he does, I hear a little 'meow'.

I turn to look behind us. And there, sitting in the back seat, is Cat.

63

Cat purrs from my lap as the road hums beneath us, and I know she's not mine, that I'll probably have to give her back, but right now she's exactly what I need. My hands shake as I check my phone before it dies. Nothing more from Es. Just one new message from Daphne. It's a picture of her in a bronze bikini, sitting in a bright blue indoor pool and drinking from a bottle of Veuve, with the text: *HAPPY NEW YEAR!!!! Gonna be so hungover tomorrow. LOVE YOU!*

I type back: *Love you too!*

Then I put my phone back in my bag and look out the window, watching the New Year's Eve stragglers singing drunkenly at the top of their lungs, linking arms with friends, or puking in a rose bush, beneath a moon I've seen 55,026 times now, a moon I thought I'd never see again. The moon might be the same, but everything about *me* changed tonight.

I mean, I killed four people, for one.

And I liked it.

Oscar turns on his indicator and changes lanes, then reaches into the console for a little earpiece and presses something on his phone, calling someone.

His hands tighten around the steering wheel, his jaw clenches and then someone must answer because he says, 'We have a problem.' He reels off Jonathan's address, listens for a little bit and then he says, 'Yes, there's a cage upstairs and possibly other things I missed. I think they were from one of those hunting sites ... Deal with it thoroughly ... I don't care how.'

Then he hangs up.

'Who was that?' I ask.

'Hans. He'll deal with it.' His eyes stay trained on the road ahead.

Hans.

A flash of him sitting down on that bench in the park, the same night I was turned, then taking me under his wing. All these years later and Oscar still has him cleaning up the messes he doesn't want to 'deal' with.

'How did you find me tonight?' I ask glancing over at him.

'There was an envelope in your flat with an address on the back. I went to that address, and the roommate told me where Olivia was,' he says, his voice hard and clipped. Then he looks over at me, his eyes flame. 'Jesus, Aubrey, I knew you'd do something stupid like this. They were from that site you joined, weren't they? I told you to be more careful.'

I bristle. Is he seriously angry with me? 'This isn't my fault,' I say. 'None of it is.'

But he ignores me, and just turns up the music and stares ahead like he's furious and trying to control himself. And screw him.

I glare out the window, stroking Cat, thinking: *I was only on that site because I was looking for you. I didn't know Jonathan killed me because you lied about everything, all of this is YOUR fault.*

Houses turn to paddocks, and the wide roads turn to those narrow streets. And then we're back at Oscar's gate. And now I'm furious. Because all he had to do was tell me the truth and I wouldn't have been there tonight. But as I watch the gate shudder open, seething, I tell myself not to be confrontational. If I want answers—and I do, I need them—I'm going to have to ask gently. With Oscar that's the only way.

All the other cars are gone, the lights are off, and the dashboard clock reads 3.27 am.

We park in silence.

Oscar gets my suitcase from the boot and pulls it over the gravel and Cat purrs as I take her inside. The house is still a mess from the party; glasses and bottles and streamers lying everywhere. Mr and Mrs Parker have gone for the night.

'Where are Rupert and Carmilla?' I ask, looking around for them.

'They've gone,' Oscar snaps as he closes the door. Then he turns to look at me and says, 'Come.'

We go through to the drawing room. The Christmas tree is still up, the little lights blinking, and the fire is crackling. I take off my coat and sit down on a sofa and Cat finds a spot on another chair. As he pours us both a stiff drink, to the top of the glass, Oscar's phone beeps with a message.

He looks down at it, then puts his phone in his pocket and sits down next to me, handing me my drink. 'Hans dealt with the scene. So don't worry about any of that.'

I take a gulp. Then another. It's warm in my throat and in my stomach.

When I look up, he's watching me.

Be measured. Just have a calm and adult conversation, I tell myself. But there's something about the calmness in his aura and the blame in his eyes that's making my insides hot and my throat tight. And I'm so sick of the lies, of the way he manages me. So I blurt out, 'I almost died tonight because of you. I want to know the truth, Oscar. About all of it. Now. No more lies.'

He swallows hard and downs the rest of his drink, then gets up and silently pours himself another one. He takes his time, like he's deciding whether to answer me. It's annoying.

'Oscar?' I say.

He lets out a big breath. 'There's not that much to tell, Aubrey,' he says.

Frustration bubbles up inside me. Because he clearly knows more than he's told me, and this is my life. I deserve to know.

'Well,' I say, trying to control my tone. 'Just start at the beginning. How did we meet?'

He blinks. 'Here,' he says, slowly. 'We met here. You lived in the village and came to a dance.'

I think of that feeling I had, walking through the village with Rupert and Carmilla, like it was familiar somehow …

'You wore that red dress, the same one you ruined on Christmas Eve. And a hairpin in your hair that caught the light.'

A flash of the way that dress made me feel when I first saw it. Like a part of me knew that already. *No wonder it fit so well.* But this is all information Oscar could have offered up to me sooner, but didn't. Why not?

'And then … you seduced me? Had me cheat on my husband? And when he found out, he killed me?' I ask, my voice cracking. 'Because I know he did. I saw that tonight.' My voice jumps a few notes. 'Is tha—'

'He was already hurting you,' Oscar says calmly, but definitively. 'I wanted you to leave, but it was a different time, it wasn't that easy. You didn't want to be all alone and you couldn't be with me, for obvious reasons.'

'Obvious reasons?' I echo, with a sardonic laugh. 'What, because you couldn't be bothered?'

He clenches his jaw like he doesn't appreciate me calling a spade a spade, and I take a deep breath. *Stay calm, stay calm.* I look down and I see the blood on my pink jumper and then I think of that cage and the chains around me and the stake in my back and …

'I should never have been there tonight,' I spit out. 'I wouldn't have been if you'd just told me the truth. Because I saw visions from when I was married to Jonathan in his last life, but I didn't know he'd murdered me because you let me think you killed me.' My breath gets quicker and quicker. 'I thought he was my fucking soulmate. I was dating him!'

So much for staying calm. My voice is so loud it scares even me.

But it's like I can't control the rage inside me anymore. Like it's been building for too long; I've put up with too much. Appeased too often. I don't *want* to control it anymore. Let him see it, feel it. He did this to me.

Oscar just looks at me. 'That wasn't my fault,' he says, still calm. And the fact that he's so calm is making me even more angry. 'How was I to know that you were seeing him again? I knew there was *someone*, Daphne told me that night in the club, someone who you might tell things to, the way you did that chap, Freddie.'

Reality warps around me.

He knew about Freddie?

'I did *not* want a repeat of that,' he tells me. 'I got to him just before he went to the police. Had to scrub his dimwit little mind clean and tell him to sign up to war.'

That's why Freddie never wanted to talk about it, acted like he barely knew me ... Oscar wiped his mind.

'I wasn't going to let you do that again with anyone,' he continues. 'Especially not without the tools to protect yourself. Not with all the growing dangers out there. But how was I meant to know it was *him*? Or what he was planning? Or that you'd seen him in a vision? You weren't exactly an open book either, Aubrey. If I'd known any of that, I would have ripped his heart out all over again.'

He's staring at me, his eyes blazing.

Again?

'You killed Jonathan last time? In his last life?'

'Of course I did. Do you really think I would have let him get away with harming you?'

I let out a furious laugh. 'Are you kidding me? *Him*, harming me? What about you? You put me in a room with a tiger! And you've lied to me about almost everything. I mean, I saw Emma tonight, alive and well. So don't pretend to be some hero. You're selfish, you play games with me for your own amusement. But this is my life Oscar, and it's not fair. It's cruel. You can't imagine what it feels like. Never knowing who you are, what you've been through.'

Something cracks behind his eyes, and he nods and looks down at the ground. His knuckles get white, his fists are clenched so hard.

'Perfect, say nothing.' I let out a short huff and start to laugh. 'I can't believe I ever loved someone like y—'

'Fuck Aubrey,' he snaps, staring me down. 'Maybe I *wanted* you to hate me, ever think of that?'

The air around us seems to stop moving altogether.

'Oh, I know you did,' I say, my voice hard, even though my ribs ache. 'Rupert told me that "forbidden" thing was bullshit. You didn't need to lie about all that either, Oscar. You didn't need to make my whole life miserable just so, what, I wouldn't fall in love with you again, cramp your style …' I pause. 'Rest assured, you're safe. I will *never* love you like that again.'

'Great,' he says.

'Great.'

I sit there, seething, my breath quick, imagining myself getting up and storming out. Would he let me go? I bet he would. My lower lip quivers but I clench my jaw to stop it. I can feel his eyes on me and my cheeks get hot.

'I'm sorry,' he whispers. 'It was never meant to be this hard for you. It was only meant to be hard for me.'

'Hard for *you*?' I retort. 'How has any of this *ever* been hard for you?'

He breathes heavily, and I stare at him, needing an answer.

'I'm not as awful as you think I am,' he says. 'I needed you to hate me so you wouldn't love me. Because we couldn't be together, Aubrey. And I didn't trust myself to *not* be with you, if you wanted to. I was trying to protect you—from me. From everything around me. Not because it's forbidden, but because I bring bad things. You wouldn't have been safe.'

'You bring "bad things"?' I let out an angry laugh. 'That's such bullshit. You just didn't want the hassle. But if you didn't want to take care of me, you shouldn't have turned me into a fucking vampire,' I yell.

'You think you know everything, Aubrey,' he says, resignation and sadness in his eyes. 'You always did. I didn't *want* to turn you. You begged me to.'

'No, I fucking did not!' I say. *He's lying, like he lies about everything. He has to be.*

'You did.' There's no give in his voice. 'Many times.'

'Well, you shouldn't have listened!'

He looks right at me. 'You're right, I shouldn't have. But you were going to die.' There's a heat in his eyes. 'I was going to lose you forever, and in that moment, I was weak.'

I frown.

'So, your solution to not losing me forever was turning me into a vampire and then not talking to me for one hundred and fifty years?' I ask.

'I was trying to do the right thing. It was better that way, better than—'

'Than what?'

'Than me putting you in danger and you dying. For real. Because like I told you, vampires don't get reincarnated. I knew that if you died as a vampire, I'd lose you *forever*.'

A ping rings out beneath my ribs.

'That has happened to me before,' he continues. 'I couldn't

go through it again. Not with you—that pain would be unbearable. The end of me.'

'I don't believe you,' I say, with more conviction than I feel.

He reaches out and touches my face. His pupils flare. My stomach clenches. And in comes a flash, just like last time. In technicolour, with sound, like I'm stepping into one of his memories. I look around.

I'm in a room, and it's a long time ago. Before my time, even. The only light in the room is coming from a candelabra and a fireplace. On the rug, in front of the fireplace, stand three men. Two of them are restraining a woman. The other holds a stake. A mirror has been set up in Oscar's eye line, like they want him to witness how weak and helpless he is—and he IS helpless. Bound in chains, and drawn, like he hasn't fed properly in months. The woman is fighting to free herself, and Oscar is pulling against the chains, his arms straining, his eyes flaming. But he's so weak, they barely move. And as he watches, pain crackling behind his eyes, the man grins at him, then drives the stake through her heart.

I gasp. He lets go of me and the images cut to black. I swallow.

'She's the only person I ever turned before you, and I swore to myself I would never do it again. But then that night, the night you died … I could feel something was wrong. I went straight to you, but I was too late. You were lying there, unconscious and covered in blood. I could hear your heart about to give in, and I just couldn't let it happen. To make a vampire, you have seven short seconds after the last heartbeat to feed them vampire blood. Aubrey, I had just seven seconds to make the biggest choice of both of our lives. And he had killed you because of me, because of us. I should have protected you. I should have forced you to leave him. When it came down to it, I just couldn't lose you. But I also couldn't let you be near me. I needed to protect you, no matter the cost. I owed you that.'

My heart stutters and thoughts swirl around.

'I couldn't bear to lose you the same way,' he continues. 'The vampires who did that to Juliette are still around. They hurt her to hurt me, I knew it could happen again …' He swallows and looks down. 'My best option was to let you go.'

As I take in his words, the world spins a little slower. All this time I thought we were so different. But he's been doing the same thing I have, just trying to get by in this world of absurdity. While I've been holding so tightly to my humanity, like that might save me, he's shut his out altogether lest it cause him more pain. Thinking *that* might save him.

He looks over at me, torment in his eyes. 'And I thought you'd be okay. I thought you'd just forget me. I whispered into your ear that you needed blood, that you needed to never tell anyone what you were, and that you needed to leave that house and go to the gardens nearby. I took your necklace, the one I gave to you on Christmas, to remember you by. From then on, I watched over you. I know it wasn't perfect, but I protected you in my own way.'

'You could have just told me all this. I would have understood.'

'No, you wouldn't. You would have done what you're about to do right now.' His eyes look straight into me. 'Tried to convince me we can be together.'

My breath shudders.

'Would that be so bad?'

His eyes shift, like he can't look at me.

'Oscar?'

'If we were together and something happened to you because of me …'

'So I should just spend eternity alone, with no love, and no meaning? How is that a life?'

His eyes look deeply into mine; something burns behind them. 'I don't know anymore. There's a packet of cigarettes beside him and he lights one and takes a drag. I reach for it and take a drag too—my final 'fuck you' to Jonathan. I blow out a big cloud of smoke and hand it back to him.

'Did you know I'd found those pictures?' I ask him. 'Is that why you were so hot and cold?'

He shakes his head. 'Not until you told me. But I was worried you'd figure out how I felt, that it was obvious. I couldn't have that. Because I knew then we'd end up having this exact chat.' He smirks, exhaling a cloud of smoke as he watches me. 'I'm sorry about Tina, though. You were never in any danger; I would never let something happen to you. I just needed you to buy into it. Because I could feel you softening, falling again.'

'Oh my god, you have the biggest ego,' I say, and he starts to laugh.

'You really haven't changed at all.'

'But is that a good thing or a bad thing?' I ask, as my eyes meet his.

He lies down on the sofa and says, 'The best thing.'

And somehow, the only thing for me to do then is to lie down beside him and put my head on his shoulder. As I do, it feels like the most natural thing in the world. Like I've done it a thousand times before—and maybe I have.

We stay there for a little while, smoking. Saying nothing. Cat, not wanting to be left out, meows and stretches and comes over, settling by my feet and purring. And I think: *Of all the ways I saw myself starting New Year's Day, this one seemed the most unlikely* …

'I haven't done this for a long time,' he says eventually, in a croaky voice. 'Just laid down next to somebody.' He strokes my hair. 'Not since you.'

'What did we used to talk about?'

He takes a drag and blows out a cloud of smoke. 'You'd say: "Would you want to be with me if the world was going to end?"' His voice cracks.

'And what would you say?' I ask.

'I'd say, "Yes." The truth is, I don't care if the world ends. I've been alive for more than seven hundred years, I just want to have a good time while I'm here. But I do care if *you* end.'

I prop myself up on my elbows so I can see his face.

'Tell me the rest,' I say, looking into his eyes. 'About me. About who I was. I've always wanted to know.'

He lets out a sigh and stares deep into my eyes. 'I know that Aubrey was your maiden name, and that you missed having it as your own. I'd call you that. I know that you were beautiful. And that I loved you, really loved you,' he says, his voice husky. 'I still love you.'

It hits me in the centre of my chest. Those words I've always wanted to hear.

All this time, I thought Aubrey was just a link to my human-self, to the light and the version of me I couldn't let go. But it was *also* a link to him. To a love that has lasted through many lifetimes.

As I look at him, my heart opens, it opens so wide I couldn't stop it even if I wanted to. And I hear myself say. 'I love you too.'

He reaches forward and touches my face. 'I know, and that's the problem. When people love each other like we do ... it's never simple.'

I take a deep breath and think about what he's just said. 'What was my first name, then?' I ask.

'Tabitha,' he says.

I snort. 'Really?' I ask. He grins and my heart squeezes 'Like *Bewitched*?'

He nods. And I really like the name, but it's not *me*. Aubrey is.

'What else?' I ask, my voice almost a whisper. 'What did I like?'

'I wish I knew more, Aubrey, but I tried my hardest to keep my distance. I knew I couldn't get too close, I could feel myself being drawn to you.'

'But what about us, our story? You must know that,' I ask, as he takes a final drag and stubs out the cigarette on the ashtray. 'How did we fall in love? And what was that piece you were playing on the cello? Because it felt like I knew it. It made me want to cry.'

He smiles, reaches for my face and touches my cheek.

'I wrote that piece for you,' he says. 'As for how we fell in love …' He smiles again, and it's more beautiful than all the dawns I thought I was missing out on, combined. 'It was, tumultuous, to say the least.'

'What do you mean?'

'You hated me on sight. You'd heard the rumours about me bedding half the town's women, which were all true, and you weren't having a bar of it. But there was something about you that my soul recognised immediately, even though my mind didn't know you, didn't understand why I felt tied to you. I couldn't shake it. One day, I saw why.'

I'm thinking of everything my soul remembered that my mind forgot. Even Jonathan's soul had a memory of me that he was unaware of. Something that drove him towards me.

Maybe that's the way it is for all of us, humans and vampires alike. Our souls are timeless, they carry scars and links to others that our minds cannot accept or understand. Some bonds are of love, some are of trauma, and it can be hard to tell the difference.

I frown. 'But how could your soul recognise mine?' I ask. 'Had we met before, in another life?'

He nods. 'Yes, a long time ago now. When I was still human. It was in France—I was a knight, and you were my wife. My memory of it all dissolved when I was turned, of course, so I only know pieces of that from what I've seen in your memories.'

As he says this, all I can think is: *Oh*.

And that kaleidoscope shifts once more, the pattern reconfigures but the sands remain the same.

Because now it's so obvious. All this time, I *did* have a soulmate. Someone who had loved me in multiple lifetimes.

It just wasn't Jonathan. Now that I think about it, Oscar *has* given me love. Real love. The kind that sees you, really sees you, and loves you anyway. He has fought for me, protected me, sacrificed for me.

'What did you see? Can you show me?' I ask, gazing into his eyes. 'What happened to us in that life?'

He lets out a sigh. 'We have a lot of time, Aubrey,' he says, and his voice is tired. 'And it's been a big night.'

So, I lie down, my head on his chest, as the fire crackles and Cat purrs.

Because he's right, we have time. We have all the time in the world. We have eternity.

I have eternity. And I meant what I thought in that cage: I'm going to use it.

So as the sun starts to rise outside, I let my eyelids get heavy and for the first time in 150 years, I fall asleep calm and … happy. Knowing I'm exactly where I'm meant to be. I don't know how any of it will work out, but I do know that Jonathan was right about one thing: *There are far, far better things ahead than any we leave behind.* That life has a million surprises in store for me. There will be chaos and magic and glitter and darkness, cigarettes and yearning and silk and moonlight, dancing and tears and laughter and blood and make-up sex and photo albums and even the fear of death. There will be everything and nothing all at once.

And for the first time in my life, I can't wait.

Screw control.

I cannot wait to live.

Title: ARCHWAY: FOUR DIE IN SUBURBAN BLAZE–ONE OF OUR OWN!!!!

Location: London

Posted by: @MrJones

Four people have been found dead after a house fire in Archway in the early hours of New Year's Day. Firefighters were called to the scene by neighbours just before 4 am and fought tirelessly to contain the blaze, heroically saving surrounding properties.

'This appears to be a tragic accident,' said a spokesperson for the police. 'A New Year's Eve party gone wrong.'

But neighbours witnessing the scene have other thoughts. 'There was stuff inside,' said one elderly neighbour. 'A cage and metal fixtures, my grandson took a look and said it was a sex swing and other BDSM paraphernalia. I bet they were doing something perverted with fire. They put us all at risk!'

Another neighbour told *The Evening Standard*: 'They were a secretive bunch. Their blinds always shut, boarded up one of their windows and all, never a word for the neighbours. I think they were into drugs.'

Police are working to identify the victims, and urge anyone with information to contact Crimestoppers immediately.

Comments:

@MrJones: OMFG. One of our members @Riley was in this fire! And guys, he said he was onto a vamp, some chick named Aubrey who worked at Selfridges. He showed me a video of her zooming around and climbing through a second-storey window! I bet she did this!

@HenryD: Who were the others?

@MrJones: Not sure

@Vampitup, replying to @MrJones: Why didn't Riley tell us about her? If she worked at Selfridges maybe she had something to do with Kenneth Brawley????

@MrJones, replying to @Vampitup: He told me in secret, it was something he was working on with other members but you know Riley, he never could keep a secret.

@Vampitup, replying to @MrJones: You should have said!

@HenryD: Should we tell the police?

@BloodyGoooood: Like they'd believe us.

@redflannelforever: I'm new here, but I'm totally committed. I was attacked on Boxing Day by some bitch who made me pee myself. Who knows what else she did to me? But I'm in! Whatever you want!

@HenryD: Welcome.

@Eric22: This is fucking war! Killing one of our own.

@Vampitup: We need to meet to discuss this immediately. See if we can get that video.

@Viciousdelicious: Agreed. Onward.

@Eric22: We're just getting started.

ACKNOWLEDGEMENTS

I wrote this book in a fever dream while contracted to write and deliver another, and while doing heavy promotion for a third. It was chaos of the most beautiful order, but it was also incredibly hard—on some days, it felt impossible. So thank you to everyone and everything that made it possible.

First off, thank you to my fantastic agent, Mollie Glick, for believing in this idea from the very first pages and for always being in my corner. Also to Via Romano, Sarah Harvey and Gabby Fetters.

To my wonderful editors, Roberta Ivers, April Osborn, Rachel Cramp and Vanessa Lanaway—go team! You did such a brilliant job bringing this to life with me.

To Dana Spector and Berni Vann who work behind the scenes, getting my books into the hands of film and TV people—thank you.

To the entire team at HarperCollins Publishers Australia, Hanover Square Press and Harlequin US—thank you so much for believing in this story and bringing it to the world.

To my writer friends, who did what writers do for one another: commiserate, laugh, cry, and hold each other up when it gets tough. Specifically, Vanessa McCausland, Anna Downes and Ashley Kalagian Blunt. And to Tabby and Daleya—you may be on the other side of the world, but oh how I love and appreciate you.

To my mother—thank you for always being there, for reading my first pages and for daring to read a vampire book even though you thought you didn't like vampires at all.

To my sister—who introduced me to *True Blood* (and Eric), the place where my love affair with vampires started, but certainly didn't end.

To my dad—hope you're watching from wherever you are. I miss you every single day. I love you.

To Mickey—oh, let me count the reasons why … for watching everything vampire-esque that we could find with me, for every note you left on my manuscript printout telling me to keep going, for the flowers and the read-throughs and the support. And the promise that no matter what happened, you would be there.

To the booksellers and bookstagrammers who constantly blow my mind with their support and insight and deep comprehension of the books I've put out into the world. Thank you for being on this wild, unplottable author journey with me.

To every writer of a vampire novel, every creator of a vampire TV show and every maker of a vampire film: thank you for your vision, and how fun is this?

To the loves that make us, the loves that break us, the loves that burn us to the ground … but mainly, to the love hearts we draw in the ash for ourselves.

To the best days, the worst days, to all the nothing moments in between that aren't nothing at all.

To life.